"*OVER THE EDGE* IS MORE THAN A SOLID, GRIPPING, PAGE-TURNING MYSTERY."*

"The case begins with the maniacal middle-of-the-night call from a young former patient of [Alex Delaware's]. Within hours the teenager has been arrested at the scene of the mutilation murders of his mentor and lover, and an anonymous street hustler. The case is not nearly as simple as it seems. Perhaps the best of Kellerman's books . . . a triumph . . . complex plot twists . . . believable characters . . . so vividly drawn Kellerman approaches the boundary of the psychological horror story."   —*The Washington Post*

"*Over the Edge* is startling. Jonathan Kellerman's third Alex Delaware novel is also his best. . . . As a result, a great many people who have so far not been lucky enough to meet Alex are going to make a wonderful reading discovery. . . . Kellerman has reinvented the private-eye story, and maybe just in time. . . . Filled with insight. . . . If you've got a weak stomach, enter Alex's world carefully, but *do* enter."
—Stephen King

"Harrowing. . . . The work of a novelist of uncommon insight and storytelling skill."   —*Los Angeles Times*

"*Over the Edge* is a sleek and high-powered performance. . . . Delaware is no ordinary psychologist. . . . He has demonstrated that he is also a born detective, and in *Over the Edge* he returns to the trail. It leads him into some dark places, through three generations of jealousy and greed . . . drugs and blackmail . . . a wide variety of sexual deviations and a great deal of money."   —*The New York Times*

continued . . .

JONATHAN KELLERMAN

OVER THE EDGE

An Alex Delaware Novel

A SIGNET BOOK

SIGNET
Published by New American Library, a division of
Penguin Putnam Inc., 375 Hudson Street,
New York, New York 10014, U.S.A.
Penguin Books Ltd, 80 Strand,
London WC2R 0RL, England
Penguin Books Australia Ltd, Ringwood,
Victoria, Australia
Penguin Books Canada Ltd, 10 Alcorn Avenue,
Toronto, Ontario, Canada M4V 3B2
Penguin Books (N.Z.) Ltd, 182–190 Wairau Road,
Auckland 10, New Zealand

Penguin Books Ltd, Registered Offices:
Harmondsworth, Middlesex, England

Published by Signet, an imprint of New American Library, a division of Penguin
Putnam Inc. This is an authorized reprint of a hardcover edition published by
Atheneum Publishers. The hardcover edition was published simultaneously
in Canada by Collier Macmillan Canada, Inc. For information address Atheneum
Publishers, an imprint of Simon and Schuster, 1230 Avenue of the Americas,
New York, NY 10020.

First Signet Printing, March 1988
First Signet Printing (Kellerman Afterword), January 2002
10 9 8 7 6 5 4 3 2 1

Copyright © Jonathan Kellerman, 1987
Afterword copyright © Jonathan Kellerman, 2002

Printed in the United States of America

PUBLISHER'S NOTE
This is a work of fiction. Names, characters, places, and incidents either
are the product of the author's imagination or are used fictitiously,
and any resemblance to actual persons, living or dead, business
establishments, events, or locales is entirely coincidental.

As always, to my family.

And to Barney Karpfinger,
Agent Extraordinaire.

Have mercy, Heaven! When here I
cease to live
And this last act of
wretchedness forgive!

Thomas Chatterton
("The Marvellous Boy")
Last Verses
August 24, 1770

Many thanks to Michael Tolwin, M.D., tour guide

1

IT WAS my first middle-of-the-night crisis call in three years.

A thousand days out of practice, and there I was, bolted upright in the darkness, clutching the receiver with sleep-slowed fingers, queasy and drowsy but ready for action—my voice soothingly professional even as my brain struggled for a toehold in its climb toward consciousness.

Slipping into the old role with autonomic ease.

There was a stirring from the other side of the bed. The phone had wrenched Robin from sleep, too. A blade of lace-filtered starlight striped her face, the perfect features restfully blank.

"Who is it, Alex?"

"The service."

"What's the matter?"

"I'm not sure. Go back to sleep, hon, I'll take it in the library."

She looked at me questioningly, then rolled away in a swaddle of covers. I threw on a robe and left the bedroom. After switching on the lights and wincing at the glare, I found paper and pencil and picked up the receiver.

"I'm back."

"This one sounds like a real emergency, Doctor. He's breathing real hard and not making much sense. I had to ask him several times for his name before he caught on, and then he screamed it at me. I'm not sure, but it sounded like Jimmy Catmus or Cadmus."

"Jamey Cadmus." Uttering the name brought me completely awake, as if by incantation. Memories that had been buried for half a decade surged forth with the clarity of yesterday. Jamey was someone you didn't forget.

1

"Put him on," I said.

The phone line crackled.

"Hello, Jamey?"

Silence.

"Jamey? This is Dr. Delaware."

I wondered if the connection had gone through.

"Jamey?"

Nothing, then a low moan and labored, shallow breathing.

"Jamey, where are you?"

The reply was a strangled whisper: "Help me!"

"Of course, Jamey. I'm here to help. What's the matter?"

"Help me hold it together. Together. Together. It's all . . . coming apart. The stink of it. Stinkflesh of all seasons . . . stinking lesions . . . ripped apart by the reeking blade—"

Until then I'd conjured an image of him as I'd seen him last: solemnly prepubescent, blue-eyed, milky-skinned, hair black and shiny as a helmet. A twelve-year-old boy. But the voice on the telephone was a tortured baritone, undeniably masculine. The juxtaposition of visual and aural was bizarre, unsettling—the boy lipsynching the words of an adult ventriloquist.

"Easy, Jamey. It's all right." Taking special care to be gentle: "Where are you?"

More silence, then jumbled spurts of words, as erratic and staccato as automatic-weapons fire: "Stop telling me that! Always telling me that stink. I hear you lying telling me the sudden burst of valve arterial . . . plumes of the nightbird . . . I am so . . .—Shut up! I've heard enough stink! The dark has gone stink—masturbating master . . ."

Word salad.

A gasp and his voice trailed off.

"I'm here, Jamey. I'm staying right with you." When there was no reply, I went on: "Have you taken something?"

"Dr. Delaware?" Suddenly he seemed calm, surprised at my presence.

"Yes. Where are you—"

"It's been a long time, Dr. D.," he said mournfully.

"Yes, it has, Jamey. It's good to hear from you."

No answer.

"Jamey, I want to help you, but I need to know what's going on. Please tell me where you are."

The silence stretched to an uncomfortable length.

"Have you taken anything? Done anything to hurt yourself?"

"I'm in hellstink, Dr. D. Hell's bells. A glass canyon."

"Tell me about it. Where is this canyon?"

"*You* know!" he snarled. "*They* told you! *They* tell me all the time! An abyss—a piss!—glass and steelstink."

"Where, Jamey?" I said softly. "Tell me exactly."

His breathing quickened and grew louder.

"Jamey—"

The cry was sudden, wounded, a pain-filled whisper.

"Oh! The earth stinking, soaked scarlet . . . opening lips. . . . The plumes are rankstink. . . . *They told me so, the stinking liars!*"

I tried to break through, but he'd retreated absolutely into a private nightmare. Maintaining the eerie whisper, he held a rambling dialogue with the voices in his head, debating, cajoling, cursing the demons that threatened to engulf him until the curses gave way to abject terror and impotent sobbing. Powerless to stem the hallucinatory flow, I waited it out, my own heartbeat hastened now, shivering despite the warmth of the room.

Finally his voice dissipated in a funnel of sucking breaths. Taking advantage of the silence, I tried to reel him back.

"Where's the glass canyon? Tell me exactly, Jamey."

"Glass and steel and miles of tubing. Serpentine . . . Rubber snakes and rubber walls . . ." More shallow breathing. "Goddamn white zombies bouncing bodies off the walls . . . needle games . . ."

It took me a moment to process that.

"Are you in a hospital?"

He laughed hollowly. The sound was frightful. "They call it that."

"Which one?"

"Canyon Oaks."

I knew the place by reputation: small, private, and very expensive. I felt momentary relief. At least he hadn't overdosed in some dark alley.

"How long have you been there?"

He ignored the question and started crying again.

"They're killing me with lies, Dr. D.! Programming

painlasers through the tender flesh! Sectioning the cortex—draining the juices raping the tender gender flesh—stinkpiece by stinkpiece!"

"Who—"

"Them! . . . flesh eaters . . . white zombies . . . dead-climb all up out of the towerful torrent-shit . . . shit plumes . . . shit birds . . . out of the wetflesh . . . *Help me, Dr. D.*—fly here help me hold it together . . . beam down! Suction me into another sphere into clean. . . ."

"Jamey, I want to help you—"

Before I could finish, he was at it again, his whispers as agonized as if he were being boiled alive. I drew my robe tighter and tried to think of the right thing to say when he landed back on earth. Suppressing feelings of helplessness, I concentrated on what little I could do: Go with the hallucinations, accept them, and try to work from within to calm him down. The important thing was to keep him on the line, not to lose his trust. To ride it out for as long as it took.

It was a good plan, the only sensible one under the circumstances, but I never got a chance to use it.

The whispering rose in pitch as if responding to the twist of an unseen dial, spiraling higher as relentlessly as an air-raid siren. At the top of the spiral was a plaintive bleat, then a scream amputated by a dull click as the line went dead.

THE NIGHT operator at Canyon Oaks Hospital informed me that incoming calls wouldn't be accepted until 8 A.M. —almost five hours away. I used my title, told her it was an emergency, and was connected to a flat contralto who identified herself as the night shift nursing supervisor. She listened to what I had to say, and when she answered, some of the flatness was seasoned by skepticism.

"What did you say your name was, sir?"

"Dr. Alex Delaware. And you're Ms.—"

"*Mrs*. Vann. Are you a member of our staff, Doctor?"

"No. I treated him several years ago."

"I see. And you say he called you?"

"Yes. Just a few minutes ago."

"That's highly unlikely, Doctor," she said with some satisfaction. "Mr. Cadmus is on a locked—he has no phone access."

"It was him, Mrs. Vann, and he was in real distress. Have you checked his room recently?"

"No, I'm on the opposite wing of the hospital." A pause. "I suppose I could call over there."

"I think you should."

"Very well. Thank you for the information, Doctor. And good night."

"One more thing—how long has he been hospitalized?"

"I'm afraid I'm not allowed to give out confidential patient information."

"I understand. Who's his attending doctor?"

"Our director, Dr. Mainwaring. But," she added, protectively, "he's not available at this hour."

Muffled noises came on in the background. She put me on hold for a long time, then returned to the line, sounding stressed, and told me she had to go. It was the second time in ten minutes I'd been cut off.

I switched off the lights and went back to the bedroom.
Robin turned toward me and propped herself on her
elbows. The darkness had transformed the copper in her
hair to a strangely beautiful lavender. Her almond eyes
were half closed.

"Alex, what was that all about?"

I sat on the edge of the bed and told her about the call
from Jamey and my conversation with the night nurse.

"How strange."

"It *is* weird." I rubbed my eyes. "I don't hear from a
kid in five years, and out of the blue he calls, talking
gibberish."

I stood up and paced.

"He had problems in those days, but he wasn't crazy.
Nowhere near crazy. His mind was a work of art. Tonight he was a mess—paranoid, hearing voices, talking
nonsense. Hard to believe it's the same person."

But intellectually I knew it was possible. What I'd
heard over the phone had been psychosis or some kind of
bum trip. Jamey was a young man by now—seventeen or
eighteen—and statistically ripe both for the onset of schizophrenia and for drug abuse.

I walked to the window and leaned on the sill. The
glen was silent. A faint breeze ruffled the pinetops. I
stood there for a while and stared out at velvety layers of
darkness.

Finally she spoke:

"Why don't you come back to bed, honey?"

I crawled back between the sheets. We held each other
until she yawned and I felt her body go slack with fatigue. I kissed her, rolled away, and tried to fall asleep,
but it didn't work. I was too wound up, and both of us
knew it.

"Talk," she said, slipping her hand into mine.

"There's really nothing to talk about. It was just so
strange to hear from him like that. And then getting the
cold shoulder from the hospital. The hag I spoke to
didn't seem to give a damn. She was a real ice cube,
acted as if *I* were a nut case. Then, while I was on hold,
something happened that upset her."

"You think it had something to do with him?"

"Who the hell knows? The whole thing is so bizarre."

We lay side by side. The silence began to feel oppressive. I looked at the clock: 3:23. Raising her hand to my lips, I kissed the knuckles, then lowered and released it. I pushed myself out of the bed, walked around to her side, leaned over, and covered her bare shoulders.

"I won't be able to sleep tonight. No reason to keep you up."

"Gonna read?" she asked, knowing my usual way of coping with occasional insomnia.

"No." I went to the closet and began selecting clothing in the dark. "I think I'll take a drive."

She rolled over and stared, eyes open wide.

I fumbled a bit before finding flannel slacks, cordovans, a turtleneck, and a mediumweight Harris tweed sportcoat. Sufficiently professional. Quietly I got dressed.

"You're going out there—aren't you?—to that hospital."

I shrugged.

"The kid's call was a cry for help. We once had a good relationship. I liked him a lot. Now he's falling apart, and there's probably nothing I can do, but it'll make me feel better to get some closure."

She looked at me, started to say something, and sighed.

"Where is this place?"

"Out in the West Valley. Twenty-five minutes at this hour. I'll be back soon."

"Be careful, Alex, okay?"

"Don't worry, I'll be fine."

I kissed her again and said, "Go back to sleep."

But she was wide-awake as I crossed the threshold.

Winter had come late to Southern California and had hung on tenaciously before dying. It was cold for early spring, and I buttoned my coat as I stepped onto the terrace and walked down the front steps. Someone had planted night-blooming jasmine several years ago; it had flourished and spread, and now the glen was heavy with perfume from March through September. I breathed deeply and, for one brief moment, thought of Hawaii.

The Seville was in the carport, next to Robin's Toyota longbed. It was coated with dust and in need of a tune-up, but started up faithfully. The house sits atop a twisted old bridle path, and it takes a bit of maneuvering to get a Cadillac through the tree-shaded curves without a scratch. But after all these years I can do it in my sleep, and after backing out with a lurch, I wheeled around quickly and began the winding descent.

I turned right on Beverly Glen Drive and barreled downhill toward Sunset. Our part of the glen is rural chic—small clapboard houses on stilts gussied up with insets of stained glass, SAVE THE WHALE bumper stickers on old Volvos, a market specializing in organic produce—but just before Sunset it turns into gated estates. At the boulevard I hooked right and headed toward the San Diego Freeway. The Seville sped past the northern border of the UCLA campus, the south gate of Bel Air, hypertrophied haciendas on million-dollar lots. A few minutes later the 405 overpass came into view. I pointed the Seville at the on-ramp and flew onto the freeway.

A couple of tankers groaned in the slow lane, but otherwise all five lanes were mine. The blacktop rose before me, vacant and glistening, an arrowhead aimed infinitely at the horizon. The 405 is a section of the artery that traverses California vertically, running parallel with the ocean from Baja to the Oregon border. At this part of the state it tunnels through the Santa Monica mountain range, and tonight the highlands that had been spared hovered darkly, their towering, dusty haunches breaded with the season's first vegetative stubble.

The asphalt humped at Mulholland, then dipped toward the San Fernando Valley. A breathtaking view—the pulsating rainbow of distant lights—appeared suddenly, but at seventy miles per, it dissolved in an instant. I swung to the right, got onto the Ventura Freeway West, and increased my speed.

I zipped through twelve miles of valley suburbia: Encino; Tarzana (only in L.A. could a bedroom community be named after the apeman); Woodland Hills. Keyed up and bright-eyed, I kept both hands on the wheel, too edgy to listen to music.

Just before Topanga the blackness of night surrendered to an explosion of color, a winking panoply of scarlet, amber, and cobalt blue. It was as if a gigantic Christmas tree had been planted in the middle of the freeway. Mirage or not, I braked to a halt.

Few vehicles had been cruising the freeway at that hour. But there were enough of them—logjammed and static, bumper to bumper—to create a 4:00 A.M. traffic jam.

I sat for a while with the motor idling, then realized that the other drivers had turned off their engines. Some had exited and could be seen leaning against trunks and hoods, smoking cigarettes, chatting, or simply gazing up at the stars. Their pessimism was overwhelming, and I turned off the Seville. In front of me was a silver Porsche Targa. I got out and walked up to it. A ginger-haired man in his late thirties sat in the driver's seat, chewing on a cold pipestem and perusing a legal journal.

"Excuse me, could you tell me what's going on?"

The Porsche driver raised his eyes from the magazine and looked up at me pleasantly. From the smell of things it wasn't tobacco that filled the pipe.

"Smash-up. All lanes are blocked."

"How long have you been here?"

A quick look at a Rolex.

"Half hour."

"Any idea when it'll clear up?"

"Nope. It's a nasty one." He put his pipe back in his mouth, smiled, and returned to an article on maritime shipping contracts.

I continued walking along the left shoulder of the freeway, past half a dozen rows of cold engines. Rubbernecking had slowed traffic on the opposite side to a crawl. The stench of gasoline grew stronger, and my ears picked up an electric chant: multiple police radios barking in independent counterpoint. A few yards more, and the entire scene was visible.

A huge truck—twin transport trailers over eighteen wheels—had jackknifed across the freeway. One trailer remained upright and was positioned perpendicular to the dotted white lines; the other had flipped on its side, a good third of it suspended over the side of the highway. The linkage between the two vans was a severed sprig of twisted mesh. Pinned beneath the sprawling metal carcass was a shiny red compact car crushed like a used beer can. A few feet away sat a larger sedan, a brown Ford, its windows blown out, its front end an accordion.

The lights and noise came from a pair of hook and ladders, half a dozen ambulances, and a platoon of fire department and highway patrol cars. Half a dozen uniforms huddled around the Ford, and a strange-looking machine outfitted at the snout with oversized tongs made repeated passes at its crumpled passenger door. Blanketed bodies on stretchers were being loaded into ambulances. Some were hooked up to intravenous bottles and handled gingerly. Others, encased in body bags, were treated like luggage. From one of the ambulances came a moan, unmistakably human. The freeway was littered with glass, fuel, and blood.

A line of CHP officers stood at parade rest, shifting their attention constantly from the carnage to the waiting motorists. One of them saw me and motioned me back with a curt hand wave. When I didn't comply, he marched forward, grim-faced.

"Go back to your car immediately, sir." Up close he was young and big with a long red face, a skimpy fawn-colored mustache, and thin, tight lips. His uniform had been tapered to show off his muscles, and he sported a tiny, foppish blue bow tie. His name tag said BJOR-STADT.

"How much longer do you think we'll be here, Officer?"

He stepped closer, one hand on his revolver, chewing an antacid and giving off an odor of sweat and wintergreen.

"Go back to your car immediately, sir."

"I'm a doctor, Officer. I've been called out on an emergency and have to get through."

"What kind of doctor?"

"Psychologist."

The answer didn't seem to please him.

"What kind of emergency?"

"A patient of mine just called in crisis. He's been suicidal in the past and is at high risk. It's important that I get to him as quickly as possible."

"You going to this individual's home?"

"No, he's hospitalized."

"Where?"

"Canyon Oaks Psychiatric—just a few miles up."

"Let me see your license, sir."

I handed it over, hoping he wouldn't call the hospital. The last thing I needed was a powwow between Officer Bjorstadt and sweet Mrs. Vann.

He studied the license, gave it back, and looked me over with pale eyes that had been trained to doubt.

"Let's just say, Dr. Delaware, that I follow you to the hospital. You're saying that once we get there, they're going to verify the emergency?"

"Absolutely. Let's do it."

He squinted and tugged on his mustache. "What kind of car are you driving?"

" 'Seventy-nine Seville. Dark green with a tan top."

He studied me, frowning, and said finally: "Okay, Doctor, coast through *slowly* on the shoulder. When you get to this point, you can stop and stay put until I tell you to move. It's a real disaster out here, and we don't want any more blood tonight."

I thanked him and jogged to the Seville. Ignoring hostile stares from the other drivers, I rolled to the front of the line, and Bjorstadt waved me through. Hundreds of flares had been laid down, and the freeway was lit up like a birthday cake. It wasn't until the flames disappeared in my rear-view mirror that I picked up speed.

The suburban landscape receded at Calabasas, giving way to softly rolling hills dotted with ancient gnarled scrub oak. Most of the big ranches had long been subdivided, but this was still upper-crust horse country—high-priced "planned communities" behind gates and one-acre spreads designed for weekend cowboys. I got off the freeway just short of the Ventura County line and, following the arrow on the sign that said CANYON OAKS PSYCHIATRIC HOSPITAL, swung south over a concrete bridge. After passing a self-serve filling station, a sod nursery, and a Christian elementary school, I drove uphill on a one-lane road for a couple of miles until another arrow directed me westward. The pungence of ripe manure clogged the air.

The Canyon Oaks property line was marked by a large flowering peach tree shadowing low, open gates meant more for decor than security. A long, winding lane bordered by boxwood hedge and backed by shaggy eucalyptus led me to the top of a knoll.

The hospital was a Bauhaus fantasy: cubes of white concrete assembled in clusters; lots of plate glass and steel. The surrounding chaparral had been cleared for several hundred yards, isolating the structure and intensifying the severity of its angles. The collection of cubes was longer than tall, a cold, pale python of a building. In

the distance was a black backdrop of mountain studded
with pinpoints of illumination that arced like low, shoot-
ing stars. Flashlights. I parked in the near-empty lot and
walked to the entrance—double doors of brushed chrome
centered in a wall of glass. And locked. I pressed the
buzzer.

A security guard peeked through the glass, ambled
over, and stuck his head out. He was middle-aged and
potbellied, and even in the dark I could see the veins on
his nose.

"Yes, sir?" He hitched up his trousers.

"I'm Dr. Delaware. A patient of mine—James Cadmus—
called in crisis, and I wanted to see how he was."

"Oh, *him*." The guard scowled and let me in. "This
way, Doctor."

He led me through an empty reception room decorated
in insipid blue-greens and grays and smelling of dead
flowers, turned left at a door marked C Ward, unlocked
the dead bolt, and let me pass through.

On the other side was an unoccupied nursing station
equipped with personal computers and a closed-circuit
TV monitor displaying video oatmeal. The guard passed
the station and continued to the right. We entered a
brief, bright corridor checkered with blue-green doors,
each pocked with a peephole. One door was open, and
the guard motioned toward it.

"Here you go, Doc."

The room was six-by-six, with soft white vinyl walls
and low, flat ceilings. Most of the floor space was taken
up by a hospital bed fitted with leather restraints. There
was a single window high up on one wall. It had the filmy
look of old Plexiglas and was barred with steel posts.
Everything—from the commode to the nightstand—was
built in, bolted down, and padded with blue-green vinyl.
A pair of crumpled white pajamas lay on the floor.

Three people in starched white crowded the room.

An obese blond woman in her forties sat on the bed,
head in hands. By her side stood a big, broad black man
wearing horn-rimmed glasses. A second woman, young,
dark, voluptuous, and sufficiently good-looking to pass
for Sophia Loren's kid sister, stood, arms folded across
her ample chest, at some distance from the other two.

Both women wore nurse's caps; the man's tunic buttoned to the neck.

"Here's his doctor," announced the guard to a trio of stares. The fat woman's face was tear-streaked, and she looked frightened. The big black narrowed his eyes and went back to looking impassive.

The good-looking woman's eyes narrowed with anger. She shouldered the black man aside and stomped over. Her hands were clenched, and her bosom heaved.

"What's the meaning of this, Edwards?" she demanded in a contralto I recognized. "Who is this man?"

The guard's paunch dropped a few inches.

"Uh, he said he was Cadmus's doctor, Mrs. Vann, and, uh, so I—"

"It was a misunderstanding." I smiled. "I'm Dr. Delaware. We spoke on the phone—"

She looked at me with amazement and swiveled her attention back to the guard.

"This is a *locked ward*, Edwards. It's locked for two reasons." She gave him a bitter, condescending smile. "Isn't it?"

"Yes, ma'am—"

"What are those reasons, Edwards?"

"Uh, to keep the loon—to maintain security, ma'am, and, uh—"

"To keep the patients *in* and strangers *out*." She glared at him. "Tonight you're batting oh-for-two."

"Yes, ma'am. I just thought since the kid—"

"That's enough thinking on your part for one night," she snapped. "Return to your post."

The guard blinked rheumily in my direction.

"You want me to take him—"

"*Go*, Edwards."

He looked at me hatefully and shuffled away. The fat woman on the bed put her head back in her hands and began to snuffle. Mrs. Vann shot her a sidelong glance full of disdain, batted her long dark lashes in my direction, and held out a finely boned hand.

"Hello, Dr. Delaware."

I returned the greeting and tried to explain my presence.

"You're a very dedicated man, Doctor." Her smile was a cold white crescent. "I suppose we can't fault you for that."

"I appreciate that. How's—"

"Not that you should have been let in—Edwards will answer for that—but as long as you're here, I don't imagine you'll do much harm. Or good, for that matter." She paused. "Your former patient's no longer with us."

Before I could respond, she went on:

"Mr. Cadmus escaped. After assaulting poor Miss Surtees here."

The fat blonde looked up. Her hair was a stiff, platinum meringue. The face under it was pale and lumpy and mottled with pink. Her eyebrows were plucked flat, canopying small, olive drab, porcine eyes rimmed with red. Thick lips greasy with gloss tensed and trembled.

"I went in to check on him"—she sniffled—"just like I do every night. All this time he's been such a nice kid, so I undid the cuffs like I always do—give the boy a bit of freedom, you know? A little compassion doesn't hurt, does it? Then the massage—wrists and ankles. What he always does is he drifts right off in the middle of the massage and starts smiling like a baby. Gets a good sleep sometimes. This time he jumped up real crazy, screaming and frothing at the mouth. Punched me in the stomach, tied me with the sheet, and gagged me with the towel. I thought he was gonna kill me, but he just took my key and—"

"That's enough, Marthe," said Mrs. Vann firmly. "Don't upset yourself any further. Antoine, take her to the nurses' lounge, and get some soup or something into her."

The black man nodded and propelled the fat woman out the door.

"Private-duty nurse," said Mrs. Vann when they were gone, making it sound like an epithet. "We never use them, but the family insisted, and when big bucks are involved, the rules have a way of getting bent." Her head shook, and the stiff cap rustled. "She's a float. Not even registered, just an LVN. You can see the good she accomplished."

"How long's Jamey been here?"

She came closer, brushing my sleeve with her fingertips. Her badge had a picture that didn't do her justice and, under it, a name: Andrea Vann, R.N.

"My, but you're persistent," she said archly. "What

makes you think that information is less confidential than it was an hour ago?"

I shrugged.

"I had the feeling when we spoke on the phone that you thought I was some sort of crank."

The frigid smile returned.

"And now that I see you in the flesh I'm supposed to be impressed?"

I grinned, hoped it was charming. "If I look the way I feel, I wouldn't expect you to be. All I'm trying to do is make some sense out of the last hour."

The smile turned crooked and, in the process, somehow grew more amiable.

"Let's get off the ward," she said. "The rooms are soundproofed, but the patients have an uncanny way of knowing when something's up—almost an animal type of thing. If they catch on, they'll be howling and throwing themselves against the walls all shift."

We went into the reception room and sat down. Edwards was there, shuffling around miserably, and she ordered him to fetch coffee. He screwed up his lips, swallowed another gallon of pride, and complied.

"Actually," she said, taking a sip and putting the cup down, "I did think you were a crank—we get plenty of them. But when I saw you, I recognized you. A couple of years ago I attended a lecture you gave at Western Peds on childhood fears. You did a nice job."

"Thanks."

"My own kid was having bad dreams at the time, and I used some of your suggestions. They worked."

"Glad to hear it."

She pulled out a cigarette from a pack in the pocket of her uniform and lit it.

"Jamey was fond of you. He mentioned you from time to time. When he was lucid."

She frowned. I interpreted it:

"Which wasn't very often."

"No. Not very. How long did you say it's been since you last saw him?"

"Five years."

"You wouldn't recognize him. He—" She stopped herself. "I can't say more. There's been enough rule bending for one night."

"Fair enough. Can you tell me how long he's been missing?"

"A half hour or so. The orderlies are out in the hills with flashlights."

We sat and drank coffee. I asked her what kinds of patients the hospital treated, and she chain-lit another cigarette before answering.

"If what you're asking is, Do we get lots of escapes, the answer is no."

I said I hadn't meant that at all, but she cut me off.

"This isn't a prison. Most of our wards are open—the typical stuff: acting-out adolescents, depressives past the high-risk period, anorexics, minor manics, Alzheimer's, cokeheads, and alkies on detox. C Ward is small—only ten beds, and they're rarely all full—but it creates most of our hassles. C patients are unpredictable—agitated schizos with impulse control problems; rich psychopaths with connections who weaseled out of jail by checking in for a few months; speed freaks and cokers who've taken it too far and ended up paranoid. But with phenothiazines, even they don't act up much—better living through chemistry, right? We run a tight ship."

Looking angry again, she stood, adjusted her cap, and dropped her cigarette into cold coffee.

"I'm gonna have to get back, see if they found him yet. Anything else I can do for you?"

"Nothing, thanks."

"Have a nice drive back, then."

"I'd like to stick around and talk to Dr. Mainwaring."

"I wouldn't do that if I were you. I called him right after we discovered Jamey was missing, but he was in Redondo Beach—visitation with his kids. Even if he left right away, that's a long drive. You'll be stuck here."

"I'll wait."

She adjusted her cap and shrugged.

"Suit yourself."

Once alone, I sank back down and tried to digest what I'd learned. It didn't add up to much. I sat restlessly for a while, got up, found the men's room, and washed my face. The mirror bounced back a tired visage, but I felt full of energy. Probably running on reserves.

The clock in the reception room said 4:37. I thought of

Jamey wandering in the darkness and grew taut with anxiety.

Trying to put him out of my mind, I sat back and read a copy of the hospital throwaway, *The Canyon Oaks Quarterly*. The cover article was on the politics of mental health financing—lots of talk about HMOs, PPOs, PROs, and DRGs. The gist of it was to urge families of patients to lobby legislators and insurance carriers for more money. Briefer pieces dealt with anticholinergic syndrome in the elderly—old people misdiagnosed as senile because of drug-induced psychosis—the fine points of occupational therapy, the hospital pharmacy, and a new eating disorders program. The entire back page was an essay by Guy Mainwaring, M.D., FACP, medical director, entitled "The Changing Role of the Psychiatrist." In it he asserted that psychotherapy was of relatively minor value in dealing with serious mental disorders and best left to nonmedical therapists. Psychiatrists, he stressed, were physicians and needed to return to the medical mainstream as "biochemical engineers." The article ended with a paean to modern psychopharmacology.

I put the paper down and waited restlessly for half an hour before hearing the rumble of an engine and the sizzle of gravel under rubber. A pair of headlights beamed through the glass surrounding the front doors, and I had to shield my eyes from the glare.

The headlights went off. After my pupils had adjusted, I made out the waffled contours of a Mercedes grille. The doors swung open, and a man charged in.

He was fiftyish and lean, with a face that was all points and angles. His hair was gray-brown and thin and brushed straight back over a generous crown. A widow's peak marked the center of a high, wide brow. His nose was long and sharp and slightly off-center; his eyes were restless brown marbles set deeply in shadowed sockets. He wore a heavy gray suit that had cost a lot of money a long time ago, a white shirt, and a gray tie. The suit hung loosely, trousers bagging over dull black oxfords. A man unconcerned with frills and niceties, a perfect match for the Bauhaus building.

"Who are you?" The accent was crisp and British.

I stood up and introduced myself.

"Ah, yes. The psychologist. Mrs. Vann told me about Jamey's call to you. I'm Dr. Mainwaring."

He shook my hand vigorously but mechanically.

"It was good of you to drive all the way out here, but I'm afraid I can't talk with you at length. Have to put things in order." Then, as if contradicting himself, he leaned closer. "What did the boy have to say over the phone?"

"Not much that made sense. He was extremely anxious and seemed to be experiencing auditory hallucinations. Pretty much out of control."

Mainwaring made a show of listening, but it was obvious that nothing I'd said surprised him.

"How long's he been this way?" I asked.

"Quite some time." He looked at his watch. "Sad case. Apparently he was extremely bright once."

"He was a genius. Off the scale."

He scratched his nose. "Yes. One wouldn't know it now."

"That bad?" I asked, hoping he'd say more.

"Quite."

"He was moody," I recalled, trying to get a dialogue going. "Complex—which you'd expect, given his intellectual level. But there was no indication of psychosis. If I had predicted anything, it would have been depression. What precipitated the breakdown? Drugs?"

He shook his head.

"Sudden onset schizophrenia. If I understood the etiologic process"—he smiled, revealing an Englishman's tea-stained teeth—"I'd be waiting for the call from Stockholm."

The smile faded quickly.

"I'd best be off," he said, as if talking to himself, "to see if he's turned up. I've avoided drawing the authorities into this—for the sake of the family. But if our people don't find him soon, I may have to call the police. It gets quite cold in the mountains, and we can't have him catching pneumonia."

He turned to go.

"Would you mind if I waited around to see him?"

"I'm afraid that wouldn't be advisable, Dr. Delaware—confidentiality and all that. I appreciate your concern and regret your driving out here for nothing. But before anything else, the family needs to be notified—which may take some doing. They're in Mexico on holiday, and you know the phones down there." His eyes darted distractedly. "Perhaps we can chat at some later date—once the proper releases have been signed."

He was correct. I had no right—legally or professionally—to a shred of information on Jamey. Even the moral prerogatives were vague. He'd called me for help, but what was that worth? He was crazy, incapable of making rational choices.

And yet he'd been rational enough to plot and carry out his escape, sufficiently intact to obtain my number.

I looked at Mainwaring and knew that I'd have to live with the questions. Even if had the answers, he wouldn't be doling them out.

He took my hand again and pumped it, muttered something apologetic, and rushed off. He'd been cordial, collegial and had told me nothing.

I stood alone in the empty waiting room. The sound of shuffling feet made me turn. Edwards, the guard, had waddled in, somewhat unsteadily. He threw me a feeble imitation of a tough guy stare and fondled his billy club. From the look on his face it was clear he blamed me for all his troubles.

Before he could verbalize his feelings, I saw myself to the door.

3

I GOT home at five forty-five. Robin was sleeping, so I sat in the living room and watched the sun wipe the tarnish from a sterling silver sky. By six-fifteen she was up and humming, draped in a wine-colored kimono. I went into the bedroom, and we embraced. She drew away and cupped my chin with her hand. Taking in my unshaven face and rumpled clothes, she looked at me, incredulous.

"You've been up all this time!"

"I got back a few minutes ago."

"Oh, honey, you must be exhausted. What happened?"

"When I got there, he was gone. Escaped. I stayed for a while, hoping they'd find him."

"Escaped? How?"

"He knocked out his nurse, tied her up, and split. Probably went up into the foothills."

"That's spooky. Is this kid dangerous, Alex?"

"He could be," I admitted reluctantly. "The head nurse implied as much without coming out and saying so—told me the ward he was on was reserved for unpredictable patients. On the phone he was ranting about flesh eaters and reeking blades."

She shuddered. "I hope they find him soon."

"I'm sure they will. He couldn't get too far."

She began laying out her clothes. "I was going to make breakfast," she said, "but if you're beat, I can grab something in Venice."

"I'm not hungry, but I'll keep you company."

"You sure? You look awfully beat."

"Positive. I'll sleep after you leave."

She dressed for work in jeans, chambray shirt, crew-neck sweater, and Top-Siders, making the outfit look as elegant as an evening gown. Her long auburn-tinted hair has the kind of bouncy, soft curl obtainable only from

20

nature. This morning she wore it loose, glossy ringlets tumbling over delicate shoulders; at work she would bunch it up under a cloth cap. All sixty-two inches of her moved with a liquid grace that never ceased to catch my eye. Looking at her, you'd never know she was an ace with a circular saw, but that was part of what had attracted me to her in the first place: strength and mastery in a totally feminine package, the ability to forge beauty amid the roar of lethal machinery. Even covered with sawdust, she was gorgeous.

She sprayed herself with something floral and kissed my chin. "Ouch. You need a sanding."

Arms around each other, we went into the kitchen.

"Sit," she ordered, and proceeded to prepare breakfast— bagels, marmalade, and a pot of decaffeinated Kona coffee. The room was sun-filled and warm, soon seasoned by the burgeoning aroma of the coffee. Robin laid out two place settings on the ash-burl trestle table she'd built last winter, and I carried the food in on a tray.

We sat opposite each other, sharing the view. A family of doves cooed and pecked on the terrace below. The gurgle of the fish pond was barely audible. Robin's heart-shaped face was lightly made up—just a trace of shadow over eyes the color of antique mahogany—the olive-tinted skin smooth and burnished by the last remnants of summer tan. She spread marmalade on half a bagel with quick, sure strokes and offered it to me.

"No, thanks. Just coffee for now."

She ate slowly and with obvious pleasure, rosy, alert, and bristling with energy.

"You look raring to go," I said.

"Uh-huh," she replied between mouthfuls. "Got a big day. Bridge reset on Paco Valdez's concert box, finish a twelve-string, and get a mandolin ready for spraying. I'm gonna come home stinking of varnish."

"Great. I love a smelly woman."

She'd always been industrious and self-directed, but since returning from Tokyo, she'd been a dynamo. A Japanese musical conglomerate had offered her a lucra-tive position as a design supervisor, but after much delib-eration she'd turned it down, knowing she preferred craftsmanship to mass production. The decision had re-

newed her dedication, and twelve-hour days at the Venice studio were becoming the rule.

"Hungry yet?" she asked, holding out another bagel
half.

I took it and chewed absently; for all I tasted it could
have been warm modeling clay. I put it down and saw
her shake her head and smile.

"Your lids are drooping, Alex."

"Sorry."

"Don't be. Just get yourself into bed, fella."

She finished her coffee, stood, and began clearing the
table. I retreated to the bedroom, peeling out of my
clothes in transit. After drawing the drapes, I slunk between the sheets and lay on my back. I'd been staring at
the ceiling for several minutes when she stuck her head
in.

"Still up? I'm going now. Be back around seven. How
about dinner out?"

"Sure."

"I have a craving for Indian. Does varnish go with
tandoori chicken?"

"It does if you've got the right wine."

She laughed, fluffed her hair, came over, and kissed
my forehead. "Catch you later, sweetie."

After she left, I slept for a couple of hours. I awoke
feeling fuzzy, but a shower and a glass of orange juice
made me feel semihuman.

Dressed in jeans and a polo shirt, I went into the
library to work. My desk was stacked with papers. It had
never been like me to procrastinate, but I was still unac-
customed to being busy.

Three years earlier, at thirty-three, I'd fled burnout by
retiring prematurely from the practice of psychology. My
plan had been to loaf and live off investments indefi-
nitely, but the leisurely life ended up being far more
exciting—and bloody—than I could have known. One
year and a reconstructed jaw later, I crawled out of my
cave and began working part-time—accepting a few court-
ordered custody evaluations and short-term consultations.
Now, though still not ready for the commitment of long-
term therapy cases, I'd increased my consult load to
where I felt like a workingman again.

I stayed at the desk until one, finishing two reports to judges, then drove into Brentwood to have them typed, photocopied, and mailed. I stopped at a place on San Vicente for a sandwich and a beer and, while waiting for the food to arrive, used a pay phone to call Canyon Oaks. I asked the operator if Jamey Cadmus had been found yet, and she referred me to the day shift supervisor, who referred me to Mainwaring. His secretary told me he was in conference and wouldn't be available until late afternoon. I left my service number and asked him to return the call.

My table was near the window. I watched joggers in peacock-hued sweat suits huff along the grassy median and picked at my lunch. Leaving most of it on the plate, I paid the check and drove back home.

Returning to the library, I unlocked one of the cabinets under the bookshelves. Inside were several cardboard cartons packed with the files of former patients. It took a while to find Jamey's—I'd vacated my office with haste, and the alphabetization was haphazard—but soon I had it in my hands.

Sinking down in the old leather sofa, I began to read. As I turned the pages, the past materialized through the haze of data. Soon vague recollections began to take on shape and form; they rushed in noisily, like poltergeists, evoking a clamor of memories.

I'd met Jamey while consulting on a research study of highly gifted children conducted at UCLA. The woman who ran the grant had a thing about the genius-insanity stereotype: She was out to disprove it. The project emphasized intensive academic stimulation of its young subjects—college-level work for ten-year-olds, teen-agers earning doctorates—and though critics charged that such superacceleration was too stressful for tender minds, Sarita Flowers believed just the opposite: Boredom and mediocrity were the real threats to the kids' well-being. ("Feed the brain to keep it sane, Alex.") Certain that the data would support her hypothesis, she asked me to monitor the mental health of the whiz kids. For the most part, that meant casual rap groups and a counseling session now and then.

With Jamey it had evolved into something more.

I reviewed my notes from our first session and recalled how surprised I'd been when he showed up at my door wanting to talk. Of all the kids in the project, he'd seemed the least open, enduring group discussions with a distant look on his pale, round face, never volunteering information, responding to questions with shrugs and noncommittal grunts. Sometimes his detachment stretched to retreating between the pages of a volume of poetry while the others chattered precociously. I wondered, now, if those asocial tendencies had been a warning sign of things to come.

It had been a Friday—the day I spent on campus. I'd been examining test data in my temporary office when I heard the knock, soft and tentative.

In the time it took me to get to the door he'd backed away into the corridor, and now stood pressed against the wall as if trying to recede into the plaster. He was almost thirteen, but slightness of build and a baby face made him appear closer to ten. He wore a blue and red striped rugby shirt and dirty jeans and clutched a book bag stuffed so full the seams had spread. His black hair was worn long with the bangs cut ruler-straight, Prince Valiant style. His eyes were slate-colored—blueberries floating in milk—and too large for a face that was soft and round and at odds with his skinny body.

He shifted his weight and stared at his sneakers.

"If you don't have time, forget it," he said.

"I have plenty of time, Jamey. Come on in."

He nibbled his upper lip and entered, standing back stiffly as I closed the door.

I smiled and offered him a seat. The office was small, and the options were limited. There was a musty, moth-eaten green couch of Freudian vintage on the other side of the desk and a scarred steel-framed chair perpendicular to it. He chose the couch, sitting next to his book bag and hugging it as if it were a lover. I took the chair and straddled it backwards.

"What can I do for you, Jamey?"

His eyes took off in flight, scanning every detail of the room, finally settling on the tables and graphs crowding the desk top.

"Data analysis?"

"That's right."

"Anything interesting?"

"Just numbers at this point. It'll be awhile before patterns emerge—if there are any."

"Kind of reductionistic, don't you think?" he asked.

"In what way?"

He fidgeted with one of the straps on the book bag. "You know—testing us all the time, reducing us to numbers, and pretending the numbers tell the truth."

He leaned forward earnestly, suddenly intense. I didn't yet know why he'd come but was certain it hadn't been to discuss research design. A great deal of courage building had preceded the knock on my door, and no doubt, a rush of ambivalence had followed. For him the world of ideas was a safe place, a fortress against intrusive and disturbing feelings. I made no attempt to storm the fortress.

"How so, Jamey?"

He kept one hand on the book bag. The other waved like a pennant in a storm.

"Take IQ tests, for example. You pretend that the scores mean something, that they define genius or whatever it is we're supposed to be. Even the name of the study is reductionistic. 'Project 160.' Like anyone who doesn't score a hundred sixty on a Stanford-Binet can't be a genius? That's pretty lame! All the tests do is predict how well someone will do in school. They're unreliable, culturally biased and according to my reading, aren't even that good at predicting—thirty, maybe forty percent accuracy. Would you put your money on a horse that came in a third of the time? Might as well use a Ouija board!"

"You've been doing some research," I said, suppressing a smile.

He nodded gravely.

"When people do things to me, I like to understand what it is they're doing. I spent a few hours in the psych library." He looked at me challengingly. "Psychology's not much of a science, is it?"

"Some aspects are less scientific than others."

"You know what I think? Psychologists—ones like Dr. Flowers—like to translate ideas into numbers in order to look more scientific and impress people. But when you do that, you lose the essence, the"—he tugged at his bangs and searched for the right word—"the *soul* of what it is you're trying to understand."

"It's a good point," I said. "Psychologists themselves have been arguing about it for a long time."

He didn't seem to hear me and continued expounding in a high, child's voice.

"I mean, what about art—or poetry? How can you quantify poetry? By the number of verses? The meter? How many words end with *e?* Would that define or explain Chatterton or Shelley or Keats? That would be *stupid.* But psychologists think they can do the same kind of thing to people and come up with something meaningful."

He stopped, caught his breath, then went on.

"It seems to me that Dr. Flowers has a *fetish* for numbers. And machines. She loves her computers and her tachistoscopes. Probably wishes we were mechanical, too. More *predictable.*" He worried a cuticle. "Maybe it's because she herself needs contraptions to live a normal life. What do you think?"

"It's a theory."

His smile was mirthless.

"Yeah, I forgot. The two of you are partners in this. You have to defend her."

"Nope. When you guys talk to me, it's confidential. Test data—the numbers—go into the computer, but anything else stays out. If you're angry at Dr. Flowers and want to talk about it, go ahead."

He took his time digesting that.

"Nah, I'm not angry at her. I just think she's a sad lady. Didn't she used to be an athlete or something?"

"She was a figure skater. Won a gold medal at the 'sixty-four Olympics."

He was silently pensive, and I knew he was struggling to visualize the transformation of Sarita Flowers from champion to cripple. When he spoke again, his eyes were wet.

"I guess that was a cruel thing to say—about her needing machines and all that."

"She's open about her disabilities," I said. "She wouldn't expect you to pretend they don't exist."

"But jeez, there I was going on about reductionism,

and I went and did the same thing to her—pigeonholed her as a gadget freak because she walks with braces!"

He dug the nails of one hand into the palm of the other.

"Don't be too hard on yourself," I said gently. "Looking for simple answers is just one way we try to make sense out of a complicated world. You're a critical thinker, and you'll be all right. It's people who don't think who sink into bigotry."

That seemed to provide some comfort. His fingers relaxed and spread on whitened denim knees.

"That's an excellent point, Dr. Delaware."

"Thank you, Jamey."

"Uh, could I ask you one more thing about Dr. Flowers?"

"Sure."

"I don't understand her situation—her physical condition. Sometimes she seems pretty strong, almost normal. Last week I actually saw her take a couple of steps by herself. But a few months ago she looked really bad. Like she'd aged years overnight and had no strength at all."

"Multiple sclerosis is a very unpredictable disease," I explained. "The symptoms can come and go."

"Is there any treatment for it?"

"No. Not yet."

"So she could get worse?"

"Yes. Or better. There's no way to know."

"That's hideous," he said. "Like living with a time bomb inside you."

I nodded. "She copes with it by doing work she loves."

The water in the blue-gray eyes had pooled. A single tear rolled down one soft cheek. He grew self-conscious, wiped it away quickly with his sleeve, and turned to stare at a faded ocher wall.

He remained silent for a few moments, then sprang up, grabbing the book bag and hefting it over his shoulder.

"Was there anything else you wanted to talk about, Jamey?"

"No," he said, too quickly. "Nothing."

He walked to the door. I followed and placed a hand on his skinny shoulder. He was quivering like a pup whisked from the litter.

"I'm glad you came by," I said. "Please feel free to do it again. Anytime."

"Sure. Thanks." He flung the door open and scurried away, footsteps echoing faintly down the high, arched corridor.

Three Fridays went by before he showed up again. The book bag was gone. In its place he lugged a graduate-level abnormal psychology text that he'd tagged in a dozen places with shreds of tissue paper.

Plopping down on the couch, he began flipping pages until he came to a frayed scrap of tissue.

"First," he announced, "I want to ask you about John Watson. From what I can gather the man was a total fascist."

We discussed behaviorism for an hour and a half. When I grew hungry, I asked him if he wanted something to eat, and he nodded. We left the office and walked across campus to the Coop. Between mouthfuls of cheeseburger and gulps of Dr Pepper, he kept the dialectic going, moving sequentially from topic to topic, attacking each one as if it were an enemy to be vanquished. His mind was awesome, astounding in its ability to mine slag heaps of data and emerge with essential nuggets. It was as if his intellect had assumed an identity of its own, independent of the childish body in which it was housed; when he talked, I ceased to be aware of his age.

His questions came at me, as rapid and stinging as hailstones. He seemed to have barely assimilated one answer before a dozen new lines of inquiry had been formed. After a while I started to feel like a Sunday batter facing a pitching machine gone berserk. He fired away for a few minutes more, then, just as abruptly as he'd begun, ended the conversation.

"Good." He smiled with satisfaction. "I understand now."

"Great," I said, and exhaled wearily.

He filled half his plate with ketchup and dragged a bunch of soggy french fries through the scarlet swamp. Stuffing them in his mouth, he said:

"You're fairly intelligent, Dr. Delaware."

"Thank you, Jamey."

"When you were a kid, were you bored in school?"

"For the most part. I had a couple of teachers who were inspiring. The rest were pretty forgettable."

"Most people are. I've never really attended school. Not that Uncle Dwight didn't try. When I was five, he sent me to the snobbiest private kindergarten in Hancock Park." He grinned. "Three days into the semester it became clear that my presence was"—he mimicked a histrionic schoolmarm—*"upsetting to the other children."*

"I can imagine."

"They were doing *reading readiness* exercises—color matching, learning the alphabet, stuff like that. I thought it was mind-numbing and refused to cooperate. As punishment, they put me in the corner by myself, which was no punishment at all because my fantasies were terrific entertainment. Meanwhile, I'd gotten hold of an old paperback copy of *The Grapes of Wrath* that someone had left lying around at home. The cover was really interesting, so I picked it up and started to read it. Most of it was pretty accessible, so I really got into it, reading in bed at night with a flashlight, stashing it in my lunch box and taking it to school. I'd sneak in a few pages during snack time and when they stuck me in the corner. After a month or so, when I was halfway through the book, that bitch of a teacher found it. She freaked out, snatched it out of my hands, so I attacked her—punching, biting, a real fight. They called Uncle Dwight down, and the teacher told him I was hyperactive and a discipline problem and needed professional help. I jumped up, accused her of being a thief, and said she was oppressing me the same way the farm workers had been oppressed. I still remember how their jaws dropped—like robots that had become unhinged. She shoved the book in front of me and said, *'Read!'*—just like a Nazi storm trooper ordering a prisoner to march. I buzzed through a couple of sentences, and she told me to stop. That was it—no more kindergarten for Master Cadmus."

He stuck out his tongue and licked ketchup from his lower lip. "Anyway, so much for school days." He looked at his watch. "Oops. Gotta call my ride." And with that, he was off.

The Friday afternoon visits became regular after that, a floating crap game with ideas as the dice. We talked in the office, in the graduate reading room, over junk food

in the Coop, and while strolling the shaded walkways
that webbed the campus. He was fatherless and, despite
the guardianship of an uncle, seemed to have little awareness of what it meant to be male. As I fielded countless
questions about myself, all framed in the hungrily naïve
manner of an immigrant seeking morsels of information
about a new homeland, I knew I was becoming his role
model. But the questioning was one way; when I attempted to probe into his personal life, he changed the
subject or emitted a blitzkrieg of irrelevant abstractions.

It was an ill-defined relationship, neither friendship
nor therapy, for the latter implies a contract to help, and
he had yet to confess the existence of a problem. True,
he was intellectually alienated, but so were most of the
kids on the project; alienation was assumed to be a
common trait of those in the cosmic range of intelligence.
He sought no help, wanted only to talk. And talk. About
psychology, philosophy, politics, literature.

Nevertheless, I never relinquished the suspicion that
he'd shown up that first Friday to unburden himself of
something that bothered him deeply. I'd observed his
moodiness and periodic anxiety, bouts of withdrawal and
depression that lasted for days, had noticed the sudden
dark look or wet eye in the midst of a seemingly neutral
conversation, the acute constriction of throat and involuntary tremble of hand.

He was a troubled boy, plagued, I was sure, by significant conflict. No doubt it was buried deep, wrapped, like
a mummy, in a gauzy cocoon of defenses, and getting to
the core would be no mean task. I decided to bide my
time: The science of psychotherapy is knowing what to
say, the *art* is knowing when to say it. A premature
move, and all would be lost.

On the sixteenth Friday he arrived carrying a load of
sociology books and started to talk about his family,
spurred on, supposedly, by a volume on family structure.
As if lecturing from that text, he ejected the facts, helter-
skelter, in a voice devoid of emotion: The Cadmuses
were "rolling in money"; his paternal grandfather had
built an empire in construction and California real estate.
The old man was long gone, but people spoke of him as
if he were some kind of god. His other grandparents

were dead, too. As were both his parents. ("Almost like a hex, huh? Sure you wanna stick around with me?")

His mother had died in childbirth; he'd seen pictures but knew little about her. Three years later his father had committed suicide by hanging himself. The responsibility of raising an orphaned toddler had fallen to his father's younger brother, Dwight. This had translated to the hiring of a succession of nannies, none of whom had stuck around long enough to mean anything to Jamey. A few years later Dwight had married and fathered two daughters, and now all of them were one happy family—this last comment pronounced with bitterness and a look that warned against further questions.

His father's suicide was one subject I was determined to broach eventually. He'd indicated no self-destructive thoughts or impulses, but I considered him at elevated suicidal risk; the moodiness concerned me, as did his extreme perfectionism, sometimes unrealistic expectations, and fluctuating self-esteem. When you added a history of parental suicide, the odds tipped further upward; the possibility that he'd choose, one bleak day, to imitate the father he'd never known couldn't be ignored.

It came to a head midway through our twentieth session.

He liked to quote poetry—Shelley, Keats, Wordsworth— and was particularly enamored of a poet named Thomas Chatterton, of whom I'd never heard. My questions about the man were evaded with contentions that a poet's work spoke for itself. So I did a little library research of my own.

An afternoon spent slogging through dusty volumes of literary criticism produced some interesting facts: The experts considered Chatterton a genius, the chief poet of England's eighteenth-century Gothic revival and the major precursor to the Romantic movement, but in his day he'd been alternately ignored or vilified.

A tormented, tragic figure, Chatterton lusted for fortune and fame and was denied both. Frustrated at the lack of appreciation for his own works, he perpetrated a major literary fraud in 1768, producing a group of poems supposedly written by a fifteenth-century monk named Thomas Rowley. But Rowley never existed; he was a figment of Chatterton's imagination, his name cribbed from a tombstone at St. John's Church in Bristol. Ironi-

cally, the Rowley poems were well received by the lite-
rati, and Chatterton enjoyed a brief, vicarious adul-
ation—until the hoax came to light and its victims ex-
acted their revenge.

Excommunicated from the literary scene, the poet was
reduced to pamphleteering and menial jobs and, eventually, to begging for scraps of food. There was a final,
morbid twist: Though penniless and denied bread on
credit by local merchants, the starving Chatterton com-
plained to a benevolent apothecary of rat infestation in
his garret and was dispensed arsenic.

On August 24, 1770, Thomas Chatterton swallowed
poison, a suicide at the age of seventeen.

The next time Jamey quoted from him I reported what
I'd learned. We were sitting on the rim of the inverted
fountain that fronted the psych building. It was a clear,
warm day, and he'd taken off his shoes and socks to let
the water trickle over bony white feet.

"Uh-huh," he said glumly. "So what?"

"Nothing. You got me curious, so I looked him up. He
was an interesting fellow."

He moved several feet away and stared into the fountain, kicking one heel against the concrete with enough
force to redden the skin.

"Something the matter, Jamey?"

"Nothing."

Several minutes of tense silence passed before I spoke
again.

"You seem angry about something. Does it bother
you that I looked up Chatterton?"

"No." He turned away disgustedly. "That's not what
pisses me off. It's that you're so smug—thinking you
understand me. Chatterton was a genius, Jamey's a genius; Chatterton was a misfit, Jamey's a misfit. Click,
click, click. Putting it all together like some fucking case
history!"

A pair of passing students heard the anger in his voice
and turned to stare. He didn't notice them and gnawed
on his lip.

"You're probably worried I'm gonna snarf rat poison
up in some attic, right?"

"No. I've—"

"Bullshit. You shrinks are all the same." He folded his arms across his chest, kept smashing at the fountain. Pinpoints of blood sprouted on his heel.

I tried again.

"What I was saying is that I've wanted to talk to you about suicide, but it has nothing to do with Chatterton."

"Oh, really? And what *does* it have to do with?"

"I'm not saying you're suicidal. But I have concerns, and I wouldn't be doing my job if I didn't bring them up, okay?"

"Okay, okay. Just spit it out."

"All right," I said, choosing my words carefully. "Everyone has bad days, but you're depressed way too much of the time. You're an exceptional person—and I don't mean just your intelligence. You're sensitive, caring, and honest." The compliments might have been slaps across the face from the way they made him flinch. "Yet you don't seem to like yourself very much."

"What's to like?"

"A lot."

"Right."

"That's part of what worries me—the way you put yourself down. You set extremely high standards for yourself, and when you succeed, you ignore the success and immediately raise your standards. But when you fail, you won't let go of it. You keep punishing yourself, telling yourself you're worthless."

"So what's the point?" he demanded.

"The point," I said, "is that you're setting yourself up for constant misery."

He avoided eye contact. The blood from his heel trickled into the water and disappeared in a pink swirl.

"None of this is meant as criticism," I added. "It's just that you're going to encounter disappointment throughout your life—everyone does—and it would be good to know how to cope with it."

"Sounds like a great plan," he said sarcastically. "When do we start?"

"Whenever you want."

"I want *now*, okay? Show me how to cope. In three easy lessons."

"First I need to know more about you."

"You know plenty."

"We've talked plenty, but I really don't know much at all. Not about the things that bother you or turn you on—your goals, your values."

"Life and death stuff, huh?"

"Let's say important stuff."

He faced me, smiling dreamily.

"You wanna know how I feel about life and death, Dr. D.? I'll tell you. Both suck. Death's probably quieter."

Crossing his legs, he examined the bloody heel as if studying a biology specimen.

"We don't have to talk about this now," I said.

"But I want to! You've been leading up to it all these months, right? This is what all the buddy-buddy stuff has been about, right? Building rapport so you can head-shrink more effectively. So let's talk about it now, okay! You want to know if I think about killing myself? Sure. Once or twice a week."

"Are they passing thoughts, or do they stay with you for a while?"

"Six of one, half dozen of the other."

"Do you ever think about a method?"

He laughed out loud, closed his eyes, and began reciting in a low voice:

Since we can die but once, what matters it,
If rope or garter, poison, pistol, sword,
Slow wasting sickness or the sudden burst of valve
arterial in the noblest parts,
Curtail the misery of human life?
Tho' varied is the cause, the effect's the same
All to one common dissolution tends.

The eyes opened.

"Tom C. had an answer for everything, didn't he?"

When I didn't respond, he laughed again, forcing it.

"Not amused, Dr. D.? What do you want, catharsis and confession? It's my life, and if I decide to bow out, it's my decision."

"Your decision will affect other people."

"Bullshit."

"No one lives in a vacuum, Jamey. People care about you. I care about you."

"What textbook did you pull that out of?"

The fortress seemed impenetrable. I searched for a wedge.

"Suicide is a hostile act, Jamey. You, of all people, should appreciate that."

His reaction was sudden and extreme. The blue eyes ignited, and his voice choked with rage. Jumping up, he turned on me, shouting shrilly:

"My father was *dog shit!* And so are you for bringing him up!"

He bobbled a shaky finger in front of my face, sputtered, and ran barefoot across the courtyard. I picked up his shoes and socks and took off after him.

Having crossed the science quad, he swung left and disappeared down a flight of steps. Catching up wasn't difficult because his gait was clumsy, spindly legs knocking against one another like syncopated chopsticks.

The steps ended at the loading dock of the chemistry building, an empty concrete rectangle, oil-slicked and darkened by brick walls on three sides. There was only one exit, a green metal door. He tried the latch, but it was locked. Turning to run, he saw me and froze, panting. His face was white and tear-streaked. I put down the shoes and approached.

"Go away!"

"Jamey—"

"Leave me alone!"

"Let's work this out—"

"Why?" he screamed. "Why bother?"

"Because I care about you. You're important to me, and I want you to stick around."

He broke into sobs and looked as if he were going to crumple. I came nearer, put my arm around his shoulder, and held him.

"You're important to me, too, Dr. D." He sniffled into my jacket. I felt his arms go around my waist, small hands caressing my back. "You really are. 'Cause I love you."

I stiffened. It was the wrong thing to do, the worst thing to do. But it was reflexive.

He cried out and twisted free, the young face a mask of hatred and pain.

"There! Now you know! I'm a little faggot! I've been one for years, and now I have the hots for you!"

The shock had worn off, and I was in control again, ready to be therapeutic. I stepped forward. He shrank back.

"Get away, you lame fuck! Leave me the fuck alone! If you don't, I'll scream for help!"

"Jamey, let's talk—"

"*Help!*" he wailed. The sound reverberated in the emptiness of the dock.

"Please—"

He screamed again.

I put the shoes and socks down and walked away.

Over the next few weeks I made repeated attempts to talk to him, but he shunned me. I played the scene over and over in my head, wondering what I could have done differently, wishing for magic while cursing the limitations of words and pauses.

The more I thought about it, the more I worried about suicide. After much deliberation I broke confidentiality and phoned his uncle. Knowing it was the right thing to do didn't make it any easier.

I talked my way through an army of underlings and finally reached Dwight Cadmus at his office in Beverly Hills. Introducing myself, I kept the betrayal to a minimum, mentioning nothing about homosexuality, addressing only my concerns for the boy's safety.

He listened without interruption, answered in a voice that was dry and deliberate.

"Hmm, I see. Yes, that is of concern." A ruminative pause. "Is there anything else, Doctor?"

"Yes. If you have guns in the house, unload them, hide the ammunition, and put them away."

"I'll have that done immediately."

"Lock up your medicines. Try to keep him away from knives—"

"Certainly."

"—and ropes."

Strained silence.

"If that's all, Doctor—"

"I want to reemphasize how important it is to get him

some professional help. If you need a referral, I'd be happy to provide you with a couple of names."

"Thank you. I'll discuss this with my wife and get back to you."

I gave him my number, and he thanked me again for my concern.

I never heard from him.

4

I PUT the file back and called Canyon Oaks again. Mainwaring hadn't returned to his office, but his secretary assured me he'd gotten the message.

In the silence of the library my thoughts wandered. I knew if I sat around long enough, they'd return to roost in dark places. Rising, I searched for the cordless phone and found it in the living room. With the phone hooked to my belt, I stepped out onto the terrace and descended the stairs to the Japanese garden.

The koi were swimming lazily, a concentric rainbow. The sound of my footsteps brought them to the rock-edged rim of the pond, gulping hungrily and churning the water in anticipation.

I tossed a handful of pellets into the water. The fish thrashed and bumped against one another to get at the food. Their scales threw off sparks of scarlet, gold, platinum, and tangerine, the roiling bodies fiery amid the tranquil hues of the garden. Kneeling, I fed the more assertive carp by hand, enjoying the tickle of their barbels against my palm.

When they were sated, I put the food away and sat cross-legged on a cushion of moss, tuning my ears to small sounds: the gurgle of the waterfall; the tiny kissing sounds made by the fish as they nipped at the algae coat on the smooth wet rocks that rimmed their pool, a warm breeze gently agitating the branches of a flowering wisteria. Evening approached and shrouded the garden in shadow. The jasmine began to emit its perfume. I watched colors give way to contours and worked at shrouding my mind.

I'd grown meditatively calm when the phone on my belt whistled and beeped.

"Dr. Delaware," I answered.

"Pretty formal, Alex," said a youthful voice speckled with static.

"Lou?"

"None other."

"How are you? The formality's 'cause I was expecting someone else."

"*I'm* peachy. I trust you're not too disappointed."

I laughed. The static grew louder.

"The connection's weak, Lou. Where are you calling from, ship or shore?"

"Ship. Got a boatload of prospective investors heading for the Turks and Caicos, a hold full of bluefin and wahoo, and enough rum to render the inhibitions flaccid."

Lou Cestare held a long-term lease on a warm spot in my heart. Years ago, when I was earning more money than I knew what to do with, he'd shown me what to do with it, guiding me through a series of real estate and securities investments that would allow me to live comfortably without ever having to work again—if my life-style remained reasonable. He was young and aggressive, a clean-cut, fast-talking, blue-eyed, northern Italian. At the age of twenty-seven he'd been written up by the *Wall Street Journal* as a superstar stock picker. By thirty he was top dog in a large investment firm and heading higher. Then, abruptly, he made a change in *his* life-style, quitting the corporate world, selling a Brentwood spread, packing up a young wife and baby, and moving to northern Oregon to work for himself and a select group of clients. Most were megarich; a few, like myself, he kept on for sentimental reasons. He alternated, now, between a home office in the Willamette Valley and a hundred-foot yacht christened *The Incentive*. Both were outfitted with a fortune in computer gizmos that enabled him to talk to an international army of floor traders by modem.

"Your portfolio came up on-screen the other day, Alex. I've got everything tagged, just like a dentist. Time for a midyear checkup."

"What's up?"

"You've got two hundred eighty K in tax-frees at an average yield of eight-point-seventy-three percent, producing a yearly income of twenty-four thou four hundred forty that Uncle Sam can't touch. Ninety K of that matures over the next few months. It's generally the older stuff with a slightly lower yield—seven-point-nine percent average. The question is, Do you want more munis or should I get you high-yield corporates or T bills? They'd be taxable, but if you're not earning much, the higher rates would put more bucks in your pocket. According to my records, you pulled in forty-two grand last year doing odds and ends. What about this year?"

"I'm working a little more. About six thousand a month."

"Gross or net?"

"Gross."

"Any big deductions?"

"Not really."

"Last year's rentals and interest income were thirty-one K. Any reason for that to change?"

"None that I can foresee."

"So you're pulling a little over a hundred thou, still in a healthy fifty percent bracket. Unless you need to be liquid or feel like gambling, the munis are the way to go."

"What kind of gambling are you talking about?"

"Brand-new over-the-counter issues, mostly unlisted. I've got a laser imaging firm based in Switzerland that looks promising, a Pennsylvania scrap conversion syndicate, and something right up your alley: a Carolina outfit specializing in booby hatches."

"Booby hatches?"

"You bet. This group—Psycorp—contracts for mental health services in medium-sized communities. Mostly down South and Midwest, but it's expanding. Very aggressive marketing, and the demographics look good. Lots of crazies out there, Alex. Bet you never thought of yourself as a high-growth industry."

"I think I'll stick with bonds. What kinds of rates are you getting?"

"I've got a line on some ten and a half percent stuff at par from an estate sale, but you'll have to go out long-term—thirty years minimum. Your net increase in income will be approximately"—I heard keys clicking in the background—"two thousand three hundred and forty dollars. Don't spend it all in one place."

"Double A?"

"These are rated triple B—which is still investment quality—but I expect an upgrade to A in a few months. I don't take ratings that seriously anymore; the services have gotten lazy. Look at the WPPSS debacle—from triple A to the toilet, and they never saw it until it was too late. Best thing is to bird-dog each issue yourself. Which I do—assiduously. The one I've got in mind for you is very kosher. Conservative beach community with a heavy tax base. Long-overdue public utility financing, no controversy. You want in?"

"Sure. How much can you get?"

"Two hundred and fifty thou. I'm committed for a hundred to someone else. You can have the other one fifty."

"Get me a hundred even. Ninety from the maturing bonds, and I'll wire you ten thousand tomorrow. Oregon or the West Indies?"

"Oregon. Sherry's handling transactions while I'm gone."

"How long are you planning to be away?"

"A week, maybe longer. Depends on the fishing and how long it takes for the rich folk to get on each other's nerves. By the way, we got your thank-you note for the coho. Good stuff, huh?"

"That was terrific salmon, Lou. We invited friends over and barbecued it like you suggested."

"Good. You should see the bluefin we've been hauling in. Three-hundred-pounders with meat like purple butter. Got a plate of it sashimied right here in front of me. I'll save you some fillets."

"That would be great, Lou."

"Whoa!" he called out. "Pardon me, Alex, some kind of action starboard. *Jesus God, look at that monster!*" He took a sip of something and came back on the line, swallowing. *"Haul it in, Jimbo!* Pardon me, *again*. Everything okay by you?"

"Just great."

"Terrific. Then I'd best be signing off and heading down to charm the customers."

"Bye, Lou. Think of me over crab cocktails."

"Conch," he corrected. "Marinated in lime juice. Eat it; then play Miles Davis with the shell."

A beep came on the line.

"That your end or mine?" he asked.

"Mine. Call waiting."

"I'll let you go, Alex. Roger, over and out."

I depressed the button and connected to the waiting call.
"Alex? This is Milo, and I gotta make it quick."
"Milo! Good to hear from you. What's up?"
"I've been talking to someone who says he knows you.
Fellow by the name of James Wilson Cadmus."
"Jamey! Where is he?"
"So you do know him?"
"Sure I do. What's—"
"He said something about calling you this morning."
"Yes, he did."
"What time was that?"
"Around three-fifteen."
"What did he have to say?"
I hesitated. Milo is my best friend. I hadn't heard from
him for longer than usual and had started to wonder
about it. Under different circumstances, I would have
welcomed his call. But his tone of voice was far from
friendly, and I became acutely aware of what he did for a
living.
"It was a crisis call," I hedged. "He wanted help."
"With what?"
"Milo, what the hell is this about?"
"Can't explain, pal. Catch you later."
"Wait a second—is the kid okay?"
It was his turn to hesitate. I could visualize him running his hands over his big, scarred face.
"Alex"—he sighed—"I really gotta go."
Click.
It was no way to treat a friend, and I was stiff with
anger. Then I remembered the case he'd been working
on, and anxiety washed over me like toxic surf. I called
his extension at the West L.A. station and, after getting
the runaround from the police bureaucracy, learned nothing more than that he was at a crime scene. Another call
to Canyon Oaks elicited barely muted hostility from
Mainwaring's secretary. I was starting to feel like a pariah.
The thought that Jamey might be mixed up with Milo's
current case was sickening. But at the same time it gave
me some direction. The case had received lots of press
coverage, and if Milo wouldn't tell me what was going
on, perhaps the media would.
I reached for the radio and spun the dial, tuning in
each of the two all-news AM stations in turn. Not a

word. Further spinning produced nothing but audio garbage. The TV news was all blow-dried hair and moist white teeth—happy talk and phony ad libs interspersed with hefty servings of murder and mayhem on blue plate special.

Plenty of horrors but not what I was looking for.

I spied the morning *Times* rolled up on the desk and seized it. Nothing. I knew two people on the paper, the chess editor and Ned Biondi at the Metro Desk. I found the reporter's number on my Rolodex and dialed it.

"Doc! How the hell are you?"

"Just fine, Ned. How about yourself?"

"Super. Ann Marie just started grad school at Cornell. Education."

"That's terrific, Ned. Next time you talk to her give her my best."

"Will do. We couldn't have done it without you."

"She's a great kid."

"No debate from me on that. So, what kind of scoop do you have for me today? The last one wasn't half bad."

"No scoops," I said. "Only questions."

"Ask away."

"Ned, have you heard about anything breaking on the Lavender Slasher case?"

"Not a damn thing." His voice edged a notch up the register. "Something drift your way?"

"Nothing."

"Just random curiosity, huh?"

"Something like that."

"Doc," he implored, "that case has been bone dry for a month. If you know something, don't hold back. Prick teasing went out with the Pill."

"I really don't know anything, Ned."

"Uh-huh."

"Sorry to bother you. Forget I called."

"Sure," he said edgily. "My mind's a goddamn blank."

"Bye, Ned."

"Sayonara, Doc."

Neither of us believed for a moment that the issue had died with the conversation.

Robin came home in a great mood, showered, put on jewelry, and changed into a slinky little black dress. I dressed in a tan linen suit, blue pinpoint oxford shirt with a white spread collar, navy and claret tie, and calfskin loafers. Very stylish, but I felt like a zombie. Arm in arm we walked out onto the terrace and down to the Seville.

She settled in the passenger seat, took my hand, and squeezed it. Reaching up, she opened the sunroof and let warm California air flow over her face. She was in fine spirits, fairly glowing with anticipation. I leaned over and kissed her cheek. She smiled and lifted her lips to mine.

The kiss was warm and prolonged. I mustered all the passion at my disposal but was unable to clear Milo's call from consciousness. Dark, disturbing thoughts kept peeking around the empty corners of my mind. I struggled to contain them and, feeling like a louse for failing, vowed not to ruin the evening.

I started the engine and slipped Laurendo Almeida on the tape deck. Soft Brazilian music filled the car, and I started the engine and tried to summon forth imagery of carnivals and string bikinis.

We dined at a dark, saffron-saturated place in Westwood Village, where the waitresses wore belly dancer costumes and looked as Indian as Meryl Streep. Despite the cheap theatrics, the food was excellent. Robin made her way— daintily but inexorably—through lentil soup, tandoori chicken, cucumbers in yogurt dressing, and a dessert of sweetened milk balls coated with candied silver foil. Hoping she wouldn't notice the masochism, I punished my palate with extra-hot curry.

I let her do most of the talking and contented myself with nods and smiles. It was a continuation of the deception born with the kiss in the car—I was miles away—but I pushed aside my guilt by rationalizing that knavery conceived in love was sometimes kinder than honesty. If she saw through it, she said nothing, perhaps engaging in a loving artifice of her own.

After dinner we cruised Wilshire to the beach and looped down to Pacific Coast Highway. The sky was inky and starless; the ocean, a rolling meadow of black satin. We drove in silence toward Malibu, and the breakers provided a rhythm section for Almeida as he coaxed a samba out of his guitar.

We stopped at Merino's, just past the pier. The interior of the club was hazy with smoke. From a corner stage a four-piece group—drums, bass, alto sax, and guitar—was embroidering Coltrane. We ordered a brandy apiece and listened.

When the set ended, Robin took my hand and asked me what was on my mind. I told her about Milo's call, and she listened gravely.

"The kid's in trouble," I said. "If it has anything to do with the Slasher, huge trouble. The hell of it is I don't know if he's a survivor or a suspect. Milo wouldn't give me the time of day."

"That doesn't sound like Milo," she said.

"Milo hasn't seemed like Milo for a while," I reflected. "Remember how he didn't show up for the New Year's thing and never called to explain. Over the last few weeks I've phoned him at work and at home, must have left a dozen messages, but he hasn't returned one of my calls. At first I thought he was on some kind of under-cover thing, but then his face was all over the tube when they found the last Slasher victim. It's obvious he's dis-tancing himself from us—from me."

"Could be he's going through a rough time," she said. "Working on that case has got to be incredibly stressful for someone in his position."

"If he's stressed, I wish he'd turn to his friends for support."

"Maybe he just can't open up to someone who hasn't been through it, Alex."

I sipped my brandy and thought about it.

"You might be right, I don't know. I've always as-sumed the gay thing wasn't any big deal for him. When our friendship took hold, he brought it up, said he wanted to clear the air, claimed he'd made his peace with it."

"What did you expect him to tell you, honey?"

There was a half inch of brandy left in the snifter. I rolled the stem between my fingers and watched the liquid shift like a tiny golden sea at storm.

"Think I've been insensitive?" I asked.

"Not insensitive. Selectively unaware. Didn't you once tell me that people do that all the time, that we use our minds as filters, to keep things sane?"

I nodded.

"You have to admit, Alex, it's unusual for a straight guy and a gay guy to be as close as you two. I'm sure there are whole segments of Milo that he keeps to himself. Just as you do. Both of you have had to do some heavy denying to keep the relationship going, haven't you?"

"Like what?"

"Like do you ever actually think about what he and Rick do in bed?"

I was silent, knowing she was right. Milo and I talked about everything but sex. Up, down, over, and around the topic, but never squarely on it. It was denial of the first order.

"The funny thing," I said, "is that this afternoon, when I was reviewing my notes on Jamey and asking myself if I could have done anything differently, I fantasized about introducing him to Milo. The kid is gay—or thought he was then—and I wondered if having him meet an adult homosexual who'd made a good adjustment would have been helpful." I frowned. "Pretty damned naïve."

My throat was tight, and the last of the brandy went down hot and rough.

"Anyway," I said bitterly, "the two of them got together without any help from me."

We cleared our heads with a walk along the beach, got back in the Seville, and drove home in silence. Robin rested her head on my shoulder; the burden was comforting. It was just past midnight when I pulled north onto Beverly Glen, ten after when I unlocked the front door.

An envelope fluttered in the draft and settled on the parquet. I picked it up and examined it. It had been hand-delivered by a Beverly Hills messenger service at 11:00 PM. Inside was an urgent request to phone the law offices of Horace Souza as soon as possible next morning ("Re: J. Cadmus") and a number with a mid-Wilshire exchange.

Finally there was someone who wanted to talk to me.

5

RISING EARLY, I had the paper in my hands a minute after it landed. There was a teaser at the bottom of the front page—"POSSIBLE BREAK IN LAVENDER SLASHER CASE"—but it contained no new information other than that LAPD, the Beverly Hills police, and the sheriff's department were expected to announce new developments at a joint press conference later in the day. The rest was rehash—stale facts, interviews with the victims' still-aching families, a dispassionate chronology of the serial murders that had begun a year before and continued with bimonthly regularity.

The Slasher's victims were boy hookers, ranging in age from fifteen to nineteen. Most were runaways from Middle America. All six had been garroted with lavender silk and mutilated after death. The killings had been carried out at an unknown place, the bodies then dumped at various locations around the city. There was a westerly pattern to the dumping, with the first corpse discovered in a back-alley trash bin off Santa Monica Boulevard, in the heart of Boystown, the sixth near a hiking path in Will Rogers State Park. Four bodies had been found in West Hollywood—the sheriff's bailiwick—the last two in West L.A. Division. Geographically Beverly Hills was sandwiched between the two turfs like a sweetmeat, but it had been passed over.

I put the paper down and called Horace Souza's office. It must have been a private line because he picked up the phone himself.

"Doctor, thank you for returning my call so promptly."

"What can I do for you, Mr. Souza?"

"A former patient of yours, James Cadmus, is a client of mine. I'm representing him in a criminal case and would greatly appreciate talking to you about it."

"What's he charged with?"

"I'd prefer to discuss the matter in person, Doctor."

"All right. I can be at your office in an hour. Where are you located?"

"Don't fuss with directions, Doctor. I'll have someone pick you up."

At eight the doorbell rang. I opened it and came face-to-face with a chauffeur in gray livery. He was in his early thirties, tall and rangy, with a strong nose and a weak chin. In the shadow of the nose a thick black mustache had sprouted, covering most of his mouth. His face was pale and freshly shaved and bore several razor nicks along the jawline. His peaked cap had been pushed back so that it rested precariously atop a thatch of long brown hair that flowed over his collar. Satin-edged trousers tapered to needle-toed bullhide cowboy boots. His eyes were dark and, at first glance, lazy. But when they locked onto mine, I sensed plenty of analysis despite the absence of movement.

"Dr. Del'ware? I'm Tully Antrim, here to take you to Mr. Souza. I didn't wanna scratch the car, so I parked it a ways down."

I followed him off my property and down the access road, walking quickly to keep up with his long stride.

A hundred yards above Beverly Glen was a turnaround shadowed by tall trees. On it sat twenty feet of Rolls-Royce—a gleaming, black Phantom IV limousine. I'd seen a picture of one like it in a spread on Prince Charles and Lady Di's wedding. That car had belonged to the mother of the groom.

The chauffeur held open the door to the passenger area and, when I was settled, closed it carefully, walked around, and got into the driver's seat.

The car was big enough to dance in. The interior was gray felt with the feel of cashmere and lots of wood, all of it madly burled and polished to a mirror finish. Crystal bud vases in silver filigree holders were bracketed to the cloth behind each passenger door. Each held a fresh American Beauty rose. The side windows were etched lightly with a floral motif and partially concealed by pullback velvet drapes.

The glass partition separating driver from passenger

was closed. Locked in hermetic silence, I watched the chauffeur go through a series of pantomimes: straightening his cap; turning the ignition key; fiddling with the radio; swaying to what I assumed was the ensuing music.

The Rolls wheeled smoothly toward Beverly Glen. Morning commuter traffic from the Valley was thickening; Antrim was skillful, edging the huge car seamlessly into the flow. He drove south to Wilshire and headed east.

I sat back, feeling like a child amid the grand scale of the limousine. The chauffeur's shaggy head was bopping to music I couldn't hear. There were several ivory buttons on the armrest, each labeled with a tiny silver plaque. I pushed the one that said DRIVER.

"Yes, sir?" he responded without looking back or breaking rhythm.

"Why don't you open the partition? I'd like to hear the music."

"You've got an automatic tape system back there. Controls right on the armrest. Easy listening."

"That'll put me back to sleep. What are you tuned to?"

"KMET. ZZ Top."

"I'll take it."

"Yo." He pushed a button, and the glass slid open. The car was filled with eardrum-rupturing rock-and-roll—the Texas trio rhapsodizing about a girl with legs who knew how to use them. Antrim sang along in a whiny tenor.

The song was followed by a commercial for an abortion clinic selling itself as a feminist health center.

"Some car," I said.

"Yeah."

"Must be pretty rare."

"Probably. Used to belong to some Spanish guy, buddy of Hitler."

"Franco?"

"That's the one."

"How does it drive?"

" 'Sall right for a big car."

Van Halen came on the radio and demolished the potential for further conversation. We hit a red light at Rexford during a news break. While he lit a cigarette, I asked him, "Is this typical treatment?"

"Whaddya mean?"

"Picking people up in limousines."

"Mr. Souza tells me to do something, I do it," he said irritably, then found another rock station and cranked up the volume.

We passed through Beverly Hills and the Miracle Mile and entered the mid-Wilshire financial district. The buildings lining the boulevard were Deco-tinged columns of pink and white granite, seven to ten stories tall, built in the forties and fifties, when people took earthquakes seriously and shied away from genuine skyscrapers.

The structure we stopped at was older and smaller, four stories of red-roofed Italianate wedding cake, a rare remnant from the turn of the century, when Wilshire had been residential. The chauffeur swung up the circular driveway in front of the mansion and parked. The entry door was a nine-foot nest of gargoyles in mahogany. To its right were two discreet brass plates. The first said SOUZA AND ASSOCIATES, A LEGAL CORPORATION. The second listed Souza's name and those of a dozen other lawyers.

Antrim ushered me into an arched hall decorated with dried plants and western art, down a corridor floored in black-and-white marble checkerboard, and through the open doors of a small elevator. He operated it with an old-fashioned lever and unlatched the door at the fourth floor.

We exited to a landing carpeted in silver plush, at the top of a winding carved staircase. High, spotless windows offered a view of what once were formal gardens and now served as the parking lot. In the distance were the elegant, shaded avenues of Hancock Park.

The chauffeur beckoned toward a doorway and led me into an anteroom hung with more western art. In the center of the room was a small writing desk, unoccupied. To the right was a large oil of a depressed-looking Indian on an equally morose horse; to the left, a carved door. He knocked on the door.

The man who answered was medium-sized, sixtyish, and balding, with a wide, blocky body and large, thick hands. He was heavy without being fat, and his low center of gravity suggested he'd be hard to topple. His features were broad and strong—he'd photograph better than life—his skin was steam room pink, and what hair he did have was cropped, coarse, and sandy. He was in shirtsleeves. The shirt was white Egyptian cotton, mono-grammed on the pocket and tucked into navy blue trousers of exquisite cut. Navy suspenders banded a barrel chest. His tie was muted blue and yellow paisley; his shoes were as glossy and black as the Rolls.

"Here's the doc," said Antrim.

"Thank you, Tully," said the bald man sonorously, "you can go now." He stepped forward, emitting a light citrus scent, and grasped my hand.

"Dr. Delaware, I'm Horace Souza. Thank you so much for coming on such short notice."

"No problem. How's Jamey?"

He gave my hand a hard squeeze and let go.

"I saw the boy a couple of hours ago. Psychologically he's at rock bottom. And this is just the beginning. Once the police hold their press conference, he'll cease to be James Cadmus and will don a new persona: the Lavender Slasher. Monster of the Month."

I experienced a sudden, sinking feeling, like being dropped down one of those bottomless shafts that crop up in bad dreams. It wasn't shock, or even surprise; since I'd talked to Milo, the worst-case scenario had slithered in and out of my brain like some nasty little snake. But now the serpent had emerged brazenly, bared its fangs, and struck, murdering hope.

"I can't believe it," was all I could say.

"I've had trouble believing it myself. I was at his christening, Doctor. He was a fat little babe, a handful and a half."

He kneaded his chin between thumb and forefinger.

"I'm very worried about him, Doctor. He's been un-stable for some time, and once the arrest is made public, any remaining coherence will shrivel. You know the times we're living in. The public wants blood. He'll be lynch mob fodder. The DA is in the process of filing on two counts of murder one with six more to follow shortly. Multiple homicide is special circumstances, which means the gas chamber if it's not handled correctly. By *correctly*, I mean organization, teamwork. Can I count you on my team, Doctor?"

"Just what is it you think I can do?"

"Let's discuss that. Please come in."

His sanctum was a large corner room brightened by French doors and ringed by a balcony. On the balcony were pots brimming with azaleas and camellias. The walls were carved architectural paneling brightened by still more frontier art—these paintings looked like original Remingtons—and topped by ornate white molding and a domed white ceiling. The floor was bleached oak, over which a Navaho rug had been laid. In one corner sat a Chippendale table holding a china tea set. The rest was standard high-price law office: oversized desk; leather chairs; ten square feet of diplomas, testimonials, photographs, and gavels on plaques; a glass case filled with antiquarian legal tomes.

A man about my age sat stiffly in one of the chairs, staring at his shoes. He turned at the sound of our approach, rose unsteadily, and adjusted his tie.

Souza went to his side and placed a fatherly hand on his shoulder.

"Doctor, this is Mr. Dwight Cadmus, the boy's uncle and guardian. Dwight, Dr. Alexander Delaware."

Showing no sign of recognizing my name, Cadmus held out a hand that was soft and moist. He was tall and stooped, with thinning brown hair and soft, defeated eyes blurred by thick glasses and rouged by grief. His features were regular but vague, like a sculpture that had been abraded. He wore a brown suit, white shirt, and brown tie. The clothes were expensive, but they looked as if they'd been slept in.

"Doctor," he said, barely looking at me. Then, inexplicably, he smiled, and I saw, in the humorless upturning of petulant lips, the resemblance to Jamey.

"Mr. Cadmus."

"Sit down, Dwight," said Souza, exerting pressure with his hand. "Rest yourself."

Cadmus sank like a stone.

Souza gestured to a chair. "Make yourself comfortable, Doctor."

He seated himself behind the desk and rested his elbows on its tooled leather top.

"First let me lay out the facts, Doctor. If I cover familiar ground, please bear with me. Yesterday, in the early hours of the morning, James escaped from his hospital room. Shortly after, he phoned you from a vacant conference room. Do you remember the time of the call?"

"Around three-fifteen."

He nodded.

"That jibes with the reports of the hospital staff. Unfortunately it doesn't help our case from a time frame perspective. In any event, subsequent efforts to locate him on the grounds were unsuccessful. A call was dispatched to Dwight in Mexico, and he and his family flew back up immediately. Upon landing, they contacted me. We held an emergency conference with Dr. Mainwaring, during which a list was compiled of any locations Jamey'd been known to frequent. Attempts were made to contact each by phone."

"What kinds of locations?"

"Homes of acquaintances mostly."

"It was a short list," said Cadmus in a near whisper. "He hasn't liked people for a long time."

There was a brief, uncomfortable silence. The attorney glanced at Cadmus, who kept his gaze on his wing tips.

"We've wrestled with the boy's emotional problems for a long time," explained Souza. "It's been a strain."

I nodded sympathetically.

"One of the parties we tried to reach was an Ivar Digby Chancellor of Beverly Hills. Jamey had developed a—friendship with him, though to our knowledge it had ended some time ago."

"Damned deviate," muttered Cadmus.

Souza looked at him sharply and went on:

"Despite the fact that the relationship had been put to rest, it seemed possible he'd return to Chancellor's house. However, no one answered there. None of the other calls was fruitful either. Finally we called in the police. They took our list and visited each address. Sometime later—around eight in the morning—the boy was located at the Chancellor residence."

Souza stopped and looked at the uncle, as if expecting another interruption. Cadmus kept quiet, seemingly oblivious of both of us.

"The police walked into a bloody scene, Doctor. Chancellor was dead, strangled and stabbed repeatedly, as was a second party, a sixteen-year-old male prostitute known as Rusty Nails—given name, Richard Ford. According to the report, Chancellor's body had been trussed up, Ford's was prostrate, and Jamey was sitting cross-legged on the floor between the two corpses, clutching a long-bladed knife and a swatch of lavender silk. He seemed in a trance, muttering incoherently—something about bursting arteries and zombies—but went wild at the sight of the officers. It took several policemen to subdue him, and he was put in restraints before being taken away."

I remembered the boy's phone call, the terrible images.

Souza kept reciting:

"They booked him in the county jail, placed him in isolation, and phoned me. I set out immediately to do all the lawyerly things at my disposal in order to obstruct the investigation: filed a writ prohibiting interrogation because of mental incompetence, protested the lack of adequate medical care at the jail, and demanded release on bail or immediate transfer to a psychiatric facility. The writ was complied with—a minor victory because he's too incoherent to be interrogated anyway. The medical care issue was handled by allowing Dr. Mainwaring to visit him and administer medication under supervision. In view of the boy's escape and the enormity of the charges, you can imagine how the bail transfer request was received. He remains at the jail, curled in his cell like a fetus, mute and unresponsive."

The attorney sat back in his chair, picked up a fountain pen, and suspended it between his index fingers. As promised, he'd laid out the facts with the precision of a draftsman. The end result was the blueprint of a nightmare. I searched Dwight Cadmus's face for reaction, found only arctic immobility.

Souza got up from behind the desk and straightened one of the cups in the tea set. Instead of returning to his chair, he stood with his back to the French doors, outlined squarely against the glass.

"I've done some research into your background, Doctor. Your scholarly credentials are impeccable, you have a reputation for honesty, and you've had an impressive amount of courtroom experience as an expert witness— though I don't believe any of it was in a criminal trial."

"That's right," I said. "I testified at the Casa de los Niños trials as a material witness. My expert testimony's been limited to child custody issues and personal injury cases."

"I see." He thought for a moment. "If it sounds as if I'm quizzing you, forgive me. How familiar are you with the notion of insanity?"

"I know it's a legal concept, not a medical or psychological one."

"Exactly," he said, obviously pleased. "A defendant may be a stark, raving lunatic and still be judged legally sane. The essential question is the capacity to distinguish right from wrong. Diminished capacity dictates the absence of guilt. I want your help in constructing a dim cap defense for Jamey."

"I thought the legislature eliminated psychiatric testimony in dim cap cases."

He smiled tolerantly.

"The Twinkie defense hubbub? Not at all. Psychiatrists and psychologists are no longer allowed to get up on the stand and draw conclusions about diminished capacity, but they're permitted to present clinical data from which those conclusions can be drawn. For the purpose of this case the distinction is insignificant."

"Despite that," I said, "I have lots of problems with the concept of diminished capacity."

"Really? What bothers you about it, Doctor?"

"For one, it asks us to go beyond our training and pull off the impossible—crawling into someone's head and reconstructing the past. It's little more than officially sanctioned guesswork, and laymen are starting to see through it. On top of that, it lets too many bad guys off the hook."

Souza nodded, unperturbed.

"That's all very fine, in theory. But tell me, when you spoke to Jamey on the phone, how did he sound?"

"Agitated, confused, hallucinating."

"Psychotic?"

"I can't diagnose from a phone call, but most probably."

"I appreciate your professional caution, but believe me, he's psychotic. Severe paranoid schizophrenia. He's been ill for quite some time. He hears voices, sees visions, is overtly delusional, and has been deteriorating steadily. Dr. Mainwaring hasn't been encouraging about the prognosis. The boy's out of control. Do you think it fair that he be called to answer for acts that are rooted in that kind of madness? That he be viewed as a *bad guy?* He needs care, not punishment. The insanity defense is his only hope."

"You're assuming, then, that he committed eight murders."

He pushed a wing chair opposite me and sat down, so close that our knees almost touched.

"Doctor, I've managed to obtain an early look at everything the police have put down on paper. The time frame is incriminating, and the physical evidence is overwhelming. Following a violent escape from Canyon Oaks, he was found at the scene of the crime with the murder weapons in hand. His fingerprints were all over the Chancellor house. And there'll be more evidence to follow, I guarantee you. They won't slip up on this one. We won't be able to fight the facts. In order to keep him off Death Row, our strategy must be to show that his mental state had deteriorated to the point where free will was impossible."

I remained silent. Souza leaned close enough for me to smell his breath.

"It won't be a fishing expedition, I assure you. There are robust medical and social histories, a verified pattern of prior deterioration. In addition, genetics are on our side. His grandmother and his father—"

Cadmus shot out of his chair.

"Stay away from that angle, Horace! We'll be dragged through the muck enough without getting into that!"

Souza straightened his thick legs, stood, and faced the younger man. His eyes glinted with anger, but he spoke softly.

"Forget about privacy for the foreseeable future, Dwight. You're a public figure now."

"I don't see why—"

Souza cut him off with the wave of a hand.

"Go home and rest, son. You've been under tremendous strain."

Cadmus protested, but feebly.

"I want to know what's going on. He's my—"

"And you will. The doctor and I need to talk about technical matters. When we've reached a meeting of the minds, you'll be the first to know. Now, go and get some sleep. I'll have Tully drive you home."

End of discussion.

The attorney went behind his desk and pushed a button. Moments later the chauffeur appeared. Souza gave the order, and Cadmus followed Antrim out the door.

When we were alone, Souza shook his head pityingly. "You should have known his father," he said, "a great, snorting bull of a man. Chewed up life and swallowed it whole." He paused. "Sometimes I wonder if blood isn't like wealth, growing progressively more dilute with each new generation."

He pressed another button and summoned a smart-looking young woman in a feminized version of a business suit.

"Some tea, please, Veronica. Coffee for you, Doctor?"

"Tea would be fine."

To the secretary:

"A full pot, dear."

"Certainly, sir." She removed the pitcher from the china tea set, handling it as if it were spun sugar, and walked out. Souza watched her departure before returning his attention to me.

"As I was saying, there's no lack of data to back up a dim cap. I'm not asking you to go out on a limb."

"You've got Mainwaring," I said. "Why do you need me?"

"I'll use Dr. Mainwaring's testimony if I have to, but there are problems with him as a witness."

"What kinds of problems?"

He chose his words.

"First and foremost, the boy escaped while under his care, which will leave him open to a good barbecuing by the prosecution."

He stood, hooked his fingers in his suspenders and began orating in a deep, theatrical voice:

" 'Dr. Mainwaring, you've just stated that Mr. Cadmus is incapable of distinguishing right from wrong. If that's so, how in the world did you allow him to get loose? To run amuck and commit two ghastly murders?' Pause for dramatic emphasis, during which I'll object vociferously but the damage will have been done. The jury will view

him as lacking good judgment, and his testimony will
work against us."

When I was sure the performance was over, I said:

"You referred to 'problems,' in the plural. What else?"

Souza smiled as if to say "You caught me."

"Over the years Dr. Mainwaring has acquired a reputation as a defense psychiatrist, one who puts forth biological theories that excuse a multitude of sins. Those
theories haven't always met with agreement by other
experts or juries."

"In other words, he's a whore who's been on the losing
side too many times."

"In other words."

"Why, then, was he the one treating Jamey?" The
anger in my voice surprised both of us.

"There's been no error committed, Doctor. He's very
well regarded as a clinician. As a legal expert, however,
he leaves much to be desired."

The secretary knocked and came in with the teapot.
She poured two cups and brought them to us on a silver
tray, poured cream for Souza, which I declined, and left.
The attorney sipped. The delicate cup was a mismatch
with his fleshy hand.

"You, on the other hand, Dr. Delaware, would be an
asset to our team."

"I'm flattered," I said, "but it doesn't make sense. I
have no experience in criminal cases, I'm far from an
expert on psychosis, and I told you how I feel about the
insanity defense."

Souza looked at me warily through swirls of steam.

"I suppose," he said, "that candor is called for."

"Without it we have nothing further to talk about."

"All right. Candor it is. First, let me emphasize that
when I talked about checking you out and learning your
credentials were first-rate I was being truthful. I've found
out quite a bit about you: You received your doctorate at
twenty-four, wrote an important textbook at twenty-nine,
could have been a full professor by thirty-four. You were
at the peak of an outstanding career when you dropped
out. You've been described to me repeatedly as brilliant
but stubborn, often to the point of obsessiveness. The
brilliance is important because it means you can quickly
fill the gaps in your knowledge. The obsessiveness ap-

peals to me, too, because it means that if I can get you over to my side, you'll be one hell of a gladiator. But in all truthfulness there's no shortage of psychiatric expertise at my disposal, and even if you join my team, I may call on others to augment your testimony."

He leaned forward.

"There are, Dr. Delaware, factors other than your professional attributes that are relevant to my strategy. First of all, you treated Jamey years ago, before he became psychotic. I have no doubt that if I sit on my hands, the prosecution will try to get you on their team, to have you testify that the boy had his wits about him and was perfectly in control. They'll use your testimony to support their claim that his psychosis is a fabrication of recent vintage; the insanity defense, some kind of legal stunt. As you mentioned, the layman is suspicious of psychiatric testimony, so the burden of proof will be upon us. I'm going to have to show that the roots of madness were laid long ago. You can play a valuable role in that regard.

"Second"—he smiled—"you have ties to the police; you've consulted to them. You even have a personal relationship with one of the investigators on this case, Detective Sturgis. That will allow me to paint you as a law-and-order man, a hardhead who's unlikely to be fooled. If *you* feel capacity was diminished, it must be so."

He replaced his cup in its saucer.

"Simply put, Dr. Delaware, I want to co-opt you."

"You're talking about pitting me against a friend. Why should I do it?"

"Because you care about Jamey. You drove out at three-thirty in the morning in response to his plea for help. Skepticism notwithstanding, you know he's sick, not evil. And you couldn't live with yourself if he met his death and you hadn't done all you could to prevent it."

"Death? They haven't executed anyone in this state for a long time."

"Come now, Doctor. You don't really believe the boy would survive the penitentiary, do you? He's *crazy*. Suicidal. As I was saying before Dwight got all huffy, self-destruction runs in the family. Within weeks he'd find a way to open his veins or hang himself with a bed sheet. I'm plenty concerned right now about his confinement at the jail, but at least Mainwaring's providing one-on-one care. In San Quentin the only personal care he'd get would be a nightly anal battering." He lowered his voice. "He needs to be in a *hospital.* And I'm asking you to help me get him into one."

I took a moment to digest everything he'd said, then told him:

"You've put me in a difficult position. I need to think about it."

"That's fine," he answered quickly. "I don't expect you to decide on the spot."

"If I agree to work with you, Mr. Souza, it will have to be on my terms. I have a strong aversion to doing things halfway. You're asking me to reconstruct Jamey's frame of mind. To do that, I'd need to reconstruct his life, to make sense out of the events leading up to his deterioration. I'm not yet convinced that's possible, but if it is, I'd need access to everyone—family members, Mainwaring, anyone I deem relevant—and all records."

"Every door will be open to you."

"There'll be times when my questions get intrusive. From what I just saw, Dwight Cadmus would have problems with that."

"Don't worry about Dwight. Just tell me what you want and when you want it, and I'll see to it that he cooperates."

"There's something else to consider," I said. "Even if I work with you, I won't promise the outcome. It's possible I'll investigate and feel capacity wasn't diminished."

He nodded.

"I've thought of that, Doctor. Of course, I don't want it to happen, and I'm certain that the facts will support me. But should you decide you can't back me up, the only thing I ask is that you invoke confidentiality, so the prosecution can't use the information."

"Fair enough."

"Good. Then can I count on your help?"

"Give me twenty-four hours to decide."

"Fine, fine. There is, of course, the matter of payment. What's your fee?"

"A hundred twenty-five dollars per hour, including phone calls and travel time portal to portal. Just like a lawyer."

He chuckled.

"As it should be. Would an advance of ten thousand dollars be acceptable?"

"Let's hold off until it's clear we'll be working together."

He stood and shook my hand.

"We will be, Doctor, we will be."

He buzzed for Antrim, was told the chauffeur hadn't returned from dropping off Cadmus, phoned him in the Rolls, and gave him his new assignment. While we waited, he poured more tea. When he'd finished his cup, he said:

"One more thing. The police know about Jamey's call and will probably want to interview you about it. Feel free to discuss it with them. If you find it within your heart to emphasize the psychotic aspect of the conversation, please do so. I'd prefer that you didn't talk about your treatment of the boy."

"I wouldn't even if you hadn't asked. Our sessions were confidential."

He nodded approvingly.

With those issues out of the way the conversation deteriorated to small talk, which neither of us enjoyed. Finally the chauffeur stood in the doorway, cap in hand, materializing suddenly, as if out of the ether.

Souza walked me out to the anteroom. The writing desk was now occupied by the smart-looking young secretary. He thanked me again while smoothing nonexistent strands of hair atop his shiny crown and smiled. It looked like an egg cracking open.

I followed Tully Antrim out of the building, eager to get home. All the talk of teams and strategy had gotten to me. I had plenty to think about, and the last thing I wanted to do was play games.

6

Souza had researched me. I decided to follow his example.

I phoned Mal Worthy, a Beverly Hills divorce lawyer with whom I'd worked on several custody cases. Mal was a high roller with a tendency toward glibness, but he was also a solid legal talent, bright and conscientious. More important, he seemed to know everyone in L.A.

His secretary's secretary told me he was out for an early lunch. I managed to cadge out of her the fact that he was at Ma Maison and called him there. He came to the phone still munching.

" 'Lo, Alex. What gives?"

"I need some information. What do you know about an attorney named Horace Souza?"

"You with him or against him?"

"Neither, at the moment. He wants me on his team, quote unquote."

"His team is *him*. Which is more than enough. He's got a slew of other guys working under him, but he runs the show. If you like winning, stick with Horace." He stopped talking for a moment and swallowed. "I didn't think he was doing much family law."

"This is a criminal case, Mal."

"Expanding your horizons?"

"I'm still trying to decide. Is the guy straight?"

"Is any good lawyer straight? We're henchmen. Souza's an ace, been in business a long time."

"From the way he was talking he'd been working with the defendant's family a long time. They're old money, not career criminals. The office reeks of gentility. Looks like a place for estate planning, not criminal law."

"Souza's one of that rare and dying breed—an old-school generalist who can pull it off. He's a self-made Bakersfield boy—cut his teeth in the military, worked on the Nuremberg trials, made lots of contacts, and set up shop in the late forties. Big white house on Wilshire."

"He's still there."

"Some place, huh? He owns it and a good mile of the boulevard on either side. Guy's loaded. Works 'cause he loves it. I remember a speech he gave before the bar association, talked about the good old days, when L.A. was a tough town. How he'd be defending murderers and rapists one day, probating a robber baron's will the next. You don't see that anymore. What kind of case does he want you for?"

I hesitated, knew he'd read about it in the papers anyway, and told him.

"Whoa! Nasty stuff! You're gonna be famous."

"Spare me."

"Not in the mood for celebrity? Everyone else in this city is."

"I feel out of my element. I've never done a criminal case, and I'm no fan of diminished capacity."

"Beginner's jitters? Listen, Alex, most of the so-called psychiatric experts are bullshitters and whores. They come across so pompous and stupid in court, you'll shine by comparison. As far as your feelings about dim cap, all I can say is try to put them aside. My first year out of law school I got a job in the public defender's office. Worked my ass off representing incredible scumbags. Ninety-nine percent were guilty. If they'd all been aborted, the world would have been a better place. It was a fucking zoo. I'm not saying I liked it—I pulled out soon enough—but while I was doing it, I resolved to give the assholes my best shot, pretended they were virgin martyrs. I put my feelings in one box, my job in another. A hell of a lot more than ninety-nine percent of those assholes walked.

"I can't promise that kind of pigeonholing will work for you, Alex, but you should consider it. There's a scrap of paper under glass at the National Archives that grants everyone the right to a fair trial and a competent defense. Getting involved in that process is nothing to be ashamed of. Okay?"

"Okay," I said, eager to end the conversation. "Thanks for the pep talk."

"No sweat. Bye now. Gotta get back to the duck salad."

*   *   *

At five o'clock an unmarked pulled up in front of my house. Two men, one large and bulky, the other short and slender, got out. At first I thought the big one was Milo, but as they climbed up the steps to the terrace, I could see he was a stranger.

I opened the door before they knocked. They flashed their IDs in unison.

The larger one was a downtown sheriff's homicide investigator named Calvin Whitehead. He wore a light blue suit, royal blue shirt, and navy tie with a repeating pattern of gold horseshoes. His complexion was fair— freckles, hazel eyes, and dishwater hair cut short and parted on the right side. He had wide shoulders, a small head, girlish lips, jug ears, and the sour look of a high school jock who hadn't heard cheers for a long time and resented it. The small one was a Beverly Hills PD detective named Richard Cash. He was dark, wore tinted aviator glasses and a beige Italian-cut suit, and had a fox face dominated by a wide, lipless wound of a mouth.

I invited them in. They unbuttoned their jackets, and I saw their shoulder holsters. Whitehead sat on the sofa. Cash took an armchair and looked over the living room.

"Nice place," he said. "Any slide trouble?"

"Not yet."

"My brother's a doctor, bought a place up in Coldwater Canyon a couple of years ago. Last big rain half the backyard melted away."

"That's too bad."

"Insurance covered most of it."

Whitehead cleared his throat.

"Sir," he said, "we're here to talk about an alleged perpetrator by the name of James Wilson Cadmus."

"Where's Milo?" I asked.

They looked at each other.

"He's tied up right now." Cash smiled.

"With other aspects of the case," added Whitehead.

"It's a three-territory case," explained Cash. "We split up responsibilities." He smiled again and added: "He said to send regards."

I was certain the last statement was a lie.

Whitehead's face clouded with impatience. The pace of

his gum chewing picked up. I wondered if it was good cop–bad cop time.

"Sir," he said, "we know Cadmus called you several hours before he was arrested."

"That's correct."

"What time was that, Doctor?" asked Cash, pulling out a pen and pad.

"Around three-fifteen."

"How long did the conversation last?"

"About ten minutes."

"What did the two of you talk about?"

"He talked, I mostly listened. He wasn't making much sense."

"Not making sense about what?" asked Whitehead quickly. He had an unpleasant way of making questions sound like accusations.

"About anything. He was agitated, seemed to be hallucinating."

"Hallucinating," he repeated, as if he'd never heard the word before. "You mean, seeing things?"

"Most of the hallucinations were auditory; he seemed to be hearing voices. He was convinced someone was out to kill him. He may have been seeing things also."

"Try to remember everything he said, sir," he said imperiously.

I repeated as much of Jamey's ramblings as I could recall—flesh eaters, white zombies, reeking blades, the glass canyon, the preoccupation with stink. Cash scribbled as I talked. When I got to the part about the burst of valve arterial, I realized it was a phrase from the Chatterton poem on death that he'd recited during our last session. Not wanting to get into the past, I kept that to myself.

"Sounds pretty violent," said Cash, scanning his notes. "And paranoid."

"Like he was priming himself for something," agreed Whitehead. "Premeditating."

"He was scared," I said.

Whitehead narrowed his eyes.

"Of what?"

"I don't know."

"Did he sound paranoid?"

"Are you asking for a diagnosis?"

"Sure."

"Then the answer is, I don't know. His doctor could tell you more about his mental state."

"I thought he was your patient, sir."

"*Was* is correct. Five years ago."

"How often have you seen him since?"

"Never. That phone call was the first I'd heard from him."

"Uh-huh," he said absently. "You're a psychiatrist?"

"Psychologist."

"And you can't tell if he was paranoid or not?"

"He was frightened. If the fear was irrational, it could be paranoia. If he had something to be afraid of, it wouldn't be."

"So you're saying he had something to be afraid of."

"No. I'm saying I don't know."

Cash broke in:

"It's like that bumper sticker, Cal. 'Even paranoids have enemies.' " He laughed, but no one joined in.

Whitehead pressed on.

"What were you treating him for five years ago?"

"That's confidential patient information."

The girlish lips twisted into a tight, liver-colored blossom.

"All right," he said, smiling ferociously. "Let's back it up. You said he thought people wanted to kill him. Which people?"

"He didn't say."

"Do you think he meant the zombies—what's the wording, Dick?"

Cash flipped a page and read out loud:

"Flesh eaters and white zombies."

"Great title for a movie, huh?" Whitehead grinned. When I didn't reply, he continued. "Did he think these flesh-eating white zombies were the ones out to get him?"

"I don't know. At the time I thought the white zombies might have referred to the hospital staff."

"Did he say anything about wanting to get even with the staff? For cooping him up?"

I shook my head. "From your questions it sounds like you think he was talking normally. It wasn't like that at all. His speech was disjointed. He came nowhere near to developing a train of thought."

"Uh-huh. Did he talk about wanting to kill people?"

"No."

"Or cut them up with a stinking blade?"

"Reeking blade," corrected Cash.

"Whatever," said Whitehead. "Did he say stuff like that?"

"No."

"What do you think he meant by flesh eaters?"

"I have no idea."

"Uh-huh. What I'm thinking," he said, "is that you could take flesh eating literally, as in darkies munching on missionaries, or . . ."

"Metaphorically," suggested Cash.

"Yeah. Metaphorically. As in *cocksucking*." He flashed the shit-eating grin of a kid who'd gotten away with saying a dirty word, then looked at me expectantly.

I remained silent.

"We know," he continued, "that Cadmus is a deviate. Deviates like to talk about eating each other. *Flesh eating* could mean deviant sex. Does that make sense to you?"

"Your guess is as good as mine."

"I was hoping, sir"—he smiled sourly—"that yours would be better."

I didn't answer.

"How long have you been a psychiatrist, sir?"

"Psychologist. About thirteen years."

"Pretty interesting work?"

"I enjoy it."

"Treat a lot of people with sexual problems?"

"No. I work mostly with children."

"Deviant children?"

"All kinds of children."

"Where'd you go to school?"

"UCLA."

"Great school."

"I agree."

"The kids you treat, any of them do violent things— chop up small animals, tear the wings off of flies?"

"I can't talk to you about my cases."

"Go to any Bruin games?"

"Once in a while."

"What about Cadmus? Was he into sports?"

"How would I know that?"

"You ever know him to do anything violent or weird—besides being sexually deviant?"

"Not to my knowledge."

"Nothing like that ever came up in treatment?"

"That's confidential."

He cracked his gum and looked annoyed.

"This is a homicide investigation, sir. We can do the paper work and get the information anyway."

"Then you'll have to do that."

He flushed with anger.

"You want to know who you're protecting? He butchered those—"

"Cal"—Cash broke in—"the doctor's only doing what he has to." He smiled at me over tinted lenses. "Got to play it by the book. Right, Doctor?"

On the surface it seemed a hackneyed skit, standard good cop–bad cop stuff, but the hostile stare Whitehead threw at the other man made me wonder.

"Right," I said, looking away to avoid the appearance of camaraderie.

Whitehead pulled a pack of Juicy Fruit out of his pants pocket, unwrapped two sticks, and added them to the cud in his mouth. His jaws made little wet noises.

"Sure," he said, giving me a cold, knowing smile. "By the book. Tell me, sir, how long have you known he was sexually deviant?"

I didn't answer.

He stared at me hard. Then, suddenly, like a dog peeing to mark his turf, he made a show of getting comfortable: leaning back; spreading his arms along the back of the couch; stretching and crossing his legs. His shins were coated with ginger-pink hair.

"You know," he said, "you can always tell a fag cutting. They slice deeper and more often. Seventy, eighty, a hundred wounds on one body. Why do you suppose that is, sir?"

"I wouldn't know."

"No?" he said with mock disappointment. "I thought you might. One of the psychiatrists I asked about it said it had something to do with repressed rage. All those pretty boys act sweet and gentle, but they've got this shitload of rage boiling inside. So they chop each other into hamburger. That make sense to you?"

"No single rule ever explains an entire group."

"Uh-huh. Just thought you might have an opinion on it."

He rolled his tongue inside his cheek and feigned contemplation. "What about Cadmus? Do you see him as someone carrying around a lot of repressed rage?"

"Like I said before, no diagnoses from a phone call."

"You tell that to Horace Souza, too?"

"My conversation with Mr. Souza is—"

"Confidential," he mimicked. "You're a pretty stubborn guy, sir."

"It's not a matter of stubbornness. It's professional ethics."

"Doctor-patient stuff?"

"Right."

"But he's not your patient anymore?"

"Correct."

"What is he then?"

"I don't understand what you're asking."

The cold smile surfaced again.

"He called you even though he's not your patient. Are you friends or something?"

"No."

"So the call was out of the clear blue?"

"I'm not sure why he called. Maybe he remembered me as someone he could talk to."

"After five years."

"Right."

"Uh-huh. Tell me, did he ever mention the name Ivar Digby Chancellor?"

"No."

"Richard Emmet Ford?"

"No."

"Darrel Gonzales? Matthew Higbie?"

"No."

"Rolf Piper? John Henry Spinola? Andrew Terrence Boyle? Rayford Bunker?"

"None of those."

"How about these: Rusty Nails, Tinkerbell, Angel, Quarterflash?"

"No."

"Never mentioned any of them?"

"Not a one."

"You know who those people are?"

"I assume they're victims of the Lavender Slasher."

"They're victims all right. Of little Jimmy Cadmus. Your *former patient.*"

He'd shot questions at me that were oblique and out of context in an attempt to throw me off guard and establish psychological dominance. I was familiar with the technique, having seen it used by Milo and some of the more devious psychotherapists. But while Milo was a virtuoso who capitalized upon an uncanny ability to appear stupid and inept before moving in for the kill, Whitehead seemed genuinely inept. His tangents had led nowhere, he'd learned close to nothing, and now he was frustrated.

"This guy you're protecting," he said angrily, "let me tell you what he did. First he strangled them; then he cut their throats ear to ear. The 'second smile' the lab boys call it. He gave 'em all nice big smiles. After that he went to work on the eyes. Popped 'em out with his fingers and puréed 'em. Then down to the other balls."

He recounted the details of the killings, growing progressively angrier with each lurid disclosure, glaring at me as if I'd wielded the knife. I found the intensity of his hostility puzzling. I hadn't been able to help him because I knew next to nothing. He was convinced I was stonewalling, and I could understand his frustration. But frustration alone didn't account for the naked contempt in his eyes.

When the recitation of horrors was over, he took Cash's notes from the smaller man's lap and read them slowly. The Beverly Hills detective looked bored and began fidgeting, a one-man band of narcissistic mannerisms— smoothing his razor-cut; scrutinizing his manicure; removing his rosy glasses, holding them up to the light, spitting on them, and wiping them lovingly. Then he got up and walked around the room.

"This is very nice," he said, eyeing a collection of framed ivory miniatures. "Indian?"

"Persian."

"Very nice."

He inspected paintings, examined books on the coffee table, fingered upholstery fabric, and checked his reflection in a Victorian beveled mirror.

"Great room," he pronounced. "Did you use a decorator?"

"No."

"Just kinda did it yourself?"

"Over the years."

"Has a good feel to it," he said. "Coherent." He smiled. I thought I detected a mocking edge to his words, but I couldn't be sure: the tinted lenses did a good job of masking his emotions.

"All right, sir," said Whitehead, "let's go over that phone call again. From start to finish."

It was busywork. I considered protesting but knew it would only make things more difficult. Feeling like a kid kept after school, I complied. Whitehead removed a plum-sized lump of dead gum from his mouth, wrapped it in a handkerchief, and stowed the mess in his pocket. After filling his mouth with a fresh wad, he resumed the interrogation.

It was a stultifying process. He repeated old questions and tossed in a batch of new ones. All ranged from pointless to irrelevant. As we trudged farther along the road to nowhere, Cash continued to check out the room, interrupting several times to comment on my good taste. Whitehead acted as if he weren't there.

I decided this was no good cop–bad cop routine. This was no routine at all.

They hated each other.

By a quarter to six the interrogation was dead. At ten to, Robin came home. When I introduced her to them as my fiancée, their eyes widened in amazement.

Suddenly I understood it all: Whitehead's antipathy and pointed comments about deviates; Cash's preoccupation with my interior decoration.

They'd assumed I was gay.

When you stopped to think, it made a kind of narrow-minded sense: I was friends with a homosexual cop; I'd treated—and had shown human concern for—a homosexual teen-ager. I had a well-decorated home. Utilizing a mindless formula that approached life as simple arithmetic, they'd done their calculations and had come up with a neat little answer:

One plus one equaled queer.

As they fumbled and prepared to leave, I filled with

anger. Not at being mistaken for a homosexual but at being categorized and dehumanized. I thought of Jamey. His whole life had been one categorization after another. Orphan. Genius. Misfit. Pervert. Now they said he was a monster, and I didn't know enough to dispute it. But I realized, at that moment, that I couldn't walk away from learning more.

Souza had foisted a tough choice upon me. The two policemen had helped me make my decision.

7

I CALLED the attorney the next morning and, after re-
minding him of my terms, agreed to work with him.

"Good, Doctor," he said, as if I'd made the only
rational decision under the circumstances. "Just tell me
what you need."

"First I want to see Jamey. After that I'll take a
complete family history. Who'd be the best person to
start with?"

"I'm the most knowledgeable historian of the Cadmuses
you could find," he said. "I'll give you an overview, and
then you can talk with Dwight and anyone else you
choose. When would you like to see the boy?"

"As soon as possible."

"Fine. I'll arrange it for this morning. Have you ever
visited the jail?"

"No."

"Then I'll have someone meet you and orient you.
Bring ID that states you're a doctor."

He gave me directions and offered to messenger over
the ten-thousand-dollar retainer. I told him to keep the
money until my evaluation was complete. It was a symbolic gesture, bordering on pettiness, but it made me feel
less encumbered.

The County Jail was on Bauchet Street, near Union
Station, in a neighborhood east of downtown that was
half industrial, half slum. Truck yards, warehouses, and
machine shops shared the area with twenty-four-hour bail
bondsmen, crumbling fleabags, and dusty stretches of
vacant lot.

Entry to the facility was through a subterranean parking structure. I found a space in the dimness next to a
decrepit white Chrysler Imperial blotched with rust spots.

Two kerchiefed and haltered young black women got out of the big car, solemn-faced.

I followed them up a flight of iron stairs and into a small, silent courtyard created by the U-shaped intersection of the parking structure with the jail. On the left arm of the U was a door stenciled OWN RECOGNIZANCE COURT. Running through the yard was a short strip of grimy sidewalk bordered by parched, yellowing lawn. A large spruce tree grew on one side of the lawn; from the other sprouted a spruce seedling—stunted, tilted, and stingily branched—that resembled nothing so much as the big tree's neglected child. The walkway ended at double doors of mirrored glass set into the high, windowless front wall of the jail.

The building was a study in cement slab—massive, sprawling, the color of smog. The expanse of raw, flat concrete was crosshatched overhead by concrete beams at the seam of the union with the parking garage. The junction yielded a maze of right angles as cruelly stark as monochrome Mondrian that cast cruciform shadows across the courtyard. The sole concession to ornament was the scoring of the concrete into parallel grooves, as if an enormous rake had been dragged through the cement before it had dried.

The women reached the double doors. One of them pulled a handle and the mirror parted. They preceded me into an incongruously tiny room with glossy pale yellow walls. The floors were worn linoleum. Adorning the right wall was a patch of tarnished hand lockers. Blue letters over the lockers instructed anyone carrying a firearm to deposit it within.

Straight ahead was more one-way mirror, shielding a booth similar to that of a movie house ticket taker. In the center of the silvered glass was a grilled speaker. Below the speaker was a stainless steel trough. To the right of the booth was a gate of iron bars painted blue. Over the gate were painted the words SALLY PORT. Beyond the blue bars was empty space backed by an opaque metal door.

The women stepped up to the booth. A voice barked through the speaker. At the end of the bark was a question mark. One of the women said, "Hawkins. Rainier P." Another bark elicited the deposit of two driver's licenses through the trough. Several moments later the bars slid open. The women trudged through, and the blue gate clanged shut behind them with earsplitting finality. They waited silently in the sally port, shifting their weight from hip to hip, looking too tired for their ages. In response to a third bark they passed their purses to the left, answered more questions, and waited some more. When the rear metal door opened suddenly, a beefy tan-uniformed sheriff's deputy stood in the opening. He nodded perfunctorily, and the women followed him through the door. When they'd disappeared, it slammed shut, loud enough to echo. The entire procedure had taken ten minutes.

"Sir," barked the speaker.

I stepped up and announced myself. Up close I could make out movement on the other side of the glass, shadowy reflections of young, sharp-eyed faces.

The speaker asked for identification, and I dropped my hospital badge from Western Pediatric into the trough.

A minute of scrutiny.

"Okay, Doctor. Step into the sally port."

The holding area was the size of a walk-in closet. On one wall was a key-operated elevator. To the left were tinted glass sliding windows set over a steel barrier. Behind the glass sat four deputies—three mustachioed men, one woman. All were fair and under thirty. The men looked up at me briefly before resuming their examination of a copy of *Hustler*. The woman sat in a swivel chair and peered at a hangnail. The booth was papered with county memoranda and outfitted with a panel of electronic equipment.

I waited restlessly, suspended between freedom and what waited on the other side of the metal door. I was no prisoner, but for the time being I was trapped, at the mercy of whoever pushed the buttons. I started to feel antsy, the anticipatory anxiety of a kid being strapped into a roller coaster seat, unsure of his fortitude and just wanting it to be over.

When the opaque door opened, I was looking at a young Hispanic man in civilian clothes—pale blue shirt and blue-green tartan tie under a sleeveless maroon V-neck sweater, gray corduroy slacks, crepe-soled buckskin oxfords. A picture ID card clipped to the collar of the shirt said he was a social worker. He was tall, narrow, and long-limbed. Glossy brush-cut hair capped a long, pale face. Large, elfin ears created a striking resemblance to Mr. Spock that didn't dissipate when he spoke: His voice was flat, as emotionless as Morse code.

"Dr. Delaware, I'm Patrick Montez. I'm supposed to orient you. Please come with me."

On the other side of the door was a wide, empty yellow corridor. As we entered it, one of the deputies in the glass booth stuck his head out and scanned the hallway in both directions. Montez took me to an elevator. We rose several flights and exited into more glossy yellow, trimmed with blue. I caught a glimpse of rumpled hospital beds through an open door at the end of the corridor.

"My office is over there," he said, pointing across the hall.

A slatted wooden bench ran the length of the wall outside the office. Two men in yellow pajamas sat slumped at opposite ends. The nearer one was a squat dark Mexican in his sixties with rummy eyes and a fallen face. The other was a young man with a full head of surfer-blond curls—tan, muscular and scarcely out of his teens. His face was male-model perfect except for the tics that caused his features to jump like Galvani's frog. As we passed, the wino looked away. But the blond boy turned toward us. Something feral slithered into his eyes, and his mouth twitched into a snarl.

Suddenly he strained to rise. I looked quickly at Montez, but he seemed unperturbed. The blond boy grunted and raised his buttocks an inch from the bench before snapping back sharply, as if forced down rudely by an invisible hand. Then I saw the shackles around his wrists—metal cuffs chained to stationary bolts running through the bench seat.

A deputy appeared, nightstick in hand. The blond boy cried out gutturally. The deputy stood watch from a distance as the prisoner slammed his back several times against the slats, then sank back down, breathing hard and mouthing silent obscenities.

"Come on in, Doctor," said Montez, as if nothing had happened. He took out a ring of keys, unlocked the door, and held it open.

The interior of the office was standard county issue:

desk chairs and table of gray-painted metal; a corkboard
pinned with layers of official documents. The room was
windowless and ventilated by a ceiling fan. A table beside the desk held a thriving potted devil's ivy and a
police scanner that hissed and spit until the social worker
leaned over and turned it off.

"This is the largest jail system in the world," he said.
"Official maximum capacity is fifty-one hundred inmates.
Right now we've got seventy-three hundred. On a good
weekend, when the city really gets down to partying, we
process sixteen thousand."

He reached into a drawer and pulled out a roll of Life
Savers.

"Want one?"

"No, thanks."

He popped a candy into his mouth and sucked on it.

"You're a psychologist?"

"Right."

"In theory there are two parallel systems here: mental
health and custody. We're supposed to work together. In
actuality mental health is a guest. The jail is run by the
sheriff's department, and the main emphasis is on processing and maintaining criminals. Psychiatric input is
viewed as another tool to make that work."

"Makes sense," I said.

He nodded.

"I start out with that spiel because I always get questions from mental health people about our treatment
philosophy, modes of therapy—all that good stuff. The
truth of it is this is a giant corral: We lock them up and
work at keeping them alive and reasonably healthy until
trial. Even if we had time for psychotherapy, I doubt it
would help most of our guys. About fifteen percent are
seriously psychiatrically disturbed—more impaired than
the patients at County Hospital. Bona fide psychotics
who're also murderers, rapists, armed robbers. If you
include your everyday ambulatory sociopath—guys judged
to be too dangerous to be released on bail—triple that
figure. On top of that are the derelicts and gomers who
do something especially outrageous and can't make ten
percent of a seventy-five-dollar bail. Most of them are
head cases, too."

"Do you medicate them?"

"If the inmate has a private psychiatrist who's willing to administer and monitor dosages—like Cadmus—he gets medicated. Otherwise no. We're not staffed for it— one part-time psychiatrist who comes in once in a while and a handful of nurses for the entire jail. The deputies aren't qualified to handle it."

I considered the notion of a thousand or so mentally disturbed felons cooped up without treatment and asked how long the average stay was.

"Usually it's days, not weeks. Again, it's a matter of processing; we have to move out as many as we move in or there'd be no place to put 'em. As is, we've got inmates sleeping on the roof in the summer and in the aisles when it cools down. Once in a while you come across someone who should have been released a month ago but wasn't because the paper work got lost and his lawyer was incompetent. Plenty of attorneys do a lot of screaming and filing of writs, but they don't understand the system and end up causing more trouble for their clients."

"Plenty but not all," I said.

He smiled and clicked the Life Saver against his teeth.

"Two hours ago an order came down from on high to give you the grand tour. Now here we are. That should tell you something about Mr. Souza's influence."

"I appreciate your spending the time."

"No problem. Gives me a little respite from paper work."

He chewed the candy and swallowed it, took another from the roll. The ensuing silence was punctuated by a loud scream, followed by several more. Several hard thumps vibrated the wall behind us—the slatted bench being pushed repeatedly against the plaster. More screams, a blizzard of running footsteps, the whisper of a scuffle, and all was calm. Montez had sat through it without moving a muscle.

"Back to lockup for Mark," he said.

"The blond kid?"

"Yup. Comes up for trial next week. Seemed to be calming down. You never know."

"What did he do?"

"Ate a lot of PCP and tried to decapitate his girlfriend."

"A guy like that doesn't get locked in a cell?"

"He came in too disturbed and too pretty to be put on cellblock, too healthy for the infirmary. We have a thirty-five-room inpatient unit—isolation rooms for prisoners too iffy for general custody—and we stuck him there, but when he started to get lucid, we moved him out to make room for someone crazier and put him on the ward. Ward patients get to move around under supervision. He started to look a little spacey this morning, so they cuffed him. Obviously he's slipping again—pretty typical for a duster. He belongs back in isolation, but we've got no vacancies, so he'll have to go to a cellblock with twenty-four-hour lockup. If an empty room comes up, he'll be moved back here."

"Sounds like juggling," I said.

"With live grenades. But don't take that to mean it's a shlocky system. The public wants bad guys caught and put away, but no one wants to pay for a place to put 'em. Considering the situation, this is probably the best-run system in the county. You've got enough violent offenders to populate a small city, and despite that, things go smoothly. Take initial processing, for example. When a guy comes in, we've got to find out if he's a member of a street gang or a prison gang to know where to put him. Some gangs coexist; others will rip each other apart on sight. Until recently we didn't even have a computer, but screwups were rare. If they weren't, there'd be blood in the halls, and last I checked, things still looked pretty yellow."

"And blue." I smiled.

"Right. School colors. Probably some urban planner's idea of what soothes the savage breast." The phone rang. He picked it up, talked about moving Cochran from 7100 to 4500, made inquiries about a leg abscess on Lopez and Boutillier's need for twenty-four-hour nursing, put the receiver down, and stood up.

"If you're ready, we can check out the campus. Then I'll take you to see your client."

He took me to the inpatient unit first—thirty-five isolation rooms set aside for inmates with profound psychiatric problems. Five were marked COED and had been set aside for women, but men occupied three of them. Visual access was provided through a mesh window in the door of each room. A scrap of paper identifying the prisoner was taped below the window. Some of the papers bore coded messages as well.

The codes, explained Montez, referred to inmate characteristics that demanded staff vigilance: suicidal tendencies, drug addiction, unpredictability, mental retardation, assaultiveness, medical abnormalities, and physical handicaps—as in the case of the toothless double amputee in the first room I viewed, who stood on his knee stumps and stared at the floor. The code said he was unusually explosive.

The social worker encouraged me to look at the prisoners, and I did, despite some unease at being intrusive. The rooms were tiny—six-by-four. Each one contained a bed and a steel commode and nothing else. Most of the inmates lay on the beds wrapped in jumbled sheets. A few slept; others stared desolately into space. In one of the coed rooms I saw a black woman squatting on the commode. Before I could look away, our eyes met, and she grinned defiantly, spread her legs, stretched, and stroked her labia while licking her lips. A glance into another cell revealed a three-hundred-pound white man festooned with tattoos standing catatonically rigid, hands held over his head, eyes glazed over. Next door to him, a coal-colored youth with sculpted musculature and a shaved bullet head paced and worked his mouth nonstop. Soundproofing silenced the message, but I read his lips: Fuckyoufuckmefuckyoufuckme, over and over, like a catechism.

When I told him I'd seen enough, Montez took me off the unit and back to the elevator. While we waited, I asked him why Jamey wasn't in one of the inpatient rooms.

"He's been judged too dangerous. They put him on the High Power unit, which I'll explain later."

The elevator came, and we boarded. Montez punched a number and rode slouching against the door.

"What do you think so far?" he asked.

"Strong stuff."

"What you just saw was the Hilton. Every lawyer wants his client in one of those rooms, and inmates are always faking craziness to get there because it's safe—no one gets cut or raped—which isn't the case on cellblock."

"Seven thousand applicants for thirty-five spaces," I reflected. "A seller's market."

"You bet. More exclusive than Harvard."

As we neared the hub of the jail, the silence that had characterized the isolation unit was replaced by a low, insectile hum. Montez had used the word *campus,* and strangely enough, the academic analogy seemed superficially fitting—wide, bright corridors teeming with young people and bustling with activity, the energy level reminiscent of a university during registration week.

But the walls of this college were grungy and permeated with a stale, masculine stench, and there was nothing bright-eyed about its students. We walked past scores of stone-faced men, enduring a gauntlet of cold, radar stares.

The prisoners walked freely, and we were in their midst, unprotected.

They stood around singly or in small groups, wearing royal blue jump suits. Some walked purposefully, clutching sheafs of paper. Others slumped listlessly in plastic chairs or waited in line for cigarettes and candy. From time to time a uniformed deputy could be seen strolling and surveilling, but the inmates vastly outnumbered the guards, and I could see nothing to prevent the confined from overpowering their keepers and tearing them—and us—to shreds.

Montez saw the look on my face and nodded.

"I told you it was a hell of a system. Held together by prayer and spit."

We walked on. It was a young man's world. Most of the inmates were under twenty-five. The guards looked scarcely older. A profusion of bulky shoulders and bulging biceps. I knew what that meant: plenty of hard time. Pumping iron was a favorite prison yard pastime.

The prisoners clustered along racial lines. The majority were black. I saw lots of Rasta dreadlocks, cornrows, and shaved skulls, a plethora of shiny, keloid knife scars on dusky flesh. Second largest in number were the Latinos— smaller but just as husky, sporting bandanna-bound homeboy pompadours, devilish goatees, and *vato loco* swaggers. Whites were in the minority. For the most part they were biker types—hulking, bearded lugs with hog jowls, earrings, and greasy forearms blued with Iron Cross tattoos.

Despite their differences they had one thing in common: *the eyes*. Cold and dead, immobile yet piercing. I'd seen eyes like that recently but couldn't quite remember where.

Montez took me to a general population cellblock where most of the cells were empty—we'd just seen their occupants—and then to a twenty-four-hour lockup full of wild, gaunt men in yellow pajamas who tore at their faces and paced like zoo animals. A single deputy watched balefully from a glass rectangle suspended midway between the two tiers of the block. He saw us and unlocked the door.

Stepping into the booth, I felt like a diver in a shark cage. Soul music blasted the block from multiple speakers. Even in the booth it was loud. I thought of a recent article in a psych journal about the effects of constant high-volume noise on rats: The rodents had grown initially agitated, then had withdrawn into a passive psychotic-like state. I looked at the pacing men in yellow and wondered for the thousandth time about the relevance of animal research to the human condition.

A console of electronic equipment lined one wall. Above it was a rack holding two shotguns. Below, an inmate in a khaki jump suit pushed a mop over the soapy cement floor.

"Trustee?" I asked.

"Right. Everything's color-coded. Blue is mainline; khaki means trustee; transport trustees have red armbands; kitchen trustees wear white. These guys in yellow are psych cases. They never leave their cells."

"How are they different from the ones on the inpatient ward?"

"Officially they're supposed to be less disturbed, but it's really arbitrary."

The deputy spoke up. He was short and stocky with a tobacco-colored military mustache and a seamed face.

"If they're really motivated, we punt 'em over to inpatient, right, Patrick?"

Montez responded to his laughter with a faint smile.

"What he means," the social worker explained, "is they have to do something outrageous—bite off a finger, eat a pound of their own excrement—to get off block."

As if on cue, one of the prisoners on the upper tier stripped off his pajamas and began masturbating.

"No dice, Rufus," muttered the guard, "we are not impressed." He turned to Montez and chatted for a few minutes about movies. The naked prisoner reached orgasm and ejaculated through the bars. Nobody paid attention, and he slumped to the floor, panting.

"Anyway," said Montez, moving toward the door, "check it out, Dave, it's not Truffaut, but it's a good piece of cinema."

"Will do, Patrick. Where you headed?"

"Taking the doctor over to High Power."

The deputy looked at me with renewed interest.

"Gonna try to dim cap one of those clowns?" he asked.

"I don't know yet."

"Cadmus," said Montez.

The deputy snorted.

"Fat chance," he said, and pushed a button that released a pneumatic lock.

"This," said Montez, "is the top of the line as far as bad guys go."

We were standing in front of an unmarked locked door monitored by two closed-circuit TV cameras. To the left was the attorney interview room. Lawyers and clients sat opposite one another at a series of partitioned tables. To their rear were several private glass-walled rooms.

"High power is reserved for highly publicized cases, high-risk-for-escape types, and real monsters. Shoot the president, blow up a bank with the people in it, or dismember a dozen babies, and you'll end up here. There are a hundred and fifty cells, and there's a waiting list. Surveillance is constant, and the prisoner-guard ratio is high. Security is airtight; we're talking meals slid under the door, steel doors and entry codes that change randomly. You can't go in, but I'll have him brought out."

He pressed a buzzer, and the TV cameras rotated with a low whine. Several minutes later a giant red-haired deputy opened the door and squinted at us suspiciously. Montez talked to him in a near whisper. The redhead listened and disappeared behind the door without comment.

"We'll wait in there," said the social worker, pointing

to the interview room. He guided me past hushed, furtive conferences, which stopped as we walked by, resumed when we'd passed. The lawyers looked as shifty-eyed as their clients. One of them, a washed-out-looking man in a polyester suit, sat stoically as the prisoner across from him, a small, balding mulatto with thick glasses, called him a motherfucker and railed on about habeas corpus.

"Court-appointed," said Montez. "A joyful assignment."

Several deputies carrying walkie-talkies patrolled the room. Montez waved one over. He was dark, rosy-cheeked, soft-looking, and prematurely bald. The social worker explained the situation to him, and he stared at me, nodded, and unlocked one of the glass rooms before stepping back out of earshot.

"Any questions?" asked Montez.

"Just one, but it's a bit personal."

"No sweat."

"How do you cope with working here full-time?"

"There's nothing to cope with," he said evenly. "I love my work. The paper work gets to be a bit much, but it'd be that way anywhere else and a damned sight more boring. In this place no two days are ever the same. I'm a movie freak, and I get to live pure Fellini. That answer it?"

"Eloquently. Thanks for the education."

"Anytime."

We shook hands.

"Wait here; it'll take awhile," he said, glancing at the balding deputy. "Deputy Sonnenschein will take care of you from this point."

I stood outside the glass room for several minutes as Sonnenschein strolled the interview area. Finally he approached in an awkward, rolling gait, as if his body were segmented and only loosely connected at the waist. His thumbs were hooked in his belt loops, and his holster flapped against his flank. Under the thinning hair was a curiously childlike moon face, and up close I saw that he was very young.

"Your patient should be here any minute," he said. "It takes time to get through High Power." He threw a backward glance at the glass room. "I've gotta search you, so let's go inside."

He held the door open and entered after me. Inside

were a blue metal table and two matching chairs, bolted to the floor. He asked me to remove my jacket, checked the pockets, ran his hands lightly over my body, returned the garment, inspected my briefcase, and had me sign a logbook. I noticed that Souza had visited at eight that morning, Mainwaring an hour earlier.

"You can sit down now," he said.

I did, and he took the other chair.

"You're here to try to dim cap him, right?" he asked.

"I'm going to talk to him and see."

"Good luck," he said.

I looked at him sharply, searched for sarcasm but found none.

"What I meant was—" His walkie-talkie spit and cut him off. He listened to it, then put it to his lips, rattled off a few numbers, and said everything was ready. Rising, he walked to the door, put his hands on his hips, and stood watch.

"You started to say something," I reminded him.

He shook his head.

"See for yourself. They're bringing him in now."

8

AT FIRST I couldn't see him. He was submerged in a phalanx of deputies, all of them huge. The red-haired giant who'd stuck his head out the door to the High Power unit led the way, checking me out and scanning the room. When he gave the okay, the rest of them entered, moving in concert like some massive tan arachnid that parted slowly to reveal the shackled boy in its grasp.

I wouldn't have recognized him had he passed me on the street. He'd grown to six feet but didn't weigh more than 130 pounds. The yellow pajamas hung loosely on his spindly frame. Puberty had stretched his face from sphere to oval. The features were regular but ascetic, the bones peaking sharply under a thin tent of flesh. His black hair was still long; it hung down over his forehead and fell in greasy clumps upon bony shoulders. His skin was the color of parchment, shadowed with unearthly overtones of gray-green. Black stubble lightly dotted his chin and upper lip. A large, florid pimple blossomed from one hollow cheek. Both eyes were closed. He gave off a sour smell.

The deputies moved with silent precision. Meaty hands remained clasped around sticklike arms. One pair propelled him to the table. Another sat him down. Wrist and ankle cuffs were secured to the stationary chair. It left him in an awkward position, but he allowed himself to be manipulated with the limp passivity of a marionette.

When they were through, the redhead came over and introduced himself as Sergeant Koocher.

"How long will this take, Doctor?" he asked.

"It's hard to tell before I talk to him."

"We'd prefer that you keep it to one hour maximum, and we'll be back to pick him up in sixty minutes. If you need more time, let Deputy Sonnenschein know before-hand. He'll be right outside."

Sonnenschein frowned and nodded assent.

"Any questions?" asked Koocher.

"No."

He signaled to the others, and they left. Sonnenschein was the last to exit. He remained on the other side of the glass, arms folded across his chest, positioned at an angle that allowed him a clear view of both the glass room and the interview area. I turned from him to the boy on the other side of the table.

"Hello, Jamey. It's Dr. Delaware."

I searched the pallid face for signs of response, found none.

"I'm here to help you," I said. "Is there anything you need?"

When he didn't answer I let the silence simmer. Nothing. I started to talk, softly, soothingly—about how frightened he must be, how glad I was that he'd reached out to me, how much I wanted to help.

After twenty minutes he opened his eyes. For an instant I was hopeful that I'd broken through. Then I looked at him closely, and hope scurried back into its burrow.

His eyes were filmed over and unfocused, the whites a soiled-linen gray shot through with red. He was looking at me without seeing.

A trickle of drool seeped from the corner of his mouth and flowed down his chin. I took out a handkerchief and wiped it away, held his chin, and tried to snag eye contact. It was futile; his stare remained vacant and lifeless.

Lowering my hand, I placed it on his shoulder. The movement caught the corner of Sonnenschein's eye. He wheeled around and stared sharply through the glass. I gave him an everything's okay look, and after a few seconds he relaxed his stance but didn't avert his gaze.

Jamey remained motionless. His pajamas were sweat-soaked. Through the moist fabric he felt stiff and cold; I might have been touching a corpse. Then abruptly he sucked in his cheeks and pursed his lips, blowing out rancid air. His head lolled, and he shuddered. The tremor coursed its way from his core to my fingertips, faded, and repeated itself. So abrupt was the surge of energy that I

had to restrain myself from pulling away. But I'd made
that mistake once before and wouldn't let it happen again.

Instead, I intensified the pressure of my fingers. A sobbing sound rose from deep within his abdomen; his shoulders
heaved, then slumped. He closed his eyes again, and his
head swung pendulously before dropping to the table. He
lay there, cheek to the metal, mouth gaping, breathing
nasally and heavily. Nothing I said or did roused him.

He slept stuporously. I watched him and felt my spirits
sink with each heave of his scrawny chest. I'd been prepared for psychosis, but for nothing this regressed. The
standard battery of mental status questions—orientation
to time and place, inquiries about distorted thought processes and scrambled perceptions—was irrelevant. On
the phone he'd responded, if only minimally. He'd told
Milo he'd called me; that meant some degree of consciousness. Now he was a zombie. I wondered if it was a
transitory phase—the severe depression that sometimes
follows a schizophrenic outburst—or something more insidious: the beginning of the end.

Schizophrenia is a baffling collection of disorders. Psychiatry's come a long way since the days when psychotics
were burned as witches, but the roots of madness remain
a locked box. Psychiatrists control schizophrenic symptoms with drugs without really understanding why they
work. It's palliative treatment that has little to do with
cure. A third of all patients recover by themselves. Another third responds favorably to medication and supportive psychotherapy. And there exists a group of
unfortunates who are resistant to any form of treatment;
no matter what is attempted, they slide inexorably
toward total mental deterioration.

I looked at the limp body splayed across the table and
wondered which group would claim Jamey.

There was a third possibility, but it was a remote one.
His symptoms—the tremors, the drooling, the sucking
and blowing—bore the earmarks of tardive dyskinesia,
nerve damage brought on by heavy doses of anti-psychotic
medication. The disorder usually appears in older patients treated over a period of several years, but in rare
cases acute dyskinesia has been noted after only minimal
drug ingestion. Souza had told me that Mainwaring was
continuing to medicate Jamey in the jail, and I made a

note to learn more about the drugs he was getting and the dosage levels.

He started to snore loudly. As he sank deeper into sleep, his body seemed to retreat from my touch, going limp, almost liquid, as if his bones had melted. His breathing slowed. I kept my hand on his shoulder and talked to him, hoping some small bit of comfort would find its way through the stupor.

We stayed that way for the rest of the hour. I let go only when the cadre of deputies arrived and carried him back to his cell.

Sergeant Koocher told Sonnenschein to escort me out of the jail.

"I see what you meant by good luck," I said as we walked. "Getting him to respond."

"Yup."

"How often is he like that?"

"Most of the time. Sometimes he starts crying or screaming. Usually he just sits and stares until he falls asleep."

"Has it been that way since he got here?"

"He was pretty hyped up when they brought him in a couple of days ago. Like a duster. We had to keep him in restraints. But it didn't take long before he started to fade away."

"Does he talk to anyone?"

"Not that I've seen."

"How about his attorney?"

"Souza? Nah. He does the whole fatherly thing—puts his arm around him, feeds him juice and cookies. Cadmus shines him on. Totally out of it."

We turned a corner and nearly collided with a group of inmates. At the sight of Sonnenschein's uniform they veered away sharply.

"I guess it's good for his case," he said.

"What is?"

"His being so—decompensated."

He noted my surprise at his use of the technical term and grinned.

"Psych major," he explained. "Got one more year for a B.A. Working here got me interested in it."

"You're saying he's faking psychosis in order to be judged incompetent."

He shrugged.

"You're the doctor."

"What about *your* opinion? Off the record."

He didn't answer right away.

"Off the record I don't know. With some clowns it's obvious what they're up to. The minute they get here they start putting on the Looney Tunes act. Only they usually overdo it because they're uneducated; everything they know about psychosis comes from TV and splatter flicks. Know what I mean?"

"Sure. Draft dodger mania."

"You got it. Cadmus doesn't pull that kind of crap, but I heard he used to be some kind of genius, so maybe he's just playing the game a little smarter."

"You said he screamed once in a while. What does he say?"

"Nothing. He just screams. No words. Like a deer that's been gutshot."

"If you do make out something, could you write it down and show it to me the next time I'm here?"

He shook his head.

"No way, Doc. If I report it to you, I've got to report it to the DA. If I do it in this case, everyone will start to ask. After a while I'd be doing investigative freebies for everyone and neglecting my job."

"Okay," I said. "Just asking."

"No harm in that."

"Let me ask you something else then. Do you keep some kind of log—a record of the High Power inmates' behavior?"

"Sure. Incident reports, unusual occurrences. Only screaming's not unusual. Some nights it's all you hear."

We reached the elevator and waited for it to arrive.

"Tell me," he said, "do you like your work?"

"Most of the time."

"It stays interesting?"

"Very."

"Good to hear. I've really enjoyed my psych classes, especially the abnormal stuff, been thinking about going on for a master's or something. But it's a lot more school, a heavy-duty decision, so I've been asking the psychiatrists who come here if they like what they do. Last one I asked—Cadmus's other doctor—looked at me funny, like it was a trick question, like what did I *really* mean by that."

"It's an occupational hazard," I said. "Overinterpreting."

"Maybe so, but I got the feeling he just didn't like cops."

I thought of what Souza had said about Mainwaring's being tagged as a defense expert, said nothing.

A few seconds passed.

"So," said Sonnenschein, "you really do like it."

"Can't think of anything I'd rather do."

"Excellent." He smiled, then grew grave. "You know, you spend some time up here, see these guys and hear about the things they've done, makes you want to understand how people get like that, know what I mean?"

"I sure do."

The elevator doors opened. We boarded and descended in silence. When they opened again, he'd forged his face into a stoic mask. I wished him luck with his studies.

"Thanks," he said, stepping out and using his hand to keep the door from closing. "Listen, I hope you figure out what's going on with the kid. If I could help you, I would. But I can't."

I stepped into the sally port. Beyond the blue bars I saw two men in the entry room. Their backs were to me as they stashed their guns in one of the lockers. I collected my ID and stepped out as they walked up to the trough. One of them was Cal Whitehead. The other was a big man, too, heavy and droopy, with pale skin, thick black hair, and startling green eyes under shaggy black brows. The hair was clipped short around the back and sides, except for long, unfashionable sideburns, and left thick on top. A wave of it swept across his forehead. His face was broad with thick features—a prominent, high-bridged nose, fleshy ears, and full, soft lips—its boyishness marred by the acne scars that pitted the flesh. His clothes were baggy and rumpled—brown corduroy jacket with button flaps and a half belt in back, tan double-knit trousers over scuffed desert boots, brown rayon shirt, and mustard-colored tie.

"Hey, it's the psychiatrist," said Whitehead.

I ignored him and looked at the other man.

"Hello, Milo."

"H'lo, Alex," said my friend, with obvious discomfort.

An awkward silence took root and sprouted, interrupted finally by a bark from behind the glass. Milo unclipped his LAPD ID card from his lapel and dropped it into the trough. Whitehead did the same with his sheriff's ID.

"How've you been?" I asked.

"Fine," he said, looking at his shoes. "Yourself?"

"Fine."

He coughed and turned away, rubbing a big, soft hand over his face, as if washing without water.

The awkward silence blossomed. Whitehead seemed amused.

"Hey, Doc," he said, "how's your patient? Ready to spill his guts and save us a hassle?"

Milo winced and flashed me a knowing look that faded instantaneously.

"Don't tell me," taunted Whitehead, "he's totally zonked out, right? Pissing down his leg, eating his own shit, and *un-a-ble-to-tell-right-from-wrong.*"

I started to walk away. Whitehead moved his bulk between me and the door.

"Yesterday you had nothing to say, mister. Today you're an expert."

"Cool it, Cal," said Milo.

"Yeah, I forgot," said Whitehead, not budging. "He's your buddy, so when he pulls the dim cap shit, it's okay."

The door to the sally port slid open.

"Come on, Cal," said Milo, and I saw his hands clench.

Whitehead looked at me, shook his head, smiled, and stepped aside. He pivoted, stomped into the port, and Milo followed him.

The bars slammed shut. Whitehead moved immediately to the left and began kibitzing with the deputies in the booth. Milo stood by himself on the other side of the port. Before I left, I tried to catch his attention, but he'd fixed his gaze on the grimy floor and never raised his eyes.

9

SOUZA'S STEAK bled as he cut into it, forming a pinkish puddle around the meat that spread and coated the white bone china plate. He inserted a chunk of sirloin in his mouth, chewed slowly, swallowed, wiped his lips, and nodded.

"He was that way when I saw him early this morning," he said. "Stuporous."

We were alone in the dining room of his law building. The room was hushed and dim, an Anglophile's fantasy. An oval Victorian table of mahogany polished to a mirror glow stretched nearly the length of the room, ringed by matching chairs upholstered in floral brocade. An oversized stone mantel liberated from some drafty Hampshire manor dominated one wall. Above it a collection of hunting prints surrounded a framed heraldic crest. Silk Persian rugs spread over dark parquet floors. The walls were carved, waxed, knotty pine panels hung with antique Punch caricatures and more hunt scenes. Fluted pedestals in each corner supported marble busts of men of letters. Heavy drapes of the same brocade that covered the chairs had been drawn over tall, arched windows, and the sole source of light was a Waterford chandelier suspended above the table's center.

"One of the deputies told me he was agitated when he first came into the jail but has been withdrawing steadily," I said.

"That's an accurate assessment. The entire history has been one of deterioration. At the time of his commitment to Canyon Oaks he displayed long stretches of lucidity—days at a time. Anyone talking to him during those periods would have wondered what he was doing there. He was a brilliant boy before the . . .troubles, and his facility with the language was damn near awe-inspiring.

He'd use his intellect to try to convince others that he'd been wrongfully committed. He was so good that even I found myself questioning the wisdom of the decision once or twice. But eventually, if you spent enough time with him, the psychosis emerged."

"In what way?"

"A misplaced word here, a jumbled thought there. The pairing of topics that bore no logical relation to one another. He'd begin a sentence and trail off into silence or add details that didn't fit. Attempts to question him about it made him acutely upset, often to the point of hysteria—jumping to his feet; making outrageous accusations; screaming. Eventually the lucid periods diminished, and he became more confused, less predictable. It became impossible to hold a normal conversation with him. *Profoundly paranoid* is the phrase Dr. Mainwaring used. Now"—he shook his head and sighed—"apparently it's gotten even worse."

"By *less predictable,* do you mean violent?"

"Not really, though I suppose unrestrained, he might have been able to do some damage. He'd flail out, jump up and down, clutch his face, tear at his hair. He may have been mildly assaultive on one or two occasions, but before the escape he had never hurt anyone. No one ever considered him homicidal, if that's what you mean."

"This morning he was drooling and trembling and making sucking motions with his mouth. Have you seen that before?"

"I noticed it for the first time yesterday. Of course, I haven't been in close enough contact with him to be certain he hasn't been that way before. What do those symptoms mean?"

"I'm not sure yet. I'll need a detailed record of any treatment he's received—medication, electroconvulsive therapy, psychotherapy, everything."

His eyebrows rose.

"Are you implying some kind of toxic reaction?"

"At this point I don't know enough to imply anything."

"Very well," he said with some disappointment. "I'll set up a meeting with Mainwaring, and he can fill you in. Be sure to let me know if you feel there's brain damage of any sort. It could prove useful."

"I'll keep you posted."

He looked at the untouched meal on my plate.

"Not hungry?"

"Not right now."

After lifting a glass of ice water to his mouth, he sipped and put it down before speaking.

"The severity of his condition has gotten me thinking, Doctor. I'd originally considered petitioning for a delay based upon incompetence to stand trial but decided against it. At that time I felt the chance of success was nil. He was disturbed but still verbal with occasional flashes of brilliance; a psychiatrist talking to him at the wrong time might have mistakenly assumed malingering. In a highly publicized case judges tend to play it conservative; few of them have the gumption to cope with the hue and cry certain to result from a delay. Now, however, I don't know. If he maintains this level of deterioration or gets worse, even the prosecution psychiatrists may agree he's incompetent. What do you think?"

"Have you yourself suspected him of malingering?"

He'd begun cutting another piece of meat, and the question stilled his knife and fork and caused him to look up.

"No, not really. I know he's quite ill."

"But not so ill that he couldn't pull off eight murders that required careful planning."

He put the utensils down.

"You come right to the point, don't you, Doctor? No matter, I like that. Yes, you're right. We're not dealing with one cathartic explosion of bloodlust; the slashings were carried out with a perverse kind of care and attention to detail. That suggests detachment and the ability to think analytically, which poses a problem for the whole notion of an insanity defense. But I believe I have a way of dealing with that problem, which I'll come to later. In any event, what's your opinion regarding a petition for delay?"

"What would a delay mean in practical terms?"

"Involuntary commitment until such time as he's judged competent, which in this case may be *if,* not when. But would the boy's interests be best served by such a move? The commitment would have to be at a state hospital, and those places are horrors. He'd end up on a back ward, which might be a death sentence in itself. If I take the case to trial and the diminished capacity defense is successful, there'd be more flexibility in arranging his subsequent care."

I knew what he had in mind. Another private hospital, where the family's money would play a major role in influencing treatment and discharge decisions. There Jamey could be put away long enough for the furor to die down and then quietly released as an outpatient in the care of his guardians.

A chilling scenario ran through my head. Would he end up yet another psychological time bomb let out on the street with little more than a prescription for Thorazine and an appointment with a therapist because some expert had misread behavioral suppression as significant improvement? If so, the gradual fade to noncompliance was depressingly predictable—pills not swallowed, appointments not kept—as were its consequences: the inexorable return of the demons. Confusion, pain. Night walks. The sudden lashing out fueled by paranoiac fury. Blood.

Up to this point I'd been able to involve myself in Jamey's case—to sit across from him and feel compassion—because I'd disassociated myself from the crimes of which he'd been accused, denying the possibility that he'd butchered eight human beings. But even Souza, it seemed, assumed he was guilty, and listening to him talking strategy and discussing flexibility of care was forcing me to confront the consequences of my involvement.

If Jamey had done what they said he had, I didn't want flexibility. I wanted him locked up forever.

Which made me a hell of a defense expert.

Mal Worthy had talked about the emotional balm that resulted from cutting off one's feelings, from detaching values from actions. But I was no attorney and could never be. I watched Souza slice a wedge of steak and pop it in his mouth and wondered how long I'd last on his team.

"I don't know," I said. "It's a tough question."

"Well, Doctor"—he smiled—"it's my problem, not yours."

He pushed aside his plate, and the lower part of his face disappeared, momentarily, behind a cloud of white linen.

"I can ring the kitchen for something else if you'd like—some fruit or coffee?"

"No, thanks."

There was a brass dish filled with after-dinner mints next to the water pitcher. He offered it to me and, after I'd declined, took a mint himself. A button under the table edge summoned a black-uniformed Filipino woman who cleared the dishes.

"Now then," he said, when she was gone, "what would you like to know about the Cadmus family?"

"Let's start with Jamey's caretaker history and the significant relationships in his life, including the details of his parents' deaths."

"All right," he said contemplatively. "To understand all of that, it's best to go back a generation and start with his grandfather."

"Fine." I pulled out a notepad and pen.

"I met John Jacob Cadmus in Germany right after the war. I was a legal officer assigned to the War Criminals Investigation Section, and he was a field representative for the adjutant general's office in charge of processing the bastards. He'd begun the war as an infantry private, served heroically in several major battles, and ended up a colonel at the age of twenty-seven. We became friends, and when I returned to California, Black Jack—he was called that because of his black Irish coloring—decided to come with me. He was from Baltimore, but his roots were shallow, and the West was the land of opportunity.

"He was a visionary, foresaw the postwar baby boom and the housing shortage it would bring. Back in those days the San Fernando Valley was undeveloped—a few ranches and orchards, some federal acreage set aside for military bases that were never built, the rest dust and scrub. Jack set about buying up as much Valley land as he could. He borrowed himself heavily into debt but managed to stall the creditors long enough to educate himself about architecture and construction and hire work crews. By the time the boom arrived he'd built dozens of huge housing tracts—thousands of units, mostly five-room bungalows on forty-by-eighty lots. He made sure each one had a fruit tree—orange, lemon, apricot—and advertised nationally, selling the California dream. The houses sold as fast as he could put them up, and by the age of thirty he was a millionaire several times over. Eventually he expanded to commercial and industrial projects, and by 1960 Cadmus Construction was the third largest builder in the state. When he died, in 'sixty-seven, the company had initiated major projects in Saudia Arabia, Panama, and half of Europe. He was a great man, Doctor."

It was a paean to a dead man, and I wasn't sure what the point was.

"How was he as a husband and father?" I asked.

Souza was annoyed by the question.

"He loved his boys and was kind to his wife."

A strange answer. My expression reflected it.

"Antoinette was a troubled woman," he explained. "She came from an established Pasadena family that had lost its money but managed to maintain appearances and a foothold on the social ladder. Jack met her at a charity ball and was taken with her immediately. She was a beauty. Slender, very pale, very fragile, with huge, mournful blue eyes—the boy has those same eyes—but I always found her strange. Distant, extremely vulnerable. I imagine it was her very vulnerability that attracted Jack, but soon after the marriage the extent of her problems became evident."

"What kinds of problems?"

"The kinds that fall within your bailiwick. At first it seemed like severe shyness, social withdrawal. Then it became clear that she was terrified of leaving the house, terrified of life itself. I'm sure there's a technical term for it."

"Agoraphobia."

"Agoraphobia," he repeated. "That was Antoinette's problem. Back then, of course, she was thought of as physically ill. Constitutionally weak. As a wedding present, Jack set her up in a glorious Spanish mansion on Muirfield, overlooking the country club, just a few blocks from here; a Pakistani surgeon owns it now. Once ensconced, she never left the place, not even to tour the gardens. In fact, she seldom ventured out of her room, staying in bed all day, scribbling verse on scraps of paper, sipping weak tea, complaining of all sorts of aches and pains. Jack had half the specialists in town on retainer, and each of them supplied nostrums and tonics, but none of it helped. Eventually he gave up and simply let her be, accepting her weakness."

"She was strong enough to bear children," I said.

"Amazing, isn't it? Peter—Jamey's father—was born ten months after the wedding, in 'forty-eight; Dwight, a year later. Jack hoped the joys of motherhood would pull her out of her depression, but she got worse and had to be sedated for the bulk of both pregnancies. After Dwight's birth her withdrawal deepened, and she rejected the baby, refused to nurse or even to hold it. Things deteriorated to the point where she bolted her door and wouldn't see Peter or Jack. For the next two years she stayed in her room, drinking her tonics and swallowing her pills, writing poetry and napping. She'd cry out in her sleep, as if having horrible nightmares. Then she began to accuse everyone—Jack, the servants, even the children—of conspiring against her, plotting to kill her, the usual paranoid nonsense. When she stopped eating and grew downright skeletal, Jack realized she'd have to be institutionalized and made plans to have her flown to a place in Switzerland. It was supposed to be a secret, but she may have gotten wind of it because a week later she was dead, overdosed on one of her medications; apparently it contained some kind of opiate, and she ingested enough to stop her heart."

"Who took care of the boys through all this?"

"Jack hired governesses. When they were older, they were sent to boarding schools. He did the best he could under the circumstances, Doctor, which is why I answered your question about what kind of father he was the way I did."

I nodded.

"Schizophrenia is believed to be genetic nowadays, isn't it?" he asked.

"It runs in families. Probably a combination of heredity and environment."

"I view Jamey as very much the product of his genes. The superior intellect is his endowment from Jack. The rest of it comes from the other side—antisocial tendencies, paranoia, a morbid preoccupation with fantasy and poetry. Saddled with such a chemistry, how could he have turned out normal?"

He tried to look empathetic, but his rhetoric had the studied passion of a prepared oration.

Instead of answering his question, I posed one of my own:

"How did the lack of mothering affect Peter and Dwight?"

"They turned out differently, so it's hard to pinpoint an effect per se. Dwight was always a good boy, eager to please. A me-tooer. He staked out the middle road early in life and stayed on it. Peter was another story. Good-looking, wild, always testing the limits. He was bright but never buckled down to studying, and Jack had to endow a building to get him into college. Once accepted, he continued to goof off and was finally expelled after three semesters. Jack should have been more firm with him, but Peter was his favorite, so instead, he indulged him. Sports cars, credit cards, early access to a trust fund. It sliced the spine right out of the boy. Combining that type of permissiveness with the nonsense of the sixties destroyed his character completely."

"Drugs?"

"Drugs, alcohol, promiscuity—all of the counterculture idiocy fed right into Peter's natural hedonism. At the age of nineteen he had a Ferrari. He used it to cruise Sunset Boulevard and pick up girls. One night he drove to a topless bar, took a liking to one of the dancers, flashed his smile and his billfold, and whisked her away to San Francisco. This was in 'sixty-eight, with the hippie scene in full bloom up there. The two of them jumped right into it—communal living in some Haight-Ashbury dive, swallowing any drug they could get their hands on, Lord knows what else. The leeches they lived with knew a good thing when they saw it, and the trust fund started running dry."

He frowned indignantly.

"Didn't his father try to stop it?"

"Of course he did. He had me hire private detectives, who tracked them down in a matter of days. Jack flew up to talk to Peter and received the shock of his life. The boy he remembered had been outstanding-looking, meticulous to the point of vanity about dress and appearance. In San Francisco Jack came face-to-face with a creature he barely recognized. I still remember his words: 'He looked like a goddamn dead Jesus, Horace, right off the goddamn cross.' As he recounted it, Peter was dirty, smelly, and emaciated, with glazed eyes and blurred speech. His hair was as long as a girl's, tied in a ponytail, and he wore a scraggly, untrimmed beard. Jack ordered him to come home and, when Peter refused, threatened to cut off the money. Peter told him to mind his own business—said it obscenely—and the two of them came to blows. The leeches got in the act, and Jack took a pummeling. He came back to Los Angeles emotionally shattered.

"Eventually the girl became pregnant. She had the baby without benefit of medical attention, used some kind of brown rice diet and home-concocted herbal poultices. It was a difficult delivery, and afterward she bled to death. Somehow the baby survived, and Peter had enough sense scared into him to bring him to a hospital. He was suffering from bronchitis, skin rashes, and other infections but eventually recovered."

He shook his head, remembering.

"And that, Dr. Delaware, is how our boy Jamey came into this world. Not an auspicious beginning, is it?"

I paused in my note taking.

"What was the mother's name?"

"Margaret Norton," he replied absently, as if the name and its owner were inconsequential. "She called herself Margo Sunshine. We did some background investigation on her. A runaway, from New Jersey. One relative: a mother dying of alcohol poisoning. When Peter spotted her dancing naked, she was seventeen. Just another one of the aimless kids who drift out here. But she was in the right place at the right time and ended up a Cadmus."

And dead, I thought, keeping it to myself.

Souza examined his cuff links and kept talking.

"You can see from all this why I feel the history will support a dim cap defense. Look at what we've got: atrocious genes, prenatal malnutrition, and parental drug abuse, which could certainly lead to some kind of subtle, inborn brain damage, couldn't it? Add to that traumatic birth, early infection, and maternal deprivation, and it's a litany of disasters."

"Who raised Jamey?" I asked, ignoring the speech.

"Peter did. Not that he was cut out for it. But for a while he seemed to be growing up, meeting his responsibilities. There'd been some doubt in Jack's mind about the baby's paternity; but the resemblance to Peter was striking, and when they came home, he accepted both of them with open arms, paid for the best doctors, nurses, and nannies, built an elaborate nursery. At first the baby seemed to be bringing Jack and Peter together. They worked hard at amusing him—no easy task because he was colicky and cried constantly. When Peter's patience ran out, Jack was there to step in. They were closer than they'd ever been. Then in November of 'sixty-nine Jack became ill. Pancreatic cancer. He was gone in a matter of weeks.

"We all were stunned, but the most severely affected was Peter. He was in shock, confronted suddenly by the enormousness of his obligations. For twenty-one years his father had blunted all the rough edges for him, but now he was on his own. In addition to the baby, there was the business to run. Jack was your typical charismatic leader, poor at delegating, kept things in his head or on scraps of paper. His affairs were a mess, and poor Peter was left with the task of sorting it out.

"On the day of the funeral he came to me literally shaking with terror, wondering how he was going to run the company and raise an infant when he couldn't even run his own life. The pathetic truth was, he was right. He had no head for business. Dwight had shown some talent along those lines—he was a business major at Stanford—but he was barely twenty, and I encouraged him to stay in school.

"I set about hiring professional managers, and they reorganized the company on a more conventional basis. It took a year to get it done. All the while Peter was at loose ends. He tried getting involved in corporate affairs but was easily bored. My suggestion that he return to college was shrugged off. There was no purpose in his life, and he sank into depression and started to pull away from the baby. It was history repeating itself, and I urged him to seek psychiatric help. He refused and went rapidly downhill. I'm certain he started taking drugs again. His eyes took on a wild look, and he lost a lot of weight. He'd spend days in his room brooding, then go roaring off in one of his cars and not return for days."

"How did Jamey react to the changes in his father?"

"He seemed to develop independent of Peter's ups and downs. It was obvious early on that he was unusually bright. He'd come toddling around, making precocious remarks clearly aimed at engaging his father's attention. But rather than charm him, the precociousness frightened Peter, and he reacted by rejecting Jamey, actually pushing him away physically.

"I've never been a parent myself, but I knew what that could do to a young child. I talked to Peter about it, but he grew angry and called Jamey a freak, said he was 'spooky.' He worked himself up into a fury talking about it, so I backed off, out of fear for the child's safety."

"Was he always that volatile?"

"Until then, no. Like Jack, he had a short fuse, nothing serious. But it began to get out of hand. Minor things—the little messes children create—that would have annoyed a more stable person enraged him. He had to be restrained more than once from striking out at Jamey with a closed fist. The nannies were instructed to keep a close watch at all times. When he lost all interest in fatherhood, no one tried to talk him out of it."

"Was there ever any actual physical abuse?"

"No. And once Peter refused to be a father, the child was safe, because the withdrawal was absolute. As his mother had done, he shut his door on life and became a hermit. And just as she had, he ended his misery by taking his own life."

"How'd he do it?"

"Hanged himself. The house had a ballroom with high, vaulted ceilings and thick oak crossbeams. Peter stood on a chair, threw a rope over one of the beams, looped it around his neck, and kicked the chair away."

"How old was Jamey when it happened?"

"That was in 1972, so he must have been around three. We shielded him from the details. Do you think he could remember that far back?"

"It's possible. Has he ever talked about it?"

"Only in general terms—not having a father, philosophical questions about suicide. I spoke to Dwight and Heather, and as far as they know, he's never asked for the gory details nor been given any. Did he ever mention anything about hanging to you?"

"No. He was very closed about personal matters. Why is it important?"

"It may be relevant in terms of setting up a defense. The circumstances surrounding the slashings—especially the Chancellor murder—have made me wonder about the influence of early memories upon adult behavior. All the victims were strangled before being cut, and Dig Chancellor was found suspended from a crossbeam. I'm not a strong believer in coincidence."

"So you're suggesting the murders were symbolic acts of patricide?"

"You're the psychologist, Doctor. I defer to your interpretation."

"Wouldn't it hurt your case to supply motivation for the murders? Make the crimes look more purposeful?"

"Not if the motivation's shown to be illogical and psychotic. Jurors' minds abhor a vacuum. Given no motive, they'll supply their own. If I can show that the boy is a prisoner of long-buried morbid impulses, it will help steer them my way. In general, the more psychology I can inject into the trial, the better our chances of success."

Always thinking strategically.

I put aside the invitation to play Freud and asked him who reared Jamey after his father's suicide.

"Dwight did. He'd received his M.B.A. by then and was working at Cadmus Construction as an executive trainee. Of course, the physical caretaking continued to be carried out by governesses and babysitters, but Dwight extended himself—took the boy on outings, taught him to play catch. Certainly gave him more attention than Peter ever had."

"You said 'governesses,' plural. How many were there?"

"Quite a few. They came and went in a stream. None stayed longer than several months. He was a difficult child, cranky and moody, and his intelligence actually made matters worse because he knew how to use his tongue as a weapon of intimidation. Several of the women left in tears."

"Where did they live during this period?"

"In the house on Muirfield. Dwight had moved back home after graduation—shortly before Peter's death. When he and Heather married, they sold it and bought a more manageable place nearby."

"How did Jamey adjust to the marriage?"

For the first time in the conversation Souza hesitated, if only for a second.

"I suppose there were difficulties—logic dictates there would be—but outward appearances were calm."

"How did Jamey and Heather get along?"

Another pause.

"Just fine, as far as I could see. Heather's a lovely girl."

During most of the interview he'd narrated with authority. Now he seemed tentative. I commented on it.

"That's correct," he said. "I felt confidence in Dwight, and once he took over, my involvement in personal matters lessened. He and Heather are in a better position than I to answer questions about recent events."

"All right."

He rang for the black-garbed waitress and ordered tea. She left and reappeared with a cart that held the china service from his office. This time I accepted a cup.

"You seem," I said between sips, "to have been much more than a family attorney."

He put down his cup and licked his lips with a brief, saurine movement of his tongue. In the dimness his complexion glowed rosy, and I watched it deepen angrily as he spoke.

"Black Jack Cadmus was the best friend I ever had. We came up together the hard way. When he began purchasing land, he offered me a fifty percent buy-in. I was cautious, had trouble believing all that scrub would turn into city, and turned him down. Had I accepted, I'd be one of the richest men in California. When the money started pouring in, Jack insisted I receive a substantial sum anyway, claiming I'd helped him with the legal end of it—title searches, drawing up deeds. That was true as far as it went, but he paid me much more than my services were worth. That money financed the establishment of this firm, the purchase of this building, everything I own, which I'm not ashamed to say is substantial."

He leaned forward and a pinpoint of light from the chandelier reflected off his naked cranium.

"Jack Cadmus is responsible for who I am today, Doctor. You don't forget something like that."

"Of course not."

It took several seconds for the broad features to settle back into professional repose. My comment had been innocent—curiosity about the degree of his involvement with a client. Yet answering it had evoked a strong reaction. Maybe he didn't believe that a comment from a psychologist could ever be innocent. Or perhaps he was peeved at having his privacy invaded. An overreaction, it seemed, but people who earn their livings rooting in the psychic refuse of others often develop an obsession with personal secrecy.

"Anything else?" he asked, pleasant again, and I stopped surmising.

"Yes. I want to know more about Ivar Digby Chancellor. The papers have been describing him as a prominent banker and gay activist, but that doesn't tell me much. In your office Dwight Cadmus called him a damned deviate. Were he and Jamey lovers?"

"Once again we're in an area where Dwight and Heather could be more helpful, but I'll do my best to describe things in general terms. Yes, there was some kind of intimate relationship, but I don't know that I'd call it love."

His mouth puckered as if he'd eaten something spoiled. "Pederasty maybe."

"Because Jamey was a minor?"

"Because the whole thing smacked of exploitation," he said angrily. "Dig Chancellor had other fish to fry. He didn't need to seduce an impressionable, disturbed boy. For God's sake, Doctor, the man was old enough to be his father. In fact, Chancellor and Peter had been classmates in military school."

"So the families have known each other for a long time."

"They were neighbors, lived a block apart, ran in the same social circles. The Chancellors are prominent in accounting and banking. Big, strapping people—even the women are large. Dig was the largest—six-five, shoulders like a mountain, loved football, squash, polo. Married an heiress from the Philadelphia Main Line. A man's man—or so everyone thought. No one suspected he was queer until after the divorce. Then the rumors started spreading— the nasty kind of thing passed behind hands at cocktail parties. They might have faded, but Dig turned them into fact by going public. Showed up at one of those marches for gay rights holding hands with two hairdresser types. It made the front page of the papers and was picked up by the wire services."

Suddenly I remembered the photo. It jogged my memory and created a mental image of a dead man: a towering, square-jawed, executive type in gray suit and rimless glasses marching down the middle of Santa Monica Boulevard, dwarfing the svelte mustachioed men on either side. Banners in the background. Under the picture a caption commenting on the melding of old money and the new morality.

"Once out of the closet, he flaunted it," said Souza disgustedly. "The family was scandalized, so he broke away and started his own bank—Beverly Hills Trust. Built it up soliciting accounts from homosexual businesses; there's a lot of money there, you know. Used his fortune and influence to buy sympathetic political candidates. Purchased an estate from a movie mogul, one of those dinosaurs north of Sunset, and let it be used for fund-raisers—ACLU, the arty crowd, male go-go dancers, that kind of thing."

"You didn't like him."

Souza sighed.

"For years I've had a box at the Hollywood Bowl. Dig had one in the same section. Inevitably we'd bump into each other at concerts, chat, trade hors d'oeuvres, compare wines. In those days he sported the finest tailored evening wear and always had a young lady on his arm. Very gallant. Then one year he showed up with his hair peroxided and curled, wearing mascara and a loose robe, like some bloody Roman emperor. Instead of a woman, he had with him a gaggle of boys straight out of a Maxfield Parrish print. He greeted me heartily, held out his hand, as if nothing were out of the ordinary. Perverse."

He stirred his tea and frowned.

"Mind you, I have nothing against homosexuals, though I'll never be convinced they're normal. Let them keep a low profile and go about their business. But Chancellor didn't show that type of discretion. He advertised his deviance, exploited the innocent. A damned predator."

He'd grown flushed again and seemed to have worked himself into a passion; this time I thought I understood why.

"That should fit perfectly into your strategy," I said.

The stirring accelerated, and he looked up sharply.

The expression on his face told me my guess had been right on target.

"Oh?"

"You said before you had a way of reconciling diminished capacity with the premeditated nature of the slashings. Painting Chancellor as the homicidal mastermind and Jamey as his dupe would be an excellent way to accomplish that. You could claim that Chancellor did the actual killing and Jamey was a passive observer. That would shift the bulk of the blame to a dead man and turn the one murder Jamey had to have committed—that of Chancellor—into a noble act, the elimination of a sadistic predator."

Souza smiled.

"Very impressive, Doctor. Yes, I have been thinking along those lines. It's no secret that all the Slasher victims were murdered elsewhere and dumped around the city. My assertion will be that the killings took place at Chancellor's estate, with Jamey no more than an observer, seduced by an older man, befuddled by psychosis. The boy allowed himself to be swept along for several months. No doubt his guilt at witnessing the butchery contributed to his breakdown and the subsequent need for hospitalization."

"During his hospitalization the slashings stopped."

He waved his hand, dismissing the point.

"We know Chancellor was a sick man. What if he were bent in more than one way, exhibitionistic as well as queer. So many of them are. I assert that he needed an audience for his crimes and tagged Jamey for the role. The boy and he had a twisted relationship, no doubt about that. I won't claim Jamey is a total innocent. But it's the leadership role that's crucial. Who led the way? Who premeditated? A powerful, domineering older man or a confused teen-ager? Even the escape can work in our favor. I've got investigators searching for witnesses, someone who saw the boy that night. If we can show that Chancellor broke Jamey out of Canyon Oaks, we can claim he abducted him in order to have him witness another blood orgy. Took him home and slaughtered Richard Ford. But this time Jamey was overcome by the savagery of what he saw. They argued, struggled, and the boy managed to kill the butcher."

When he'd enlisted my participation in Jamey's defense, Souza had made the case sound hopeless. Now, barely two days later, he was trumpeting a neat psychodrama that transformed Jamey from monster to mind slave and, finally, to dragon slayer. But I wondered how much confidence he really had in the Svengali strategy. To my mind, there were plenty of holes in it.

"You said Chancellor was a very large man. Jamey's a wraith. How could he overpower him and hoist him over a crossbeam?"

"Dig was taken by surprise," he said, unperturbed, "and Jamey was strengthened by the release of pent-up fury; I'm sure you're aware of the power of adrenaline. With the proper fulcrum it's surprising what even a small person can lift. I know a prominent physicist who'll testify to that."

The look on his face invited further questioning.

"Chancellor had an estate," I said, "which means servants. The slashings were messy affairs. How could he conceal that kind of thing from them?"

"He employed a day staff—gardeners, maid, cook—but only one man lived on the premises, a combination bodyguard majordomo named Erno Radovic. Radovic is an unstable character, used to be a policeman until he was booted off the force. I employed him once or twice as an investigator before I realized what kind of troublemaker he was. In fact, it wouldn't surprise me if he were in on all of it, but for the time being he's in the clear, alibied for the night of the murder. Seems Thursday was his day off. He'd leave mornings and return Friday by noon. Slept once a week on a boat he had moored in the Marina. He produced a woman who said she'd been with him all last Thursday. All of which strengthens my theory because each of the Slasher victims was dumped on a Friday, in the early-morning hours, and, according to the forensics lab, killed several hours before. On Thursday night. Now we know the reason. With Radovic gone there'd be no witnesses."

"Has the forensics lab produced any evidence that Chancellor wielded the knife?"

"Not to my knowledge. But neither is there proof that Jamey wielded it. The handle was blood-smeared, no clean fingerprints. In any event, whether or not it actu-

ally happened that way is hardly relevant, is it? The key is to provide the jurors with a reasonable doubt. To get them to consider a different scenario from the one the prosecution will present."

He gazed at me steadily, awaiting a response. When I gave none, he turned away and ran a blunt finger around the rim of his saucer.

"You ask good questions, Doctor. Answering them helps keep me on my toes. Anything else?"

I closed my notepad. "Given Jamey's history, I'm concerned about suicide."

"So am I. It was one of the first things I mentioned when I petitioned for release to an institution prior to trial. The DA's office said the High Power lockup featured twenty-four-hour suicide watch and was safe. The judge agreed."

"Is that true?"

"For the most part. You couldn't get tighter security anywhere. But can suicide ever really be prevented?"

"No," I conceded. "If someone's determined, he'll eventually succeed."

He nodded.

"Right now he seems too lethargic to damage himself. Nevertheless, if you pick up any danger signs, please inform me immediately. What else?"

"Nothing for now. When can I talk to Dwight and Heather Cadmus?"

"They're in seclusion with friends in Montecito, avoiding the press. Dwight should be returning in a couple of days. Heather was planning to stay longer. Is it necessary that you see them together?"

"No. In fact, individually would be better."

"Excellent. I'll have it arranged and phone you. I've got a call in to Mainwaring, and I'll try to set up a time for you to meet with him and review the records within the next few days."

"Fine."

We stood simultaneously. Souza buttoned his suit jacket and walked me out the door of the dining room and down the corridor to the building's entrance. It was late afternoon, approaching dusk, and the rotunda was full of immaculately turned-out young men and women—associates and ancillary staff leaving for the day, trailing wisps of perfume and cologne, designer loafers and stiletto heels tattooing the checkered marble. The sight of Souza evoked reflexive smiles and servile nods. He ignored them and drew me away from the crowd, placed a hand on my shoulder, and smiled.

"Coming up with my Chancellor strategy was first-rate thinking, Doctor, as was your little interrogation. Perhaps you're in the wrong profession."

I backed out of his grasp and moved toward the door.

"I don't think so," I said, and walked away.

On the way home I stopped at the Pico kosher deli near Robertson and bought provisions: a pound of corned beef, new pickles, coleslaw, and a loaf of caraway rye sliced thick. The evening traffic was chromium soup, but I made it to the glen by six-thirty. Once settled, I fed the koi, glanced at the mail, and went into the kitchen, where I prepared sandwiches and set them on a platter in the refrigerator. When Robin's truck pulled into the carport, I was waiting on the terrace, Grolsch in hand. She'd been sawing and planing for most of the afternoon and looked tired; when she saw the food, she cheered.

After dinner we sat in the living room, put our feet up, and shared the *Times*. I got as far as page three before Jamey's face jumped out at me.

The picture was a head shot, formally posed, that looked to be a couple of years old. Black-and-white photography had turned his blue eyes murky. In another context the downward turn of his lips might have seemed sad; under the present circumstances it took on a sinister cast. The article surrounding the photo described him as the "scion of a family prominent in the construction industry" and made note of his "history of serious psychiatric problems." A paragraph at the end said the police were delving into Ivar Digby Chancellor's background. Souza worked fast.

10

THE NEXT morning I put on jeans, a polo shirt, and sandals, took my briefcase, and walked down the glen toward UCLA. The road was choked with cars—commuters making the daily pilgrimage from homes in the Valley to West Side business districts. Watching them inch forward, I thought of Black Jack Cadmus and wondered how many of them had fruit trees in their backyards.

I crossed Sunset, continued south on Hilgard, and entered the campus at Strathmore. A short hike brought me to the northern edge of the Health Sciences Center—a complex of brick behemoths rumored to house more corridor space than the Pentagon. I'd misspent a good deal of my youth in those corridors.

Entering at ground level, I made a familiar right turn. The hallway leading to the Biomedical Library was lined with glass display cases. This month's exhibit was on the history of surgical instruments, and I glanced at the array of therapeutic weaponry—from crude, stone trepans exposing the cerebral tissue within a mannikin's skull to lasers traversing arterial tunnels.

The library had just opened and was still quiet. By noon the place would be jammed with medical students and those aspiring to be medical students, sleep-deprived residents, and grim-faced graduate students hiding behind hillocks of reference material.

I sat down at an oak table, opened my briefcase, and pulled out the volume of *Fish's Schizophrenia* that I'd brought from home. It was the third edition, relatively new, but after two hours of study I'd read little I hadn't already known. Putting the book aside, I went searching for more current information—abstracts and journal articles. Half an hour of peering into microfiche viewers and shuffling index cards and three more hours hunched in the stacks made my eyes blur and my head buzz. I took a break and headed for the vending machines.

Sitting in an outdoor courtyard, I drank bitter coffee, chewed on a stale sugar doughnut, and realized how few facts I'd found floating in a sea of theory and speculation.

Schizophrenia. The word means "split mind," but it's a misnomer. What schizophrenia really represents is the disintegration of the mind. It's a malignant disorder, cancer of the thought processes, the scrambling and ero sion of mental activity. Schizophrenic symptoms—delusions, hallucinations, illogical thinking, loss of touch with reality, bizarre speech and behavior—embody the layman's notion of *crazy.* They occur in one percent of the population in virtually every society, and no one knows why. Everything from birth trauma to brain damage to body type to poor mothering has been suggested as a cause. Nothing has been proved, although much has been disproved, and as Souza had pointed out gleefully, the evidence suggests a genetic predisposition to madness.

The course of the disease is as unpredictable as that of a flash fire in a windstorm. Some patients experience a single psychotic episode that never recurs. Others recover after a series of attacks. In many instances the disorder is chronic but static, while in the most severe cases deterioration progresses to the point of total breakdown.

Despite all this ambiguity, the relationship between madness and murder is clear: The vast majority of schizophrenics are harmless, less violent than the rest of us. But a few are stunningly dangerous. Paranoid, they lash out in sudden bursts of rage, often maiming or killing the very people working hardest to help them—parents, spouses, therapists.

Schizophrenics don't commit serial murders.

The sadism, premeditation, and ritual repetition of the Lavender Slashings were the trademark of another denizen of the psychiatric jungle.

He's the beast who walks upright. Meet him on the street, and he'll seem normal, even charming. But he roams those streets, parasitic and cold-eyed, stalking his prey behind a veneer of civility. The rules and regulations that separate humans from savages don't concern him. "Do unto others as you damn well please" is his creed. He's a user and a manipulator, and he lacks empathy or conscience. The screams of his victims are at best irrelevant, at worst a source of pleasure.

He's the psychopath, and psychiatry understands him even less than it does the schizophrenic. The symptoms of madness can often be altered with medication, but there's no therapy for evil.

Madman or monster, which was Jamey?

Sonnenschein, with a cop's natural cynicism, had suspected the latter. I knew he spoke from experience, because the first thing psychopaths often attempt after being caught is feigning insanity. The Yorkshire Ripper had tried it, as had Manson, Bianchi, and Son of Sam. All had failed, but not before fooling several experts.

Over the years I'd examined a fair share of budding psychopaths—callous, shallow kids who bullied the weak, set fires, and tortured animals without a shred of remorse. Seven-, eight- and nine-year-olds who were downright scary. They followed a pattern that Jamey hadn't fit; if anything, he'd seemed overly sensitive, too introspective for his own good. But how well had I really known him? And though the decompensation I'd witnessed in the jail had seemed the farthest thing from fraud, could I be absolutely certain that I was immune from subterfuge?

I wanted to believe Souza, to be certain I was on the side of the good guys. But at this point I had nothing to go on besides wishful thinking and the Cadmus family history the attorney had given me—a propaganda piece that may or may not have been accurate.

It was homework time. I needed to plumb the past in order to bring the present into focus, to conduct a psychological autopsy that illuminated the fall of a young genius.

The meetings with the Cadmuses and Mainwaring were days away. But the psychology building was a short sprint across the science quad.

I found a pay phone, dialed the psych department, and asked the receptionist to connect me with Sarita Flowers's extension. Seven rings later a cool young female voice answered.

"Dr. Flowers's office."

"This is Dr. Delaware. I'm a former associate of Dr.

Flowers. I happen to be on campus and wonder if I could drop by and talk with her."

"She's tied up with meetings for the rest of the afternoon."

"When will she be free?"

"Not until tomorrow."

"She might want to talk to me before then. Could you please reach her and ask?"

The voice tightened suspiciously.

"What did you say your name was?"

"Delaware. Dr. Alex Delaware."

"You're not a reporter, are you?"

"No. I'm a psychologist. I used to consult to Project 160."

Hesitation.

"All right. I'm going to put you on hold."

Several minutes later she was back, sounding resentful.

"She'll see you in twenty minutes. My name is Karen. Meet me at the fourth-floor elevators."

She rounded the corner just as I got off, tall and angular, wearing a red and white Diane von Furstenberg dress that dramatized the blackness of her skin. Her hair had been trimmed to a half-inch nap, accentuating tiny ears and high cheekbones. Ovals of ivory dangled from each ear, and ivory bracelets segmented one ebony forearm.

"Dr. Delaware? I'm Karen. Come this way."

She led me down the hall to a door labeled A.D. OBSERVATION—DO NOT DISTURB.

"You can wait in here. She should be out in a minute."

"Thanks."

She nodded coolly. "Sorry for hassling you before, but the press has been hounding her ever since the Cadmus thing. We had to call campus security to eject a guy from the *Enquirer* this morning."

"Don't worry about it."

"Want any coffee or anything?"

"No, thanks."

"Okay, then. I'll be off." She put her hand on the doorknob but stopped before turning it. "You're here about Cadmus, too, aren't you?"

"Yes."

"What a crazy thing to happen. It's created some real problems for the project. She's been under a lot of stress anyway, and this just makes it worse."

Not knowing what to say, I smiled sympathetically.

"A real crappy thing," she repeated, opening the door and walking off.

The room was dark. A microphone dangled from the ceiling, which, like three of the walls, was layered with acoustical tile. The fourth wall was a one-way mirror. A woman in a wheelchair sat looking through the glass. In her lap was a clipboard, stuffed with papers. She turned toward me as I entered and smiled.

"Alex," she whispered.

I bent over and kissed her cheek. She emitted a cool, clean California scent—suntan lotion and chlorine.

"Hello, Sarita."

"It's so good to see you," she said, taking my hand and squeezing it hard.

"Good to see you, too."

She sat tall in the chair, dressed casually but formally, in a navy blazer, pale blue silk blouse, and spotless white slacks that couldn't conceal the withered outlines of atrophied legs.

"I'll be through in just a few minutes," she said, and pointed toward the mirror. On the other side was a brightly lit windowless room floored with linoleum and painted white. In the center of the floor sat a child in front of an electric train set.

He was about six or seven, dressed in jeans, a yellow T-shirt, and sneakers, chubby and chipmunk-cheeked with caramel-colored hair. The miniature railroad was an elaborate setup: shiny cars; silver track; a papier-mâché landscape of bridges, lakes, and rolling hills; wooden depots and semaphores; built-to-scale two-story houses rimmed with matchstick picket fences.

Pasted to the boy's forehead and scalp were several electrodes trailing black cables that snaked along the floor and fed into an electroencephalogram monitor. The machine spewed out a slow but steady stream of paper patterned with the peaks and troughs of a line graph.

"Pull up a seat," said Sarita, picking up a pencil and making a notation.

I sat in a folding chair and watched. The boy had been

fidgeting, but now he sat stock-still. A low hum sounded, and the train began to roll steadily around the track. The boy smiled, wide-eyed; after a few moments his attention wandered again, and he began to move restlessly and look away. The train stopped. The boy returned his eyes to the locomotive and seemed to go into a trancelike state, face immobile, hands folded in his lap. There were no control switches in sight, and when the train started up again, it appeared to do so of its own accord.

"He's doing very well," said Sarita. "On task fifty-eight percent of the time."

"Attentional deficit?"

"Severe. When he first came in, he was all over the place, just couldn't sit still. The mother was ready to kill the kid. I've got another dozen just like him. We're running a study on teaching AD kids selfcontrol."

"Biofeedback?"

She nodded.

"We found most of them were pretty tense, and I thought the train would be a fun way to teach them to relax. It's hooked up to the EEG monitor through a wire under the floor. When they go into alpha state, the train runs. When they come out, it stops. One kid hates trains, so we use a tape recorder and music. The schedule of reinforcement can be programmed so that as they get better, they're expected to sit still for longer periods. Besides the attentional benefits, it makes them feel more in control, which should translate to higher self-esteem. I've got a grad student measuring it for a dissertation."

A buzzer went off on her wristwatch. She turned it off, scribbled a few notes, reached up, and pulled down the mike.

"Very good, Andy. You really kept it going today."

The boy looked up and touched one of the electrodes.

"It itches," he said.

"I'll be right in to take it off. One second, Alex."

She wheeled toward the door, yanked it, and rolled through. I followed her into the hallway. An old-faced young woman in halter top and shorts stood near an unmarked door, leaning against the wall. One hand twisted a strand of long dark hair. The other held a cigarette.

"Hello, Mrs. Graves. We're just about through. Andy did beautifully today."

The woman shrugged and sighed.

"I hope so. I got another report from school today."

Sarita looked up at her, smiled, patted her hand, and opened the door. After wheeling to the boy, she removed the electrodes, tousled his hair, and repeated that he'd done well. Reaching into the pocket of her blazer, she drew out a miniature toy car and handed it to him.

"Thank you, Dr. Flowers," he said, turning the gift over with pudgy fingers.

"My pleasure, Andy. Keep up the good work. Okay?"

But he'd run out of the room, engrossed in the new toy, and didn't hear her.

"Andy!" said his mother sharply. "What do you say to the doctor?"

"I already *did!*"

"Then say it again."

"Thank you." Begrudgingly.

"Bye now," said Sarita as they walked away. When they were gone, she shook her head. "Lots of stress there. Come on, Alex, let's go to my office."

The room was different from what I remembered, Spartan, less professorial. Then I realized that she'd altered it to accommodate her disability. The bookshelves that once lined one wall from floor to ceiling had been exchanged for low plastic modules that ran around three walls. The massive carved desk that had served as the room's centerpiece was gone; in its place was a low table that fit into one corner. The wall behind the table had once borne dozens of photographs—a pictorial essay of her athletic career. Now it was nearly blank; only a few pictures remained. A pair of folding chairs stood propped against the wall. What was left was mostly empty space. When the wheelchair entered, the space disappeared.

"Please," she said, pointing to the chairs. I unfolded one and sat.

She maneuvered around the table and put down the clipboard. While she checked her messages, I looked at the photos she'd left hanging: a beaming teen-ager receiving the Gold Medal at Innsbrück; a faded and yellowed program from the 1965 Ice Capades; an arty black-and-white shot of a lithe young woman gliding on ice, long blond hair streaming; the framed cover of a women's magazine promising its readers health and beauty tips from Skating Superstar Sarita.

She swiveled around, and her pale eyes circled the office.

"The minimalist look." She smiled. "Gives me easy access and keeps me sane. Since I've been in this thing, I find myself getting claustrophobic. Hemmed in. This way I can close the doors and spin around like a nut. Dervish therapy."

Her laugh was throaty and warm.

"Well, dear boy," she said, looking me over, "time has treated you kindly."

"You, too," I said automatically, and immediately felt like a jerk.

The last time I'd seen her had been three years ago at an APA convention. She'd been recovering from an MS attack that had left her enfeebled but able to walk with the aid of a cane. I wondered how long she'd been in the wheelchair; from the look of her legs it had been a while since she'd stood upright.

Observing my embarrassment, she pointed to her knees and laughed again.

"Hey, except for these I'm still first-class merchandise, right?"

I took a good look at her. She was forty but had the face of a woman ten years younger. It was an all-American face, sunny and open under a mop of thick blond hair, now cut in a pageboy, skin deeply tanned and lightly dusted with freckles, eyes open and guileless.

"Absolutely."

"Liar." She chuckled. "Next time I'm depressed I'll call you up for supportive prevarication."

I smiled.

"So," she said, growing serious, "let's talk about Jamey. What do you need to know?"

"When did he first start to look psychotic?"

"A little over a year ago."

"Was it gradual or a sudden thing?"

"Gradual. Insidious, really. You worked with him, Alex. You remember what a strange kid he was. Moody, hostile, defiant. Stratospheric IQ, but he refused to channel any of it. All the others got heavily involved in their studies. They're doing beautifully. The few classes he started he dropped out of. Failure to enroll was a clear violation of the project contract, and I could have dropped him, but I didn't because I felt sorry for him. Such a sad little boy, no parents, I kept hoping he'd work it through. The only thing he seemed to care about was poetry—reading, not writing. He was so obsessive about it that I kept thinking he might eventually do something creative, but he never did. In fact, one day he dropped poetry cold and developed an overnight interest in business and economics. Never went anywhere after that without the *Wall Street Journal* and an armload of finance texts."

"When was this?"

She thought for a moment.

"I'd say around eighteen months ago. And that wasn't the only change he made. Since I'd known him, he'd been a real junk food junkie. It was a kind of running joke, how he'd eat a buffalo chip if you put Cool Whip on it. Suddenly all he wanted was sprouts, tofu, whole grains, and unfiltered juice."

"Any idea what led up to the change?"

She shook her head.

"I asked him about it, especially the interest in economics, because I thought that might be a positive sign, an indication that he was getting serious about his studies. But he just gave me one of his get-out-of-my-face looks and walked away. A couple of months went by, and he still hadn't registered for classes or done much of anything but bury himself in the business library. I decided at that point to drop him. But before I had a chance to tell him, he started to act really strange.

"At first it was the same old stuff, but more so. Moodier, more depressed and withdrawn—to the point where he just stopped talking. Then he began to have anxiety attacks: flushed face; dry mouth; shortness of breath; palpitations. Twice he actually fainted."

"How many attacks were there?"

"About half a dozen over a one-month period. Afterward he'd get really suspicious, look at everyone accusingly and slink away. It upset the other kids, but they tried to be sympathetic. Since he kept to himself, it didn't create as big a problem as it could have."

She stopped, bothered about something, and brushed a

strand of hair away from her face. Her eyes narrowed, and her jawline hardened.

"Alex, diagnostics has never been my strong suit—even in grad school I stayed away from the crazies and concentrated on behavioral technology—but I'm not blind. I didn't just go about my business and let him fall apart. It wasn't as dramatic as it's coming out. The kid had a history of nonconformity, attention-seeking. I thought it was a temporary thing. That it would self-limit and he'd go on to something else."

"He called me the night he escaped," I said. "Flamingly psychotic. Afterward I did the guilt thing, too. Wondering if I'd missed something. It was counterproductive. There's nothing either of us could have done. Kids go crazy, and no one can prevent it."

She looked at me, then nodded.

"Thanks for the vote of confidence."

"Anytime."

She sighed.

"It's not like me to introspect, but I've been doing a lot of it lately. You know how hard I've had to fight to keep the project going. A genius-insanity scandal was the last thing I needed, but I got it in spades. The irony is that preventing bad PR was one of the reasons I kept him here longer than I should have. That and being a soft-hearted sucker."

"What do you mean?"

"The fact that I kept him on. As I said before, just before he started to fall apart, I'd decided to ask him to leave the project. But when he started to look emotionally fragile, I delayed the decision because I was worried it might cause some kind of dramatic reaction. The project grant was up for renewal. The data were beautiful, so scientifically I was in good shape, but because of budget cuts, the political bullshit was flying hard and heavy: Why give money to geniuses when the retarded need it more? Why hadn't more blacks and Latinos been included? Wasn't the whole concept of genius elitist and racist in the first place? All I needed was Jamey freaking out and the papers getting hold of it. So I tried to wait it out, hoping it would blow over. Instead, he got worse."

"Did you get renewed?"

"Only for one year, which is garbage, stringing me

along until they decide to cut the funds. It means not being able to sink my teeth into anything of substance."

"I'm sorry."

"It's all right," she said without heart. "At least I've got some time to scrounge up alternative funds. The odds looked good until this thing blew up." She smiled bitterly. "The foundations don't like it when even one of your subjects hacks up eight people."

I steered the conversation back to Jamey's deterioration.

"What happened when he got worse?"

"The suspiciousness turned into paranoia. Once again it was gradual, subtle. But eventually he was claiming someone was poisoning him, railing on about the earth's being poisoned by zombies."

"Do you remember anything more about his delusions? Phrases he used?"

"No, just that. Poisoning, zombies."

"White zombies?"

"Maybe. It doesn't ring a bell."

"When he talked about being poisoned, did he suspect anyone specifically?"

"He suspected everyone. Me. The other kids. His aunt and uncle. *Their* kids. We were all zombies, all against him. At that point I called the aunt and told her he needed help and couldn't continue on the project. It didn't seem to surprise her. She thanked me and promised to do something about it. But he showed up the next week anyway, looking really uptight, muttering under his breath. Everyone stayed away from him. The big surprise was when he came to group—probably the first time in a year. He sat quietly through half of it and then jumped up in the middle of the discussion and started yelling. From what he said it sounded as if he were hallucinating— hearing voices, seeing grids."

"What kinds of grids?"

"I don't know. That's the word he used. He was holding his hand in front of his eyes, squinting and screaming about bloody grids. It was frightening, Alex. I rushed out, called security, and had him taken to the med center. I spent the rest of the session calming the other kids down. It was agreed that we'd keep the whole incident quiet so as not to hurt the project. I never saw him again and thought that was the end of it. Until now."

"Sarita, as far as you know, did he ever take drugs?"

"No. He was a straight arrow, kind of stuffy, really. Why?"

"The grid hallucination. It's typical of an LSD trip."

"I seriously doubt it, Alex. As I said, he was conservative, overcautious. And toward the end, when he was into health foods, obsessed with his body, it would make even less sense for him to be tripping out."

"But if he was doping," I said, "you might not have known about it. It's the kind of thing kids don't talk about with adults."

She frowned.

"I suppose so. Nevertheless, I just don't believe he was into acid or any other drug. Anyway, what difference would it make? Drugs couldn't make him psychotic."

"No. But they might have put him over the edge."

"Even so."

"Sarita, he went from a troubled kid to a homicidal maniac. That's a hell of a fall from grace, and my job is to make some sense out of it. I'd like to talk to the other kids on the project to see if they knew anything about it."

"I'd rather you didn't," she said. "They've been through enough."

"I'm not planning to add to the stress. On the contrary, it could make them feel better to talk about it. I counseled all of them at one time or another, so it wouldn't be like a stranger coming in."

"Believe me," she insisted, "it's not worth it. They don't know anything that I haven't told you."

"I'm sure you're right, but I'd be irresponsible if I didn't interview the people who've been his friends for the last five years."

At the word irresponsible she winced. When she spoke, her voice was tight and subdued, but she tried to cover it with a smile.

"He had no friends, Alex. Not in any real sense. He was a loner. No one got close to him."

When I didn't answer, she shrugged absently.

"You'd need consent from all five of them. A couple are still minors, so the parents would have to consent as well. I can't promise their cooperation. It would be a real hassle for very little payoff."

"I'll take that risk, Sarita. The paper work will be taken care of by the defense attorney, a guy named Horace Souza."

She wheeled away from me and folded her arms across her chest.

"I've talked to Mr. Souza," she said. "He's a pushy, manipulative man, heavily into control. I suppose if I refused, he'd find some way to coerce me."

"Come on, Sarita. It doesn't have to come to that."

She exhaled and spun around. The wheels of the chair made squeaking sounds, like the chirp of a hatchling.

"Since the headlines broke, I've been fighting to keep out of the limelight, but I can see now it's a losing battle. It's really strange, Alex, weathering challenge after challenge to keep the project alive just to see it end like this."

"Who says it's ended?"

"It's dead, Alex. Jamey murdered it just as surely as he did those boys."

I shook my head.

"I don't doubt the press will have a field day with his IQ, just as they did with Leopold and Loeb. But your real enemy is ignorance. Folk myths about genius. If you stonewall it and the facts don't come out, people will revert to those myths. The more open you are about it, the better your chances of outlasting the publicity and getting your message across."

She was silent for several moments.

"All right," she said curtly. "I'll arrange it. Now if you'll excuse me, there's work I have to do."

"Thanks for your time," I said, standing.

Her handshake was cursory; her parting smile, mechanical. She closed the door after me quickly, and as I walked away, I heard an abrasive, groaning sound, rubber on vinyl. Spinning. Over and over.

11

SOUZA WAS surprised at my request.

"Doctor, all you're going to see is a large blood-spattered room, but if you think it's necessary, it can be arranged."

"It would be helpful."

He paused long enough for me to wonder if we'd been cut off.

"In what way, Doctor?"

"If he's ever lucid enough to talk about the murders, I want to be as knowledgeable as possible about the details."

"Very well," he said skeptically. "I've never had an expert ask for it, but I'll talk to the police and have them clear you for a visit."

"Thank you."

"On a more conventional note, I'd like to hear about any progress you've made in your evaluation."

I gave him a summary of my interview with Sarita Flowers. He latched immediately on to the grid hallucination and my inquiries about drug use.

"What are these grids exactly?"

"People on LSD sometimes report seeing brightly lit multicolored checkerboard designs. But Jamey spoke of seeing *bloody* grids, so it may have been something totally different."

"Interesting. If he did in fact see these grids, how significant is it?"

"Probably not at all. While visual hallucinations aren't as common in schizophrenia as auditory disturbances, they do occur. And Dr. Flowers seemed fairly certain that he never took drugs."

"But seeing this kind of thing is common in LSD users?"

"Yes, but not exclusive to them."

"It raises possibilities, Doctor."

"That Chancellor fed him drugs and turned him into a robot?"

"Something along those lines."

"I wouldn't push that theory yet. The facts strongly support a diagnosis of schizophrenia. Schizophrenics often exhibit severe distortions of language; words acquire new, bizarre definitions. It's called verbal paraphasia. To him, *bloody grids* could have meant 'spaghetti.' "

"I don't require scientific certainty, Doctor, only implied possibilities."

"At this point you don't have even that. There are no other indications he took any kind of drugs. Mainwaring must have run tests when he admitted him. Did he say anything about substance abuse?"

"No," he admitted. "He said it was a clear-cut case of schizophrenia. That even if the boy had taken drugs, they couldn't have made him crazy."

"That's an accurate appraisal."

"I understand all that, Doctor. But should you come across other evidence of drug abuse—anything at all— please call me immediately."

"I will."

"Good. Incidentally, Dwight will be able to see you this afternoon at three."

"Three will be fine."

"Splendid. If you have no objection, he'd prefer to meet at Cadmus Construction. Away from prying eyes."

"No problem."

He gave me the corporation's Westwood address and made another offer to pay me. My first impulse was to refuse, but then I told myself I was being childish, confusing self-denial with independence. Money or no money, I was involved in the case and had come too far to turn back. I told him to send me half the retainer, and he said he'd write out a check for five thousand dollars the instant we got off the phone.

I arrived at the jail at eleven and was kept waiting in the entrance lobby for forty-five minutes without explanation. It was a hot, smoggy day, and the pollution had seeped indoors. The chairs in the room were hard and unaccommodating. I grew restless and asked about the delay. The voice from the mirrored booth claimed ignorance. Finally a female deputy arrived to take me to the High Power block. In the elevator she told me that an inmate had been knifed to death the day before.

"We have to double-check procedures, and it slows everything down."

"Was it gang-related?"

"I'd imagine so, sir."

A stocky black deputy named Sims took over at the entrance to the High Power block. He ushered me to a small office and searched me with a surprisingly light touch. When I got to the glass room, Jamey was already there. Sims unlocked the door, waited until I was seated before leaving. Once outside, he stayed close to the glass and, just as Sonnenschein had, kept an unobtrusive but watchful eye on the proceedings.

Jamey was awake this time, straining and twisting agains this shackles. His lips were pursed, the eyes above them careening like pinballs. Someone had shaved him, but it had been a slapdash job, and dark patches of stubble checkered his face. His yellow pajamas were clean but wrinkled. The pungence of stale body odor quickly filled the room, and I wondered when they'd last bathed him.

"It's me again, Jamey. Dr. Delaware."

The eyes stopped moving, froze, then sank slowly until they settled on me. A brief flicker of clarity illuminated the irises, as if lightning had flashed within the orbital sockets, but the blue quickly filmed over and remained glassy. Not much of a response, but at least he was showing minimal awareness.

I told him I was glad to see him, and he broke out into a sweat. Beads of moisture mustached his upper lip and glossed his forehead. He closed his eyes again. As the lids fluttered shut, the cords of his neck grew taut.

"Jamey, open your eyes. Listen to what I have to say."

The lids remained fastened tight. He shuddered, and I waited for other signs of dyskinesia. None came.

"Do you know where you are?"

Nothing.

"What day is it, Jamey?"

Silence.

"Who am I?"

No response.

I kept talking to him. He rocked and fidgeted, but unlike the movements he'd displayed during the first visit, these appeared to be voluntary. Twice he opened his eyes and stared at me cloudily, only to close them again quickly. The second time they remained shut, and he showed no further response to the sound of my voice.

Twenty minutes into the session I was ready to give up when his mouth began to work, churning, the lips stiff and extended, as if he were struggling to talk but unable to do so. The effort made him sit straighter. I leaned close. In the corner of my eye I saw a khaki blur: Sims edging closer to the glass and peering in. I ignored him, kept my attention fixed on the boy.

"What is it, Jamey?"

The skin around his lips puckered and blanched. His mouth became a black ellipse. Out came several shallow exhalations. Then a single word, muttered under his breath:

"Glass."

"Glass?" I moved within inches of his mouth, felt the heat of his breath. "What kind of glass?"

A strangled croak.

"Talk to me, Jamey. Come on."

I heard the door open. Sims's voice said:

"Please move back, sir."

"Tell me about the glass," I persisted, trying to build a dialogue out of one whispered word.

"Sir," said Sims forcefully, "you're too close to the prisoner. Move back."

I complied. Simultaneously Jamey retreated, hunching his shoulders and bowing his head; it seemed a primitive defense, as if self-reduction would make him unappealing prey.

Sims stood there, watching.

"It's all right," I said, glancing over my shoulder. "I'll keep my distance."

He stared at me stolidly, waiting several seconds before returning to his post.

I turned back to Jamey.

"What did you mean by glass?"

His head remained lowered. He swung it to one side so that it rested unnaturally on his shoulder, like a bird preparing for sleep by tucking its beak in its breast.

"The night you called me you talked about a glass

canyon. I thought that meant the hospital. Was it something else?"

He continued withdrawing physically, managing, despite the restraints, to curl into fetal insignificance. It was
as if he were disappearing before my eyes, and I was
powerless to stop it.

"Or are you talking about this room—the glass walls?"

I kept trying to reach him, but it was useless. He'd
turned himself into a nearly inert bundle—pallid flesh
wrapped in sweat-soaked cotton, lifeless but for the faint
oscillation of his sunken chest.

He remained that way until Sims entered and announced
that my time was up.

The Cadmus Building was on Wilshire between Westwood and Sepulveda, one of those high, mirrored rectan-
gles that seem to be cropping up all over Los Angeles—
narcissistic architecture for a city built on appearances. In
front was a sculpture made of rusty nails welded together
to create a grasping hand three stories high. The title
plate said STRIVING and assigned the blame to an Italian
artist.

The lobby was a vault of black granite, air-conditioned
to the point of frigidity. In the corners sat oversized
dieffenbachias and ficus trees in brushed steel planters.
To the rear was a granite counter shielding a pair of
security guards, one heavy-jowled and gray-haired, the
other barely out of his teens. They looked me over as I
checked the directory. The building was filled with attorneys and accountants. Cadmus Construction occupied the
entire penthouse.

"Can I help you, sir?" asked the older one. When I
told him my name, he asked for identification. After
confirming it with a sotto voce phone call, he nodded,
and the young one accompanied me to the elevators.

"Security always this tight?"

He shook his head. "Just this week. Got to keep out
reporters and nuts."

He pulled a ring of keys from his belt and unlocked an
express elevator that whisked me up in a matter of seconds. The door opened, and I was greeted by the corporate logo: a small red C nestled in the belly of a larger
blue one. The reception area was decorated with Albers

prints in chromium frames and architectural models in
Plexiglas cases. A willowy brunette was waiting for me
there, and she led me through a foyer that forked. To
one side was the secretarial pool—rows of frozen-faced
women pounding nonstop on word processors—to the
other were metal double doors marked PRIVATE. The
brunette opened the doors, and I followed her down a
silent corridor carpeted in black. Dwight Cadmus's office
was at the end of the hallway. She knocked, opened the
door, and let me in.

"Dr. Delaware here to see you, Mr. Cadmus."

"Thanks, Julie." She left, closing the door after her.

It was an enormous room, and he was standing in the
middle of it, stooped, jacketless, shirtsleeves rolled up to
the elbows, wiping his eyeglasses with a corner of his tie.
The inner walls were brownish gray plaster, and from
them hung architectural renderings and a painting of a
caravan of Arabs riding camels across a wind-carved dune.
The outer walls were floor-to-ceiling smoked glass. I
thought of the single word Jamey had whispered, speculated, and put the thoughts aside.

The glass walls were a backdrop for a low, flat desk of
lacquered rosewood, its top piled high with blueprints
and cardboard tubes. Perpendicular to the desk was a
large wet bar; facing it, a pair of armchairs upholstered in
textured black cotton. A suit jacket was draped over one
of them.

"Make yourself comfortable, Doctor."

I sat in the empty chair and waited until he finished
polishing. Sunlight had turned the darkened glass to amber; the city below seemed brassy and remote.

Placing his spectacles on his nose, he walked behind
the desk and sat down in a swivel chair, glancing at the
blueprints and avoiding eye contact. His hair was especially thin on top, and he patted it as if seeking reassurance that some remained.

"Can I get you anything?" he asked, looking at the
bar.

"No, thanks."

A cacophony of honking horns rose twenty stories. He
raised his eyebrows, turned, and stared down at the
street. When he faced forward again, his expression was
blank.

"What is it I'm supposed to do for you exactly?"

"I want you to tell me about Jamey, to trace his development from birth until the present."

He looked at his watch.

"How long is this supposed to take?"

"We don't have to do it in one sitting. How much time do you have?"

He waved his hand over the blueprints.

"Never enough."

I looked at him with reflexive disbelief. He met my eyes and tried to remain impassive, but his face sagged.

"That probably didn't come out right. I'm not trying to punt. I'm more than willing to do anything I can to help. Christ knows that's all I've been doing since I found out. Trying to help. This thing's been a nightmare. You do your best to live a certain way, to keep things organized. You think you know where you stand, and boom, everything's blown to hell overnight."

"I know it's tough on you—"

"It's tougher on my wife. She really cares about him. Both of us do," he added quickly, "but she was the one who was home with him all the time. In fact, if you really want details, she could tell you more about him than I could."

"I plan on talking with her, too."

He played with the knot of his tie.

"Your name's familiar," he said, looking down again.

"We spoke on the phone five years ago," I said.

"Five years ago? What was it about specifically?"

I was certain that he remembered the conversation clearly but recounted it, nonetheless. He interrupted me midway.

"Aha. Yes, it's coming back. You wanted me to make him see a psychiatrist. I did give it a try, talked to him about it; but he fought it tooth and nail, and I didn't want to force him. It's not my nature to force things. I'm a problem solver, not a problem creater. Forcing him to do things had created problems in the past."

"What kinds of problems?"

"Conflict. Fights. Mouthing off. My wife and I have two little girls, and we don't like them exposed to that kind of thing."

"It must have been a tough decision to have him involuntarily committed."

"Tough? No. At that point there was no other way. For his sake."

He got up, went to the bar, and fixed himself a scotch and soda.

"Sure I can't get you anything?"

"Nothing, thanks."

He carried the drink back to the desk, sat down, and sipped. The hand that held the glass shook almost imperceptibly. He was nervous and defensive, and I knew he'd try to find another way to divert the interview. Before he could, I started talking.

"You began taking care of Jamey after your brother died. What was he like then?"

The question perplexed him.

"He was a little kid." He shrugged.

"Some little kids are easy going; others are irritable. What kind of temperament did Jamey have?"

"Cranky sometimes, quiet others. I guess he cried a lot—more than my girls anyway. The main thing you noticed right away was how damned smart he was. Even as a baby."

"Did he talk early?"

"You bet."

"At what age?"

"Christ, that's a long way back."

"Try to remember."

"Let's see—it had to be under a year. Six months maybe. I remember one time I was home on semester break and Father and Peter were trying to change his diaper, and this little thing pipes up and says, 'No diaper.' And I mean *clearly*, no baby talk. It was bizarre hearing words come out of something that small. Father made some joke about 'give the midget a cigar,' but I could tell he was upset by it."

"What about Peter?"

"It bothered him, too. What does any of this have to do with the situation at hand?"

"I need to know as much about him as possible. In what other ways was he precocious?"

"Everything."

"Can you give me some examples?"

He frowned impatiently.

"It's like he was moving at seventy-eight rpm when everyone else was going thirty-three and a third. By the time he was a year old he could go into a restaurant and order a sandwich. We had a maid who spoke Dutch. All of a sudden he was talking Dutch. *Fluently,* just by listening to her. He taught himself to read when he was about three. This was around the time I took him in. I walked in one evening and saw him with a book, asked him if he wanted me to read it to him. He looked up and said, 'No, Uncle Dwight. I can read it myself.' I thought he was faking, so I said to him, 'Let me hear you.' Sure enough, the kid could read. Better than some of my employees. By the age of five he could pick up the daily paper and read it front to back."

"Tell me about his schooling."

"I was tied up full-time with the company, so I sent him to nursery school. He drove the teachers crazy. Probably because he was so much smarter than they were. They expected him to do what the other kids were doing and his attitude was basically 'You're stupid, screw you.' After I got married, my wife worked hard at finding him the right school. She looked around for a long time—visited lots of places, interviewed teachers, the works—until she came up with the right one. It was the best kindergarten in Hancock Park, full of good kids from good solid families. He mouthed off so much they kicked him out after two months."

"For talking back?"

"For bucking the system. He wanted to read adult books—I don't mean porno. Faulkner, Steinbeck. They thought it would bend the other kids out of shape and you can see their point. A school's a system. Systems are based on structure. But too much slack in a system, and things fall apart. He needed to give in, but he wouldn't.

"When they tried to lay down the law, he gave them lip, pulled tantrums, kicked the teachers in the shins. I think he called one of them a Nazi or something. Anyway, they finally had enough and booted him out. You can imagine how my wife felt, after putting in all that work."

"Where'd he go to school after that?"

"Nowhere. We kept him home until he was seven,

with tutors. In one year he taught himself Latin, about five years' worth of math, and the entire high school English curriculum. But my wife pointed out that socially he was still a baby. So we kept trying different schools. Even one in the Valley for gifted kids. He never could adjust. He always thought he was smarter than anyone else and refused to follow rules. I don't care what your IQ is, that kind of attitude won't get you anywhere."

"So he never really had much conventional classroom education?"

"Not really, no. We would have liked to see him with normal kids, but it didn't work out."

He tilted his head back and drained his glass.

"It was a curse."

"What was?"

"Being too damned smart for his own good."

I turned a page of my notepad. "How old was he when you married?"

"We've been married thirteen years, so he was five."

"How did he react to the marriage?"

"He was happy. We let him be the ring bearer at the wedding. Heather had plenty of little boy cousins who wanted to do it, but she insisted on Jamey, said he needed the special attention."

"And he and Heather got along well from the beginning?"

"Sure. Why not? She's a great gal, terrific with kids. She's given him a hell of a lot more than lots of natural mothers. This thing is tearing her apart."

"Did caring for such a difficult child place stresses on your marriage?"

He picked up the whiskey glass and rolled it between his palms.

"Have you ever been married?"

"No."

"It's a great institution, you should try it. But it takes work to keep it going. I used to race yachts in college, and it seems to me marriage is like a big boat. Put the time into maintaining it, and it's something to see. Get lax, and it goes to hell in a handbasket."

"Did Jamey cause any additional maintenance problems?"

"No," he said. "Heather could handle him."

"What kinds of things did she have to handle?"

He drummed his fingers on the table.

"I have to tell you, Doctor, this line of questioning is really starting to bother me."

"In what way?"

"Your whole approach. Like the way you just said 'In what way?' Prefab. Scripted. I feel like I'm on the couch being analyzed. I don't see what my marriage has to do with getting him into a hospital instead of a jail."

"You're not a patient, but you are an important source of information. And information's what I need to lay the foundation for my report. Just as you do when you build a building."

"Yeah, but we don't dig our foundations one inch deeper than the geologists say we have to."

"Unfortunately my field's not as precise as geology."

"That's what bothers me about it."

I closed my book.

"Perhaps this isn't the right time to talk, Mr. Cadmus."

"There isn't going to be a better one. I just want to stay on the topic."

He folded his arms across his chest and stared out at a point over my shoulder. Behind the glasses his eyes were flat, as unyielding as armor plate.

"There's something you need to bear in mind," I said evenly. "A trial is a spectacle. The psychological equivalent of a public flogging. Once the lawyers get going, no area of Jamey's life or yours will be off-limits. Your mother's illness, the relationship between your parents, your brother's marriage and suicide, your marriage—everything will be fair game for journalists, spectators, the jury. If it's juicy enough, some author may even write a book about it. Compared to that, this interview's a piece of cake. If you can't handle it, you're in real trouble."

He reddened, clenched his jaw, and his mouth began to twitch. I watched his shoulders stiffen, then slump. Suddenly he looked helpless, a kid playing dress up in the executive suite.

When he spoke again, his voice was choked with rage.

"We put ourselves on the line for the little bastard. Year after year after year. And then he goes and does something like this."

I got up and walked to the bar. For his drink he'd used

Glenlivet, which suited me just fine. After pouring a couple of fingers for myself, I fixed him another scotch and soda and brought it to him.

Too numb to speak, he nodded thanks and took the glass. We drank in silence for several minutes.

"All right," he said finally. "Let's get it over with."

We picked up where we'd left off. He repeated his denial that raising Jamey had affected his marriage, though he admitted the boy had never been easy to live with. The lack of conflict he credited to his wife's patience and talent with children.

"Had she worked with kids before?" I asked.

"No, she studied anthropology. Got a master's and started work on her doctorate. I guess she's just a natural."

Shifting gears, I had him trace the development of Jamey's psychosis. His account was similar to the one Sarita Flowers had given me: a gradual but steady descent into madness that escaped notice longer than it should have because the boy had always been different.

"When did you start to get really worried?"

"When he started to get really paranoid. We were afraid he'd do something to Jennifer and Nicole."

"Had he ever threatened them or gotten physical?"

"No, but he began to get mean. Critical and sarcastic. Sometimes he called them little witches. It didn't happen often because he'd been living in our guesthouse over the garage since the age of sixteen and we hardly saw him, but it concerned us."

"Before that he was living in your house?"

"That's right. He had his own room with a private bath."

"Why did he move to the guesthouse?"

"He said he wanted privacy. We talked it over and said fine; he'd always kept to his room anyway, so it wasn't as if this were a major change."

"But he continued to come into the main house and harass your children?"

"Once in a while, maybe four or five times a month, mostly to eat. The guesthouse has a kitchen, but I never saw him cook. He'd forage in our refrigerator, take out bowls of leftovers, and eat standing up at the sink, bolting it down like an animal. Heather offered to set a nice table for him, cook him a decent meal, but he refused.

Later he became a health nut and the scrounging stopped, so we saw him even less, which was a blessing, because the first thing he always did when he came in was bitch, putting everything down. At first it just seemed like snottiness; then we realized he was going off the deep end."

"What made you realize that?"

"As I said before, the paranoia. He'd always been a suspicious kid, looking for ulterior motives behind everything. But this was different. The minute he'd enter the kitchen, he'd sniff at the food like a dog, start screaming that it was poisoned, that we were trying to poison him. When we'd try to calm him down, he'd call us all kinds of names. He'd get all flushed, and his eyes would get this really wild look, spaced out, nodding, as if he were in another world, listening to someone who wasn't there. Later we found out from Dr. Mainwaring that he'd been hallucinating voices, so that explained it."

"Can you remember any of the names he called you?"

He gave a pained look.

"He'd say we stank, that we were ravagers and zombies. One day he pointed his finger at Jennifer and Nicole and called them zombettes. At that point we knew we had to do something."

"Before he became psychotic, what kind of relationship did he have with your daughters?"

"When they were little, pretty good actually. He was ten when Jennifer was born, twelve when Nikki came along—too old to be jealous. Heather encouraged him to participate in taking care of the babies. He fastened a mean diaper, was really good at making them laugh. He could be creative when he wanted to, and he used to put on puppet shows for them, invent fantasy stuff. But when he got older—fourteen or so—he lost interest. I know it bothered the girls because until then he'd given them all this attention, and now he was saying, 'Go away, leave me alone'—and not saying it all that nicely. But both of them are great little gals—very popular, plenty of other fish to fry—so I'm sure they put it out of their minds pretty fast. They avoided him without our telling them to do so. But we still worried."

"And that was what prompted you to have him committed."

"That's what started us thinking about it. The straw that broke the camel's back was when he destroyed our library."

"When was this?"

He took a deep breath and let it out.

"A little over three months ago. It was at night. We'd already gone to bed. All of a sudden we started hearing these incredible noises from downstairs; screaming; yelling; loud crashing. Heather called the police, and I grabbed my gun and went down to check it out. He was in the library, naked, hurling books off the shelves, ripping them up, shredding them, screaming like a maniac. It was something I'll never forget. I yelled for him to stop but he looked right through me, as if I were some kind of . . . apparition. Then he started coming at me; the gun didn't bother him a bit. His face was red and puffy, and he was breathing hard. I backed away and locked him in. He went back to destroying the place; I could hear him smashing and tearing. Some of these books were old and worth a fortune; they were left to me by my dad. But I had to let him destroy them to prevent someone from getting hurt."

"How long was he in there?"

"Maybe fifteen minutes. It seemed like hours. Finally the police came and restrained him. It was tough because he fought them. They thought he was on PCP or something and called for an ambulance. They were ready to take him to County General Hospital, but we'd talked to Mainwaring the week before, and we said we wanted him to go to Canyon Oaks. There was a bit of a hassle, but then Horace showed up—Heather had called him, too— and smoothed things out."

"Who referred you to Dr. Mainwaring?"

"Horace. He'd worked with him in the past and said he was topnotch. We called him, woke him up, and he said to come right over. An hour later Jamey was committed to Canyon Oaks."

"On a seventy-two-hour hold?"

"Yes, but Mainwaring let us know right away he'd be staying there for a while."

He looked at his empty glass, then longingly at the Glenlivet bottle on the bar.

"The rest, as they say," he said tersely, "is goddamn history."

He'd been answering my questions cooperatively for more than an hour and looked worn out. I offered to quit and come back another time.

"Hell," he said, "the day's shot anyway. Keep going."

He looked at the bar again, and I told him to feel free to mix another drink.

"No"—he smiled—"I don't want you thinking I'm some kind of lush and putting it in your report."

"Don't worry about it," I said.

"Nah, it's okay. I'm past my limit. Now, what do you want to know?"

"When did you first realize he was homosexual?" I asked, bracing myself for another bout of defensiveness. To my surprise, he remained calm, almost sanguine.

"Never."

"Pardon me?"

"I never realized he was homosexual because he's not homosexual."

"He's not?"

"Hell, no. He's a mixed-up kid who has no idea what he is. Even a normal kid can't know what he is at that age, let alone a crazy one."

"His relationship with Dig Chancellor—"

"Dig Chancellor was an old faggot who liked to bugger little boys. I'm not saying he didn't bugger Jamey. But if he did, it was rape."

He looked to me for confirmation. I said nothing.

"It's just too damned early to tell," he insisted. "A kid that age can't understand enough about himself—about life—to know he's queer, right?"

His face constricted pugnaciously. The question wasn't rhetorical; he was waiting for an answer.

"Most homosexuals recall feeling different since early childhood," I said, omitting the fact that Jamey had described those feelings to me years before he had hooked up with Chancellor.

"Where do you get that? I don't buy it."

"It comes up consistently in research studies."

"What kind of research?"

"Case histories, surveys."

"Which means they tell you and you believe them?"

"Basically."

"Maybe they're lying, trying to justify their deviance as some inborn thing. Psychologists don't know what causes queerness, do they?"

"No."

"So much for science. I'll go with my nose, and my nose tells me he's a mixed-up kid who got led down the wrong road by a pervert."

I didn't debate him.

"How did he and Chancellor meet?"

"At a party," he said with a strange intensity, removing his glasses. Suddenly he was on his feet, rubbing his eyes. "I guess I was wrong, Doctor. I am feeling pooped out. Some other time, okay?"

I gathered up my notes, put my glass down, and rose.

"Fair enough. When's a good time?"

"I have no idea. Call my girl, and she'll set it up."

He walked me to the door quickly. I thanked him for his time, and he acknowledged it absently, casting a sidelong glance at the bar. I knew with almost clairvoyant certainty that the moment I was gone he'd head straight for the scotch.

A FERRARI Dino had stalled at Westwood and Wilshire. Two middle-aged beachboys in shorts and tank tops struggled to push it to the side of the boulevard, ignoring uptilted fingers and blaring horns and turning the afternoon traffic to sludge. Sitting in the Seville, I mulled over the interview with Cadmus and decided it had yielded meager pickings. Too much time had been spent dealing with his defensiveness, not enough on substance; a host of topics hadn't even been broached. I wondered what secrets he was laboring to conceal—it's the ones with the most to hide who build psychic fortresses—and lacking a ready answer, I decided to pursue other avenues before approaching him again.

The Dino finally reached the curb, and the automotive snarl untangled gradually. At the first opportunity I turned left and cut through the side streets of Westwood until I reached Sunset. Five minutes later I was home.

An envelope from a Beverly Hills messenger service was in the mailbox along with a lot of junk. Inside the envelope was a check for five thousand dollars and a note to call someone named Bradford Balch in Souza's office.

The unproductive interview and the zeros on the check combined to make me feel uneasy. I'd accepted Souza's offer with ambivalence that had never dissipated. Now the doubts rose within me like a rainswelled river.

I'd developed a rationale for my interviews: By knowing Jamey's past, I'd be able to understand and somehow to help him. I'd believed it when I said it, but now the words seemed hollow. Although history can provide the comfort of hindsight, by itself it seldom unravels the mystery of madness. I wondered if I would ever accumulate enough knowledge to comprehend his deterioration truly, and—more important—if I did, to what use could the knowledge be put? Playing retroprophet, as Souza wanted? Using my doctorate to coat sorcery with a veneer of science?

Even the most brilliant psychiatrist or psychologist who abandons scientific rigor to step into the bog of speculation called diminished capacity can be made to look like a complete idiot on the witness stand by a prosecutor of only moderate capabilities. Yet there's no shortage of psychiatrists and psychologists willing to subject themselves to this type of humiliation. Some are whores, purchased for the day, but most are honorable men and women who've been seduced into believing they're mind readers. I'd always viewed their testimony as institutionalized quackery, but now I was in danger of joining their ranks.

I couldn't take an oath and say anything definitive about Jamey's state of mind a week, a day, or even a minute ago. No one could.

What the hell had I gotten myself into?

I knew right then, as I'd known deep down from the beginning, that Souza wouldn't get what he wanted from me. Although I'd made him no promises, I had left the door open for collaboration, and continuing the pretense would be manipulative—his type of game, not mine. I'd have to deal with it soon, but not yet. I simply wasn't ready—out of compulsiveness, sentimentality, or guilt—to walk away from the case, from Jamey.

I stood there, pondering my options, folding and unfolding the check until it began to look like abstract origami. Finally I reached a compromise of sorts: I'd finish my interviews, knowing all the while that I was working for myself, but not take the money. Placing the check back into its envelope, I went into the library and locked it in a desk drawer. When the time was right, I'd give it back.

I realized suddenly that the house was hot and stuffy. Slipping out of my clothes, I put on running shorts, threw open some windows, and got a Grolsch out of the refrigerator. Bottle in hand, I called Bradford Balch, who turned out to be one of Souza's associates. He sounded like a young man, overly eager, with a high, nervous voice.

"Uh, yes, Doctor, Mr. Souza asked me to call to let

you know that the police have approved your visit to the Chancellor estate. Do you still want to go?"

"Yes."

"All right then. Please be there tomorrow morning at nine."

He gave me the address, thanked me for calling, and hung up.

I thought about the phone call. It was the first time Souza hadn't called me directly, and I knew why.

For the past week he'd wooed me like an NBA scout pursuing a lightning-reflexed, eight-foot teen-ager: flattery, the chauffeured Rolls, lunch in his private dining room, and, most important, casting aside the usual crush of underlings and remaining personally accessible. He'd wanted me on his team, but on his terms: He was the captain, and I was supposed to know my place. My insistence upon seeing the murder site had been a bit of unwelcome independence, and although he'd gone along with it, he'd made sure to express his disapproval by having a subordinate deliver the message.

Subtle but pointed. It gave me a small taste of what it would be like to be on his bad side.

When the smog is especially heavy in Southern California, the terrain takes on the illusory look of a photograph shot through a vaseline-smeared lens. The skies darken to grimy bronze, contours of buildings dissolve into the haze, and the vegetation assumes a malignantly fluorescent hue.

It was that kind of morning as I drove east on Sunset toward the Beverly Hills city limits. Even the grandest mansions seemed to shimmer and soften in the filthy heat, melting columns of Neapolitan ice cream garnished with marzipan palms.

The Chancellor estate sat on five million dollars' worth of acreage, on a hill north of the boulevard, overlooking the Beverly Hills Hotel. Six feet of stone wall topped with three more feet of wrought-iron bars surrounded the property. The bars terminated in gold-plated arrowhead finials that looked sharp enough to eviscerate the overly curious climber.

Arched iron gates bisected the wall. They were flung wide open and guarded by a uniformed Beverly Hills patrolman. I drove the Seville to within an inch of his outstretched palm and stopped. He walked over to the driver's side and, after I'd given him my name, stepped back and muttered into his walkie-talkie. A moment later he nodded and waved me through.

All that was immediately visible beyond the gate was a hairpin curve of gravel drive shadowed by walls of burgundy eugenias. As I rounded the curve, the eugenias gave way to low borders of white sun azaleas and the drive flattened to a broad S that cut through a rising swath of emerald lawn. At the peak of the lawn sat a Greek Revival mansion the size of a stadium—marble steps leading up to a wide colonnade; a formal reflecting pool perpendicular to the steps; strategically placed statuary, all of it celebrating the male figure. Despite the smog, the place shone blindingly white.

The landscaping favored geometry over spontaneity: circular beds of white roses; barbered privet hedges; ball-on-pedestal topiary; marching columns of Italian cypress. It was the kind of stuff that required constant attention, and attention had been lacking recently, as evidenced by stray shoots, wayward boughs, wilted petals, and dry patches that seemed especially scabrous against the velvet of the lawn.

A black-and-white, an unmarked Plymouth, and a pearl gray Mazda RX-7 were parked at the base of the steps. I pulled up next to the Mazda, got out, and walked through an open courtyard toward white-lacquered double doors. A man and woman were standing by the doors, leaning against a replica of Michelangelo's David, laughing and smoking. The woman wore a BHPD uniform, snugly tailored; the man, a hound's-tooth jacket over black slacks. I picked up a snatch of conversation ("Yeah, Sagittarians are always like that") before they heard me and turned. The man's eyes were obscured by aviator shades. I recognized him: Richard Cash, the detective who'd come to my house with Whitehead.

"Hey, Doc," he said amiably, "ready for the grand tour?"

"Anytime you are."

"Okay," he said, and ground out his cigarette on the marble floor. Turning to the female officer, who was young and blond, he smiled and smoothed back his hair. "All right, Dixie, let's definitely do it, catch you later."

"Sounds exceptional, Dick." She grinned and, after tucking a loose strand of hair under her hat, saluted and walked away.

Cash observed her retreating form and gave a low whistle.

"Love that affirmative action." He winked and pulled open one of the doors.

We walked into a snowdrift. Everything—walls, floors, ceilings, even the woodwork—had been painted white. Not a subtle off-white softened by hints of brown or blue but the pure, pitiless gleam of calcimine.

"Pretty virginal, huh?" said Cash as he led me past a circular staircase, under a marble arch and through a bright, wide foyer that divided a cavernous living room from an equally cavernous dining room. The milk-bath motif continued: white furniture; white carpeting; white mantel; white porcelain vases filled with albino ostrich plumes. The only exceptions to the glacial surfaces were occasional patches of mirror and crystal, but the reflections they projected accentuated the absence of color.

"There are thirty-five rooms in this place," said Cash. "I assume you don't want to see all of them."

"Just where it happened."

"Righto."

The foyer ended at a wall of glass. Cash hooked to the right, and I followed him into a large atrium backed by a pillared loggia. Beyond the loggia was an acre of terraced lawn and more topiary. Below the terrace an Olympic-sized rectangular swimming pool sparkled turquoise. The decking around the pool was white marble, and naked cherubs were stationed at either end. Each cherub held aloft an urn brimming with white petunias. A white sea horse had been painted at the bottom of the pool, which ran to the edge of the property and appeared to float into the sky. The cityscape below was obscured by brownish pinkish vapor.

"Here we are," said Cash in a bored voice.

There were no plants in the atrium. The room was high-ceilinged, floored with hardwood painted white and furnished in white rattan. Several chairs were overturned, and a leg on one of the sofas was broken. Suspended from the ceiling were whitewashed crossbeams. An inch-wide gray mark bisected one of them.

"That where the rope was knotted?"

"Uh-huh."

The white walls were mottled with rusty stains that repeated themselves across the glossy floor in Rorschach splotches and pinpoint spatters. So much blood. Everywhere. As if a washerwoman had entered with a mopful of it and splashed with abandon. Cash watched me take it in and said:

"Finally some color, huh?"

The outline of a human body had been drawn across the floor, but instead of white chalk, a black grease pencil had been used. The outer perimeters of the outline were smeared with rust. An especially large dark stain was situated below the rope mark. Speckles of blood dotted the crossbeam. Even in this desiccated state the stains conjured up horrific images.

I walked forward. Cash restrained me with his arm.

"Look, no touch." He smiled. Starbursts of light bounced off his shades. The arm smelled of Brut.

I drew back.

At the rear of the atrium were sliding glass doors. One had been left slightly ajar, but no breeze entered from the loggia. The room smelled stale and metallic.

"All of it happened here?" I asked.

"Basically."

"Was there any ransacking elsewhere?"

"Uh-huh, but that's off-limits."

"Anything taken?"

He smiled, condescendingly.

"This was no burglary."

"Where'd the rope come from?"

"One of the pool lifesavers."

"What kinds of weapons were used?"

"Stuff from the kitchen: butcher knife; meat skewer; cleaver. A little purple silk thrown in for fun. Hellacious wet scene."

"Multiple wounds?"

"Uh-huh."

"Same as the other Slasher murders?"

Cash's thin lips parted. His teeth were cosmetically perfect but nicotine-mottled.

"Love to get into that with you, but I can't."

I stared some more at the room, then let my gaze wander through the glass doors. Dead leaves and brown-edged petunia petals floated on the surface of the pool. Somewhere in the distance a crow squawked.

Cash took out a cigarette and lit it. Casually he let the match fall to the floor.

"That about do it?" he asked.

I nodded.

I drove back home, went down to the garden, sat on a moss-bordered rock, and fed the koi. The sound of the waterfall lulled me into a trancelike torpor—alpha state, like one of Sarita Flowers's hyperactive train runners. Sometime later the sound of human voices snapped me out of it.

The noise was coming from the front of the house. I climbed halfway up the terrace—high enough to look down but still out of sight.

Milo and another man were talking. I couldn't make out what they were saying, but their body postures and the looks on their faces said it wasn't a friendly chat.

The other man was in his early forties, deeply bronzed, medium-sized, and solidly built. He wore designer jeans and a glossy black windbreaker over a flesh-colored T-shirt that nearly succeeded in simulating bare skin. His hair was coarse and dark and cut military-short. A full, thick beard covered two-thirds of his face. The chin hairs were gray, the rest of the beard reddish brown.

The man said something.

Milo responded.

The man sneered and said something else. He shifted his hand toward his jacket, and Milo moved with incredible quickness.

In a second the man was down, flat on his stomach, with Milo's knee in the small of his back. Deftly the detective jerked his arms back and cuffed him, patted him down, and came up with a gravity knife and a nasty-looking handgun.

Milo hefted the weapons and said something. The man arched his back, raised his head, and laughed. He'd scraped his mouth going down, and the laughter emerged through bloody lips.

I climbed back down, quickly jogged back through the garden, and out to the front of the house.

The man on the ground was still laughing. When he saw me, he laughed harder.

"Hey, Dr. Delaware, look at this fucking police brutality!"

His beard was purpled with blood, and as he talked, he emitted a fine pink spray. Craning back to look up at Milo, he taunted:

"Ooh, sweetie pie, such fury!"

"Beretta nine-two-six," said Milo, ignoring him and examining the gun. "Sixteen rounds. Figuring on a shoot-out, Ernie?"

"It's registered and legal, faggot."

Milo pocketed the weapons and drew out his service .38. Standing, he jerked the bearded man to his feet.

"Stay back, Alex," he said, and jabbed the revolver into the man's kidneys.

"Alex?" the man giggled. "How cozy. He's one, too?"

"Move it," barked Milo. With one hand on the scruff of the man's neck and the other on his weapon, he prodded his prisoner down the hill. I followed several paces behind.

Two cars were parked on the turnaround: Milo's un-marked bronze Matador and the gray RX-7 I'd seen at the Chancellor house. Milo's eyes searched the area, then settled on a eucalyptus. Keeping the .38 pressed into the bearded man's sacrum, he pushed him against the trunk of the tree, face forward, and kicked the in-sides of his feet until they spread. Then he undid the cuffs and slammed one of the man's arms around the tree.

"Hug it," he ordered.

The man embraced the eucalyptus, and Milo cuffed him again and slipped his hand inside a pocket of the man's jeans.

"Ooh, feels heavenly." The man laughed.

Having taken out a set of car keys, Milo walked to the RX-7 and unlocked the driver's door.

"Illegal search," hollered the man.

"File a complaint," said Milo, squeezing his big body inside the sports car. After several minutes of rummaging, he exited emptyhanded and walked around to the rear. After opening the hatchback, he lifted the storage deck and pulled out a hard-shell case. He put it on the ground and unlatched it.

Inside was a disassembled Uzi.

"A regular arsenal, Ernie. Concealing this is going to get you in deep shit."

"Fuck you. It's in Mr. Chancellor's name. He got it okayed by the muckamucks."

"Chancellor was a gun freak?"

"No, asshole. He wanted first-class protection."

"Which you really gave him."

"Go butt-fuck yourself, Fruitfly."

Milo smiled tightly.

"If I were you, I'd worry about my own anal sphincter, Ernie. You'll be spending tonight behind bars, and we both know how former gendarmes do in lockup."

The man clamped his jaws shut. His eyes were wild.

Milo took the weapons and locked them in the trunk of the Matador. Then he got into the front seat and called for backup.

The man started growling. He looked at me and laughed.

"You're a witness, *Alex*. I just came here to talk to you and Fruitfly sucker-punched me."

Milo came out of the car and told him to shut up. The man responded with a stream of invective. I tried to talk to my friend.

"Milo—"

He held up his hand to silence me, took out a notebook, and started writing. A moment later a black-and-white with its lights flashing roared up the hill and came to a sudden stop. A second squad car followed seconds later. Two patrolmen jumped out of the first car, one out of the second. All three had their hands on their holsters. Milo waved them over and gave them instructions. As he talked, they looked at the man cuffed to the tree and nodded. The man started swearing. One of the cops went over and stood by him.

The prisoner started to laugh and taunt his guard, who remained impassive.

The conference broke up. A second patrolman joined

the one guarding the bearded man. Together they unlocked the cuffs, freed his arms, drew them behind his
back, recuffed him, and pushed him down into the rear
of the Matador. One of them got in next to him. Milo
waited until they'd settled, then slid across the front seat.
The remaining officer walked toward me. He was young
and dark and had a strong cleft chin. His badge said
DesJardins.

"I'd like to take your statement, sir."

"There's not much to tell."

"Whatever, sir."

I told him the little that I knew and asked him what
was going on.

"A little disturbance, sir."

He turned to leave.

"Who's the guy with the beard?" I asked.

"A bad guy," he said, and walked away.

Milo got out of the Matador. The uniforms removed
the bearded man from the car and transferred him to one
of the black-and-whites. One cop got in the back with
him; the other took the wheel. Milo gave DesJardins the
weapons he'd confiscated, and the young officer put them
in the trunk of his black-and-white, closed it, and got into
the driver's seat. Both drivers started up their engines
and drove off.

The road was suddenly silent. Milo leaned against the
Matador, let out a deep breath, and ran his hands over
his face.

"What the hell was that all about?" I asked.

"His name's Erno Radovic, and he's a first-class psycho."

"Chancellor's bodyguard?"

"Yeah," he said, surprised.

"Horace Souza mentioned his name. Said he was
unstable."

"That's an understatement. He followed you home
from Chancellor's place. I saw him and tagged along."

"You were there? I didn't see you."

"I was parked around the corner. Radovic's still a
suspect, and I've been keeping my eye on him."

"When you were calling in, he said he came here to
talk to me. What did he want?"

"For what it's worth he claims to be investigating Chancellor's murder on his own and wants to pump you for information about the kid."

"He's got to know I wouldn't talk to him."

"Alex, with this guy, logic doesn't enter into it. I've known him for a long time. He used to be a cop; we were in the same class at the academy. Even as a cadet he was a John Wayne crazy, used his gun as a dick. Once he got out on the streets, he was a disaster waiting to happen—five fatal shootings in seven years, a whole bunch more borderline assaults. All blacks. They put him in Vice, and he roughed up hookers. Gave him a desk job, and he alienated the brass. No one wanted him, so he was transferred from division to division. West L.A. was his last stop; he spent three months there in Records, before they kicked him out on psych disability. The day he showed up he got on my case and never got off—perfumed notes in my locker addressed to Detective Tinkerbell, that kind of crap."

"Sounds like a strange one to be working for a guy like Chancellor."

"Not really. I always figured him as latent. Maybe he got in touch with it, and it blew his mind. That's only one of the reasons we're looking at him closely. In any event, he's dangerous. If you see him, stay away."

"What's his supposed reason for investigating the case?"

"He says it's out of loyalty to Chancellor, that your guy, Souza, is setting up to sully the boss's name and he wants to keep the record straight. But who the hell knows? On top of being crazy the guy's a noted liar. Maybe he's covering his own ass 'cause he knows we're still interested in him, or maybe he's just floating through fantasyland, playing detective. He used to be a PI—after he was booted off the force, he wangled himself a license—and before Chancellor took him in and made the city a safer place, he did some work for lawyers. But he didn't last at it. Too goddamned volatile, used muscle instead of manners. Did you notice how he laughed all the time?"

I nodded.

"He does it when he's pissed. Weird." He tapped his head. "The wiring's not right up there, Alex. You'd know more about it than I would. The main thing is keep your distance. I've filed enough paper to keep him behind bars for a couple of days, but he'll be out eventually. So watch out."

"I hear you."

"I know you do—right now. But we both know you have this tendency to get obsessive and forget little things like personal safety. Okay?"

He gave me a sour look and opened the door of the Matador.

"Where are you going?" I asked.

"Back on the job," he answered, looking away.

"Just like that, huh?"

He shrugged, got in the car, and closed the door. The window was rolled down, and I leaned in through the opening.

"Milo, what the hell is going on with you? A month goes by, and I don't hear from you. I try to reach you, and you don't return my calls. For all I know, you've crawled into some cave and rolled a rock across the opening. Now you show up, bust some maniac on my property, and play the it's-all-in-a-day's-work routine."

"I can't talk about it."

"Why the hell not?"

"We're working opposite sides of the Cadmus case. Just being seen with you is a no-no. If Radovic weren't such an explosive freak, I would have called for assistance and had someone else bust him."

"Maybe so, but that doesn't explain why you were incommunicado before I got involved in the case."

He chewed on his lip and put the keys in the ignition. Switching on the radio, he listened to it belch police calls before flicking it off.

"It's complicated," he said.

"I've got time."

He shot out his wrist, glanced at his Timex, then stared out the windshield.

"I really can't stay here, Alex."

"Some other place, then. Where we won't be spotted."

He smiled. "Cloak and dagger, huh?"

"Whatever it takes, my friend."

Gazing at the dashboard, he used his hands to slap a nervous drumbeat against his thighs. Several seconds passed.

"There's this place," he said finally, "near the airport, on Aviation. The Golden Eagle. You sit and get soused and listen to the pilots gab with the control tower. I'll be there at nine."

My first thought was: A cocktail lounge, he's off the wagon.

"See you there," I said.

He started up the Matador, and I held out my hand. He looked at it as if it were some kind of rare specimen. Then suddenly his Adam's apple bobbed, and he reached out with both his big padded paws, squeezed my fingers hard, and let go. A minute later he was gone.

13

THE GOLDEN Eagle was a one-story trapezoid of chocolate stucco on a bleak industrial stretch stacked with
warehouses and chain-linked auto storage lots. The lounge
squatted in the shadows of the San Diego Freeway overpass, so close to the LAX runways that the jet roar
caused the glasses above the bar to quiver and tinkle like
keys on a vibraphone. Despite the location, the place was
jumping.

The gimmick was aural voyeurism: Cushioned headsets
wired into the sides of each hexagonal table enabled the
tipplers to eavesdrop on cockpit banter, and a wall of
plate glass exposed a lateral view of the runway.

I got there at nine and found the place dark and
smoke-filled. All the tables were taken; Milo wasn't at
any of them. The bar was a pine semicircle coated with
an inch of epoxy resin and padded with sausage-colored
vinyl. Smiling salesmen bellied up to it, drinking, eating
nachos, and tossing lines at stewardesses on layover.
Waitresses in salmon-colored microdresses and seamed
mesh stockings pardoned their way through the crowd,
trays aloft. In a corner of the room was a small plywood
stage. A skinny middle-aged man in a kelly green suit,
open-necked lime green shirt, and stacked-heel oxblood
patent oxfords sat in the middle of it, tuning an electric
guitar. Nearby were a microphone and an amplifier. Atop
the amplifier was a synthesized rhythm box; in front of it,
a propped cardboard sign that read THE MANY MOODS OF
SAMMY DALE in gilt-edged calligraphy. Sammy Dale wore
a goatee and a dark toupee that had come slightly askew,
and he looked as if he were in pain. He finished tuning,
adjusted the rhythm box until it emitted a rumba beat,
and said something unintelligible into the microphone.

Eight beats later he was crooning a mock-Latin rendition
of "New York, New York" in a whispery baritone.

I retreated to a corner of the bar. The bartender looked
like a moonlighting college boy. I ordered a Chivas straight
up and, when he brought it, tipped him five dollars and
asked him to get me a table as soon as possible.

"Thanks. Sure. We've got a couple of campers tonight,
but that one over there should be clearing soon."

"Great."

I got the table at nine-fifteen. Milo showed up ten
minutes later, wearing beige jeans, desert boots, a brown
polo shirt untucked, and a bold plaid sportcoat. He scanned
the room as if searching for a suspect, found me, and
shambled over. A waitress followed him like a lamprey
pursuing a bass.

"Sorry I'm late," he said, sinking into the chair. A 747
was coming in for a low landing, and the plate glass was
vibrating and awash with light. At the next table a black
couple wearing headphones pointed up at the plane and
smiled.

"Can I get you something?" asked the waitress.

He thought for a moment.

"Beefeater and tonic, easy on the tonic."

"G and t, Beef, low t," mumbled the waitress, scribbling. Looking at my half-empty glass, she smiled.

"Another for you, sir?"

"No, thanks."

She hurried off and returned quickly with the drink, a
cardboard coaster, and a bowl of nachos. Milo thanked
her, ate a handful of chips, and fished the lime wedge
from his glass. After sucking on it thoughtfully, he raised
his eyebrows, ate the pulp, placed the rind in an ashtray,
and swallowed half the drink.

"Radovic's in for forty-eight hours tops."

"Thanks for the tip."

"Anytime."

We drank in silence. Waves of bar chatter filled the
room, as impersonal as white noise. Sammy Dale, having
inexplicably programmed the rhythm box to a slow waltz,
was singing about doing things his way.

"Is he a serious suspect?" I asked.

"You're in the enemy camp," he said, smiling faintly,

"and I'm not supposed to be fraternizing with you, let alone handing out investigative details."

"Forget I asked."

"Nah," he said, finishing his drink and calling for another. "It's nothing Souza doesn't already know. Besides, I don't want you building up false hope about Cadmus's being innocent and chasing after Radovic, so I'll tell you: No, he's not a serious suspect; Cadmus is still our main man. But Radovic's crazy enough for us to want to keep an eye on him, at least as a coconspirator. Okay?"

"Okay."

He met my glance, then stared at the tabletop.

"What I can't understand," he said, "is how you let yourself get roped into doing a dim cap."

"I'm not roped into anything. I'm collecting facts without obligation."

"Oh, yeah? Word has it Souza considers you a prize witness—to the tune of ten grand."

"Where'd you hear that?" I asked angrily.

"DA's office. Don't be so surprised; news travels fast on a case like this. They dragged me in the other day and pumped me for information about you, weren't a bit happy when I told them you weren't a sleaze. Not that my say-so will stop them from trying to make you look like the ultimate whore if you take the stand."

I told him of my intention to return the money.

"Very noble. But you won't start smelling sweet until you walk off the case."

"I can't do that."

"Why not?"

"Professional obligation."

"Aw, come on, Alex, when's the last time you saw the kid? Five years ago? What do you owe him?"

"I could have done better by him five years ago. I want to be sure I do my best now."

He leaned forward scowling. In the stingy light of the lounge his complexion seemed ghostly.

"Pretty abstract, pal. And pure crap. You never did a half-assed job in your life. Besides, no matter what he was then, he's a bad guy now, and nothing you do is gonna change that."

"In other words, you're sure he's guilty."

"Hell, yes," he answered through a mouthful of ice.

The second drink arrived. As I watched him down it, I realized how worn out he looked.

"Speaking of walking off the case," I said, "why haven't you? Working with a couple of homophobes like Whitehead and Cash can't be a barrel of laughs."

He laughed bitterly.

"Like I have a choice."

"I thought you had flexibility in assignments."

"That's the way it used to be, when Don Miller was in charge. But Miller died a couple of months ago."

His face sagged, and he tried to hide it behind his glass. I knew he'd been fond of his captain, a tough but tolerant man who'd recognized his ability as a detective and hadn't let his homosexuality get in the way.

"What happened?"

"He keeled over on the twelfth hole at Rancho Park. Clogged arteries, probably had chest pains for a while but never told anyone." He shook his head. "Forty-eight years old, left a wife and five kids."

"That's terrible. I'm sorry to hear it, Milo."

"A lot of folks were sorry. The man was a prince. Damned inconsiderate of him to check out early like that. The asshole they replaced him with is a piece of garbage by the name of Cyril Trapp. Used to be the biggest boozehound, pillhead, and whore freak in Ramparts Division. Then he found Jesus and became one of those born again scrotes who thinks everyone who doesn't agree with him deserves the gas chamber. He's opined in public that faggots are moral sinners, so needless to say, he adores me."

He tilted his head back and emptied the last drops of gin down his throat. When the waitress walked by, he flagged her and ordered a third.

"It wouldn't be that bad if he were blatant about it— good old honest hostility. I could quietly put in for a transfer on the basis of personality conflict and maybe squeak through. I like working West L.A., and it wouldn't do wonders for my personnel file, but I could handle it. But a transfer wouldn't satisfy Trapp. He wants me off the force, period. So he takes the subtle approach—

psychological warfare. Puts on the polite act and uses the duty roster to make my life miserable."

"Bad cases?"

"*Faggot* cases!" He raised his big fist and put it down hard on the table. The black couple looked over. I smiled, and they returned to their headphones.

"For the last two months," he went on in a low voice, starting to slur, "I've had nothing but gay cuttings, gay shootings, gay stompings, gay rapes. Faggot DOA, call Sturgis, captain's orders. It didn't take long to see the pattern, and I protested right away. Trapp put down his Bible, smiled, and said he understood how I felt but that my experience was too valuable to waste. That I was a *specialist*. End of discussion."

"It doesn't sound all that subtle," I said. "Why don't you file for transfer anyway?"

He twisted his lips into a frown.

"It's not that easy. Trapp's manipulated it so what I do in bed would be the issue. Once he gets a piece of that, he won't let go, and I'd have to go public or keep eating it. No doubt the fucking ACLU would love to help me, but I don't wanna be a headline. It's not that I'm denying what I am—you know I worked that through a long time ago—but I've never been one for airing my skivvies in public."

I thought back to what he'd once told me about his childhood, what it had been like to grow up as a shy, oversized, overweight boy in a working-class family in southern Indiana, son to a macho father, the youngest of five boisterous macho brothers. Though outwardly one of them, he knew he was different, had been terrifyingly aware of it since the age of six. The secret gnawed at him like a tapeworm, but when he heard his brothers joke contemptuously about fairies and queers, he knew that its release would mean disaster—perhaps, his young imagination suggested, even death. So he laughed at the jokes, went as far as cracking some of his own, churning inwardly but surviving. Learning early the value of privacy.

"I know that," I said, "but it doesn't sound like the alternative's any too good."

"Yeah, that's what Rick says. He wants me to assert myself, to put up a fight. But first I have to get *in touch with how I feel* about the whole thing. To *unburden* myself. Which is therapy talk, right? He's been seeing a shrink; now he wants me to go with him. I've resisted, so it's a major issue between us."

"If you're that unhappy," I said, "therapy could be helpful."

The waitress came over with his drink. He took it from her before she had a chance to lay it down. The moment she walked away he began gulping, and when he lowered the glass, most of the drink was gone.

"I doubt it," he said, swallowing. "All the talking in the world isn't going to change the facts: Being a cop and being gay don't mix in this millennium. I knew it would be tough when I joined the force, and I made a pact with myself that no matter what happened, I'd emerge with my dignity intact. And there was plenty to test my resolve—fascist instructors, abusive shitheads like Radovic. Mostly it's been cold silence. Ten years of heavy-duty social isolation. The last few in Homicide were the best because Miller's attitude filtered down to the troops, and I got respect for doing the job well—which is all I care about. I couldn't give a good goddamn if they invited me to double-date. But since Trapp's been running things, it's let-the-dogs-out-on-Milo time."

The third drink disappeared.

"The hell of it is"—he smiled, woozily—"that down deep I'm a closet homophobe myself. Show me a guy in drag or all decked out like the May Queen, and my gut reaction is *oh, no!* You remember that gay solidarity march in West Hollywood last summer? Rick and I went and stood on the sidelines, too chicken to join the show. It was a goddamn freak show, Alex. Guys with tails glued to their butts, guys with half a dozen socks studded in their jocks or dildos hanging outside their pants, guys in cute little hot pants outfits and panty hose, guys with purple hair and green beards. Can you imagine the feminists or the blacks dressing up like morons to make a political point?"

He looked around for the waitress.

"And it's the same goddamn exhibitionism when it comes to homocide. When gays off each other, they've gotta do it freakier and bloodier than anyone else. I pulled one squeal where the body had a hundred and fifty-seven stab wounds. Think of that. There was maybe enough skin left to cover a postage stamp. The guy who did it weighed ninety-seven pounds and looked like Peter Pan. The victim was his lover, and he was sobbing like a baby 'cause he missed him. Then there was one where some joker took a handful of roofing nails, made a fist, shoved it up another guy's ass, let go, and twisted until the poor sucker ruptured and bled to death. There's plenty more I could tell you about, but you get the point. It's a goddamn *toilet* out there, and Trapp's been shoving my head into it without flushing, day after day."

He caught the waitress's eye and waved her over.

"Another, sir?" she said doubtfully.

"No." He smiled unevenly. "I need vitamins. Bring me a double screwdriver."

"Yes, sir. Still nothing for you, sir?"

"I'll have a cup of coffee."

He waited until she was gone before continuing.

"The gospel according to Trapp is that I can relate to that toilet because I swim in it anyway. Even if he was sincere about it, it's total bullshit. As if the witnesses are supposed to know I like guys and open up to me. Right. When I walk in, they get that suspicious look in their eyes and clam up just like they would with any other cop. What am I supposed to do, start off an interview by announcing my sexual preference—slice myself open in the name of doing the goddamn job?"

The coffee and screwdriver came. I sipped, and he raised his glass. Before he put it to his lips, he looked at me guiltily.

"Yeah, I know. Not to mention the six-pack I put away for dinner."

I was silent.

"What the hell, I'm a minority of one, I'm entitled. Cheers."

By the time he finished the screwdriver his head was starting to loll. He called for another and threw it back in one shot. When he put down the glass, his hands were shaking and his eyes were shot through with scarlet threads.

"Come on," I said, standing and dropping some bills on the table, "let's get out of here while you can still walk."

He resisted, claiming he'd only just begun, and began humming the tune of the same name, but I finally managed to steer him out of the Golden Eagle and into the night air. The parking lot was dark and smelled of jet fuel, but it was a welcome change from the boozy humidity of the lounge.

He walked with a drunk's exaggerated caution, and I worried he'd fall. The notion of hoisting and dragging 230 pounds of inebriated detective didn't thrill me, and I was thankful when we reached the Seville. Guiding him to the passenger side, I opened the door, and he stumbled in.

"Where to?" he asked, stretching out his legs and yawning.

"Let's take a drive."

"Peachy."

I opened the windows, started up the engine, and drove onto the 405 north. Traffic was light, and it didn't take long to connect to the 90, but by the time I exited at Marina Del Rey, he was asleep. I cruised along Mindanao Way, passed a couple of upscale shopping centers, and hooked toward the harbor. The breeze was damp and saline and bore just a trace of stench. A flotilla of pleasure craft bobbed silently in the glossy black water, masts as plentiful as reeds in a marsh. The moon broke against the surface of the bay in cream-colored fragments.

A sharp gust of wind blew into the car. Milo opened his eyes and straightened up, grunting. He looked out the window and turned to me, perplexed.

"Hey," he said, in a voice still thickened by alcohol, "I thought I told you to be careful."

"What are you talking about?"

"This is Radovic country, pal. Fucker's got an old Chris Craft moored in one of the slips."

"Oh, yeah," I recalled, "Souza mentioned something about that."

He swayed closer, smelling of sweat and gin.

"And you just happened to coast down here, huh?"

"Don't get paranoid, Milo. I thought the sea breeze might clear your besotted brain."

"Sorry," he mumbled, closing his eyes again, "I've gotten used to checking my back."

"That's a hell of a way to live."

He managed a shrug, then suddenly retched. I glanced over and saw him doubled up with pain and holding his belly. Quickly I pulled onto the shoulder of the road and braked the Seville. Running around to the passenger side, I opened the door just in time. He sagged forward, lurched, heaved, and vomited repeatedly. I found a box of tissues in the glove compartment, grabbed a wad, and, when it looked as if he was through, wiped his face.

Exhausted and breathing hard, he pulled himself up, leaned his head back, and shivered. I closed the door and got back in the driver's seat.

"Did I sully your paint job?" he asked hoarsely.

"No, you missed. Feel any better?"

He groaned in response.

I turned the car around, found Lincoln Boulevard, and drove north through Venice and into Santa Monica. He coughed dryly, slumped down in the seat, and let his head drop to his chest. Within moments he was sleeping again, snoring through his mouth.

I drove slowly through streets slick with coastal fog, breathing in the ocean air and collecting my thoughts. It was after eleven, and except for drifters, derelicts, and Mexican dishwashers leaving darkened chophouses, the sidewalks were deserted. Turning right on Montana, I found an all-night doughnut stand embedded in an empty asphalt lot, glowing Edward Hopper yellow and reeking of sweetened lard. Pulling up close, I left Milo dozing, got out, and bought a jumbo cup of black coffee from a pimpled kid wearing a Walkman.

When I brought it back to the car, Milo was sitting up, hair disheveled and eyelids drooping with fatigue. He took the cup, held it with both hands, and drank.

"Finish it," I said. "I want to get you back to Rick in one piece."

He constructed a stoic façade, then let it collapse.

"Rick's in Acapulco," he said. "Been there for a couple of weeks."

"Separate vacations?"

"Something like that. I've been acting like a son of a bitch and he needed to get away from me."

"When's he coming back?"

Steam rose from the coffee in wisps and swirls, misting his face and obscuring his expression.

"It's open-ended. I haven't heard from him except for one postcard that talked about the weather. He's on leave from the ER and has plenty of bucks saved up, so theoretically it could be a long time."

He lowered his face and sipped.

"I hope it works out," I said.

"Yeah. Me, too."

A gasoline truck rumbled by seismically, leaving silence in its wake. Behind the counter of the doughnut shop the acned kid checked the deep fryers while bopping to his Walkman.

"If you ever need someone to talk to," I said, "be sure to call. No need to be a stranger again."

He nodded.

"I appreciate that, Alex. I know I've been hibernating. But it's a funny thing about solitude—at first it hurts; then you acquire a taste for it. I get home from a day when everyone's been talking at me and the sound of another human voice is *grating,* and all I want is silence."

"If I worked with Cash and Whitehead, I'd want silence, too."

He laughed.

"The gruesome twosome? A couple of superstars."

"They thought I was gay because I'm your friend."

"Classical case of limited thinking. It's why neither of them will ever be worth much as a detective. Sorry if they hassled you."

"They weren't that bad," I said, "more ineffectual than anything. I just don't see how you can work with them."

"Like I said before, do I have a choice? No, actually it hasn't been as bad as it could've been. Whitehead's a dolt and antigay, but he's anti everything—Jews, blacks, women, conservationists, vegetarians, Mormons, the PTA—so it's hard to take it personally. On top of that he keeps his distance, probably worried about catching AIDS. Cash wouldn't be half bad if he gave a damn about anything other than chasing pussy and cultivating his tan."

"Real workaholic, huh?"

"Dickie-poo? Oh, yeah. I don't know if you ever heard

about it, but a couple of years ago Beverly Hills PD had this federally funded project to bust the coke dealers who were supplying the movie stars. Cash pulled undercover on that. They bought him a wardrobe from Giorgio, leased him an Excalibur and a place up in Trousdale, handed him a fat expense account, and set him up as King Shit, the independent producer. For six months he went to parties, balled starlets, and bought blow. At the end of it they busted a couple of small-timers, and even that was dismissed due to entrapment. A real triumph for law enforcement. When it was over, Cash got to keep the clothes, but everything else went. Coming back down to earth was traumatic. He'd had this taste of something sweet, and now it was yanked out of his mouth. Real work started to seem like a life sentence, so he dealt with it by becoming a goldbrick. Half the time the guy isn't even on the job. Supposedly he's interviewing sources, developing leads, but he always comes back a shade darker with the car full of sand, so we know about that, right? Even when he does show up, all he talks about is this screenplay he's working on—real-life *detective* stuff. Warren Beatty loves it, you see, but they're just waiting for their agents to get together to cut a deal, blah-blah-blah."

"Sounds like the L.A. blues."

"You got it."

He was talking clearly and seemed alert, so I started the car and headed back south. Talking about Cash had triggered an association to the bloodstained room he'd shown me this morning.

"Can we talk about the case?" I asked.

He was surprised by the abrupt turn in the conversation but collected himself quickly. Finishing the last of the coffee, he crumpled the cup and tossed it from hand to hand.

"Like I said before, no investigative details. Besides, what's there to talk about?"

"Open-and-shut, huh?"

"Close enough to it to answer my prayers."

"Doesn't that bother you?"

"What, success? Sure, but I'm learning how to cope with it."

"I'm serious, Milo. Half a dozen homicides that have

baffled the police for a year suddenly solve themselves. Don't you find that strange?"

"It happens."

"Not very often and not in serial murders. Isn't a big part of the kick for serial killers hide-and-seek, playing ego games with authorities? They may throw out hints and tease the police, but they go out of their way to avoid detection. And plenty of them—Jack the Ripper, Zodiac, the Green River Strangler—kill for years and never get caught."

"But plenty of 'em do, pal."

"Sure, through bad luck or carelessness—like Bianchi and the Yorkshire Ripper. But they don't just sit there holding the knife and wait to get picked up. It doesn't make sense."

"Slicing people into cold cuts doesn't make sense, either, but it happens—more often than you'd like to know. Now, can we change the subject?"

"There's something else that bothers me. Nothing in Jamey's history indicates sadism or psychopathy. He's profoundly psychotic, much too muddled to plan and carry out those slashings."

"You're getting abstract again," he said. "I don't give a damn how you diagnose him; the bottom line's the evidence."

"Let me ask you one more thing. Before you arrested him, did you have any other leads on the slashings?"

"You've gotta be kidding."

"Did you?"

"What's the difference if we had four hundred leads? The case is solved."

"Humor me. What were they?"

"Forget it, Alex. That's exactly the kind of stuff I don't wanna get into."

"The defense has access to investigative records. I can get it from Souza, but I'd rather hear it from you."

"Oh, yeah? Why's that?"

"Because I trust you."

"I'm flattered," he growled.

We drove in silence.

"You're a persistent bastard," he said finally, "but you don't try to change me, so I won't try to change you. If I tell you, will you drop it?"

"Sure."

"All right. No, we didn't have any leads to speak of. In a case like this you get plenty of information—people turning in their neighbors or ex-lovers. All of it dead-ended. The closest we got to anything of value was that three of the victims were seen going off with biker types before they disappeared. Now don't get excited. I said closest only because we cross-referenced everything and bikers came up three separate times. But if you know Boystown, you know that's no big deal; leather freaks abound, and the chickens pull ten, fifteen tricks a night, so they're bound to interact with some tough-guy types. Nevertheless, being dutiful public servants, we hit the pavement, checked out all the leather bars, and came up empty. Satisfied?"

"What kinds of bikers?"

"Bikers. Slobs on choppers. No names, no colors, no club ID, no physical description. It came to zilch because the parties responsible weren't cruising around all night on Harleys, Alex. They were hacking and choking pretty boys in the privacy of a big white house in Beverly Hills. All right?"

"All right."

We arrived back at the Golden Eagle just before midnight.

"What are you driving?"

"The Porsche. It's over there."

The bone white 928 was sandwiched between two Japanese compacts in a far corner of the lot, gleaming like a slice of moonlight. A young couple was admiring it, and when I coasted to a stop at the rear bumper, they looked up.

"Nice wheels," said the man.

"Yeah," said Milo, leaning out the window, "crime pays."

The couple looked at each other and hurried away.

"It's not nice to frighten the citizens," I said.

"Gotta protect Dr. Rick's bitchin' *wheels*."

"Think of it as a positive sign," I said. "You don't leave fifty grand worth of car with someone you're not planning on seeing again."

He considered that.

"Collateral on the relationship, huh?"

"Sure."

He put his hand on the door handle.

"It was good seeing you, Milo," I said.

"Ditto. Thanks for the shoulder and keep out of trouble."

We shook hands, and he stepped out of the Seville, hitched up his jeans, and searched through jangling pockets for the car keys. Retrieving a gold-plated set, he looked back at the Porsche and smiled.

"Or at the very least, alimony."

14

It was twelve-twenty when I got home, but Robin was still up, wearing a T-shirt over nothing and reading in bed.

"After you left, I went back to the shop," she explained. "Rockin' Billy phoned from New York; he's coming into town and wants another custom guitar."

I kissed the top of her head, undressed, and slipped in beside her.

"More fruit? What was it last time—a mango?"

"A six-stringed papaya." She laughed. "For the Tropical Dreams LP. No, this time he's gone high-tech. He's releasing a song next week called 'Buck Rogers Boogie' and he wants a solid body shaped like a ray gun to take on tour—chrome paint, LED readouts, synthesizer interface, the works."

"Ah, art!"

"It's antiart, which is even more fun. Sometimes when I'm in the middle of one of his jobs and I start to feel silly, I pretend Marcel Duchamp is sitting in a corner of the shop, nodding approvingly."

It was my turn to laugh.

"I'd like to see the thing when it's done," I said, "risk my life and blast off a few chords."

"Come by when Billy picks it up. You might enjoy meeting him. Despite his looks, he's not your typical burned-out rocker. More of a long-haired businessman really."

"Maybe I should meet the guy. You spend enough time with him."

"Don't worry, darling, he's not my type. Too skinny." She grew serious. "How's Milo?"

I told her.

"Poor man," she said. "Down deep he's such a softy. Isn't there something we could be doing for him?"

"He knows he can come to us, but I think he's going to go the loner route for a while. And besides, getting together is awkward as long as we're working opposite sides of the Cadmus case."

"That's awful. How much longer will you have to be involved with it?"

"I don't know."

The noncommittal answer raised her eyebrows. She looked at me and let it ride.

"Speaking of which," she said, "a call came in on the service from Horace Souza. He insisted on leaving the message personally, so I took it. He's a charming old goat, isn't he?"

"I've never seen him in that light."

"Oh, but he is, honey. Very courtly, very old-world. Like a benevolent uncle. Some women go for that type."

"To me he's just manipulative and calculating. Everything he does is framed in terms of strategy, of winning the game."

"Yes, I could see that," she said. "But wouldn't you want someone like that defending you if you were in trouble?"

"I guess so," I said grumpily. "What did he want?"

"Dr. Mainwaring can see you tomorrow at ten. If he doesn't hear from you, he'll assume it's on."

"Okay, thanks."

She propped herself up and looked into my eyes. Soft, fragrant curls brushed across my cheek.

"Poor Milo," she said again.

I was silent.

"Are you cranky, Alex?"

"No. Just tired."

"Not too tired, I hope." The tip of her tongue grazed my lower lip. A jolt of pleasure coursed through my body.

"Never too tired," I said, and wrapped my arms around her.

In the daylight the high concrete walls of Canyon Oaks Hospital were a sickbed gray that had been rendered white by the mercy of darkness. They rose, like tombstones, out of the verdant hills.

Mainwaring wasn't in his office at ten, and his secretary implied that his absence was premeditated. She led me to a small reading room down the hall and handed me Jamey's chart.

"Doctor said to read this first. He'll be ready for you by the time you're through."

The room was pale and windowless, furnished with a tufted black vinyl sofa, an ersatz-wood end table, and an aluminum pole lamp. An ashtray on the table was filled with cold butts. I sat down and opened the chart.

Mainwaring's notes for the night of Jamey's initial admission to Canyon Oaks were detailed and punctilious. The patient was described as agitated, confused, physically assaultive, and unresponsive to the psychiatrist's mental status evaluation. Note was made of the fact that he'd been transported by an emergency ambulance and accompanied by the police. Mainwaring had conducted a gross neurological exam that had revealed no evidence of brain tumors or other organic abnormalities, though he'd included an addendum emphasizing that the patient's lack of cooperation had made a comprehensive evaluation impossible. Plans for a CAT scan and an EEG were charted. Analyses for drug ingestion had ruled out the presence of LSD, PCP, amphetamines, cocaine, or opiates. Psychiatric and medical histories had been taken from Mr. Dwight Cadmus and Mrs. Heather Cadmus, legal guardians, in the presence of Horace Souza, attorney-at-law. The medical history was unremarkable. The psychiatric history documented a pattern of progressive mental deterioration including delusions of persecution and probable auditory hallucinations combined with evidence of a premorbid schizoid or borderline personality type. The working diagnosis was "schizophrenic disorder with mixed features (paranoid type, DSM#295.3x, possibly evolving to undifferentiated type, DSM#295.6x)" for which Mainwaring prescribed hospitalization and an initial regimen of chlorpromazine—the generic name for Thorazine—a hundred milligrams orally, four times a day.

Appended to the intake report were copies of the police report and court documents validating the hospital's right to hold the boy involuntarily for seventy-two hours and the subsequent long-term commitment, as well as a CAT scan conducted two days after admission by a consulting neuroradiologist, which confirmed the absence of organic pathology. The radiologist recounted—with barely disguised irritation—how difficult it had been to administer the scan because of the patient's assaultive behavior and stated that conducting an EEG wouldn't be advisable until the patient grew more cooperative. The brain wave test was unlikely to yield much of value, he added, because the patient was clearly psychotic and EEG tracings on psychotics were inconclusive. Furthermore, the patient had already been medicated; that would invalidate the exam completely. He thanked Mainwaring for the referral and signed off the case. In the note that followed, Mainwaring thanked the radiologist for his consultation, concurred with his findings and recommendations, and noted that the severity of the patient's psychosis had "dictated prompt chemotherapeutic treatment prior to encephalographic monitoring."

Past that point, the notes thinned considerably. Mainwaring had visited Jamey once or twice daily, but the contents of those contacts hadn't been recorded. The psychiatrist's remarks were brief and descriptive—"patient stable, no change" or "increased hallucinatory activity"—followed by orders to adjust drug dosages. As I read on, it became clear that Jamey's response to medication had been uneven and that adjustments had been frequent.

For a brief period following admission, he'd appeared to be reacting favorably to the Thorazine. The psychotic symptoms lessened in both frequency and severity, and twice Mainwaring recorded that "brief conversation with the patient" was possible, although he didn't specify what he and Jamey had spoken about. Soon after, however, there was an acute relapse, with Jamey growing highly agitated and lashing out physically. Mainwaring upped the dosage and, when the boy got worse instead of improving, kept increasing it steadily, searching for an "optimal maintenance dose."

At fourteen hundred milligrams daily there followed another period of improvement, although at this level of medication the patient was numbed and sleepy and progress was judged by the absence of unpredictable behaviors rather than by coherence. Then came another sudden relapse; the hallucinations this time were more "florid" than ever before, the patient so assaultive that full-time restraints were ordered. Mainwaring dropped the Thorazine and switched to other phenothiazine tranquilizers— haloperidol, thioridazine, fluphenazine. With each drug the fluctuating pattern repeated itself. Initially Jamey had appeared to grow sedate, the quiescent periods ranging from a few days to one or two weeks at a time. Then, without warning, he'd become intractably agitated, paranoid, and confused. Toward the end of the notes, repetitive movements of the lips, tongue, and trunk had begun to appear—symptoms of tardive dyskinesia similar to the ones I'd noticed at the jail. In addition to not responding favorably to the drugs, he was developing toxic reactions to them.

It was a baffling cycle, and at one point Mainwaring's frustration emerged through his curt prose. Faced with the latest relapse, he speculated that Jamey was suffering from a highly atypical psychosis, possibly related to some kind of seizure disorder—a "subtle limbic abnormality that would not be revealed by the CAT scan." The fact that dyskinesia had developed so quickly, he wrote, supported the notion of an abnormal nervous system, as did the patient's bizarre response to phenothiazines. Quoting journal references, he noted reports of success in other atypical cases through the use of anticonvulsant medication. Emphasizing that such treatment was experimental in nature, he suggested a trial dosage of carbamazepine, an anticonvulsant, once written consent from the guardians had been obtained and an EEG had been conducted. But before this could take place, Jamey got better again, growing more calm and compliant than he'd been since admission and able once again to converse in brief sentences. Along with this came significant emotional depression, but this was deemed less important than the absence of psychotic symptoms. Mainwaring was pleased and kept him on the same medication.

Two days later he escaped.

The nursing notes weren't much help. Excretory functions, nutritional data, fluid intake, and temperature were dutifully recorded in the input-output log. Jamey was described by the nurses as either "nonresponsive" or "hostile." Only M. Surtees, LVN, had something positive to say, recording his occasional smiles and noting, proudly, his appreciation of the nightly back rub in a gaily corpulent cursive flow replete with bubble-dotted I's. But her optimism was invariably negated by the notes that followed on the next shift and ignored by the summation of the charge nurse, A. Vann, RN, who stuck to vital signs and avoided commentary.

As I closed the chart, the door opened and Mainwaring walked in. So precise was his timing that I wondered if I'd been observed. Standing, I searched the room for a hidden camera. None was visible.

"Dr. Delaware," he said, and pumped my hand. He wore a long white coat over a white shirt, a black tie, tweed trousers, and black suede oxfords. His jumpy brown eyes shone brightly in his thin, wolfish face as they examined me, head to toe.

"Good morning, Dr. Mainwaring."

He looked at the chart in my hand.

"I trust you were able to decipher my penmanship."

"No problem," I said, giving him the folder. "It was very educational."

"Good. One does try to be thorough."

"I'd appreciate a photocopy for my files."

"Certainly. I'll have it mailed to you." He backed toward the door, opened it, and held it ajar. "Thoroughness notwithstanding, I assume you have questions."

"A few."

"Fine. Let's go to my office."

A short walk led us to the door with his name on it. The room was a monument to disorder, piled high with papers and books and haphazardly furnished. He removed a stack of journals from a straightbacked chair, dropped them on the floor, and offered me the seat. Maneuvering his way behind a simple wooden desk, he sat down, leaned forward, and reached for a circular pipe rack partially obscured by stacks of billing forms. Pulling a leather pouch from a coat pocket, he selected a bulldog briar, filled it, and went through a ritual of lighting, tamping, and relighting. Within moments the room was fogged with bitter smoke.

"So," he said, talking around the pipestem, "I suppose we'll be coordinating our reports."

I hadn't thought in terms of collaboration and avoided a direct answer by saying that it was a complex case and that I was far from being able to report anything.

"I see. Have you worked with many schizophrenics, Doctor?"

"It's not my specialty."

He sucked on the pipe and blew out an acrid plume. After following the smoke as it rose toward the ceiling, he lowered his eyes, then turned up his lips until they formed a wide slash of a smile. "Well, then," he said, "what is it that you'd like to know?"

"It's clear from the chart that Jamey was incoherent during most of his hospitalization. But you did record a few lucid periods during which he could carry on a con-versation. I'd be interested in knowing what kinds of things he talked about."

"Um-hmm. Anything else?"

"You recorded both auditory and visual hallucinations. Do you think that's significant? And during the halluci-natory periods how did he describe what he was hearing and seeing?"

He laced his fingers contemplatively. His fingernails were long, almost womanish, and coated with a clear polish.

"So," he said, "basically what you're interested in is *content*. May I ask why?"

"It might reveal something about what was going on in his mind."

It was the answer he'd expected, and the lipless smile reappeared.

"It's clear," he said, "that we're operating from very different theoretical backgrounds. Since we'll be working together, it's best that I lay my cards on the table. You're suggesting a classical psychodynamic approach: People's problems are caused by unconscious conflicts. Interpret the content of their ramblings in order to bring the uncon-scious to consciousness, and everything works itself out." Puff, puff. "Which is all very fine, I suppose, in cases of minor adjustment disorders. But not at all relevant to schizophrenia. The psychoses, Dr. Delaware, are essen-tially *physiologic* phenomena—chemical imbalances with-in the brain. What the patient has to *say* while in the throes of that imbalance has very little, if any, clinical significance."

"I'm not suggesting we psychoanalyze every nuance," I said, "and I respect the data on the biology of schizophrenia. But despite the fact that they sink into patterns, psychotics are as individual as anyone else: They have feelings. And conflicts. It can't hurt to learn as much as we can about Jamey as an individual."

"A holistic approach?"

"Just a thorough one."

"Very well," he said somewhat testily, "let's get on with it. What was it that you wanted to know? Ah, yes, visual and auditory hallucinations, do I think that's unusual? Statistically, yes. Clinically, no. An atypical pattern has been the hallmark of this case from the beginning. Are you suggesting hallucinogenic abuse?"

"It's the obvious differential."

"Of course it is, but it's been ruled out. I admit that when he was brought in, my first impression was that of a PCP user. The uncle and aunt were unaware of drug use, but that didn't impress me; one could hardly expect the boy to have told them about that kind of thing. However, the tests were clearly negative."

The pipe had gone out. He used the miniature spoon on his pipe tool to scoop out the top layer of ashes, tamped, and relit.

"No," he said, "I'm afraid this isn't a case of drug abuse. The diagnosis of schizophrenia is firm. While visual hallucinations are unusual in psychosis, they're not unheard of, especially in combination with auditory disturbances. Which leads me to an important point. The boy was typically incoherent and difficult to understand. He appeared to be hearing *and* seeing things, but I couldn't state with certainty that such was the case. All of it may very well have been auditory."

"What did he appear to be seeing and hearing?"

"Back to content, eh?" He removed the pipe from his mouth and played with it long enough for me to wonder if he was stalling. Finally he frowned and spoke. "To be frank, I don't recall precisely what he said."

"Souza told me he appeared quite sharp in the beginning, claiming the commitment was a mistake and being pretty convincing about it."

"Yes, of course," he said hastily. "At first there was the usual paranoid ideation: Someone was out to kill him; he was no crazier than anyone else. Then it deteriorated to wild accusations and vague mutterings about poisons and wounds—the earth bleeding, that kind of rubbish. Considering the diagnosis, nothing extraordinary. And not at all relevant to treatment."

"And the visual problems?"

"The visual part of it had to do with color. He seemed to be seeing bright colors, with special emphasis on red." He smiled faintly. "I suppose one could interpret that as sanguinary imagery—that his perceptual field was awash with blood. In light of what's evolved, that would hardly be surprising."

"The lucid periods," I repeated. "What did he talk about?"

He shook his head.

"Excepting the period immediately following hospitalization, *lucid* is an exaggeration. *Minimally responsive* would be more accurate. If I used the term *conversation*, it was in a very limited sense. The vast majority of the time he was unreachable—autistically withdrawn. When the medication took hold, he was able to answer simple yes or no questions. But he was never able to chat."

I thought back to Jamey's crisis call. He'd taken the initiative to reach me and, once we'd connected, had been able to report his location. While most of his speech had been jumbled, he'd maintained coherence for several isolated sentences. Far from normality but a lot more than answering yes or no. I raised the issue with Mainwaring, but he remained unmoved.

"During the last remission he began to grow more verbal. It renewed my hope that the latest medication would be the right one."

"Are you treating him with it now?"

He scowled.

"In a manner of speaking. There's no one at the jail qualified to monitor his response, so I have to be extremely conservative about dosage. It's not treatment in the true sense, merely patchwork, and the pattern of uneven response has reappeared."

"That could explain what I saw when I visited him.

The first time he was barely awake and showing signs of tardive dyskinesia. The second time he seemed a bit more alert and less neurologically impaired."

The psychiatrist cleared his throat.

"I'd like to suggest," he said mildly, "that you steer clear of terms like *alertness* and *relative lucidity* and that you don't even suggest the notion of voluntary drug abuse. That kind of thing can only play right into the prosecution's hands and dilute the picture we're trying to paint."

"Diminished capacity caused by paranoid schizophrenia."

"Precisely. It's a difficult enough proposition for the layman to understand, without injecting needless complications."

For good reason, I thought, and refrained from responding. He stared at me, then began sifting through the papers on his desk.

"Is there anything else, Doctor?" he asked.

"Yes. Ms. Surtees's notes seemed more positive than anyone else's. Do you see her as an accurate reporter?"

He leaned back and put his feet up on the desk. There was a hole in the sole of one of his wing tips.

"Ms. Surtees is one of those well-meaning, maternal types who attempt to make up for what they lack in intelligence and education by becoming personally involved with their patients. The other nurses viewed her with bemusement, but she posed no problem for them. I wasn't pleased at her employment, but the family was distressed and felt one-on-one care was important, and I couldn't see her doing much harm. In retrospect, perhaps I was too permissive."

Or impressed by dollar signs.

His jaws bunched as he chomped down on the pipe. He looked at me searchingly, requesting confirmation that he hadn't mishandled the case.

"So you don't have much faith in her credibility."

"She's a baby-sitter," he said brusquely, "not a professional. Now, if that's all—"

"Just one more thing. I'd like to talk with Mrs. Vann."

"Mrs. Vann is no longer with us."

"Was she dismissed because of the escape?"

"Not at all. She left of her own accord, just a few days ago."

"Did she say why?"

"Only that she'd been here for five years and wanted a change of scenery. I was disappointed but not surprised. It's difficult work, and very few last that long. She's a fine nurse, and I'm sorry to have lost her."

"So you don't blame her for what happened."

His eyebrows merged and created a mesh of creases in his forehead.

"Dr. Delaware, this is beginning to sound like an interrogation. My impression was that you came here to be educated, not to cross-examine me."

I apologized for coming on too strongly. It didn't appear to mollify him. Pulling the pipe out of his mouth, he turned it upside down and knocked it angrily against the rim of an ashtray. A small cloud of gray dust rose, then sank, leaving a film of soot on the paper disarray.

"Perhaps you're not aware of the enormousness of our task," he said. "Convincing twelve untrained individuals that the boy wasn't responsible for his behavior will be no mean feat. The issue of blame is yet another irrelevancy that will impede us. We're expert witnesses, not judges. Why persist in digressing?"

"From where I sit, what's relevant and what's digression aren't all that clear."

"Believe me," he said with visible exasperation, "the issues aren't all that complex. The boy developed schizophrenia because of poor genetics. The disease disabled his brain and hence destroyed his so-called free will. He was programmed for disaster from birth, every bit as much a victim as the people he murdered. That's not speculation; it's based on medical data—the facts speak for themselves. However, because of the ignorance of the layman, it would be helpful to augment the argument with sociological and psychological theories. That is where, I strongly suggest, you should be directing your energies."

"Thanks for the suggestion."

"Not at all," he said airily. "I'll have that chart for you within a few days. Now let me see you out."

We rose and left the office. The corridors of the hospital were silent and empty. In the front reception room a well-dressed couple sat holding hands and staring at the floor. In the woman's lap was an unopened copy of

Vogue. A cigarette dangled from the man's lips. They looked up at the sound of our footsteps and, when they saw Mainwaring, gazed up hopefully, as if at a deity.

The psychiatrist waved, said, "One moment," and walked over to greet them. The couple stood, and he shook each of their hands energetically. I waited several moments for the conversation to end, but when it became clear that my presence had been forgotten, I slipped through the door unnoticed.

15

I HAD lunch at a café in Sherman Oaks and mentally replayed the interview with Mainwaring. For all his pharmacologic expertise, he'd given me no insight into Jamey, the person. That no doubt wouldn't have troubled him at all had it been called to his attention. He was a self-proclaimed biochemical engineer with scant interest in any organism above the cellular level. Years ago he would have been viewed as an extremist, but now he was *au courant*, well in step with the new wave in psychiatry—a love affair with biological determinism at the expense of insight. Part of the motivation behind the shift was valid; psychotherapy, by itself, had proved minimally useful in the treatment of psychosis, and drugs had wrought remarkable, if unpredictable, symptomatic control.

But some of it was also political—through reasserting themselves as physicians, psychiatrists could distance themselves from psychologists and other nonmedical therapists—as well as economic, for insurance companies were reluctant to pay for something as ambiguous as talking therapy but had no problem reimbursing for blood tests, brain scans, injections, and other medical procedures.

Psychology had its share of engineers, too—behavioral technologists, like Sarita Flowers, who steered clear of disorderly annoyances like feelings and thoughts and viewed the human condition as a set of bad habits in need of Skinnerian salvation.

Either perspective was a kind of tunnel vision, *ad extremum,* the blind worship of anything that could be quantified, combined with premature self-congratulation and a black/white view of the world. But there was a lot of gray space in the middle, and a patient could get lost there.

I wondered if that had happened to Jamey.

* * *

Arriving home at two, I called Souza and asked him to set up an appointment with Marthe Surtees.

"Ah, Marthe, a kind woman. I'll call the registry that employs her and see if I can reach her. Do you have anything to report, Doctor? I'm not asking for conclusions, only a feel for where you're going."

"Nothing yet. I'm still asking questions."

"I see. When do you envision yourself sufficiently prepared to write a report?"

"That's hard to say. Perhaps in a week or so."

"Good, good. We'll be going to court for preliminaries at the end of the month. I'd like my armory well stocked by then."

"I'll do what I can."

"Yes, I'm sure you will. By the way, we spoke previously about the possibility of some kind of drug intoxication. Have you reached any conclusions about that?"

"Dr. Mainwaring was adamant that drugs had nothing to do with Jamey's condition, and he thought even raising the possibility would damage a dim cap defense."

"Mainwaring's not an attorney. If I can show that Chancellor pushed drugs on the boy, not only wouldn't it hurt, but it would help."

"Be that as it may, there's no evidence of drug abuse, The symptoms I noticed were probably tardive dyskinesia—a reaction to the medications. He'd started to show them at Canyon Oaks. It's an atypical reaction after short-term treatment, but Mainwaring feels he's an atypical schizophrenic."

"Atypical." He thought out loud. "Framed properly, that could work in our favor, make us less dependent upon precedent. Very well, keep probing, and let me know if anything else comes up. By the way, do you have anything scheduled later on today?"

"No."

"Excellent. Heather arrived last night from Montecito, took a helicopter down at midnight in order to avoid the press. The children stayed behind, so if you want to speak to her, it would be a good time."

"Sure."

"Shall we say five o'clock then?"

"Five would be fine."

"Excellent. I know you'll find her a superb young woman. Speaking of which, I greatly enjoyed speaking with your Robin."

His words were gracious, but something in his tone betrayed an undercurrent of lechery. Nothing you could put your finger on; nevertheless, I felt my stomach tighten.

"She's terrific," I said.

"Quite. Good for you, Doctor."

He gave me the address of the Cadmus house and signed off cheerily.

Hancock Park reeks of old money.

In Beverly Hills, an unlimited budget in the absence of good taste has often produced freakish architectural excess: turreted castles, texture-coated pseudovillas, Technicolor postmodernistic monstrosities, and cheesy imitations of Tara, each costing millions, competing for applause on a single palm-lined block.

Four miles east, in Hancock Park, the quieter the better. There's some diversity of style—Tudor, Georgian, Regency, Mediterranean—but it fits together unobtrusively. Very hushed, very stately. For the most part the houses are larger than their noisy cousins in Beverly Hills, remnants of a time when multiple servants were the order of the day. They sit smugly behind expansive, knife-edged lawns, set far back from wide, maple-shaded streets. The landscaping is subdued: a solitary stately pine on the lawn, yew hedges, and an occasional splash of flower petal. Wood-sided station wagons, Volvos and Mercedes sedans in neutral shades fill the driveways. As is the case with most residential areas of L.A., the streets are ghost-town empty, save for isolated perambulators pushed by uniformed nannies or permapressed young matrons holding platinum-haired toddlers in tow. A few Jews and Asians have moved in, but for the most part Hancock Park is still WASP country. And though some of the city's meanest streets surround the neighborhood and crime is higher than anyone wants to admit, Hancock Park remains an enclave of understated wealth.

The Cadmus house was on June Street north of Beverly, not far from the Los Angeles Country Club, a two-story brick Tudor whose bricks and contrasting stone and woodwork had been painted beige. A clover-laced

flagstone path divided the lawn. On either side stood a
security guard, wearing the same gray uniform as the
men in the lobby of Cadmus Construction. But these
guards were armed with pistols and billy clubs. The reason for their presence was obvious: A flock of reporters
milled on the sidewalk. When one moved toward the
house, a guard stepped forward. The reporters kept trying,
and the guards kept reacting, a curious minuet. Off to
the side, under a porte-cochere, sat Souza's Rolls, nosed
up against a high wrought-iron gate. Standing next to the
giant car was Tully Antrim, running a chamois over its
glossy flanks while keeping one eye on the street. He saw
the Seville and gestured for me to pull behind the Phantom.

The reporters had spied the exchange, and as I swung
up the drive, they surged forward amoebically. The guards
kicked up their legs and went right after them. Taking
advantage of the diversion, one of the journalists, a young,
bespectacled man in a brown corduroy suit, made a dash
for the front door.

Antrim moved fast. In three long strides he was at the
reporter's side. One more step brought him between the
man and the door. He glared at the journalist and ordered him away. The reporter argued with him. Antrim
shook his head. The reporter moved suddenly, and the
chauffeur's right hand shot out and caught him in the
solar plexus. The young man went pale, formed a tortured O with his mouth, and clutched his gut in agony.
Antrim shoved him hard, and he tripped backward. By
this time one of the security guards had reached the
scene, and he pulled the still-gasping journalist off the
property.

I'd watched the whole thing from the car, with a flood
of shouting faces pressed against the windows and hand-
held tape recorders brandished across my line of vision.
As the man in the brown suit stumbled toward his car, he
shouted something at his colleagues that caused them to
howl in outrage at Antrim and the guards. But at the
same time they stepped away from the Seville, and I used
the opportunity to get out of the car and dash behind the
Rolls. Antrim saw me and bounded over. By the time the
reporters had stopped shouting and realized what was
happening, he'd taken me by the arm, whipped out a set
of keys, and unlocked the wrought-iron gate.

"Fucking assholes," he muttered, and pushed me through, none too gently.

The reporters pressed toward the limousine, straining to look over its towering chassis. The guards followed them, and the whine of confrontation grew louder.

Antrim led me to a side entrance and knocked. Next to the door was a small curtained window. The curtains parted, a face peered out, the curtains closed, and the door opened. A big-bellied guard was on the other side.

"It's the doctor she's been waiting to see," said Antrim, pushing past him.

The guard touched the butt of his gun and said, "Go right in," sternly, in an attempt to maintain the illusion of authority.

I followed the chauffeur through a large custard-yellow kitchen. In the center of the room was a gingham-covered table. Scattered across the tabletop were a flashlight, a thermos bottle, two plastic-wrapped ham sandwiches, and a copy of the *National Enquirer*. Draped over one chair was a gray uniform jacket. Antrim shoved a swinging door, and we passed through a butler's pantry and a dark-paneled dining room fitted with brass wall sconces. An abrupt left turn led to a domed entry hall. At the rear of the hall was a carved oak staircase. From the top of the stairs came the roar of a vacuum cleaner.

He led me across the hall and down two steps into a large oyster-colored living room, carpeted in beige wool. Blackout drapes had been drawn over every window, leaving two table lamps the sole source of illumination.

The room was expensively underfurnished: stiff sofas upholstered in dull mushroom damask; a pair of Queen Anne chairs similarly covered; spindly-legged Chippendale tables redolent of lemon oil. Off to one corner was an ebony Steinway grand. Hanging from the walls were second-rate English still lifes and landscapes framed in mahogany, their pigments faded to genteel obscurity. A limestone mantel hovered over a dead fireplace. Atop it was the room's sole incongruity: a collection of primitive sculptures—half a dozen squat, slant-eyed faces hewn of rough gray stone.

A woman sat on the sofa. She stood as I entered, tall and fashion-model thin.

"Good afternoon, Dr. Delaware," she said in a wispy,

little-girl voice. "I'm Heather Cadmus." To Antrim: "Thank you, Tully. You may go now."

The chauffeur left, and I walked toward her.

I knew she was close to her husband's age, but she looked ten years younger. Her face was long, pale, and unlined, tapering to a sharp, firm chin. Except for a hint of eyeliner, she wore no make-up. Her hair was chestnut brown, cut shoulder length, flipped at the ends, and trimmed to feathery bangs covering a high, flat forehead. Under the bangs were large, round gray eyes. Perpendicular to them was a thin but strong nose, gently uptilted, the nostrils slightly pinched—a debutante face, scrubbed, pedigreed, and girlishly pretty. The picture of casual wealth was rounded out by her attire: pink oxford shirt with button-down collar, charcoal wool A-line skirt, flat brown doeskin loafers, no jewelry save for a single diamond-studded wedding band. Her hands were small-boned and narrow, with long, tapered fingers. She held out a hand, and I took it.

"Pleased to meet you, Mrs. Cadmus."

"Heather, please," she said in that same oddly tinkling voice. "Won't you sit down?" She settled down again but remained on the edge of the sofa. Maintaining an erect posture, she smoothed her skirt and crossed her legs at the ankles. I sat in one of the Queen Annes and tried to ignore the discomfort.

She smiled nervously and folded her hands in her lap. A moment later a Hispanic maid in a black uniform appeared at the entrance to the room. Heather acknowledged her with a nod, and they talked briefly in rapid Spanish.

"Can I get you something, Doctor?"

"Nothing, thanks."

She dismissed the maid.

Muffled shouts filtered through the curtains from the street. Turning toward the sound, she winced. "It was too soon to come back. They've placed the house under siege. I'm just thankful my children don't have to see it. They've been through so much already."

"Your husband told me Jamey was very rough on them," I said, taking out my notepad.

"He was," she said softly. "They're only little girls, and he scared them so." Her voice broke. "I can't stop worrying about how all this is going to affect them. And the stress on my husband is unbelievable."

I nodded sympathetically.

"Please don't misunderstand me," she said. "I care deeply about Jamey. Just thinking about what's happened to him is . . . unbearable."

"From what I understand you and he were very close."

"I—I used to think so. I thought I'd done right by him. Now I'm not sure of anything."

Her voice broke again, and one of the hands in her lap gathered up a handful of wool and squeezed until the knuckles turned white.

"Heather, I need to ask some questions that may be upsetting. If this isn't a good time, I can come back."

"Oh, no, I'm fine. Please do what you have to."

"All right. Let's start with the time of your marriage. Jamey was five. How did he react to your entering the family?"

She flinched, as if the question had wounded her, then turned pensive, phrasing her response. "It was a difficult period for all of us. Overnight I went from single girl to instant stepmother. It's a terrible role, so fraught with evil connotations. Not the way I saw myself at twenty-four. I thought I was prepared, but I wasn't."

"What kinds of problems were there?"

"What you'd expect. Jamey was very jealous of my husband's attention, which was understandable—Dwight had been more of a father to him than anyone. Then, all of a sudden, there I was. He perceived me as his rival and did his best to try to eliminate me. From a child's perspective it must have been the logical thing to do."

"What did he do?"

"Insulted me, refused to mind, made believe I wasn't there. He could use his intelligence to be quite cruel, but I understood that it came from fear and was determined to endure. I developed a thick skin and dug in my heels. Eventually he accepted my presence, and after a while we got to the point where we could talk. Dwight was heavily involved with the company, and I stayed home; that meant I did most of the parenting. We ended up doing quite a bit of talking. Not that most of it was on a very personal level—he was a loner and kept his feelings to himself; after I had my own children, I realized how close mouthed he really was—but from time to time he even confided in me."

She paused and looked down at her hands, which were gripping her skirt like talons. Then she took a deep breath and consciously relaxed them.

"In view of what's happened, I know that doesn't sound like much, Doctor, but at the time I thought I was doing great."

Her bottom lip trembled, and she turned away. The light from one of the lamps cast an aura around her profile, giving her the look of a life-sized cameo.

"Did he ever talk to you about homosexuality?"

Her husband had reacted to the gay issue with anger and denial, but she remained outwardly unruffled.

"No. By the time he—is the expression 'came out'?—he was already spending most of his time with Dig Chancellor and having little to do with us."

"Do you think Chancellor had something to do with his coming out?"

She gave that some thought.

"I suppose he might have eased the way by serving as a role model. But if you're asking if he bent a straight twig, no, I don't believe that."

"Then you do feel he's homosexual?"

The question surprised her.

"Of course he is."

"Your husband believes quite differently."

"Doctor"—she sighed—"my husband is a very fine man. Hardworking, a dedicated father. But he can also be very stubborn. When he gets an idea in his head, even one that's illogical, it's impossible to budge him. He loves Jamey deeply; until recently he thought of him as a son. The idea that he isn't sexually normal is something he just can't face up to."

In view of the much harsher realities about Jamey, I wondered why the boy's sexual proclivities loomed so large in the assault upon Cadmus's defense system. But there was no point bringing that up now.

"When did you realize he was gay?" I asked.

"I suspected it for a while. Once when I was supervising the maid as she tidied up his room, I came across some homosexual pornography. I knew if I told Dwight there'd be an explosion, so I simply threw the pictures

away and hoped it was a transitory thing. But a few
weeks later he'd replaced what I'd gotten rid of and
added to the collection. It made me realize that he really
had a problem. After that I started to put things together: how he'd never been interested in sports or playing
with other boys; the way he avoided girls. We're quite
active socially, and there was no shortage of opportuni-
ties for him to meet young ladies, but when we made
suggestions or tried to introduce him to someone, he got
angry and stalked away. After he had started seeing Dig,
my suspicions were confirmed."

"How did he and Chancellor meet?"

She gnawed her lip and looked uncomfortable.

"Do we really need to get into that? It's a very . . .
sensitive issue."

"It's bound to come out at the trial."

She leaned forward and took a platinum cigarette case
from the coffee table. Next to it was a matching lighter,
which I picked up. By the time she'd placed a filter-
tipped cigarette between her lips I had a flame ready.

"Thank you," she said, sitting back and blowing out a
lacy stream of smoke. "I quit two years ago. Now I'm
putting away half a pack a day."

I waited as she consumed a third of the cigarette.
Resting what was left of it on the rim of a crystal ashtray,
she continued:

"Are you certain . . . about its becoming public?"

"I'm afraid so. Even if the prosecution doesn't bring it
up, the relationship between Jamey and Chancellor is
likely to be a key part of the defense."

"Yes," she said grimly. "Horace talked to us about
that. I suppose he knows best." She dragged once on the
cigarette and put it down. "If you must know, they met
here. At a dinner party. It was a business affair, black
tie, the inauguration of a new company project. Dig's
bank had invested in it, as had several other institutions.
Dwight's idea was to bring all the investors together in
order to make a show of unity and get things off on the
right foot. It started off as a beautiful evening—catering
by Perino's, champagne, an orchestra, and dancing. My
girls were allowed to stay up and be little hostesses.
Jamey was invited, too, of course, but he stayed in his
room all night, reading. I remember it clearly, because

I'd had a set of evening wear made up for him, as a surprise. When I presented it to him, he refused even to look at it."

"So he never joined the party?"

"Not for a second. Dig must have wandered upstairs, and somehow they ran into each other and started talking. Midway through the party Dwight found them. He'd gone up to take an aspirin and saw the two of them sitting on Jamey's bed, reading poetry. He was outraged. Everyone was well aware of Dig's . . . tastes. Dwight felt that he was abusing our hospitality. He stepped in immediately and escorted him back downstairs—politely but firmly. It ruined the party for him, though he put on a good face. That night we talked about it, and he admitted that he'd also been worried about Jamey's sexuality for quite some time. Maybe it was naïve, but at that point both of us still felt that he was a confused teen-ager who could go either way and that Dig was the last person in the world he needed. We prayed nothing would come of the chance meeting, but of course it did. Immediately. The next morning, after Dwight left for work, Dig picked Jamey up, and they disappeared together for the entire day. The same thing happened the following day. Soon Jamey was spending more time at Dig's house than here. My husband was livid—doubly so because he blamed himself for the initial meeting. He wanted to drive to Dig's place and drag Jamey away, but I convinced him it would do more harm than good."

"In what way?"

"I didn't want things to get physical. My husband's fit, but Dig was a huge man. He worked out with weights. And I was afraid of how Jamey would react if confronted."

"Were you worried about violence?"

"No. Not then. Only that he'd become verbally abusive and impossible to live with."

"Did the mental deterioration start before or after he met Chancellor?"

"Horace asked me the same thing, and I've racked my brain trying to remember. But it's hard to pinpoint. It wasn't as if he were a normal boy who had suddenly started acting bizarre. He was never like other children, so the change was more gradual. All I can say is it was around the time Dig started showing an interest in him."

"Did you or your husband ever discuss Jamey with Chancellor?"

"Not a word. We suffered in silence."

"That must have put quite a strain on your relationship with Chancellor."

"Not really. The only relationship that had ever existed had been a business one."

"Did that continue?"

The gray eyes smoldered with anger, and a flush rose in her cheeks. The delicate muscles of her jaw fluttered, and when she spoke, her voice had risen in pitch.

"Doctor, if you're suggesting that we backed off in order to put more change in our pockets, let me assure you—"

"I wasn't suggesting anything of the sort," I broke in. "Merely trying to get a picture of how the relationship with Chancellor affected the family."

"How it affected us? It tore us apart. But no, we didn't sever business connections. You don't go dismantling a multimillion-dollar project upon which thousands of people depend because of personal matters. If that were the case, nothing in this world would ever get done."

She retrieved the cigarette and puffed on it furiously. I gave her some time to cool down. When she finished smoking, she stubbed it out, patted her hair, and forced a smile.

"Forgive me," she said. "It's been very difficult."

"There's nothing to forgive. These are tough questions."

She nodded. "Please go on."

"Does your husband still blame himself for what happened between Jamey and Chancellor?"

"Yes. I've tried to tell him it would have happened one way or another, that homosexuality is inborn, not something you can be talked into, but as I mentioned before, he's a very stubborn man."

The roots of Cadmus's denial had grown clearer, and I understood why raising the issue of Jamey's relationship with Chancellor had ended my interview with Dwight.

"He's consumed with guilt," she added, "to the point where I'm concerned about his health."

I remembered the ravenous way he'd eyed the bottle of Glenlivet and guessed what kind of health problem she was worried about. Changing the subject, I asked:

"As far as you know, did Dig Chancellor use drugs?"

"As I said, I didn't know him well, so I really couldn't tell you for certain. But intuitively I'd say no. Like so many of them, he was obsessed with his body—vegetarianism, organic foods, weight-lifting; the man was the picture of health, massively muscular. He influenced Jamey to the point where he wouldn't eat in our home. So I can't see him polluting himself."

What she was saying sounded logical on the surface, but it didn't mean much; the most zealous health freaks had a way of making an exception when it came to a cocaine buzz or an amyl nitrate orgasm.

"What about Jamey? Do you know of his taking drugs?"

"When he started acting bizarrely, I wondered about it. In fact, it was the first thing I thought of."

"Why's that?"

"The way he was behaving seemed similar to a bum LSD or PCP trip, maybe even a reaction to bad speed."

The drug talk seemed out of place coming from her patrician lips. She saw my surprise and smiled.

"I volunteer at a drug rehab center sponsored by the Junior League. It's a halfway house and counseling center for teen-agers trying to get off hard drugs. We established it after the First Lady made a plea for citizen involvement. I've spent five hours a week there for the last eighteen months, and it's been very educational. Not that I was naïve about drugs—I attended Stanford in the sixties—but things have gotten a lot worse since the sixties. The stories some of the kids tell are unbelievable: ten-year-olds on heroin; designer drugs; babies born addicted. It's sensitized me to the enormousness of the problem. That is why when Jamey started acting strangely, I panicked and called one of the counselors at the center. She agreed that it could be hallucinogens but said that the possibility of some kind of mental breakdown shouldn't be overlooked. Unfortunately I heard only the part about drugs and blocked out the rest."

She stopped, suddenly embarrassed.

"What I'm going to tell you now may sound stupid, but you have to understand that he was falling apart and I was frightened, for the entire family."

"Please go on. I'm sure it's not stupid at all."

She leaned forward penitently.

"I turned into a snoop, Doctor. Kept a close watch on him for telltale signs when I thought he wasn't looking—examining his pupils, surreptitiously checking his arms for needle marks. Several times I sneaked into his room and took it apart in hope of finding a syringe or a pill or some powder—anything I could have analyzed at the center. All I found were more of his dirty pictures. Once I even borrowed a pair of his underpants, thinking a urine trace could be done from it. In the end I came up with nothing and he kept deteriorating. I finally realized it had to be mental illness."

She took another cigarette out of the case, had second thoughts, and put it down on the table.

"I've lost a lot of sleep wondering if catching it sooner would have made a difference. Dr. Mainwaring assured us that the schizophrenia was genetically programmed and would have occurred with or without treatment. What do you think?"

"Schizophrenia's not like cancer. Response to treatment has more to do with individual biology than with how quickly you start. You have nothing to feel guilty about."

"I appreciate that," she said. "I really do. Is there anything else you'd like to know?"

"You said before he confided in you—"

"Infrequently."

"I understand. During those infrequent times what kinds of things did he talk about?"

"Hurts, fears, insecurities. The usual plagues of childhood. He was curious about his parents and went through a period where he felt they'd rejected him. I tried to support him, to build up his sense of self-esteem."

"How much did he know about them?"

"Do you mean about the kind of people they were? Pretty much all of it. At first I glossed over some of the rougher parts, but he could tell I was being elusive and kept pressing me. I thought it was best to be honest. The fact that they'd used drugs really bothered him, which is another reason—now that I'm thinking rationally—that I don't believe he would have taken anything."

"Was he aware of the details of his father's suicide?"

"He knew that Peter had hanged himself, yes. He

wanted to know why, which, of course, is an unanswerable question."

"What kinds of feelings did he express about it?"

"It enraged him. He said that suicide was a wretched act and that he hated his father for destroying himself. I tried to tell him that Peter hadn't done it to hurt him, that he'd acted only out of tremendous inner pain. I emphasized his parents' good points, too—how charming and good-looking Peter had been, his mother's talent as a dancer. I wanted him to feel good about his roots and about himself."

Uttering a raw sound that was half laugh, half sob, she breathed in sharply and dabbed at her eyes.

I waited for her to calm down before continuing.

"I'd like to hear about his childhood behavior patterns."

"Certainly. What would you like to know?"

"Let's start with sleep. Was he a good sleeper as a child?"

"No. He was always restless and easy to wake."

"Did he have frequent nightmares, night terrors, or episodes of sleepwalking?"

"There were occasional bad dreams, nothing out of the ordinary. But several months before he was hospitalized, he began to wake up screaming. Dr. Mainwaring said those were night terrors and probably related to some neurological problem."

"How often did this happen?"

"Several times a week. It's one of the reasons we let him move into the guesthouse; the noise was frightening the girls. I assume they continued or got worse after he moved out, but I can't be sure because he was out of earshot."

"Did he ever say anything when he screamed?"

She shook her head.

"Only moans and shrieks." She shuddered. "Horrible."

"Did he ever wet the bed?"

"Yes. At the time of my marriage he was a bed-wetter. I tried everything to help him stop—bribery, scolding, a bell and pad machine—but nothing worked. When he was nine or ten, it stopped by itself."

"What about fire setting?"

"Never," she said, puzzled.

"How did he get along with animals?"

"Animals?"

"Pets. Did he enjoy them?"

"We've never had dogs or cats because I'm allergic. There was an aquarium full of tropical fish in the library that he used to enjoy looking at. Is that what you mean?"

"Yes. Thank you."

She continued to appear mystified, and I knew that my questions seemed disjointed. But I'd asked them for a reason. Bed-wetting is common in children and, by itself, not considered pathological. But bed-wetting, fire setting, and cruelty to animals constitute a predictive triad: Children who exhibit all three symptoms are more likely to develop psychopathic behavior patterns as adults than those who don't. It's a statistical phenomenon, and far from ironclad, but worth looking into when you're dealing with serial murder.

I finished the developmental history and asked her to review Jamey's breakdown. Her account matched her husband's with one exception: She described herself as having wanted to get psychiatric help for Jamey years before but having been stymied by Dwight's refusal. Characteristically, she followed the implicit criticism of her husband by singing his praises as a spouse and father, and excusing his resistance as well-meaning stubbornness. When she was through, I thanked her and closed my notepad.

"Is that it?" she asked.

"Unless there's something else you want to tell me."

She hesitated.

"There is one thing. Up until recently I hadn't told anyone about it because I wasn't sure if it would help Jamey or hurt him. But I talked to Horace yesterday, and he said it could be helpful in terms of establishing that Dig Chancellor was a pernicious influence. He also asked me to cooperate with you fully, so I guess I should."

"I wouldn't do anything that would hurt Jamey if that's what you're worried about."

"After meeting you, I know that's true. He called you when he was in pain, so you must have been a meaningful person in his life."

She put her hand to her mouth and bit the inside surface of one finger.

I waited.

"I had a dress," she said, "an evening gown in lavender silk. One day I looked for it in my closet, and it was gone. I asked the maid about it, checked at the cleaner's. Their records showed it had been picked up, but it was nowhere to be found. I was very upset at the time, but eventually I forgot about it. Then, one night, when Dwight was out of town and I was sitting up reading in bed, I heard a car door slam and the sound of laughter from the rear of the house. There's a balcony outside my bedroom overlooking the street. I stepped out onto it and saw Dig and a young girl, which made no sense at all. He'd parked his car in the rear driveway and was sitting in it with the motor running. I could tell it was Dig because the car was a convertible with the top down—one of those little classic Thunderbirds—and the light over the garage was directly on his face. The girl was standing by the passenger door, as if she'd just gotten out. She was a cheap sort—bleached blonde, a lot of costume jewelry—and she was wearing my gown. She was taller than I am, and on her it looked like a minidress. I was furious at Jamey for stealing it and giving it to such a tawdry little tramp. It seemed such a malicious thing to do. I stood on the balcony and watched them laugh and talk, and then the girl leaned over and they kissed."

She stopped talking. In an instant she'd snatched up the cigarette she rejected earlier, jammed it into her mouth, and picked up the lighter before I could get to it. Her hands were shaking, and it took several attempts before she produced a flame. Putting the lighter down with a clatter, she sucked greedily on the cigarette, holding the smoke down in her lungs before letting it out. Behind the haze I could see that her eyes had filled with tears. She let them brim over, and the water meandered down her cheeks in leaky rivulets.

"They kissed again," she said hoarsely. "Then the girl pulled away and looked up into the light. It was at that point I saw it wasn't a girl at all. It was Jamey, in a wig, high heels, and my lavender dress. He looked grotesque, ghoulish, like something out of a bad dream. Just talking about it makes me ill."

As if to illustrate, she had a brief coughing fit. I searched for a tissue box and spied one made of cloisonné on a

small table near the piano. I pulled out a tissue and
handed it to her.

"Thank you." She sniffed, dabbing at her eyes. "This
is terrible, I thought I'd done all my crying."

I patted her wrist and told her it was all right. It was a
while before she was able to continue, and when she did,
her voice was weak.

"I sat up all that night, frightened and sickened. The
next day Jamey packed a suitcase and took it to Dig's.
After he'd left, I rushed to the guesthouse and searched
for the dress, wanting to rip it to shreds and burn it. As if
by doing so I could destroy the memory. But it wasn't
there. He'd taken it with him. As part of some kind of
. . . trousseau."

"Did you ever talk to him about the theft?"

"No. What would have been the point?"

I had no answer for that.

"When did this happen?" I asked.

"More than a year ago."

Before the Lavender Slashings started.

She read my mind.

"A while later the murders began. I never made any
connection. But when they picked him up at Dig's house
and I found out what they were charging him with, it hit
me like a blow. The thought of my dress being used that
way—"

Her words trailed off, and she put the cigarette in the
ashtray without killing it.

"Horace says the transvestism could add to the picture
of severe mental disturbance. He also thought the fact
that the dress had been taken to Dig's was important:
That it would show the killings had taken place there and
that Dig was the mastermind. But he wanted to hear
what you had to say."

All that seemed to pale beside one essential fact: She'd
produced another bit of evidence linking Jamey—and, by
association, Chancellor—to the Lavender Slashings. Souza's
logic was starting to baffle me.

"Was I wrong to bring it up, Doctor?"

"No, but for the time being I wouldn't go any further
with it."

"I was hoping you'd say that," she said, relieved.

I put away my notepad and stood. We exchanged

pleasantries and began walking out of the room. She'd composed herself and was once more the gracious hostess. On the way out I again noticed the carvings on the mantel and went over to take a closer look. Hefting one of the heads—a half-frog, half-human visage topped by some kind of plumed helmet—I examined it. Dense and stolid, crudely fashioned yet powerful, emitting a powerful sense of timelessness.

"Mexican?"

"Central American."

"Did you pick it up while doing field work?"

She was amused.

"What gave you the idea I'd ever done field work?"

"Mr. Souza told me you were an anthropologist. And your Spanish is excellent. I played detective and guessed you'd studied a Hispanic culture."

"Horace was exaggerating. After I graduated, I took a master's degree in anthropology because I didn't know what else to do with myself."

"Cultural or physical?"

"A little of both. When I met Dwight, all that fell by the wayside. Without regrets. Making a home is what I really want to do."

I sensed that she was asking for validation.

"It's an important job," I said.

"I'm glad somebody recognizes that. The home is everything. Most of the kids at the center had no home life. If they had, they would never have gotten into trouble."

She made the pronouncement with a false bravado born of despair. The irony seemed to elude her. I kept my thoughts to myself and smiled empathetically.

"No," she said, looking up at the carving in my hand. "I got these when I was a little girl. My father was in the Foreign Service in Latin America, and I grew up there. Until I was twelve, I was totally bilingual. It may sound fluent, but actually my Spanish is pretty rusty."

I replaced the stone on the mantel.

"Why don't you use the side door again? Those vultures are still out there."

We retraced my entrance and walked through the kitchen. The heavy-set guard was sitting at the table reading the *Enquirer*. When he saw Heather he stood and said, "Ma'am." She ignored him and walked me to the door. Up close she smelled of soap and water. We shook hands, and I thanked her for her time.

"Thank you, Doctor. And please excuse my loss of control. You know"—she smiled, placing one hand on a narrow hip—"I was really dreading your visit, but I actually feel better, having spoken to you."

"I'm glad."

"Much better actually. Was it useful in terms of helping Jamey?"

"Sure," I lied. "Everything I learn helps."

"Good." She stepped closer, as if sharing a secret. "We know he's done terrible things and shouldn't be walking the streets. But we want him placed where he'll be safe and cared for. Please, Dr. Delaware, help us get him there."

I smiled, mumbled something that could have been mistaken for agreement, and took my leave.

16

I GOT home at seven and picked up a message from Sarita Flowers that had come in two hours before: If I still wanted to, I could meet with the Project 160 subjects at eight the next morning. Please confirm. I called the psych department message center and did so. Robin arrived at seven-forty, and we threw together a dinner of leftovers. Afterward we took a basket of fruit out to the terrace and munched while looking at the stars. One thing led to another, and we got into bed early.

I was up at six the next morning and walked toward the campus an hour later. A flock of pigeons had massed on the steps of the psychology building. They clucked and pecked and soiled the cement, blissfully unaware of the dangers within: basement labs filled with cellblocks of Skinner boxes. The ultimate pigeon penitentiary.

The door to Sarita's office was locked. Karen heard my knock and emerged from around a corner, gliding like an Ibo princess. She frowned and handed me two pieces of paper stapled together.

"You won't be needing Dr. Flowers, will you?"

"No. Just the students."

"Good. 'Cause she's tied up with data."

We took the elevator two flights up to the group room. She unlocked the door, turned on her heel, and left.

I looked around. In five years the place hadn't changed: the same bilious green walls encrusted with posters and cartoons; the identical sagging thrift-shop sofas and plastic-veneered tables. Two high, dust-clouded windows embedded with wire dominated one wall. Through them, I knew, would be a view of the loading dock of the chemistry building, the swatch of oily asphalt where I'd handed Jamey his shoes and let him expel me from his life.

I took a seat on one of the sofas and examined the

stapled papers. With characteristic thoroughness, Sarita had prepared a typed summary of her charges' accomplishments.

MEMO

To: A. Delaware, Ph.D.
From: S. Flowers, Ph.D., Director
Subject: ACHIEVEMENT STATUS OF PROJECT 160 SUBJECTS

Preface: As you know, Alex, six children between the ages of ten and fourteen were accepted for the project in the fall of 1982. All except Jamey participated until the summer of 1986, when Gary Yamaguchi dropped out to pursue a career as an artist. At that time Gary was eighteen and had completed three years of study toward a B.A. in psychology at UCLA. His last evaluation revealed a Stanford-Binet IQ score of 167 and verbal/quantitative skills at the postdoctoral level. Efforts to reach him regarding participation in today's meeting were unsuccessful. He has no phone and did not respond to a postcard mailed to his last known address.

You'll be talking to the following subjects:

1. Felicia Blocker: She is now fifteen years old, a senior at UCLA, and due to receive a B.A. in mathematics at the end of this year. She has been accepted into Ph.D. programs at numerous universities and is leaning toward Princeton. She received the Hawley-Deckman Prize for undergraduate achievement in mathematics last year. Most current Stanford Binet IQ score: 188. Verbal skills at the postdoctoral level: quantitative skills beyond any known rating scale.

2. David Krohnglass: He is now nineteen years old and has earned a B.S. in physics and an M.S. in physical chemistry from Cal. Tech. He was among the top ten scorers, nationally, on the M-CAT test for admission to medical school. He plans to enter a

joint M.D.-Ph.D. program at the University of Chicago next fall. Most current SB IQ score: 177. Verbal skills at the postdoctoral level: quantitative skills beyond any known rating scale.

3. Jennifer Leavitt: She is now seventeen years old and a first-year graduate student in psychobiology at UCLA. She has published three scientific papers in peer-review journals, two as sole author. She is considering attending medical school after receiving her Ph.D. and expresses a strong interest in psychiatry. Most current SB IQ score: 169. Verbal and quantitative skills at the postdoctoral level.

4. Joshua Marciano: He is now eighteen years old and a senior at UCLA, due to receive joint B.A.'s in Russian and political science. He has created a computer program that conducts simultaneous trend analyses of longitudinal changes in economics, world health, and international relations and is negotiating for its sale to the World Bank. He has been accepted into numerous graduate programs and plans to take a year off to intern at the State Department before beginning graduate studies at the Kennedy School of International Relations at Harvard, where he will pursue a Ph.D. and, subsequently, a degree in law. Most current SB IQ score: 171. Verbal and quantitative skills at the postdoctoral level.

An impressive synopsis, worthy of a grant application and, considering the purpose of my visit, gratuitously detailed, even for Sarita. But the memo's true message insinuated itself between the lines: *Jamey was a fluke, Alex. Look at what I've done with the rest of them.*

The door swung open, and two young men came in.

David, whom I remembered as undersized and soft, had turned into a linebacker—six-three, about two thirty, most of it muscle. His ginger hair was styled in a new-wave crew cut—cropped short on top with a long sunburst fringe at the nape of the neck—and he'd produced sufficient blond fuzz to constitute a droopy mustache and chin beard. He wore rimless round glasses, baggy khaki pants, black running shoes with Day-Glo green trim, a stingily collared plaid shirt open at the neck, and a ribbon of leather tie that ended several inches above his belt. His hand gripped mine like a vapor lock.

"Hello, Dr. D."

Josh had grown to lanky middle size, the teen-idol cuteness solidifying to masculine good looks: shiny black curls trimmed in a neat cap, a valance of heavy lash over large hazel eyes, chin square, strong, and perfectly cleft, skin seemingly poreless. He was dressed mainline preppy: cuffed flannel trousers, dirty bucks, button-down shirt collar peeking out over a maroon crew-neck sweater. I remembered him as one of those fortunate creatures blessed with looks, brains, and charm, and seemingly devoid of self-doubt, but this morning he looked tense.

He forced a smile and said, "It's great to see you again." The smile faded. "Too bad it has to be under these circumstances."

David nodded in agreement. "Incomprehensible."

I asked them to sit, and they slumped down across from me.

"It is incomprehensible," I said. "I'm hoping you guys can help me make some sense of it."

Josh frowned. "When Dr. Flowers told us you wanted to meet with us to learn more about Jamey, we realized how little *we* knew about him, how much he'd chosen to distance himself from the group."

"It went beyond distancing," said David, sinking lower and stretching his legs. "He excluded us. Made it very clear that he had no use for human beings in general and us in specific." He stroked his mustache and frowned. "Which doesn't mean we don't want to help him, just that we're probably a poor source of information."

"The only one he ever talked to was Gary," said Josh, "and even that was rare."

"Too bad Gary won't be here," I said.

"He's been gone for a while," said David.

"Any idea where I could find him?"

They exchanged uncomfortable looks.

"He moved out of his parents' house last summer. Last we heard he was drifting around downtown."

"Dr. Flowers said he developed an interest in art. That's a switch, isn't it?"

"You wouldn't recognize him," said Josh.

I remembered Gary as a neat, quiet Sansei boy, a perfectionist with a passion for engineering and urban planning. His hobby had been constructing meticulously designed megacommunities, and Sarita's private nickname for him had been Little Bucky Fuller. I wondered what changes time had wrought, but before I could ask about it, the door opened and a short, frizzy-haired girl stepped into the room. She held a large cloth purse in one hand and a sweater in the other and seemed confused. Hesitating, she stared at her feet, then selfconsciously began walking toward me. I got up and met her halfway.

"Hi, Dr. Delaware," she said shyly.

"Hi, Felicia. How have you been?"

"I've been fine," she singsonged. "How have you been?"

"Just fine. Thanks for coming."

I realized that I'd lowered my voice and was talking especially gently, as if to a fearful child, which was exactly what she looked like.

She sat off to the side, away from the boys. Swinging her purse onto her lap, she scratched her chin and examined her shoes. Then she started to fidget.

She was the project's youngest and most precocious subject and the only one who resembled the stereotype of genius. Small, dreamy-eyed, and timorous, she inhabited an ethereal world of numerical abstractions. Unlike Josh and David, she'd changed little. There'd been a smidgen of growth—to five feet perhaps—and some evidence of physical maturity—a pair of hopeful buds asserting themselves beneath the white cotton of her blouse, a forehead grained with patches of pimples. But otherwise she still looked childlike, the pale face broad and innocent, the pug nose saddling thick-lensed glasses that made her eyes seem miles away. Her crinkly brown hair was devoid of style and tied in a loose ponytail, her short limbs padded with lingering layers of babyfat. I wondered which would arrive first, her Ph.D. or the completion of puberty.

I tried to make eye contact, but she'd already taken out a spiral notebook and buried her nose in it. Like Jamey, she was a loner, but whereas his detachment had been born of anger and bitterness, hers was the product of constant mental activity. She was sweet-tempered and eager to please, and though her efforts to be social were generally aborted by a tendency to drift into flights of theoretical fancy, she wanted desperately to relate.

"We were just talking about Gary," I said.

She looked up, as if thinking of something to say, then returned to her book. The boys began talking to each other in low tones.

I looked at my watch. Ten after eight.

"We'll wait a few more minutes for Jennifer and then begin."

Josh excused himself to make a phone call, and David stood and began circling the room, snapping his fingers and humming off-key. A minute later Jennifer arrived, breathless and apologetic.

"Hi, Alex!" she said, bouncing over and planting a kiss on my cheek.

"Hello, Jen."

She stepped back, sized me up, and said:

"You look exactly the same!"

"You don't." I smiled.

She'd cut her long hair in a boyish bob and lightened it from dishwater to tawny gold. Heavy plastic pendants drooped from her ears, framing a high-cheeked gamin face. She wore a loose-fitting sky blue top, fashioned like a serape and cut off-center to reveal one bare shoulder. Below the top was a snug denim miniskirt that exposed long, slender legs tapering to stack-heeled plastic sandals. Her half-inch fingernails were glossy pink, with toenails to match; her skin was the color of heavily creamed coffee. At first glance, just another trend-chasing California mall bunny.

"I should hope not," she said, and sat down on a folding chair. "Well," she said, looking around the room, "at least I'm not the last one here."

"Think again." David grinned, and he went to fetch Josh.

"Sorry," she said, feigning a cringe. "I was grading papers and got stuck with one that was illegible."

"Don't worry about it."

The boys returned. Fusillades of nervous banter shot back and forth across the room, followed by silence. I looked out at four young, solemn faces and began.

"It's great to see all of you again. Dr. Flowers gave me a rundown on what you've been doing, and it's impressive."

Obligatory smiles. *Get down to business, Alex.*

"I'm here because I've been asked to participate in Jamey's defense, and part of my job is to collect information about his mental status. You're the people he spent his days with for four out of the last five years, and I thought you might remember something that could shed some light on his breakdown. But before we get into that, let me say that I know all this has to be very upsetting for you. So if anyone wants to talk about that, please feel free."

The silence continued. Surprisingly Felicia was the one to break it:

"I think it's obvious," she said, speaking in a near-whisper, "that we're all extremely upset by what's happened—on multiple levels. We empathize and sympathize with Jamey, but at the same time the fact that we spent four years with him is frightening. Were we in danger during any of that time? Could some precaution have been taken to prevent what happened? Is there anything that we, as his peers, might have done? And finally, a more egocentric issue: His crimes have raised the risk of adverse publicity for the project and threaten to disrupt our lives. I don't know about the rest of you, but I've been constantly harassed by reporters."

Josh shook his head.

"My home number's unlisted."

"So's mine," said Jennifer. "A couple of calls came in to Dr. Austerlitz's lab, but he told them I was out of the country."

"I'm in the book, and they were on my case for three days running," said David. "Mostly tabloids, very low-level stuff. Saying no had little effect—they kept calling back—so I started answering them in Latin, and that did the trick." To Felicia: "Try it next time."

She giggled nervously.

"You summed things up beautifully," I told her. "We can discuss any or all of the points you raised. Any preferences?"

Shrugs and downward glances. But I wasn't willing to let it go that easily.

They were geniuses but adolescents nevertheless, caught up in all the narcissism and fantasies of immortality that came with that territory. Time and time again they'd been reminded of their mental gifts, told they could handle anything life dished out. Now something had happened that had shattered their omnipotence. It had to be traumatic.

"Well, then," I said. "I'll start with this one: Do any of you feel you could have done something to prevent what happened to Jamey, and if so, are you feeling guilty about it?"

"It's not guilt exactly," said Jennifer, "but I do wonder if I could have done more."

"In what way?"

"I don't know. I'm sure I was the first to notice something was wrong. Perhaps I could have acted sooner to get him help."

No one contradicted her.

"He always fascinated me," she explained, "because he was so wrapped up in himself, apparently independent of input from other people yet so obviously unhappy at the core. The few times I tried to talk to him he rebuffed me, really rudely. At first I was hurt, but then I wanted to understand him. So I went searching in the abnormal psych books for something that fit his behavioral patterns. Schizoid personality seemed to be perfect. Schizoids are incapable of establishing relationships, but it doesn't bother them. They're human islands. The early psychoanalysts considered them preschizophrenic, and though later research showed that most of them don't become psychotic, they're still considered vulnerable." She stopped, embarrassed. "You don't need to hear this from me."

"Please go on."

Hesitation.

"Really, Jen."

"Okay. Anyway, I found myself observing him, searching for signs of psychosis but not really expecting to find them. So when he actually began to exhibit symptoms, it shocked me."

"When was this?"

"Several months before Dr. Flowers asked him to leave. There was a period before then when he seemed more withdrawn than usual—which I've since learned can be a prepsychotic pattern—but the first time I actually saw him do anything overtly bizarre was around three or four months before he left. On a Tuesday. I'm sure of that because Tuesday was my free day and I was studying in the reading room. It was late afternoon, and I was the only one there. He came in, went to a corner, faced the wall, and started muttering to himself. Then the muttering grew louder, and I could tell he was being paranoid, carrying on an argument with someone who wasn't there."

"Do you remember what he said?"

"He was upset at this imaginary person, accusing him—or her—of trying to hurt him, of spreading bloody plumes. At first I thought he'd said 'fumes' but then he used the word again several times. Plumes. He repeated the word *stink* a lot, too, used it as a noun: The imaginary person was full of stink; the earth was full of stink. It was fascinating, and I wanted to stay and listen; but he scared me, so I got out of there. He didn't acknowledge my leaving. I don't think he'd been aware of my presence in the first place."

"Was there anything in the hallucinations about zombies or glass canyons?"

She drummed her fingers on her knees and grew pensive. "'Glass canyons' sounds familiar." She thought awhile longer. "Yes, definitely. I remember thinking, then, that it sounded more like poetry than a hallucination. Almost pristine. Which is probably why it didn't register at first. How did you know that, Alex?"

"He called me the night he escaped. He was hallucinating and using phrases identical to the ones you just mentioned. One of the things he talked about was a glass canyon that he needed to escape. The other day I visited him in jail and he said 'glass' several times."

"How did he look?" asked Josh.

"Not good," I said.

"So it sounds," said Jennifer, "as if there's some consistency to the hallucinatory content."

"Some."

"Couldn't that indicate that the hallucinations had something to do with a major crisis or conflict?"

Not according to Guy Mainwaring, M.D.

"It's possible," I said. "Do any of you know about some event in his life that would relate to plumes or stink?"

Nothing.

"What about zombies or glass canyons?"

They shook their heads.

"I did see him talking to himself," said Felicia, "but I never got close enough to hear what he was saying. He frightened me, so whenever I saw him coming, I left immediately. One time I did notice that he was crying." She hugged herself and stared at her lap.

"Did either of you mention any of this to Dr. Flowers?" I asked.

"Not right away," said Jennifer. "That's what bothers me; I should have. But when I saw him two days later, he seemed more normal. He even said hello. So I thought it might have been a one-time thing, maybe a drug reaction. But a few days later he was doing it again—hallucinating and getting agitated. At that point I went straight to Sarita's office, but she was out of town. I didn't know who to call—I didn't want to get him in trouble—so I waited until after the weekend and told her. She thanked me and said she was aware he was having problems and I should stay away from him. I wanted to discuss it with her, but she dismissed me, which seemed pretty cold at the time. Later I realized it was because of confidentiality."

"I was going to tell her, but I didn't," said Felicia, fighting back tears. "I was terrified of what he might do if he found out."

"I noticed him talking to himself, too," said Josh. "Several times. I knew something was wrong, and I realize now that I should have said something, but he was already in trouble for not registering for classes, and I thought it might make matters worse for him." He paused and broke eye contact. "I know in retrospect it sounds like a plus four cop-out, but that was my reasoning at the time."

"My turn," said David. "I never saw a damned thing, he always gave me the creeps. Viscerally. So I went out of my way to avoid him. The first thing I noticed was when he freaked out in group."

"That was horrible," said Jennifer, and the others nodded in agreement. "The way he screamed and got all flushed, the look in his eyes. We shouldn't have let it get that far."

The atmosphere in the room turned gloomy. I chose

my words carefully, knowing a successful approach would have to appeal to their intellects as well as their emotions.

"Virtually everyone I've spoken to about this case is consumed with guilt," I said, "without justification. A human being deteriorated, and no one knows why. From a scientific point of view, psychosis is still a giant, tragic black hole and nothing makes people feel more helpless than an unsolved tragedy. We all want to feel in control of our destinies, and when events occur that rob us of that feeling of control, we seek answers, search for meaning—punishing ourselves with I-should-haves and I-could-haves. The fact is, nothing you did or didn't do caused Jamey to go crazy. Nor did it matter if you told Dr. Flowers or not because schizophrenia doesn't work that way." And I repeated the reassurance I'd given Heather Cadmus the day before.

They listened and digested, four superb data-processing systems.

"Okay," said David. "That makes sense."

"I understand what you're saying, but I don't feel any better," said Felicia. "I suppose it will take a while to integrate the information emotionally."

"Can we go on to something else?" asked Jennifer, inspecting her nails.

No one disagreed, so I said sure.

"This has been on my mind for a while," she said. "After he was arrested, I went into the library and read everything I could on serial killers. It's a surprisingly thin literature, but everything I found indicated that those types of murder are carried out by sadistic sociopaths, not schizophrenics. I know some authorities believe sociopaths are really thinly veiled psychotics—Cleckley wrote that they wore a mask of sanity—but they don't usually decompensate and turn psychotic, do they?"

"Not usually."

"So it doesn't make sense, does it?"

"Maybe he committed the murders before he decompensated," suggested Josh.

"No way," she said. "The killings started about half a year after he left the project, and he was pretty far gone by then. And the last two occurred after he escaped from the mental hospital. Unless, of course, he had some kind of remission." She turned to me for an answer.

"He did present a pattern of relapse and remission," I said. "You described some of that: acting paranoid and disoriented one day and being able to say hello two days later. But your point about psychopaths' rarely, if ever, turning into psychotics is a good one. I never observed anything sadistic or psychopathic in his nature, nor has anyone I've spoken to so far. Have any of you?"

"No," said Josh. "He was antisocial and rude, but there was nothing cruel about him. If anything, his conscience was overdeveloped."

"Why do you say that?"

"Because after he said or did something unpleasant, he always brooded. He wouldn't apologize, but you could tell he was upset."

"He didn't like himself very much," said Felicia. "He seemed burdened by life."

While the boys nodded assent, Jennifer squirmed impatiently.

"Let's get back on track," she said. "It seems obvious that there's a significant discrepancy between his diagnosis and what he's accused of doing. Has anyone seriously looked into the possibility that he didn't do the slashings? Or is it just one of those cases where they pick a scapegoat and perseverate?"

Her face had filled with indignation. And hope that I regretted having to snuff out.

"Despite the contradictions, Jen, the evidence strongly indicates he was involved in the murders."

"But the—"

"I don't see any contradiction at all," said David. "Try this hypothetical on for size: He was psychotic, and his boyfriend, Chancellor, was a psychopath who manipulated him into killing people. Presto, there goes your discrepancy."

I sat up straighter.

"What led you to that?"

"No brilliant deduction." He shrugged. "The guy used to come by and pick Jamey up. Flagrantly weird—but he had a lot of influence on Jamey."

"Weird in what way?"

"Physically and behaviorally. He was big—pumped up like Schwartzenegger—and he dressed like a banker, but his hair was permed and dyed blond, he wore mascara and pancake make-up, and he smelled and moved like a woman."

"What you're saying," interjected Jennifer, "is that he was gay. Big deal."

"No," David insisted. "Gay is one thing. This was more than that. He was . . . conspicuous about it. Theatrical. Calculating. I can't put my finger on why, but he seemed like someone who'd enjoy manipulating others." He paused and looked at me. "Does that make sense?"

"Sure. Why do you think he was a major influence on Jamey?"

"It was obvious to anyone who saw them together that there was major hero worship in progress. Jamey had no use for people. Hell, he elevated skulking to a fine art. But the moment Chancellor walked in the door, he'd light up and start to chatter like a rhesus."

"It's true," said Josh. "The change was remarkable. And after Jamey met him, he shifted his whole intellectual orientation. From poetry to business and economics, like that." He snapped his fingers.

"Chancellor even had him doing research for him," added David, "poring over books he never would have gone near before."

"What kind of books?"

"Econ, I guess. I never looked closely. That stuff bores me, too."

"I came across him one time in the stacks of the business library," said Josh. "When he noticed me, he closed his books and told me he was busy. But I saw that he'd been compiling charts and columns. It looked as if he'd been researching security ratings—stocks and bonds."

"Mind-numbing." David smiled. "If Chancellor could get him to do that, homicide would be a cinch."

"That's really tacky," snapped Jennifer. The bearded boy gave an aw-shucks look and shrugged.

"What do you think of David's theory, Jen?" I asked.

"It makes sense, I guess," she said unenthusiastically. "Conceptually it could fit."

I waited for her to say more. When she didn't, I went on.

"A few minutes ago you mentioned thinking he might be having a drug reaction. What kind of stuff was he into?"

A chilly draft of silence blew into the room. I smiled.

"I'm not interested in your private lives, people."

"Our private lives aren't the issue," said Josh. "This involves someone who isn't here."

That took a moment to assimilate.

"Gary got into dope?" I asked.

"I said before you wouldn't recognize him."

"He went through a lot of changes last summer," said Jennifer. "It's a sensitive topic around here."

"Why's that?"

David laughed cynically. "The word's come down from on high that any discussion of Mr. Yamaguchi is bad PR. A two out of six freak-out rate doesn't bode well for grant renewal."

"I'm not interested in PR either," I said. "Or in hassling Gary. But if he got Jamey into dope, I need to know about it."

"We have no proof," said Josh.

"Educated guesses will suffice."

"I'll give you mine," said Jennifer. "When Gary decided to stop being a good little boy, he got heavily into dope—speed, acid, coke, downers, ludes. He spent most of last year blitzed. It was the first time in his life he'd ever rebelled, and he went overboard, just like a new convert; each time he got stoned it was a cosmic revelation, everyone else just had to try it. Jamey didn't have any friends, but Gary was the nearest approximation. Both of them were outsiders, and when they weren't insulting each other, they liked to huddle in the corner and sneer at the rest of us. It stands to reason that Gary got Jamey on something."

Josh looked uncomfortable.

"What is it?" I asked.

"I saw something indicating they were closer than that. Once when Chancellor picked Jamey up at the library, Gary showed up, too, and left with them. The next day I overheard him teasing Jamey about being Chancellor's little harem boy."

"Is Gary gay?" I asked him.

"I never thought so, but who knows?"

"How did Jamey react to being ridiculed?"

"He just got this spacey, disoriented look in his eyes and said nothing."

"I need to talk to Gary," I said. "Where can I find him?"

This time the response was more forthright.

"I saw him a couple of months ago," said David. "Peddling grass on North Campus. He'd gone punk and was very hostile, bragging about how free he was while the rest of us slaved for Dr. Flowers. He said he was living in a loft downtown with a bunch of other artists and due to have an exhibit at one of the galleries."

"What kind of art was he into?"

Shrugs all around.

"We never saw any of it," said David. "Probably of the emperor's clothing genre."

"Alex," said Jennifer, "are you saying drugs might have had something to do with Jamey's breakdown?"

"No. At this point I don't know enough to say anything."

It was a blatant hedge, and it didn't satisfy her. Nevertheless, she didn't push it. Soon after, I ended the meeting and thanked them for their time. Felicia and the boys left quickly, but Jennifer lagged behind, taking out an emery board and making a show of filing her nails.

"What is it, Jen?"

She put down the board and looked up.

"None of it makes sense. Conceptually."

"What's bothering you specifically?"

"The whole notion of Jamey as a serial killer. I didn't like him, and I know he had serious problems; but he just doesn't fit the profile."

The human animal has a perverse way of resisting attempts to fit it into neat, predictive packages like psychological profiles. I didn't tell her that; a few more years of study, and she'd learn it on her own. But the questions she'd raised during the discussion went beyond theorization and dovetailed with my own.

"So you don't like David's scenario?"

She shook her head, and the plastic earrings swung pendulously.

"That he was manipulated by Chancellor? No. Jamey may have looked up to Chancellor, but he was an individualist, not one to be programmed. I just can't see him as a pawn."

"What if psychosis weakened that individuality and made him more vulnerable?"

"Psychopaths prey on weak-willed, low self-esteem types with personality disorders, don't they? Not schizophrenics. If Jamey was psychotic, he'd be too unpredictable to program, wouldn't he?"

She was brilliant and single-minded, her questions fueled by youthful outrage.

"You're raising good points," I told her. "I wish I could answer them."

"Oh, no," she said. "I don't expect you to. Psych's too imprecise a science to come up with pat answers."

"Does that bother you?"

"*Bother* me? It's what *intrigues* me about it."

Karen saw me walking toward Sarita's office and came forward, indignant, her body language combative.

"I thought you said you wouldn't be needing her."

"A few things came up. It won't take long."

"Perhaps I can help you with them."

"Thanks, but no. I need to talk with her directly."

Her nostrils flared, and her full lips tightened. I moved toward the office door, but she'd blocked the way with her body. Then, after the merest instant of silent hostility, she slid away gracefully, turned, and marched off. A casual observer wouldn't have noticed a thing.

My knock was greeted by the squealing and scraping of rubber wheels on vinyl, then the outward swing of the door. Sarita waited until I'd entered, then closed it herself. Palming backward, she stopped at the desk-table, which was stacked high with computer printouts.

"Good morning, Alex. Was the meeting helpful?"

"They're insightful kids."

"Aren't they?" She smiled maternally. "They've developed so beautifully. Magnificent specimens."

"It must give you great satisfaction."

"It does."

The phone rang. She picked it up, said yes and uh-huh several times, and put it down, smiling.

"That was Karen letting me know she told you I was busy but you bullied your way in here anyway."

"Pretty protective, isn't she?"

"Loyal. Which is conspicuously rare nowadays." She swung the chair around. "Actually she's a remarkable young woman. Very bright but grew up in Watts, dropped out of school when she was eleven, ran away, and lived on the streets for five years doing things you and I never dreamed of. When she was sixteen, she pulled herself together, went back to night school, and earned a high school diploma in three years. Then she read an article about the project, thought it might be an opportunity to get more education, and showed up one morning, asking to be tested. Her story was fascinating, and she did seem sharp, so I went along with it. She tested high—in the one-forties—but not, of course, sufficiently high to qualify. Nevertheless, she was too good to let go, so I hired her as a research assistant and got her enrolled here as a part-time student. She's pulling a three-point-eight and wants to go to law school at Boalt or Harvard. I have no doubt she'll make it." She smiled again and brushed nonexistent lint from her lapel. "Now, then, what can I do for you?"

"I want to get in touch with Gary Yamaguchi, and I need his latest address."

Her smiled died.

"I'll give it to you, but it won't help. He's been drifting for the past six months."

"I know. I'll give it my best shot."

"Fine," she said coldly. After swiveling sharply, she yanked open a file cabinet and drew out a folder. "Here. Copy this down."

I pulled out my notepad. Before it was open, she hurriedly recited an address on Pico near Grand, just west of downtown—a murky, downscale neighborhood that catered to illegal aliens and street people with a menu of rotting slums, sewing shops, and shabby bars. During the last year a few artists and would-be artists had illegally established living quarters in industrial lofts, trying to create SoHo West. So far L.A. wasn't buying it.

"Thanks."

"What do you expect to get from talking to him?" she demanded.

"Just trying to establish as complete a data base as possible."

"Well, you won't get very far by utilizing—"

The phone rang again. She snatched it up and said, "Yes!" sharply. As she listened to the reply, annoyance surrendered to surprise, which rapidly swelled to shock.

"Oh, no. That's terrible. When—yes, he's right here. Yes, I'll tell him."

She put down the phone.

"That was Souza, calling from the jail. Jamey tried to kill himself early this morning, and he wants you to come as soon as you can."

I jumped to my feet and put away my notepad.

"How badly is he hurt?"

"He's alive. That's all I know."

She wheeled toward me and started to say something apologetic and conciliatory, but I was moving too fast to hear it.

17

HE'D BEEN moved to one of the inpatient rooms that Montez had shown me during my tour of the jail. Three deputies, one of them Sonnenschein, stood guard outside the door. I looked through the window in the door and saw him lying face up on the bed, head swaddled in bloodstained bandages, spidery limbs restrained by padded cuffs. An IV line dripped into the crook of one arm. In the midst of the gauzy turban was a fleshy patch—a few square inches of face, battered and swollen. He was asleep or unconscious, purpled lids closed, cracked lips parted lifelessly.

Souza stood next to a short, bearded man in his early thirties. The lawyer wore a gun-metal-colored suit of raw silk that reminded me of armor. When he saw me, he walked forward and said, angrily:

"He threw himself repeatedly and forcefully against the wall of his cell." He glared at the deputies, who responded with stony looks of their own. "There are no broken bones or apparent internal injuries, but his head absorbed most of the damage, and Dr. Platt here suspects a concussion. He'll be moving him to County Hospital any minute."

Platt said nothing. He wore a rumpled white coat over jeans and a work shirt and carried a black leather bag. Clipped to his lapel was a county badge identifying him as an attending neurologist. I asked him how bad it looked.

"Hard to tell," he said softly. "Especially with the psychotic overlay. I came over on a stat call, and I don't have much in the way of instruments. His reflexes look okay, but with head injuries you never know what can happen. We'll be observing him over the next few days, and hopefully we'll have a clearer picture then."

I looked through the window again. Jamey hadn't moved.

"So much for security," said Souza, loud enough for the deputies to hear. "This puts a whole new complexion on things."

He pulled a miniature tape recorder out of his briefcase and dictated the details of the suicide attempt in a court-room voice. After walking over to the deputies, he peered at their badges and recited their names into the machine, spelling each one with exaggerated enunciation. If they were intimidated, they didn't show it.

"What's in the IV line?" I asked Platt.

"Just nutrition. He looked pretty cachectic to me, and I didn't want him dehydrating, especially if there is some internal hemorrhaging."

"Sounds as if he took quite a beating."

"Oh, yeah. He hit that wall hard."

"Nasty way to do yourself in."

"Gotta be."

"See this kind of thing a lot?"

He shook his head.

"I do mostly rehab—deep-muscle EMGs. But the doc who usually takes jail calls is out on maternity leave, so I'm filling in. She sees plenty of it, mostly PCP ODs."

"This kid never took drugs."

"So they say."

Footsteps sounded in the corridor. A pair of ambulance attendants entered with a stretcher. One of the deputies unlocked the door to the room, went in, and emerged a moment later, mouthing the word *okay*. A second deputy followed him back in. Sonnenschein remained outside, and when our eyes met, he gave a small, meaningful nod. The second deputy stuck his head out and told the attendants and Platt to come in. The attendants carried the stretcher to the threshold and, contorting, managed to get it halfway into the room. Souza moved closer to the door, glowering protectively. I followed him. After several moments of tugging and hoisting, they disconnected the IV, rolled Jamey's limp body off the bed and onto the stretcher, and reset the drip. The silence was broken by a crisp symphony of buckling and snapping.

One of them held up the IV bottle and said, "Ready when you are."

Platt nodded. "Let's roll." The other attendant and the two deputies moved forward and lifted the stretcher. Jamey's head rolled like a skiff in choppy waters.

"I'll accompany my client to the ambulance," said Souza. No one argued. To me: "I need to confer with you. Please meet me at the entrance to the jail in ten minutes."

I said I'd be there and watched them cart him away.

When we were alone, Sonnenschein raised one eyebrow and told me to come with him. He sauntered down the main corridor and led me toward a key-operated elevator. Inmates in yellow pajamas sat hunched on slatted benches, scanning us. An operatic scream echoed from around a corner. The ward smelled of vomit and disinfectant.

A turn of Sonnenschein's key, and the elevator doors rasped open. He put the car on express, and it descended to the basement. Another flick of the key held it there. He leaned against the wall of the compartment and put his hands on his hips. Staring at me, he worked hard at stiffening his moon face, concealing his uneasiness behind a veil of hostility.

"I shouldn't be opening my mouth, and if you quote me, I'll call you a liar," he said.

I nodded my understanding.

"Still want to know what he says when he freaks out?"

"Yes."

"Well, when he freaked out this morning, he was screaming about poisoned earth and bloody plumes. The rest of the time it was mostly moans and groans. Once he went on about being a wretch or something like that."

"A wretched act?"

"Maybe. Yeah. Is that important?"

"It's his term for suicide."

"Hmm." He smiled uneasily. "Then I guess he got pretty wretched this morning."

"When did he start damaging himself?"

"The screaming and yelling started around six. I went over to check, and he calmed down and looked like he was nodding off to sleep. Then, about ten minutes later,

I heard this thud—like a melon being hit with a sledge-hammer—and ran over. He was throwing himself around, whipping his head back and forth like he wanted to fling it off his shoulders, smashing it against the wall. *Thud*. The whole back of his skull was pulp. It took four of us to tie him down. A real mess."

"Is that kind of thing routine on High Power?"

"Negative. Only time you see it is in new arrivals who come in flying on something. Once they're in High Power, they stay clean. Like I told you before, there's always someone trying to look psycho, but not to the point of heavy-duty pain."

He looked troubled. I knew what was bothering him and brought it out in the open.

"Do you still think he's faking?"

After wiping his forehead with his hand, he reached for the key and turned it. The elevator gears engaged noisily and the car began its ascent.

"You wanted to know what he said, so I told you. That's as far as I go."

The elevator stopped short at ground level, and the doors opened into the gally port.

"Step forward, sir," he said, escorting me out. I did, and he backed into the elevator.

"Thanks," I said softly, looking straight ahead and barely moving my lips.

"Have a good day, sir," he said, touching his gun butt.

I turned. His face was an unmoving mask, steadily narrowed by the closing doors. I stared at him until he disappeared.

Souza was waiting outside the entrance. When he saw me, he checked his watch and said, "Come."

We walked briskly to the parking lot and descended a flight of stairs. At the bottom was the Rolls, with Antrim holding one door open. When we were settled, he closed it, got in front, and tooled silently toward the exit. The big car seemed to hover above the ground, a dark leviathan prowling a shadowy concrete reef.

"Let's have lunch," said the attorney. After that he seemed in no mood for conversation and occupied himself with consulting a series of yellow pads, then picking up the car phone, punching in a number, and barking orders in legalese through the mouthpiece.

The fashionable restaurants were to the west, penthouse affairs ringing the downtown financial district and offering cityscape views and three-martini lunches. But the Rolls headed the other way, traversing skid row and nosing into the periphery of East L.A. Antrim drove rapidly and smoothly, turning onto a rutted side street and veering sharply into a narrow parking lot shadowed by four-story warehouses. At the rear of the lot was an old Jetstream mobile home on blocks. Its corrugated sides had been whitewashed, and its roof was bedecked with ivy. Rising through the leaves was a hand-painted wooden sign featuring the legend *ROSA'S MEXICAN CUISINE* bordered by two sombreros.

Antrim stayed with the car, and Souza and I walked to the restaurant. Inside, the place was cramped and hot but clean. Along the outer wall ran six mahogany booths, three of them occupied by groups of Mexican laborers. The portholes were draped with calico pullbacks and a Dos Equis sign blinked above the door. The kitchen was open for inspection, separated from the dining area by a waist-high wooden counter. Behind it, a mustachioed fat man in T-shirt, starched apron, and blue bandanna sweated stoically over ovens, steam tables, and deep fryers. In one corner sat an equally rotund woman reading *La Opinión* behind a silver-plated register. The aroma of chilies and pork fat filled the café.

The woman saw us enter and got up quickly. She was in her seventies, with sparkling black eyes and white hair braided on top of her head.

"Mr. Ess," she said, and took both of Souza's hands.

"Hello, Rosa, Menudo today?"

"No, no, sorry, all gone. But the chicken enchilada is very nice."

We drifted to one of the empty booths. There were no menus. Souza unbuttoned his jacket and settled back.

"I'll have the albóndigas soup," he said, "two enchiladas—one chicken, one pork—a chile relleno, frijoles and rice, and a pitcher of ice water."

"Very good. And you, sir?"

"Do you have beef salad?"

"The best in town," said Souza. The woman glowed.

"Beef salad and a Carta Blanca."

She nodded approval and transmitted the order to the cook. He handed her a tray, and she brought it to the table and unloaded its contents: a plate of blue corn tortillas, lightly toasted, and a boat-shaped dish housing a slab of butter. Souza held out the plate to me and, when I declined, took a tortilla, buttered it quickly, folded it, and ate a third. He chewed rhythmically, swallowed, and took a drink of water.

"Since you're not eating," he said, "perhaps you could give me a summary of your findings."

I did so, but he seemed uninterested in the clinical details of the case. When I remarked upon it, he sighed heavily and buttered another tortilla.

"As I said before, the complexion of the case has changed. I've already begun moving aggressively for delay of trial on the basis of incompetence. What happened this morning indicates dramatically that the county cannot be trusted to ensure the boy's safety and security, and I feel a good deal more confident about securing detention in a private facility."

"Despite the notoriety of the case?"

"Fortunately for us, there's no lack of violent crime in this city, and the story has already faded from the front pages. Yesterday's *Times* ran a small piece on page twenty-seven. Today's paper carried nothing. I expect the suicide attempt will bring it back into focus for a while, but then a period of quiescence can be expected as the vultures of the fourth estate feast on new carrion."

Rosa brought the meatball soup, the ice water, and my Carta Blanca. The heat of the café had made me sweat, and the beer hit my tongue with a frigid burst. Souza swallowed a spoonful of steaming soup without apparent discomfort.

"The question is, Doctor, do you feel comfortable aiding in that strategy?"

"I haven't finished my evaluation—"

"Yes, I understand. Your thoroughness is admirable. But have you begun to form an opinion regarding competence?"

"I plan to wait until the data are in before forming any opinions."

"Hmm."

He returned his attention to his soup, sipping and savoring, emptying the bowl, and sopping up the last drops with a piece of tortilla.

The food came on heavy white Mexican china—a platter for him and a plate for me.

"Enjoy, Doctor." And he dug in.

We ate without talking, surrounded by laughter. The salad was excellent, the strips of meat tender and slightly piquant, the vegetables firm and fresh in a lemon and pepper dressing. The spice and the heat brought beads of moisture to my brow, and I felt my shirt begin to stick. Souza made his way resolutely through a mountain of refried beans, ate most of the stuffed chili, and drained the water pitcher. Rosa was quick to refill it.

When all that was left was the steam of the chili and some stray grains of rice, he pushed the plate aside. Rosa brought a plate of candied cactus chunks. I tried one and found it too rubbery. Souza nibbled at one with strong, blunt teeth, snipping off pieces until all the candy was gone. He wiped his mouth and looked straight at me.

"So you have absolutely no idea of where your evaluation will lead you?"

"No, not really. The times I've seen him, he hasn't appeared competent, but his history is one of remission and relapse, so it's impossible to know what he'll be like tomorrow."

"Tomorrow doesn't concern me. Would you sign your name today to a declaration stating that during the two occasions you attempted to interview him he wasn't competent?"

I thought about it.

"I suppose so, if the wording was sufficiently conservative."

"You may word it yourself."

"All right."

"Good, that's taken care of." He ate another candy. "Now then, as far as diminished capacity, am I correct in assuming you're choosing to opt out?"

"I was planning to evaluate further—"

"Dr. Delaware"—he smiled—"there's really no need for that anymore. If everything goes as planned—and given the outrageous negligence of the jail staff, I'm sure it will—it will be some time before he comes to trial. Though I know how ambivalent you are about the insanity defense—and wouldn't want to tax your conscience—you'll be welcome to participate in the defense at that time."

I took a long swallow of beer.

"In other words," I said, "you've found other expert witnesses who don't share my ambivalence."

He raised one eyebrow, licked a speck of sugar from his lip.

"Please don't be offended," he said lubriciously. "My obligation is to do whatever I can to help my client. When we agreed to work together, I accepted your terms, but that didn't restrict me from talking to other doctors."

"Who do you have?"

"Chapin from Harvard and Donnell from Stanford."

"Have they examined Jamey?"

"Not yet. However, from my description of the case they feel confident a dim cap will be forthcoming."

"Well, then, I guess they're your guys."

"I do want to say that I—and the Cadmus family—appreciate all you've done, therapeutically as well as evaluatively. Heather told me that talking to you lifted her spirits, and that's no mean feat, seeing what she's been through."

He called Rosa over, handed her a twenty and a ten, and told her to keep the change. She tittered gratefully and brushed his jacket with a whisk.

Back in the limousine, he reached over and patted my shoulder.

"I respect you as a man of principle, Doctor, and trust there's no ill will between us."

"Not at all." I remembered something Mal Worthy once said. "You're a warrior, and you're doing your best to win the war."

"Exactly. Thank you for seeing that." He reached into his briefcase and pulled out a large checkbook.

"How much more do I owe you?"

"Nothing. In fact, I'll be returning the first five thousand."

"Please don't do that. It will disrupt my firm's accounting schedule, but more important, it would rob our association of professionalism should it ever come under scrutiny; the court distrusts anything that's not paid for."

"Sorry. I don't feel comfortable taking it."

"Then donate it to your favorite charity."

"I have a better idea. I'll send it to you, and you donate it to your favorite charity."

"Very well," he said, the broad features constricting with anger before settling back into forced serenity.

A petty victory, but it came at the right time.

Antrim drove back to the jail. The glass partition was closed, and from the movement of his head I could tell he was listening to music. Souza saw me watching him and smiled.

"A free spirit. But the man's an excellent mechanic."

"He must be to maintain this."

"Oh, yes. This and much more."

He got on the phone again, called the office, and jotted down his messages. None was sufficiently important to merit his attention, and he instructed the secretary to pass them on to Bradford Balch.

"One more thing," he said, putting down the phone, "and I mention it as a formality only. Now that you're no longer on the case, you realize that having served as my consultant, you're forbidden to discuss it with anyone."

"I realize that," I said coldly.

"Yes, I know you do," he said, writing on a yellow pad. I made out my name amid the scrawl.

We reached the jail parking structure. The Rolls entered and cruised until coming to a stop next to my Seville.

"Well, Doctor, it's been a pleasure," said Souza, gripping my hand and squeezing it.

I smiled noncommittally.

"There's one thing I'd like to ask you, Mr. Souza."

"What's that?"

"Do you think Jamey killed all those people?"

He let go of my hand, leaned back into a sea of gray felt, and made a tent with his fingers.

"That's not a question I can answer, Dr. Delaware."

"Why's that?"

"It's simply not relevant to my role as an advocate, and even to begin to think along those lines would hamper me in the execution of my duties."

He flashed me another smile and turned away. The chauffeur came around and opened the door. I got out. Before I reached the door of my car, the limousine had vanished.

I put my attaché down and stretched. It was the first time in my life I'd ever been fired. Strangely enough, it felt damned good.

18

I DROVE out of the parking lot and reflected on my dismissal. Souza had fished me out of a sea of experts, using the twin lures of flattery and professional responsibility: I was vital to the case because of both my prior treatment of Jamey and my ostensible brilliance. Now, given the first opportunity, he'd thrown me back like some undersized hatchling, having filled his bucket with more substantive catch. I shouldn't have been surprised. We hadn't really gotten along; although we were outwardly cordial, there was an unmistakable tension between us. He was a man who thrived on manipulation, a sculptor of behavior, and I'd proved less than pliable and thus expendable. After all, he had Chapin from Harvard, Donnell from Stanford—full professors both, well published and respected. No matter that they had no problems assuring an insanity defense before examining the patient. They were the kind of expert who thrived in Souza's system.

I didn't regret leaving his team, but I rued how little I'd learned about Jamey. The case had produced far more questions than answers. The only issue that had come close to generating a consensus was his psychosis. Everyone except Sonnenschein had agreed that he was crazy, and even the deputy had relaxed his cynicism after witnessing the damage the boy had done to himself. But the crimes of which he was accused weren't those of a psychotic, as a first-year graduate student had noticed. Souza's quick answer laid the blame—not without some justification—on a dead man. In fact, both his guardians and his peers had seen Ivar Digby Chancellor as a major influence in Jamey's life. The man had steered him from sonnets to securities, from cola to sprouts. But whether that influence had extended to serial homicide was far from clear.

Upon closer inspection, not even the diagnosis of schizophrenia was free from confusion: The disease had run an atypical course, and Jamey's response to medication had been inconsistent. In addition, he'd shown some, though admittedly minor, evidence of drug use. Sarita Flowers and Heather Cadmus were certain he'd never taken dope. But the Project 160 kids thought otherwise. As far as Mainwaring was concerned, it didn't matter, and the inconsistencies could be explained by subtle brain damage. Perhaps the psychiatrist was right, but he'd never carried out a comprehensive neurological workup. And his lack of interest in anything other than dosage levels as well as his slipshod charting weakened my confidence in his judgment.

Then there was the matter of the Cadmus family history—a lineage steeped in psychopathology. Were the similarities among the declines of Antoinette, Peter, and Jamey meaningful? Had the trussing of Chancellor been a primitive attempt at symbolic patricide? Dwight Cadmus certainly merited a second interview.

There were others I wanted to talk to as well. Gary Yamaguchi and the nurses—the gushing Ms. Surtees and the caustic Mrs. Vann. The contrast between the two women was yet another rub: The private-duty nurse had described Jamey more positively than had anyone else. Yet it was she he'd attacked the night he'd bolted. Andrea Vann had viewed him as dangerously disturbed, but that hadn't stopped her from leaving the C Ward nursing station unstaffed that night. And now she'd quit.

Too many questions, not enough answers. And a battered, mad young man destined to live out his days in a nightmare world.

Souza had cut me out before I'd had a chance to look into any of it.

As I ruminated, the Seville drifted toward the Union District, not far from the address Sarita had given me for Gary.

Souza had reminded me of my ethical obligations. I couldn't discuss my findings with anyone, but that didn't stop me from evaluating further—as a free agent.

*　　*　　*

The building sat in the middle of the block, embroidered at street level with a daisy chain of dozing winos. Bottles and cans and dogshit turned my progress down the sidewalk into a spastic ballet. The doors were rusted iron, warped and dented, and set into the crumbling brick façade of the former factory like a fistula. A band of concrete striped the brick. In it was carved PELTA THREAD COMPANY, 1923. The letters were pigeon-specked and cracked. To the right of the door were two buttons. Next to each button was a slot for an address sticker. The first was unfilled; the second framed a taped-over strip of paper that read R. Bogdan. I pushed both buttons but got no response, tried the door, and found it locked. After driving around through the alley, I saw a rear entry identical to the one in the front, but it, too, was bolted. I gave up and went home.

Jamey's Canyon Oaks chart had arrived. I locked it in my desk and retrieved Souza's check. I addressed and stamped an envelope, sealed the check inside, jogged down to the nearest mailbox, and dropped it through the slot. At three-thirty the service called to deliver a message from Robin: Billy Orleans had come into town early and would be at the studio until five. After he left, we could have dinner together. I changed into jeans and a turtleneck and drove to Venice.

Robin's place is an unmarked storefront on Pacific Avenue, not far enough from the Oakwood ghetto. The exterior is covered with gang graffiti, and the windows are whitewashed over. For years she lived upstairs, in a loft she had designed and built herself, and used the main floor as a workshop. A dangerous arrangement for anyone, let alone a single woman, but it had been an assertion of independence. Now the place was alarmed and she shared my bed and I slept a lot better for it.

Both parking spaces in back of the shop were taken up by a white stretch Lincoln limo with blackened windows, gangster whitewalls, and a TV antenna on the rear deck. Three hundred hard pounds of bodyguard leaned against the side of the car—fiftyish, a sunburned bull mastiff face, sandy-gray hair, and a white toothbrush mustache. He was dressed in white drawstring pants, sandals, and a sleeveless red singlet stretched just short of bursting. The

arms folded across his chest were the color and breadth
of Virginia hams.

I coasted to a stop and looked for a place to leave the
Seville. From inside the studio came deep, pulsating waves
of sound.

"Hi, sir," said the bodyguard cheerfully, "you the shrink
friend?"

"That's me."

"I'm Jackie. They told me to be on the lookout for
you. Just leave the car here with the keys in, and I'll
watch it for you."

I thanked him and entered the shop through the rear
door. As always, the studio smelled of conifer resin and
sawdust. But the rumble of power drills and saws had
been replaced by another wall of noise: thunderous power
chords and screaming treble riffs resonating from every
beam and plank.

I walked to the rear, where the test amplifiers were
kept and saw Robin, wearing a dusty apron over her
work clothes and padded earphones half buried in her
curls, watching a gaunt man assault a silver-glitter solid-
body electric guitar shaped like a rocket ship. With each
stroke of the pick, the instrument lit up and sparkled,
and when the man pressed a button near the bridge, a
sound similar to that of a space module leaving the launch-
ing pad issued forth. The guitar was plugged into dual
Mesa Boogie amps and cranked up to maximum volume.
As the thin man ran his fingers up and down the fretboard,
it screamed and bellowed. A smoldering cigarette was
wedged between the strings just above the fretboard. The
windows shuddered, and my ears felt as if they were
about to bleed.

Robin saw me and waved. Unable to hear her, I read
her lips and made out "Hi, honey" as she came over to
greet me. The gaunt man was lost in his music, eyes
closed, and went on for a while before he noticed me.
Then his right hand rested, and the studio turned fune-
real. Robin took off the ear pads. After unplugging the
guitar, the man removed the cigarette, stuck it in his
mouth, then placed the instrument tenderly in a clasp
stand and grinned.

"Fabulous."

He was about my age, hollow-cheeked, pale, and pinch-

featured, with dyed black hair cut in a long shag. He
wore a blue-green leather vest over a sunken, hairless
chest and crimson parachute pants. A small rose tattoo
blued one bony shoulder. His shoes were high-heeled
and matched the pants. A pack of Camels extended
halfway from one of the vest pockets. He removed the
cigarette smoldering between his lips, put it out, pulled
out the pack, extricated a fresh one, and lit up.

"Billy, this is Alex Delaware. Alex, Billy Orleans."

The rocker extended a long, callused hand and smiled.
The nails of his right hand had been left long for finger
picking. A diamond was inlaid into one of his upper
incisors.

"Hello, Alex. Head doc, right? We could use you on
the road, the band's precarious mental state being what it
is."

I smiled back. "My specialty is kids."

"Like I said, we could use you on the road, the band's
blah-blah-blah." Turning to Robin: "It's fabulous, Mizz
Wonderhands. Do some fooling with the lead pickup to
get a bit more punch on the high registers, but apart from
that, perfect. When can you have it ready for takeoff?"

"How's Thursday?"

"Fine. I'm flying up to San Francisco to visit my parents and then back down here for the Friday Forum gig.
I'll send Jackie or one of the roadies to pick it up. Now
for the fun part." He unzipped one of the compartments
on the parachute pants and drew out a wad of hundred-
dollar bills.

"Filth and lucre," he said, peeling off thirty or so and
handing them to Robin. It didn't change the size of the
wad appreciably. "That do it?"

"You gave me three hundred too much," said Robin,
counting and holding out three bills.

"Keep it. Perfectionism's hard to find, and I can use
the write-off." He hefted the wad and shifted it from one
hand to another.

"Don't flash that in this neighborhood," said Robin.

He laughed and put the money away.

"It *would* be tasteless, wouldn't it?"

"I was thinking more in terms of dangerous."

"Oh. Yeah, I guess so." He shrugged. "Well, that's
why I have Jackie. He's bulletproof. Faster than a loco-

motive. Eats rivets for breakfast. I hired him after the John Lennon thing. I was nervous; lots of people were. I think he used to break legs for the Mafia or something, but all he's had to do for me so far is glare."

Robin wrote him a receipt, and we walked to the door.

"Good to meet you, Alex."

He picked up Robin's hands and kissed them.

"Keep these in good shape. In today's market visuals are everything. I'll be needing plenty more objets d'art." A diamond-lit smile. "Well, off to S.F. and a reunion with Dr. and Mrs. Ornstein."

I thought of something.

"Billy," I said, "did you grow up in San Francisco?"

"Atherton, actually," he said, naming one of the high-priced spreads just outside the city.

"Were you involved with the Haight-Ashbury scene?"

He laughed.

"When all that was going down I was a good little nerd who wanted to be an orthodontist just like Daddy. I spent the sixties memorizing biology books. Why?"

"I'm trying to find out about some people who lived in an urban commune on the Haight."

He shook his head.

"Never my scene, but I can tell you who might know. Roland Oberheim—Rolly O. He's a producer, used to play bass with Big Blue Nirvana. Remember them?"

"I think so. Sitars over a heavy backbeat?"

"Right. And pop Hinduism. They hit gold a couple of times, then got ego cancer and broke up. Rolly was one of Ken Kesey's pranksters, heavily into acid, called himself Captain Trips. He knew everyone on the Haight. Now he lives down here, doing independent gigs. I can put you in touch if you want."

"I'd appreciate that."

"Okay. I'll call him tonight and get back to you. If I forget, call me and remind me. Robin's got all my numbers."

"Will do. Thanks."

He fluffed his hair and was gone.

Robin and I looked at each other.

"Rockin' Billy Ornstein?" we said simultaneously.

The next morning I returned to the building on Pico.

This time the door was open a crack. I leaned against it and entered.

I was greeted by a flight of wide pine stairs and the aroma of pesto. At the top of the stairs were darkness and the faint muscular outlines of two Dobermans reclining, seemingly impervious to my presence.

"Hi there, fellas," I said, and went up one step. The Dobermans sprang to their feet, snarling throatily. A heavy chain ran from each of their necks to the top stairposts, too long to be of much comfort.

The dogs bared their teeth and started roaring. I couldn't say much for their tone, but the duet was full of emotion.

"Who is it? What do you want?"

The voice was loud and female, emerging from somewhere behind the Dobermans. Upon hearing it, the dogs quieted and I shouted up:

"I'm looking for Gary Yamaguchi."

A purple pear topped with grated carrots materialized between the two dogs.

"All right, honey pies, those are good boys," the pear cooed. The dogs sank submissively and licked a pair of hands. "Yes, sweeties, yes, sugar dumplings, Mama likes when you're alert."

There was a faint click, and a bare bulb crackled to life above the stairs. The pear became a young woman—early thirties, blowsily heavy, wearing a purple muumuu. Her hair was a hennaed tangle, her pale make-up laid on with a trowel. She put dimpled hands on ample hips and swayed assertively.

"What do you want with him?"

"My name is Alex Delaware. I counseled him years ago, and I need to talk to him about another one of my patients who was one of his friends."

"Counseled? You're a therapist?"

"Psychologist."

She lit up.

"I *love* psychologists. My first two husbands were psychologists. You married?"

"Yes," I lied, keeping it simple.

"No matter, you can still come up."

I hesitated, gazing up at the Dobermans.

"Don't worry"—she laughed—"they won't eat you unless I tell them to."

I trudged up warily, ankles tingling in anticipation.

The stairs ended at a large landing. To the left was a splintered door; to the right, an open doorway. From the doorway came strong wafts of basil.

"Ms. Randee Bogdan," said the woman, saluting. "With two *e*'s." We shook hands briefly. "Come on in, Dr. Alex Psychologist."

She waddled through the doorway. Inside were three thousand square feet of studio. The walls had been painted deep salmon. One of them held a linear display of sea turtle shells polished to a high gloss; the others were bare. The floor was black lacquer; the skylit ceilings were a clutter of exposed ducts painted hot pink. The furniture was eclectic, a studied mix of Deco, contemporary, and serendipity: gray Chinese vases; Lucite nesting tables; pink fainting couches piped with taupe; a high ebony armoire inlaid with abalone; a rough stone garden urn filled with silk amaryllis; lots of empty space. Apparently casual, very expensive.

Dominating the center of the studio was an enormous industrial kitchen, stainless steel and spotless. Racks of copper pots hung from an iron rail. The counters were hammered metal with insets of marble for rolling pastry. Caldrons and pans simmered on a nine-burner Wolf range. The smell of basil was almost overwhelming. Randee with two *e*'s walked into it, lifting lids and peering into the caldrons. Once or twice she sniffed and tasted, then shook a dash of something into whatever she was brewing. I picked up a pink satinized card from a stack on the corner: CATERING BY RANDEE and a Beverly Hills exchange.

"That's the answering service," she said, licking one finger. "For class. The bowels of the operation is right here, pardon my anality."

"Did Gary live next door?"

"Uh-huh," she said distractedly, looking for something on the counter, cursing cheerfully until she found it. She held it up—a piece of paper which she proceeded to read out loud: "For the Malibu soiree of Mr. and Mrs. Chester ('Chet') Lamm. Cold winter melon soup, gosling salad with raspberry vinegar, a nice sweetbread and truffles teaser, pike and crayfish quenelles, blackened chicken with ze leetle tiny pink peppercorns, the always chi-chi pasta pesto, of course, and to top it off, lightly baked goat cheese and a daring cucumber-pineapple sorbet. What a hodgepodge—pretty fucking dreadful, huh? But to the *nouvelle-nouvelle* beasties crass is class."

I laughed. She laughed back, bosoms rolling.

"You know what I'd like to be cooking? Burgers. Bur-fucking-gers. Greasy home fries, a good honest salad—no radicchio, no endives, plain old Cesar Chavez iceberg."

"Sounds good."

"Ha! Try peddling that for a hundred a head."

She jabbed a fork into a pan, and the tines came up enmeshed with pink pasta.

"Here, taste this."

I leaned over the counter and opened my mouth. The stuff was laced with basil to the point of bitterness.

"Great," I said.

"Absolutely. The lady can cook."

She offered me other samples. Even in a hungry state the experience wouldn't have been welcome. But after the hearty breakfast I'd shared with Robin it was downright assaultive.

After more false praise from me and self-congratulation from her I managed to get her talking about Gary.

"Yeah, he lived here, along with a bunch of other freaks."

"Lived?"

"That's right. Past tense. Someone broke in last night and trashed the place, and he split. Fairly typical for the neighborhood, which is why my place is alarmed. I was doing a party at A and M records, came home around one, and found their door all smashed in. My alarm hadn't been tripped, but I called my parents and borrowed Nureyev and Baryshnikov anyway. For insurance. They're real killers—last year they eliminated parenthood from a burglar's future—and I've been leaving the door open, hoping the creeps who did it will return so I can turn my sweeties loose."

"When did the . . . freaks come home?"

"About two. That's their usual schedule: sleep until noon; panhandle in front of the Biltmore; come home and party until morning. I heard them, peeked through the door, and watched them split. Your counselee looked pretty scared."

"Any idea where he went?"

"Nah. There's been a tribe of them living there free—one of the freaks' fathers owns the building—coming in and out. They wander around, putting down everything, thinking of themselves as *très* bohemian."

"Artists?"

"If they're artists, the stuff on the stove's haute cuisine. Nah, they're little kids playing nihilist. Punk stuff, you know: Life is meaningless, so I'll solder spikes in my hair and shoot speed while Daddy pays the rent. I went through the same thing in college, didn't you?"

I'd spent college studying by day and working my way through at night. Instead of answering, I asked another question.

"Were they heavily into speed?"

"I'd assume so. Isn't that what punks are into?"

She lowered the fire on one of the burners. I remembered Gary's boast to Josh and said:

"He told someone he was going to have an exhibition in one of the downtown galleries. Any idea which one?"

She put her finger to her lips and licked the tip.

"Yeah, he told me that, too. We passed on the landing one night and he insulted my food—that's the kind of little shit he is. I told him to shove his little Buddha head up his ass even if it did mean bending sideways. He liked that. Smiled and gave me a flyer for this so-called exhibit; he was one of a bunch of other freaks showing their trash at a place called Voids Will Be Voids. I said, 'Terrific, putz, but you're still just a little snotty freak to me.' He liked that, too; said something lewd." She shook her head. "Can you imagine doing it with one of those little freaks? Yucch."

I asked her how many kids had lived in the studio.

"There was him, his little girlfriend, blonde Valley Girl type, didn't look more than fourteen; Richard the Rich Kid, the landlord's boy; *his* babe, plus assorted hangers-on. The last week or so it had been only Yamaguchi and the blonde because Richard went on vacation somewhere and the hangers-on went with him. What are you expecting to get from him anyway?"

"Information."

"Don't count on it. The kid's not into helping others."

I told her she was probably right and thanked her for letting me come up.

"Do you mind if I look around his place?"

"Why should I care?"

"Could you keep Nureyev and Baryshnikov at bay while I do it?"

"Sure. They're really sweethearts anyway."

I left, and she called out after me:

"For your sake, I hope you've got nasal congestion."

Her parting shot was more than bombast. The studio smelled like an undermaintained outhouse. Most of the space was a jumble of rancid clothing, clotted food, and nasty-looking stains. The toilet was stopped up, and brownish gunk had overflowed onto the unpainted plank floor. The furniture, if you could call it that, had been knocked together from plywood and sawhorses. Whoever had broken in had upended and shattered most of it. A workbench, similarly fashioned, held an acetylene torch, an assortment of templates and molds, fish bones, a decapitated Barbie doll with the head lying off to one side, and charred chunks of plastic. One corner of the studio was devoted to six-foot piles of newspaper, sodden and mildewed, another to a collection of roach-infested cookie boxes and empty soda cans. I poked around for a few seconds, finding nothing, before the stench overtook me.

I exited to more basil, hollered a good-bye, and walked stiffly between the Dobermans. They grinned and growled but didn't move as I made my way down the stairs. Once outside, I inhaled hungrily; even the smog smelled good.

As I unlocked the Seville, a hand settled on my shoulder. I whipped around and came face-to-face with one of the winos, a black man whose tattered clothes had grimed to the point where they matched his skin. The boundaries between cloth and flesh were indistinguishable, and he resembled some naked feathered cave creature.

His eyeballs were the color of rancid butter; the irises, filmy and listless. He was anywhere between forty and eighty, toothless, stooped, and emaciated, the caved-in face coated with an iron-filing beard. His head was covered with a greasy ski cap worn over his ears. Pinned to it was one of those cute I LOVE L.A. buttons with a heart substituted for the word *love*.

Slapping his hands on his knees, he laughed. His breath

was a blend of muscatel and overripe cheese. I winced; this was the morning for olfactory torture.

"You ugly," he cackled.

"Thanks," I said, and edged away.

"No, man, you really *ugly.*"

I turned, and the hand landed on my shoulder again.

"Enough," I said, annoyed, shoving it away.

He laughed harder and did a little dance.

"You ugly! You ugly!"

I turned the doorkey. He came closer. I compressed my nostrils.

"You ugly, you ugly. You also rich."

Oh, Jesus, what a morning. I reached into my pocket and gave him whatever change I found. He examined it and smiled woozily.

"You real ugly! You real rich! I got somethin' for you if you got somethin' for me."

He was breathing on me now, showing no inclination to leave. We were ignored by the other winos, already locked in alcoholic torpor. A pair of Mexican boys walked by and laughed. He leaned closer, giggling. I could have pushed him aside, but he was too pathetic to manhandle.

"What do you want?" I asked wearily.

"You lookin' for that li'l Jap kid wit' the nails in his hay-ed, righ'?"

"How'd you know that?"

"You ugly, but you not smart." He tapped his scrawny chest. 'Mudpie heah be smart."

Ceremoniously he held out his palm, a palsied mocha slab, mapped with black lines.

"All right, Mudpie," I said, pulling out my wallet and peeling off a five, "what is it you want to tell me?"

"Sheeit," he said, snapping up the bill and secreting it among the shapeless contours of his rags, "that buy a song an' dance. You ugly an' you rich, so why don' you give Mudpie his due?"

Ten dollars and some haggling later he let it out:

"Fust you come yesterday; then you be back, sniffin' and snoopin'. But you not be the only one. There be these other whi'e boys lookin' for the Jap, too. Ugly but not li'e you. They real ugly. Whupped with a ugly stick."

"How many were there?"

"Dose."

"Dose?"

"Li'e in spic talk—*Uno, dose,* you unnerstan'?"

"Two."

"Righ'."

"When was this?"

"At nigh', mebbe the full moon, mebbe the half-moon."

"Last night?"

"Seems to be so."

"How can you be sure they were looking for the Japanese boy?"

"Mudpie be sittin' around the back, in the dark, havin' dinnah, you unnerstan', an' they walk by, be talkin' gonna get that lil slant. Then they go in and jimmy that doah and come out later sayin' 'aw, shit, aw, fuck.' "

He laughed, cleared his throat, and shot a gob of phlegm toward the boulevard.

"What did they look like?"

"Ugly." He cracked up. "Li'e two whi'e boys."

Another ten changed hands.

"One be skinny, the other be plump, you unnerstan'? They be wearin' black leathah."

"Bikers?"

He looked at me with stuporous incomprehension.

"Motorcycle riders?" I pressed. "Like Hell's Angels?"

"Seems to be."

"Were they driving motorcycles?"

"Could be." He shrugged.

"You didn't see what they were driving?"

"Mudpie be makin' himself scarce; they Nazi types, you unnerstan'?"

"Mudpie, is there anything else you remember about them—how tall they were, the way they talked?"

He nodded somberly.

"A'solutely."

"What is it?"

"They ugly."

I found a phone booth near Little Tokyo and put a call in to Milo. He was out, and I left a message. Half a phone book dangled from a chain in the booth. Fortunately it was the second half, and I found Voids Will Be Voids listed on Los Angeles Street, just south of the garment district. I called the gallery and got a taped message, an adenoidal male sneeringly informing the listener that the place didn't open until 4:00 P.M. That left six hours. I had a light sushi lunch and headed over to the main Public Library on Fifth Street. By 12:30 I was seated at the microfilm viewer, squinting and spinning dials. It took a while to get organized, but soon after that I found what I wanted.

19

THE MARRIAGE of Miss Antoincttc Hawcs Simpson of Pasadena to Colonel John Jacob Cadmus of Hancock Park had been the main feature of the July 5, 1947, *Los Angeles Times* social pages. Accompanying the rapturous description of the nuptials, which had taken place in the rosc gardcn of thc ncwlywcds' newly built "vanilla-hued manse," was a formal portrait of a storybook couple— the groom tall, heavily mustached, and square-jawed; the bride ten years younger, raven-haired, and Renoir-soft, clutching a bouquet of white tea roses and baby's-breath to a modest bosom. Among the ushers were a city councilman, a senator, and assorted scions. The best man, Major Horace A. Souza, Esq., had escorted the maid of honor, the bride's sister, Lucy, whom—the writer simpered—he'd recently squired at the Las Flores Debutante Ball.

It had been evident early on that the relationship between Souza and the Cadmus family extended beyond professionalism, a situation not uncommon for the very rich and their retainers. But nothing, until now, had suggested romantic entanglement. Souza had bristled when I'd brought up the topic, and I wondered if he'd been reacting to more than violation of privacy. Something personal, perhaps, like unrequited love.

After obtaining several more spools of microfilm, I searched for additional pieces about him and Lucy. The search led nowhere initially, with neither of them mentioned in print until a June 1948 item appeared and confirmed my hunch: the announcement of Lucy's Newport, Rhode Island, wedding to Dr. John Arbuthnot of New York City and Newport, Rhode Island.

I allowed myself a moment's satisfaction at having played armchair detective successfully, then reminded

myself that Souza's love life had nothing to do with why I
was there. There was a spirit to resurrect: that of another
Simpson girl, a shadowy, tormented figure. The donor,
according to the attorney, of whatever defective DNA
laced Jamey's chromosomes.

Backtracking, I scanned the films for anything I could
find about Antoinette. Unsurprisingly, nothing emerged
to foreshadow psychosis: a spring engagement announcement and, prior to that, the expected puffery associated
with coming-out parties, fund-raising balls, and the kind
of chaperoned altruism considered fashionable for proper
young ladies of the privileged classes.

But something unexpected did surface in a September
1946 description of a midnight yacht party that had set
out from San Pedro and floated languidly to Catalina.

The cruise had been organized to benefit wounded war
veterans, a "gay, gala affair, featuring the renowned
Continental cuisine of Chef Roman Galle of the Santa
Barbara Biltmore and the sprightly sounds of the Freddy
Martin Band." The guest list had been lifted straight out
of the L.A. blue book, and among the revelers had been
"the lovely Miss Antoinette Hawes Simpson, dancing the
night away in the arms of her admiring beau, Major
Horace A. Souza, Esq., recently home from the Euro-
pean front."

Intrigued, I kept digging and came up with three more
articles that paired the future Mrs. Cadmus with Souza.
All of them had been written during the summer of '46,
and from the reporter's breathless tone, the couple had
been a serious item: holding hands in the winner's circle
at Santa Anita; enjoying a champagne supper at the
Hollywood Bowl; weathering an August heat wave by
watching the tide roll in from the air-conditioned lounge
of the Albacore Club. But as summer faded, so, apparently, had the romance, for Antoinette was not to be
linked in print to another man until her betrothal to Jack
Cadmus, several months later.

Unrequited love, of quite another sort.

So Souza's relationship with the Cadmuses was more
tangled than I'd imagined. I wondered what had transformed him from suitor to spectator. Had there been
competition for the lady's hand, or had Jack Cadmus
simply stepped in over the embers of a dead romance?

That Souza had served as Cadmus's best man indicated the absence of rancor. But that didn't mean there'd been no joust. Perhaps his worship of John Cadmus had made the victory seem rightful; the better man truly had won. That kind of rationalization worked best within a context of low self-esteem, and the Souza I'd met seemed anything but self-effacing. Nevertheless, a lot could change over four decades, and I couldn't dismiss the possibility that once upon a time the attorney had possessed a hearty appetite for crow.

Now he'd elevated Jack Cadmus to godlike status while casting Antoinette as a pathetic misfit, biologically responsible for her grandson's psychosis and, by extension, his crimes. Was that assessment the result of a never-healed wound, or had Souza buried enough of his pain to be objective? I went around with it for a while before giving up. Any way I turned it, it sounded like ancient history, with no clear relevance to Jamey's plight.

I loaded up the viewer with spools of more recent vintage. Predictably, the society pages had nothing to say about the union of Peter Cadmus and Margaret Norton, aka Margo Sunshine. Dwight's marriage to the former Heather Palmer had, however, attracted some attention, even though the wedding had taken place in Palo Alto. The bride boasted some pedigree: her mother was a stalwart of the DAR, and her late father had been a diplomat of note, serving in Colombia, Brazil, and Panama, where the new Mrs. Cadmus had been born. Nothing I hadn't already known.

I returned the microfilms and left the library at three forty-five. Downtown traffic, always viscous at that hour, had congealed into static bands of steel. Orange-vested construction crews were ripping up the streets—some contractor had a friend at City Hall—and detour signs had been laid on the asphalt with sadistic randomness. It took forty minutes to travel the half mile to Los Angeles Street, and by the time I got there I was tense and hostile. The proper attitude, I supposed, for a confrontation with new-wave art.

Voids Will Be Voids was a one-story storefront painted a flat black that the elements had streaked watery gray. Its sign was an exercise in dysgraphia—cramped black letters over turquoise plywood windows, frosted with dirt.

The other buildings on the block were discount clothing
outlets, and the gallery appeared to have served that
same purpose before the days of artistic enlightenment.
Most of the shops were closed or closing, darkened façades
hiding behind accordion grilles. A few remained open,
luring bargain hunters with racks of downscale threads
that clogged the sidewalk. I parked the Seville in a U-pay
lot, dropped a couple of dollars into the slotted box, and
went in.

The place was a studied attempt at antiaesthetics. The
floor was filthy linoleum, sticky and peppered with discarded cigarette butts. A stale clothes-cumin odor filled
the air. The ceiling was low and sprayed with something
that looked like spoiled cottage cheese. The alleged art-
work hung haphazardly and crookedly from unpainted
drywall, lit from above by bare fluorescent tubes that
made some pieces glare reflectively while obscuring others. Cheap stereo speakers blared forth something that
sounded like a robot mating dance—synthesized squeaks
and squeals over a shifting metallic drumbeat. In the rear
right-hand corner sat a man at a school desk, doodling
and cutting newspaper. He ignored my entry.

The stuff on the walls was crude and mean-spirited. No
doubt some art critic would find it primally raw and
pulsing with vibrant youthful hostility, but to my un-
schooled eye it was just as David Krohnglass had guessed:
of the emperor's clothing genre.

Someone named Scroto had created a set of primitive
pencil drawings—stick figures and jagged lines. Develop-
mentally at the four-year level, but no four-year-old I'd
ever met had gleefully portrayed gang rape and mutilation. The pictures were drawn on cheap pulp paper so
thin that the pencil had ripped through in several places—
part of the message, no doubt—but the frames were
another story: ornate, carved gilt, museum quality.

A second collection featured sloppily done acrylic por-
traits of pinheaded men with idiotic facial expressions
and enormous penises shaped like salamis. The artist
called her/himself Sally Vador Deli and used a tiny green
pickle for the letter *l*. Next to the salami men was a
sculpture consisting of an aluminum rod taken from a
pole lamp, bedecked with paper clips and staples, and
entitled *The Work Ethic*. Beyond that hung a huge shel-

lacked collage of recipes snipped from supermarket magazines and frankly gynecologic *Hustler* centerfolds.

Gary Yamaguchi's works were at the back. He now called himself Garish, and his art consisted of a series of tableaux utilizing Barbie and Ken dolls and other assorted objects encased in amorphous rocks of clear plastic. One featured the all-American couple sitting in the body cavity of a rotted fish teeming with maggots and was titled *Let's Eat Out Tonight in Japtown: Sashimi Trashimi.* Another showed two pairs of dolls sitting, decapitated, in a red convertible, the four heads lined up neatly on the hood, a cardboard mushroom cloud filling a black crepe background. *Double Date and Heavy Petting: Hiroshima-Nagasaki.* In a third, Barbie had been given an Asian appearance—black geisha wig, slant accents around the eyes—and dressed in an aluminum foil kimono. She sat spread-legged on the edge of a bed, smoking and reading a book, oblivious of the attentions of a combat-fatigued Ken's mouth to the juncture of her plastic thighs. *Ooh, Lookie-Lookie! Kabookie Nookie!*

But it was the last and largest piece—a chunk of Lucite two feet square—that caught my attention. In it Gary had constructed a sixties teen-age bedroom scene in miniature: One-inch scraps of notepaper became lipstick-stained love letters; triangular snips of felt made football pennants; a tiny Beatles stamp served as a poster. The floor was a litter of thimble-sized pill vials, tiny photos of Barbie, and a disproportionately large cracked leather book upon which had been scrawled "Diary" in lavender grease pencil.

Amid this clutter was the centerpiece: a Ken doll hanging from a Popsicle stick rafter, a noose around its neck. Red paint had been used to simulate blood, and there was plenty of it. Someone had believed that mere hanging was too good for Ken; a toy knife jutted from the doll's abdomen. Small pink hands clutched its handle. In case anyone missed the point, a pile of bloody viscera was coiled at the corpse's feet. The intestines were fashioned from rubber tubing and glazed with something that simulated slime. The effect was disturbingly real.

The title affixed to this bit of self-expression was *Oh, Dearie, Round-Eyes Hara-Kiri: The Wretched Act.* Price tag: $150.

I turned away and walked to the man at the school desk. He had short dark hair striped maroon and electric blue on the sides, elfin ears through which safety pins had been inserted, and a hard, hungry shark face dominated by narrow, empty eyes. He was in his late twenties—too old for the teen-age rebel game—and I wondered what he'd played at before discovering that in L.A., looking bizarre could camouflage a host of bad intentions.

He drew triangles and crossed them out, continuing to ignore me.

"I'm interested in one of your artists," I said.

Grunt.

"Garish."

Snort.

"You gotta talk to the owner. I just sit here and watch the place." It was the sneering voice of the phone message.

"Who's the owner?"

"Doctor from Encino."

"When does he come in?"

An apathetic shrug punctuated by a yawn.

"Never."

"He never comes in at all?"

"No, man. This is like . . . a hobby."

Or a tax writeoff.

"I don't get down here too often," I said, "so I'd appreciate if you'd call him and say I'd like to buy one of Garish's tableaux."

He looked up, stared, and stretched. I noticed old needle marks on his arms.

"The one with the suicide scene," I continued. *"The Wretched Act.* I'd also like to talk to the artist." -

"Tableaux." He grinned. His mouth was a disaster zone, several teeth missing, the few that remained, chipped and brown. "That's *life,* man. That's *garbage.* Not any tableaux."

"Whatever. Would you make the call, please?"

"Not supposed to. He's like in surgery all the time."

"How about cash-and-carry and an extra hundred thrown in for commission?" I took out my wallet.

At that he grew sullen.

"Yeah, sure. Cash for trash." He feigned apathy, but his eyes had come alive with anticipation, and he held out a grubby hand. "You want it that bad, it's yours for two fifty."

"Talking to Garish is part of the deal. Find him for me, and we're in business."

"This is Voids," he whined, "not any freaking missing persons scam."

"Have him here by six, and the commission goes up to one fifty."

He licked his lips and tapped his pencil against the desktop.

"Think you can buy me, huh, man?"

"I'm betting on it."

"Trying to put me in your *tableau,* Mr. Suit?"

I ignored him and feigned nonchalance.

"I can find him without you," I said, "but I want to see him today. If you can arrange it, the hundred and fifty's yours."

The striped head bobbed and weaved.

"Why the freak should I know where he is?"

"You're exhibiting his stuff on consignment. If I buy the piece, you'll owe him his share. Something tells me you communicate once in a while."

He followed that with a furrowed brow. I wondered how often he sold anything.

"Get him here by six," I said. "Tell him Alex Delaware wants to buy *The Wretched Act* and talk to him."

He shook his head.

"No messages, man. I can't remember all that."

"Delaware," I said slowly, "like in the state. He knows me."

He shrugged, defeatedly, and I left knowing he'd hus tle for the money.

There was a phone booth in one corner of the parking lot. The door had been ripped off, and traffic sounds blotted out the dial tone. I covered one ear and punched in my service number. The only message of interest was a call-back from Milo.

I reached him just as he was leaving for County General Hospital.

"Heard your boy did himself up pretty good," he said.

"It was ugly. He had to have been incredibly despondent."

"Guilt can do that to you," he said, but the glibness was forced, and he softened his voice. "What's on your mind, Alex?"

I told him about the bikers breaking into Gary's loft.

"Uh-huh. And you heard this from a wino."

"He was cleverer than he looked."

"Hey, I'm not knocking it. Some of my best info's come from juiceheads." Pause. "So you're connecting it with what I told you about the Slasher victims hanging out with bikers."

"It does seem coincidental."

"Alex, this Yamaguchi kid is a punker, right?"

"Right."

"Which means ten to one he's into nasty drugs, like glue and speed. Outlaw bikers are one of the main sources of illegal speed in this state. They call it crank. You don't need much of an IQ to cook it up, which sticks it right in those scumbags' bailiwick. Yamaguchi was probably buying from them and didn't pay on time."

"He was dealing," I said.

"Even better. It was a business deal gone sour. The leather boys tend to favor violent retribution over binding arbitration."

"All right," I said, "I just thought you should know."

"You were right to call, and if you think of anything else, don't hesitate to give a toot—that is, if Souza doesn't get bent out of shape about your fraternizing with the enemy."

I considered telling him about *The Wretched Act* but knew it could be dismissed as nothing more than a pseudoartist's conception of murder, gleaned from the papers. Instead, I said:

"Souza fired me this morning."

"No use for you anymore, huh?"

"That's the general picture."

"Makes sense. The kid's gotten progressively worse since the arrest, and with the suicide attempt there's probably enough to back up a temporary incompetence order. Given sufficient shilly-shallying, the case may never come to trial."

"What kind of shilly-shallying?"

"Paper games. One delay after another."

"How long can that last?"

"Keep paying a guy like Souza, and he'll figure out how to delay sunrise. All he's got to do is keep the kid out of the public eye until nobody gives a shit about the case anymore. Great system, isn't it?"

"Terrific."

"Cheer up, pal. It's pretty clear Cadmus shouldn't be walking the streets. At least this way he'll have soft walls."

"Yeah. I guess so."

"Anyway, now that we're not on opposite sides of the skirmish, how about dinner and amusing conversation some time?"

His voice was buoyant, and I made a silent guess.

"Two or four?"

"Uh, four." Pause. "He called, and he's coming back tomorrow."

"I'm glad for you, Milo."

"Yeah, I know that. Thanks for the shoulder when I needed it."

"Anytime."

I returned to Voids Will Be Voids just before dark. When Stripehead saw me, he jumped up and began bobbing his head nervously.

"All set?" I asked.

He bobbed at a blank space on the wall where *The Wretched Act* had hung.

"Someone came in, after you were gone and outbid you, man."

"I thought we had a deal."

"Hey, man, free enterprise—"

"Who bought it?"

"Some suit."

"You can do better than that."

"That's it, man. I never look at their faces."

"How much did he pay?"

"What's the diff? You like that kind of shit, take another one."

I could have pushed it, but purchasing the sculpture had just been a ploy to get to its creator. And Stripehead was still my only link to Gary.

"That's okay. Are we still in business on the other matter?"

"Sure." Palm out. "Two hundred."

"One fifty added to the price of the sculpture. Since you ripped me off, it goes down to one twenty-five."

He screwed up his face, shoved his hands in his pockets, and paced. The promise of temporary affluence had heightened his appetite for a chemical dream.

"Fuck, no. One fifty."

I took three fifties out of the wallet, gave him one, and withheld two.

"When I see him, you get the rest."

Cursing, he snapped up the money and went back to his desk.

"Wait here. I'll tell you when it's time."

He went back to his doodling, and I spent ten stuporous minutes walking around the gallery. Nothing looked better at second glance. Finally he stood, motioned, and led me through a rear door through a storage area and out to the darkening alley. Wiping his nose on his sleeve, he held out his hand.

"Give."

"Where's Gary?"

"He'll be here soon, man."

"Then you'll get *paid* soon."

"Up yours," he hissed, but he backed off and stood in the shadows.

I looked around. The alley was a band of lacerated asphalt, checkered with tilting, overflowing dumpsters. Garbage confettied the ground, and potholes full of waste water glistened stagnantly. More stink. I thought of Jamey's use of the word and wondered what kind of decay had fueled his visions.

Within seconds there was movement from behind one of the dumpsters and scratching, rodent sounds.

Two shadows slid along the backs of buildings, then stepped out into the open. A bare bulb above the gallery's rear door spit a triangle of cold light onto the asphalt. The shadows stood away from it but absorbed enough illumination to be rendered three-dimensional.

The larger of the two was Gary. His thick black hair had been sheared off except for a Mohawk center strip, dyed aquamarine. Roofing nails had been glued to the strip and lacquered stiff, creating a high, jagged cock's comb. He wore a vest of chain mail over bare skin and filthy black jeans gouged with holes and tucked into black plastic rain boots. A rusty razor blade dangling from a steel chain formed a necklace that came to rest over his sternum, and a feathered earring stretched one lobe. His belt was a section of rope, and from it hung a clasp knife. I remembered him as severely myopic, but his glasses were gone. I wondered if he was wearing contact lenses, or did physical correction clash with his new set of values?

The girl next to him was no more than fifteen and tiny—four feet ten or eleven. She had a petulant, snub-nosed, baby-doll face graveled with acne and topped by a Medusa mop the color of borscht. Her face was powdered white, and dark rings had been penciled around her eyes, but bad living had begun to etch its own shadows. She had an overbite that made her lips hang slightly open; her lipstick was black, and beaming through the inky flesh was the silvery glint of orthodonture. I wondered if whoever had paid for the braces was still looking for her.

Despite the getup and a studied attempt at surliness, both of them looked soft and innocent, Hansel and Gretel corrupted by the witch.

"Okay, man?" pressed Stripehead.

I handed him the pair of fifties, and he scurried back inside.

"Gary?"

"Yes?" His voice was soft and flat, as emotionless as the music blaring inside the gallery.

With anyone else I'd have made an attempt at rapport, using small talk and the reeling in of memories sweetened by time. But the old Gary and I had never had much to do with one another, and the creature before me obviously had no appetite for chit-chat.

"Thanks for coming. I want to talk to you about Jamey."

He folded his arms across his chest and the chain mail tinkled.

I took a step forward, and he backed away. But his retreat was cut short as he stumbled in a rut and lurched backward. The girl caught his arm and prevented him from falling. Once he was stabilized, she held on to him protectively. Up close I saw that his eyes were strained and unfocused. No contacts.

"What do you want?" he asked. The bare bulb backlit the spikes in his hair.

"You know about the trouble he's in."

"Yes." Unmoved.

"I've been asked by his attorney to evaluate his mental status. But I'm also trying—personally—to understand what happened."

He stared at the blur that was my face, silent and impassive. His inflection and manner were mechanical, as if his personality had been excised, fed into a synthesizer, and ejected as something only partially organic. He'd never been easy to talk to, and the punk armor was yet another layer to peel. I continued, without much hope of success.

"The others at the project said that you were friends, that he talked to you more than to any of them. Do you remember his saying or doing anything that could relate to what happened?"

"No."

"But the two of you did talk."

"Yes."

"About what?"

He shrugged.

"Don't remember?"

"That's the past. Extinct."

I tried the direct approach.

"You did a sculpture that combined elements of his father's suicide and the Lavender Slashings."

"Art imitates life," he recited.

"You titled it *The Wretched Act*, Gary. That's a phrase Jamey used to describe suicide."

"Yes."

"Why? What does it all mean?"

A faint smile tiptoed across his lips, then vanished.

"Art speaks for itself."

The girl nodded and clutched him tighter.

"He's a genius," she said, and I noticed for the first time how thin they both were.

"Sometimes," I said, "geniuses aren't appreciated in their time. What percentage of each sale does Voids give you?"

He pretended not to hear the question, but something that looked like hunger filled the girl's eyes.

Starting to feel like a minifoundation, I reached into my wallet and peeled off some bills. If Gary saw the money, he chose to ignore it. But the girl reached out and took it, examined it, and tucked it in her waistband.

It didn't guarantee cooperation by a long shot, but maybe they'd use some of it for food.

"Gary," I asked, "was Jamey on drugs?"

"Yes."

The casual answer threw me.

"How do you know?"

"He tripped."

"Like on acid?"

"Yes."

"Did you ever actually see him drop acid?"

"No."

"So you're just inferring it from his behavior."

He touched the feathered fringe of his earring.

"I know tripping," he said.

"Dr. Flowers and the others were sure he was straight."

"They're low-level androids."

"Is there anything else you can tell me about his drug use?"

"No."

"Did you ever see him take anything other than acid?"

"No."

"Do you think he did?"

"Yes."

"What kind of stuff?"

"Speed. Downers. Hog."

"PCP?"

"Yes."

"And you think he took those drugs because of the way he acted?"

"Yes." Bored.

"Gary, do you think he's capable of murdering all those people?"

He broke out into hoarse, frantic laughter, as sudden and unsettling as a stab in the dark. The girl looked at him quizzically, then joined in.

"What's the joke, Gary?"

"That was an inane question."

"Why's that?"

"Is he capable of murdering?" He laughed again. "Is he capable of breathing?"

"They're the same?"

"Sure. One can be as easy as the other. It's all part of the man-beast interface."

More nods from the girl.

"Anything else you can tell me?"

"No."

He gave her a small nod, and they turned to go. I tried again.

"I stopped at your place earlier today. Someone told me the guys who tore it up were bikers—one fat, one skinny."

I waited for a response, but none came.

"No idea who they could be?"

"No."

"How about you?" I asked the girl.

She shook her head and pouted, but a bit of fear came through.

"Are you in trouble?"

"The man-beast interface," she parroted. "We're all devolving back to the slime."

They turned their backs on me.

"Where are you going?" I called out. "In case I need to talk to you again?"

Gary stopped and swiveled slowly, moving carefully to avoid the appearance of imbalance. In the diminished light of the alley, his face shone flat and pale and grim.

"We're moving to Middleville, U.S.A.," he recited. "I'll get a job on the Ford assembly line, balancing door panels on station wagons. Slit will join the PTA. We'll have three little tykes. Every day Slit will fix me a lunch complete with a thermos and a package of Oreo cookies. We'll watch TV and die in our sleep."

He stood frozen amid the garbage. Then, furiously, he grabbed the girl's arm and pulled her along and out of sight.

20

WHEN I got home, Robin was already in the kitchen, tossing a Caesar salad. She wiped her hands and gave me an anchovy-garlic kiss.

"Hi. Billy's manager called today and said Roland Oberheim can meet with you tomorrow at three. I left the address on your nightstand."

"Great," I said listlessly. "Thank him for me next time you see him."

She looked at me quizzically.

"Alex, it took some effort to set up. You could show a little enthusiasm."

"You're right. Sorry."

She returned to the salad.

"Rough day?"

"Just a joyride through the urban swamp." And I gave her a capsulized version of the last ten hours.

She listened without comment, then said:

"Gary sounds really troubled."

"He's gone from one extreme to the other. Five years ago he was as straight and compliant as they come. High energy, a compulsive worker. Now that he's rebelled, all the energy's been focused into nihilism."

"From the way you described those sculptures it sounds like he's still got plenty of compulsiveness in him. That kind of work takes meticulous planning."

"I guess that's true. The scenes were designed for shock value, but they *were* orderly—almost ritualistic."

"That's so typically Japanese. Last year, when I was in Tokyo, I saw an exhibition of street dancing by these Japanese youth gangs that dress up like fifties greasers. They're called *zoku*—tribes. There are several rival groups, and each one stakes out its own turf in Yoyogi Park on Sunday afternoon. They come on like hoods in black

255

leather, sneering and posturing, set down ghetto blasters with cassette decks and dance to Buddy Holly tapes. It shocks the older generation, which, of course, is the whole idea. But if you look closely, you can see that there's nothing spontaneous about any of it. All the dances—every movement and gesture—are rigidly choreographed. Every gang's got its set routine. No deviation, not a trace of individuality. They've turned rebellion into a Shinto ritual."

I remembered Gary's parting soliloquy about Middleville. In retrospect it seemed chantlike.

She pulled a leaf of romaine out of the bowl and tasted it, then moved away to squeeze more lemon into the salad. I sat down at the kitchen table, rolled up my sleeves, and stared at the tabletop. She tinkered for a while. Reaching for a bottle of Worcestershire sauce, she asked:

"Is something else bothering you, Alex? You look burdened."

"I was just thinking how odd it is that two out of six kids on the project deteriorated so seriously."

She came around the counter and sat opposite me, resting her chin in her hands.

"Maybe Gary hasn't really deteriorated at all," she said. "Maybe he's just going through one of those teenage identity things, and the next time you see him he'll be enrolled at Cal Tech."

"I don't think so. There was a fatalism about him that was frightening—as if he really didn't care about living or dying. And a flatness of emotion that went beyond rebellion." I shook my head wearily. "Robin, we're talking about two boys with staggering intellects who've dropped out of life."

"Which supports the old genius-insanity myth."

"According to the textbooks, it's a myth. And anytime anyone's researched it, superior intelligence seems to be correlated with better, not worse, emotional adjustment. But the subjects in those studies were in the hundred and thirty to the hundred and forty-five IQ range—people sufficiently brilliant to excel but not so different that they can't blend in. The Project 160 kids are a different breed. A three-year-old who can translate Greek is an aberration. A six-month-old baby who talks fluent English, the way Jamey did, is downright *scary*. In the Middle Ages geniuses were thought to be possessed by demons. We pride ourselves on being enlightened, but exceptional brainpower still scares us. So we isolate geniuses, push them away. Which is exactly what happened to Jamey. His own father saw him as some kind of monster. He neglected and abandoned him. Nannies came and went. His uncle and aunt pay lip service to all they've done for him, but it was obvious that they resent having been saddled with him."

She listened, dark eyes sad. I continued talking, thinking out loud.

"Someone once said that the history of civilization is the history of genius: The gifted mind creates, and the rest of us imitate. And there are plenty of prodigies who develop into superb adults. But lots of others burn out young. The crucial factor seems to be what kind of support the child gets from his parents. It takes exceptional sensitivity to raise a prodigy. Some kids are lucky. Jamey just wasn't." My voice caught. "End of lecture."

She squeezed my hand.

"What's really the matter, sweetie?"

I said nothing for several long moments, then forced the words out.

"When he showed up at my door five years ago, it was because he was starving for a daddy. The time we spent together must have created the illusion that he'd finally found one. Somehow that got turned into romantic love, and when he expressed it, I rejected him. It was a pivotal moment. Handled right, it could have led to a happier ending."

"Alex, you were caught off guard. No one could have reacted differently."

"My training should have kept me on guard."

"You were a part-time consultant, not the director of the project. What about Sarita Flowers's responsibility? Two out of six of those kids freaked out—doesn't that say something about the quality of her leadership?"

"Sarita's more engineer than psychologist—she makes no pretense at supersensitivity. That's why she hired *me* to monitor their emotional adjustment. But I was too damned sanguine, running my little rap groups and deluding myself that the bases were covered."

"You're being too hard on yourself," she said as she let go of my hand, got up, and went back to the salad. After pulling two steaks out of the refrigerator, she engaged in a silent routine of pounding and marinating while I watched.

"Alex," she finally said, "Jamey was troubled long before the project started. A moment ago you gave some of the reasons for it. It's just not logical to think that one incident could have made that big a difference. You've immersed yourself in all the horror and lost your perspective. Souza did you a favor when he let you go. Take advantage of it."

I looked at her. She was solemn, eyes heavy with concern. What a fun guy I was.

"Maybe you're right," I said, more out of consideration for her feelings than inner conviction.

I spent a good part of the next morning phoning hospitals and nursing registries. Marthe Surtees was nowhere to be found, but Andrea Vann had signed up with the ninth registry I called. I talked to the receptionist, who handed me over to the director, a man named Tubbs with an elderly voice tinged by a faint Caribbean accent. When I asked him for her current address, all the lilt went out of his speech.

"Who did you say you were, sir?"

"Dr. Guy Mainwaring." Haughtily. "The medical director of Canyon Oaks Hospital in Agoura."

Meaningful pause.

"Oh, yes," he said, suddenly obsequious. No use alienating a potential client. "I'd love to help you, Doctor, but we do have to protect our registrees' privacy."

"I understand all that," I said impatiently, "but that's not the issue here. Mrs. Vann worked for us until recently—I assume she noted that on her application."

Not having the papers in front of him, he mumbled, "Yes, of course."

"Our personnel department has informed us that she is due additional pay for unused vacation time. We mailed the check to her home, but it came back, marked addressee unknown, no forwarding. My secretary called your agency about it last week, and someone promised to get back to her, but no one did."

"I'll have to check that—"

"In any event, I decided to phone myself—cut through the red tape."

"Of course. Do you need the phone number as well, Doctor?"

"That might be helpful."

He put me on hold and returned in a minute.

"Doctor, Mrs. Vann registered with us last week, and we found two float jobs for her. But she never responded to our calls, and we haven't heard from her since."

"Typical." I sighed. "A bright, capable woman, but she tends to wander off unpredictably."

"That's good to know."

"Absolutely. Now about that address." I rustled some papers. "Our records have her living on Colfax in North Hollywood."

"No, we have her listed in Panorama City." And he gave me the information I needed.

The phone number was disconnected.

It was a twenty-five-minute freeway ride to the downscale part of the Valley. The address Tubbs had given me was on Cantaloupe Street, on a block of three-story California-fifties apartment buildings—cheaply built rhomboids painted in unlikely colors. The building I was looking for was lemon yellow texture coat flecked with sparkles. A gateless entry in the middle of the building revealed a U-shaped courtyard built around a pool. Green Gothic letters spelled out CANTALOUPE ARMS, which evoked a series of images that made my head reel. In front was a miserly patch of succulents through which sprouted a lifeless plaster fountain. A cement pathway cut through the plants to the entrance.

There was no directory, but to the immediate right of the entrance was a panel of brass mailboxes. Most of the slots were labeled, none with the name Vann. The ones belonging to units seven and fifteen were empty. I walked into the courtyard and had a closer look.

Each apartment had a view of the pool—which was kidneyshaped and cloudy—and its own entrance. The doors were painted olive green, and flimsy-looking olive iron railings ran along both of the upper walkways. Unit seven was on the ground floor, midway down the north side of the U. I knocked on the door and received no answer. A peek through the curtains revealed a small, empty living room and, on the other side of a plywood partition, a windowless kitchenette. No signs of habitation. I took the stairs one flight up to fifteen.

This time my knock elicited a response. The door opened, and a short, pretty blond woman of around twenty-five peered out sleepily and smiled. She had a pointed feline face and wore crotch-cutting jogging shorts and a terry-cloth tank top stretched by pendulous breasts. Her nipples were the size of cocktail onions. Through the open door came a breeze of strong perfume and coffee and the soft refrain of a Barry Manilow song. Over one white shoulder I saw a red velvet settee and wrought-iron occasional tables. On the wall were a framed zodiac chart and a cheap oil panting of a reclining nude who bore some general resemblance to the woman in the door.

"Hi," she said, huskily, "you must be Tom. You're a little early, but that's cool."

She moved closer, and one hand stroked my bicep.

"Don't be shy," she urged. "Come on in and let's party."

"Sorry,"—I smiled—"wrong number."

The hand dropped, and her face hardened and aged ten years.

"I'm looking for Andrea Vann," I explained.

She stepped backward and reached for the door. I shot my foot forward and prevented it from closing.

"What the hell—" she said.

"Wait a second."

"Listen, Mister, I have a date." A car door slammed, and she jumped. "That could be him. Come on, get the hell out of here."

"Andrea Vann. A nurse. Dark, good-looking."

She bit her lip.

"Big tits and a little dark-haired kid?"

I remembered what Vann had told me about my lecture's helping her with her child's sleep problems.

"That's right," I said.

"Downstairs."

"Which unit?"

"I don't know, one of the ones on that side." She

pointed north with a long-nailed finger. Footsteps echoed in the empty courtyard. The blonde panicked and leaned against the door. "Come on, that's him. Don't fuck up my day, mister."

I stepped back, and the door shut. As I headed toward the stairs, a man rose from them—young, weedy, bearded, wearing jeans and a blue workshirt with the label "Tom" over one breast pocket. He carried something in a paper bag, and when we passed, he avoided my eyes.

I went back to seven, stared at the empty living room again, and was wondering what to do when a shrill voice sounded behind me. "Can I help you?"

I turned and faced an old woman in a pink quilted housecoat and hairnet of matching hue. The hair under the net was a pewter cap that accentuated the gray in her complexion. She was short and skinny with a crooked mouth, rubbery cheeks, a strong cleft chin, and blue eyes that regarded me suspiciously.

"I'm looking for Mrs. Vann."

"You family?"

"Just a friend."

"A good enough friend to pay her debts?"

"How much does she owe you?"

"She hasn't paid rent for three months runnin'. Put me off with excuses about late child support and big doctor bills for the kid and all that sad music. I shoulda said never you mind, but instead, I gave her time. That's gratitude for ya."

"What does three months come out to?"

She adjusted the edge of the hairnet and winked.

"Well, to be honest, I got a last-month deposit and a damage deposit that shoulda been more than it is, but that still leaves a month and a half's worth—seven hundred and fifty. You of a mind to come up with a sum like that?"

"Gee," I said, "that puts us in the same boat. She borrowed quite a bit of money from me, and I came here to try and collect."

"Great." She snorted. "Lotta help you'll be." But camaraderie twinkled in her eyes.

"When did she leave?"

"Last week. Snuck out in the middle of the night like a

thief. Only reason I saw it was that it was late and the horn was blarin', so I went on back to see what was goin' on. There she was, talking with some no-accounts, leaning on the horn like nothing mattered. She saw me, got all scared and guilty-lookin', and sped off. What really ate me was that the car was a new one. She'd gotten rid of her old heap and bought one a them flashy little Mustangs. She had money for that but none to pay me. How much she into you for?"

"Plenty." I groaned. "Any idea where she went?"

"Honey, if I knew that, would I be talkin' to you?"

I smiled.

"Any of the other tenants know her?"

"Nah. If you're her friend, you gotta be the only one. In the six months she was here I never did see her talk to no one or take visitors. Course, she worked nights and slept days, so that may have been part of it. Still, I always wondered if there was somethin' wrong with her. Good-lookin' girl like that never socializin'."

"Do you know where she was working at the time she left?"

"Nowhere. I noticed it because her usual routine was to take the kid to school, then come back and sleep the day away, bring the kid home, and head off to work. Latchkey situation, which is a hell of a way to raise kids if you ask me, but they're all doin' it nowadays. Coupla times she asked me to look in on the kid; once in a while I gave him a cookie. Coupla weeks ago all that changed. The kid started stayin' home, inside with her. She'd leave during the middle of the day and take him with her. First I thought he was sick, but he looked pretty good to me. They were just vacationin', I guess. With her outa work, I shoulda suspected I wasn't gonna get my money. But that's what you get for being too trustin', right?"

I nodded sympathetically.

"Hell of it is, I always liked the girl. Quiet but classy. Raisin' that kid all by herself. Even the money wouldn'ta made me lose sleep—the owner's a fat cat, he'll survive— but it's the lyin' I can't stand. The taking advantage."

"I know what you mean."

"Yeah," she continued, placing her hands on her hips. "It's that flashy little car that's still eatin' at me."

*   *   *

I drove back on the freeway, wondering about Andrea Vann's sudden departure. The fact that she'd registered with Tubbs's agency right after quitting indicated an intention to stay in town. But something had happened to make her pack her bags in the middle of the night. Whether or not it had to do with Jamey was unclear; there was no shortage of stresses that could drive a single mother out of town. The only way to be certain was to talk to the lady, and I had no idea how to find her.

I exited at Laurel Canyon and drove south into Hollywood. Roland Oberheim's place of business was on La Brea, just south of Santa Monica Boulevard, a small two-story office building sided with herringbone cedar. The first floor was occupied by a recording studio. A separate entrance housed the stairs to the second, which was taken up by three entertainment concerns: Joyful Noise Records ("a subsidiary of the Christian Musical Network"); The Druckman Group: Professional Management; and, at the end of the cork-paneled hall, Anavrin Productions, R. Oberheim, Pres.

The Anavrin suite was a waiting room and a back office. The former was silent and decorated with twenty-year-old psychedelic posters advertising Big Blue Nirvana in Concert at various halls around the country. The spaces in between were taken up by framed PR photos of sullen-faced bands I'd never heard of. The girl hunched behind the desk wore a hot pink vinyl jumpsuit. She had short, tortured hair and heavy jaws that worked rhythmically as she read *Billboard* to the accompaniment of moving lips. When I walked in, she looked up in amazement, as if I were the first person she'd seen all year.

"Dr. Alex Delaware here to see Mr. Oberheim."

"Oka-ay." She put down the magazine, dragged herself upright, and walked a few weary steps to the office. Opening the door without knocking, she shouted in:

"Rolly, some guy named Alex to see you."

There was a mumbled reply, and she crooked her thumb toward the office and said, "G'wan."

The back room was small and dark and windowless, textured umber walls, an oak floor, the sole furniture half a dozen tie-dyed throw pillows. Oberheim squatted yoga-style on one of them, hands on his knees, smoking a conical clove cigarette. A single gold record hung on the wall over his head, creating a weird halo effect. The rest of the decor was more psychedelic posters, a goatskin rug, and a large hookah that filled one corner. Bracket shelves held stacks of LPs and a state-of-the-art stereo system. A scarred Fender bass lay flat on the rug.

"Mr. Oberheim, I'm Alex Delaware."

"Rolly O." He motioned toward the floor. "Rest."

I squatted down across from him.

"Smoke?"

"No, thanks."

He inhaled deeply on the cigarette and held the smoke in. What finally emerged was a thin, bitter stream that shimmered and made his face seem gelatinous before dissolving.

The face itself wasn't much to look at: coarse, jowly, and openpored, with small, downturned eyes flanking a rosy bulb of a nose. His chin was mottled with scar tissue, the mouth above it concealed under a drooping brush of gray mustache. He was bald as an egg, except for a thin graying fringe that ran from temple to shoulder-top. He wore a faded black Big Blue Nirvana T-shirt with a winged guitar logo and blue surgical scrub pants. The shirt was too tight and too small, exposing a hirsute tube of gut that ringed his waist. A small leather stash bag hung from the laces of the pants.

He looked me over, squinting through the smoke.

"Friend of Billy's, huh?"

"More of an acquaintance. My fiancée builds his guitars."

"Oh, yeah," he rumbled, "spaceships, popsicles, and six-string dildos, right?"

"I haven't seen any dildos yet." I grinned.

"You will, man. That's the way it's going. Away from substance, zoom into style. Strum a dildo, break platinum. Billy's a stone businessman, he knows where it's at."

He nodded his head in self-agreement.

"Fact is, even the style today has no style. Two chords on a synthesizer and a lot of filthy words. Not that I mind filth—I played my share of raunchy gigs—but to be meaningful, filth's got to go somewhere, you know? Carry the story. It ain't good enough to shock grandma."

He massaged his belly and took another hit of cloves.

"Anyway, no matter about all of that. Billy's all right; the boy can get *down* when he wants to." He coughed. "So your lady builds those toys, huh? Must be an interesting lady."

"She is."

"Maybe I should get me one of those things in a four-string model."

He pantomimed holding a bass and moved his fingers down an imaginary fretboard.

"Boom da boom, chukka boom, chukka boom. Big old furry dildo with a heavy bottom sound. What do you think?"

"It's got possibilities."

"Sure. Shoulda had one of those at the Cow Palace in 'sixty-eight." He started humming in an incongruous falsetto. "Boom boom da boom. Here I am, mama, signed, sealed, delivered, and ha-ard. Can't you just see the little girl boppers squirm?"

He finished the cigarette and put it out in a ceramic ashtray.

"Shrink, huh?"

"That's right."

"Know Tim Leary?"

"I met him once at a convention. Years ago, when I was a student."

"Whaddya think?"

"Interesting fellow."

"Man's a genius. Fucking pioneer of the consciousness."

He looked to me for confirmation. I smiled noncommittally. He recrossed his legs and folded his arms across his chest.

"So, Alexander the Grateful, what is it you want to know?"

"Billy said you knew everyone on the Haight."

"An exaggeration"—he beamed—"but not a humungous one. It was a tight scene, one big family, fluid boundaries. Rolly got tapped as one of the daddies."

"I'm trying to find out anything I can about two people who lived on the Haight back in 'sixty-six. Peter Cadmus

and Margaret Norton. She also went by the name of
Margo Sunshine."

I'd hoped the names would trigger a casual memory,
but his smile died and his color deepened.

"You're talking about dead people, man."

"You knew them personally?"

"What's the connection, man?"

I explained my involvement with Jamey, leaving out
the fact that I'd been fired.

"Yeah. I should have known. Read about the kid in
the papers. Very ugly shit. What do you want? To find
out if his parents dropped acid, so you can blame it on
twisted chromosomes, right? More witch hunts and reefer
madness. Yo, Joe McCarthy."

"I'm not interested in that. All I want to find out is
what they were like—as human beings—so I can understand him better."

"What they were like? They were beautiful. Part of a
beautiful time."

He picked up the pack of clove cigarettes, stared at it,
tossed it aside, and pulled a joint out of his stash bag.
Lovingly and slowly he lit it, closed his eyes, sucked in a
cloud of marijuana, and smiled.

"Dead people," he said after a while. "Hearing their
name's pulling up heavy-duty associations. Beaming flash-
backs on the old cerebrovideo." He shook his head.
"Don't know if I want to get into that."

"Were you close to them?"

He looked at me as if I were retarded.

"There was no close and far. Everyone was everyone.
One big collective consciousness. A la Jung. Peaceful.
Beautiful. No one ripped anyone off because it woulda
been like tearing off a hunk of your own skin."

During the summer between my freshman and sopho-
more years in college I'd gotten a job in San Francisco,
playing guitar in a dance band at the Mark Hopkins.
Flower power had been in its heyday, and I'd paid several visits to the pharmacologic bazaar the hippies had
carved out of the Haight-Ashbury ghetto. The streets of
the Haight were a crazy quilt of social outcasts living on
the edge: baby-faced bikers, whores, pimps, and other
assorted jackals. A broth seasoned with unstable ingredi-

ents that boiled over frequently into violence, the talk of peace and love a dope-inspired illusion.

But I left Oberheim his memories unchallenged and asked him the name of the group Peter and Margo had lived with.

"They used to crash with a tribe called the Swine Club. Beautiful bunch of heads, lived in an old place right off Ashbury and ran free concerts in the park. They'd get veggies from dumpsters, cook up these big batches of rice, and give it away *free,* man. To *anyone.* Big parties. Be-ins. Nirvana gigged there all the time. So did Big Brother and Quicksilver and the Dead. Righteous all-day jams that made the place *rock.* The whole world was there. Even the Angels were cool. People would get up and rip off their clothes and *dance.* Little Margo was the wildest. She had a snake body, you know?"

He inhaled, and a quarter of the joint glowed. When he finally exhaled, nothing came out but a paroxysm of dry coughing. After it stopped, he licked his mustache and smiled.

"What kind of guy was Peter?" I asked.

"Stone-beautiful. We used to call him Peter the Cad. 'Cause he was a righteous badass—an Errol Flynn, a fucking musketeer, you know? Dark and wild and beautifully dangerous. Ready for anything, man. Heavily into risk taking."

"What kinds of risks did he take?"

He waved his hand impatiently.

"Head games. Sticking one foot off the cliff and dangling, exploring the outer limits of the sensorium. A psychic pioneer. Like Dr. Tim."

He reflected on that and toked on the joint.

"Was Margo into games, too?"

He smiled blissfully.

"Margo was soft. Beautiful. Heavily into giving and sharing. She could boogie all night to just a drum and a tambura. Like a Gypsy lady, mystical and magical."

He went through two more king-sized joints before showing signs of intoxication, talking incessantly as he tooted. But it was dope talk, loosely associated and disjointed. About concerts that had taken place two decades ago, the scarcity of high-quality dope because the "mind police" had poisoned the fields with paraquat, a scheme to reassemble the original members of Big Blue Nirvana in order to plan a comeback ("Except Dawg, man. He's a fucking *lawyer* with MGM. Stay away from *that* noise"). Cannabis dreams that told me nothing.

I sat patiently, trying to pry loose morsels of information about Peter and Margo, but he just repeated that they were beautiful, then veered off into more self-satisfying meanderings about the good old days, followed by indignant diatribes about the heartlessness of the contemporary music scene.

"A hundred fucking dollars to see Duran Duran in a society where heavy blues men with righteous chops eat out of garbage cans. Fucked *up*."

The third joint was out. He opened his mouth and swallowed the roach.

"Rolly, do you remember anything about Peter's father visiting him?"

"Nope."

"How about Margo's pregnancy? Any memories of that?"

"Just that she was sick, man. She'd try to get up and dance, but after a couple of seconds she'd turn all greenish pale and start to heave. Bummer."

"How did she and Peter feel about the pregnancy?"

"Feel?" he was starting to mumble, and his head drooped drowsily.

"Emotionally. Were they happy about it?"

"Sure." His eyelids fluttered shut. "It was a happy time. Except for the war and the shit El BJ kept trying to pull, everything was a fucking giggle."

Suppressing a sigh, I played a long shot.

"You said the Angels hung around the concerts given by the Swine Club."

"Yeah. They were cool. This was before Jagger pulled that Altamont shit."

"Did Peter or Margo have any special relationship with the Angels or any other bikers?"

He yawned and shook his head. "No relationship was special. Everyone was loving. Equal."

"Did they hang out with bikers?"

"Unh-unh."

He was drifting off to sleep, and there was one question I had to ask. One that I'd been sitting on for the last hour.

"Rolly, you've described Peter as someone with a real lust for life—"

"He lived to *live*, man."

"All right. But a few years later he ended up committing suicide. What could have led to that?"

That woke him up. He opened his eyes and glared at me angrily.

"Suicide is *bullshit*, man." His head bobbed like that of a toy dog on the rear deck of a low rider.

"What do you mean?"

"It doesn't *happen*," he said, whispering conspiratorially. "A fucking figment. The establishment uses it as a label to make rockers and head saints look like cop-outs. Janis, Jimi, Morrison, the Bear. Janis didn't off herself; she died from the pain of being. Jimi didn't off himself; the government shot him up with some kind of napalm because he knew too much truth and they wanted to shut his mouth. Morrison and the Bear aren't even dead. For all I know, Buddy Holly's with'em. They're probably partying somewhere in the Greek isles. Suicide is bullshit, man. It doesn't happen."

"Peter—"

"Peter didn't off himself, man. He died in a head game. Like I told you."

"What kind of head game?"

"An ecstasy trip. Exploring the boundaries."

"Tell me more about it."

"Sure." He shrugged. "Why not? He used to play it all the time. Get naked, climb up on a chair, make this noose out of a silk rope, and put it around his neck. Bring his weight down on it so it was tight and stroke his cock till he came. He was something to see, moaning, like Jesus in ecstasy." He ran a stubby tongue over his lips and imitated a street-black patois: "He used to say the *pressure* heightened the *pleasure.*"

He was mumbling, nearly incoherent, but I was listening acutely. He was describing a phenomenon known as eroticized hanging or autoerotic asphyxia, one of the more arcane sexual kinks, custom-designed for those who consider flirtation with death an enhancement to orgasm.

Eroticized hangers masturbate while a rope or other binding constricts their carotids, gradually increasing the pressure so that at the point of climax, the arteries are shut down completely. Some use complex systems of pulleys to hoist themselves to the noose. Others fold into bizarre contortions. Any way it's done, it's a quirky game and a dangerous one: If the masturbator loses consciousness before removing the rope or positions himself in such a way that liberation is prevented or unduly delayed, death by asphyxiation is inevitable.

"A game, you dig?" Oberheim smiled. "He liked to play games. And one day he lost. But that's cool."

21

I LEFT him snoring in his office, a flaccid monument to self-absorption: The interview had been foggy and off kilter, but I'd picked up another tidbit of Cadmus' psychopathology: Peter had been an eroticized hanger, his death very possibly a kinky accident. I wondered if Souza had known about the hanging game all along and decided that he probably hadn't; in his hands, the knowledge would have been used strategically, as evidence that sexual perversion, as well as mental disturbance, ran in the family.

As I drove north on La Brea, I thought of how downbeat I'd been with Robin and realized that Oberheim wasn't the only one with a self-absorption problem. I'd been so wrapped up in the case and the guilt it had unearthed that I'd neglected her, using her as a sounding board without considering that she might need some attention herself.

Determined to make amends, I made a three-point turn at a gas station on Fountain, drove south to Wilshire, and headed west, into Beverly Hills. There was about an hour left before the shops closed, and after parking in a city lot on Beverly Drive, I spent it like a gameshow winner on a spree, buying an antique lace blouse at a boutique on Cañon, perfume and bath soap at Giorgio, a quart of Früsen Glädje raspberry chocolate ice cream, an enormous gourmet basket at Jurgensens, the copper skillet she'd wanted at Davis-Sonoma, a dozen coral roses arranged with leather fern and baby's-breath. It was no solution, just a start in the right direction.

Maneuvering through a sea of Mercedeses, I drove away from the high-rent district and made one more stop—at a fish market near Overland—before heading home. When I got there, at six-thirty, Robin's truck was

nowhere in sight, and she'd left word with the service
that she'd be home by seven forty-five.

"There's another one, too, Doctor," said the service
operator. "Do you want it?"

"Sure."

"A Jennifer Leavitt called at three. She left two
numbers."

I copied them on a scrap of paper. One was a university extension; the other, a Fairfax District exchange. I
was curious about what Jennifer wanted but not curious
enough to interrupt my plans. Making a mental note to
call her later that evening, I placed the scrap in my
pocket.

Carrying the gifts into the bedroom, I arranged them
on the bed. After changing into jeans and a well-worn
corduroy shirt, I went into the kitchen, put Joe Pass on
the stereo, an apron around my waist, and set about
preparing dinner: an appetizer of jumbo mushrooms stuffed
with garlic and breadcrumbs; a salad of butter lettuce,
pepper, and Chinese scallions; a carafe of tarragon vinai-
grette; grilled fillets of Norwegian salmon topped with
capers; fresh string beans lightly buttered; and a bottle of
sauvignon blanc—a virgin white from the vineyard of a
lady judge I'd once met. The Früsen Glädje would serve
as dessert.

She walked through the door just as I was dressing the
salad. I took her coat and portfolio, led her to the kitchen,
sat her at the table, and brought a basin and cup with
which to wash her hands.

"Whew!" She grinned broadly. "To what do I owe all
this?"

Shushing her with a kiss, I uncorked and poured the
wine and brought the mushrooms to the table, along with
a log of sourdough.

"Alex, this is terrific!"

"Wolfgang Puck, eat your heart out."

We ate slowly and tranquilly, with a minimum of
conversation.

"Delicious," she said, pushing her plate away.

"Ready for dessert?"

She groaned and patted her tummy.

"Can we wait awhile?"

"Sure. Go relax while I clean up."

"Let me help you," she said, standing. "I need to move around."

"All right, but first go in the bedroom and bring me a cooler shirt."

"Sure, hon."

She came back holding the lace blouse to her breast, smiling like a kid.

"Baby," she said.

We moved toward each other, embraced, and never separated for the rest of the evening.

The next morning, after she'd gone to the shop, I hung up my jeans and the scrap with Jennifer's numbers fell out. After picking up the phone, I dialed the university extension. A slow-talking baritone informed me that I'd reached the psychobiology lab. In the background was a wash of voices.

"This is Dr. Delaware returning Jennifer Leavitt's call."

"Who?"

"Dr. Delaware."

"No, who're you calling?"

"Jennifer Leavitt." I spelled it.

"Oh. Uh, one second." He put down the phone and shouted out her name, returned to the line even more lethargic than before. "Uh, no, she's not here."

"When do you expect her?"

"Don't know. Uh, we're right in the middle of something, so why don't you, uh, call later."

"Can you leave a message for her?"

"Uh, well, I really don't—"

"Thanks."

I hung up and dialed the Fairfax exchange. A cheerful-sounding woman answered.

"Mrs. Leavitt?"

"Yes?"

"This is Dr. Delaware. I used to work with Jennifer at project 160—"

"Oh, yes, Doctor. Jennifer was quite anxious to talk with you. She said to tell you she'll be out for the day. She and Danny—that's her boyfriend—have gone to La Jolla. But she should be back this evening. Where can she reach you?"

I gave her my home number and thanked her.

"My pleasure, Doctor. Jennifer always had wonderful things to say about you. She was so young when she entered the project, and you really helped her adjust."

"That's great to hear."

"Now she's going to be a doctor herself. Isn't that wonderful?"

"You must be very proud."

"Oh, we are, Doctor. We are."

I did some housecleaning, fed the koi, practiced karate katas, took a three-mile run and a long soak in the tub. The morning mail held the usual junk along with a subpoena to appear as an expert witness in a custody case I'd thought long resolved, but the date was a month away, so I filed it.

All the makings of a peaceful morning, but the fact that someone had outbid me for *The Wretched Act* kept slipping into my mind. Voids Will Be Voids was some surgeon's tax dodge, hardly meant to be a bustling enterprise, yet all of a sudden customers were vying for a particular sculpture. The more I thought about it, the less I liked it.

It was only twelve-thirty, several hours before the gallery opened, but I had time on my hands, so I drove back downtown in the hope of spotting Stripehead nearby. He was nowhere in sight, and the gallery was dark, so I went for lunch in Chinatown.

Belly full of dim sum, I returned at two. Voids was still closed, but I spotted my quarry picking through the rags on a rack in front of one of the clothing outlets. By the time I'd parked and walked up behind him, he'd selected a pair of mock tigerskin stretch pants, a polyethylene tank top, and an extra-large J.C. Penney white-button shirt.

"Hi," I said softly.

He jumped and dropped the clothes on the sidewalk. I picked them up and brushed them off. The Korean who owned the outlet stared suspiciously from the doorway. Stripehead absorbed the suspicion and passed it along to me.

"Whaddya *you* want, man?"

"I want to do a little more business."

"Business starts at four o'clock." He pretended to inspect the tank top.

"I'm not interested in art. Just information."

"Then call the freakin' information bureau."

The Korean came out and stood beside us. "Buy or look?" he demanded.

Before Stripehead could sneer a reply, I said: "Buy. How much?"

The Korean quoted a figure. I offered him half as much, and we settled for two-thirds. Stripehead looked on incredulously, then held the clothes out to me.

"Keep 'em," I said. "Merry Christmas."

He started walking toward the gallery, and I stayed with him.

"You Jewish or something?" he asked.

"No. Why?"

"You do business like a Chink or a Jew, and you're sure not no Chink."

"You're welcome."

"Huh?"

"Never mind."

We reached Voids. He stood with his back to the iron grating, clutching the clothes as if afraid that he who gaveth would suddenly taketh away.

"I want to know who bought *The Wretched Act.*"

"I told you, man. Some suit."

"What was the suit's name?"

"He din't give no name."

"What about a receipt?"

"He wanted cash-and-carry, just like you."

"Tell me what he looked like."

"I told you, man, I don't look at—"

The twenty under his nose stopped him mid-sentence.

"Fifty." He tried.

I pulled the money back angrily.

"Forget it. I have a friend on the police. When I leave here, I'm calling him and filing a complaint about fraudulent business practices."

"Hey, man, I didn't do nothing."

"Maybe, maybe not. But when they take one look at you, it'll be body-search time."

I turned to leave. Scrawny fingers held me back.

"Hey, man, I was just tryin' to be fair. The other suit paid me fifty not to talk, seems you should do the same."

I peeled his hand off and started walking.

"Fuck you, man! Okay, okay! Twenty."

I stopped and turned around.

"First let's hear what you have to say."

"He had a big freaking mouth."

"I need a description, not a personality assessment."

"Okay, hold on. Let's see. He was white. And tan. Like some faggot who sits in front of a sun lamp all day."

"How tall?"

"Like you, but heavier."

"Fat?"

"Muscles."

"What about his hair?"

"Short. Like some faggot who lifts weights and grooms himself all day."

"What else?"

He contorted his face, trying to remember.

"He had a beard. Yeah. That's it, man."

"What color?"

"Dark."

In his addled way he'd produced a good description of Erno Radovic.

"Did he say why he wanted the sculpture?"

"No, he, uh—sure. He said he liked art."

I showed him another twenty and said:

"Come on. Let it out."

"Hey, man, I don't wanna get in any shit over this. He was a real asshole."

"He'll never know."

He looked up and down the street, then back at the money.

"The first time you were here he came in right after you left. Asked me what you were up to. I said, 'Hey, man, this is Voids, not some information bureau.' Then he got this bizarro look on his face and produced some cash, so I told him I never saw you before, you just wanted to buy trash. I showed him which trash, and he bid you up. That's it, man. Okay?"

Milo had told me to call him if the bodyguard showed

his face. I went to the phone booth in the parking lot and punched in his number at the West L.A. station.

He was out, so I asked for Del Hardy, his occasional partner. It took a while to locate the black detective, and when he came to the phone, he was out of breath.

"Doc," he panted.

"Hi, Del. You okay?"

"Aerobics . . . stress management program . . . orders from the brass . . . dropping like flies . . . gonna lose . . . a lot of good men."

"Milo involved in it, too?"

"Supposed to be . . . but he keeps . . . making up excuses. Like trying to solve crimes."

I laughed.

"I'd like to talk to him when he gets back. It's no emergency, just something about Erno Radovic."

He exhaled, and his voice tightened.

"That racist pig? He hassling you again?"

"Not exactly. But I have reason to believe he's been following me."

"You in any trouble?"

"Not at all. Like I said, it's no emergency."

"Okay. Anyway, Milo hasn't come in today. I think he's out on a call. But he should be phoning in within the hour, and I'll make sure he gets the message. Meanwhile, if you see the motherfucker skulking around again, phone me collect."

"Thanks, Del."

I drove home, pulled out a stack of psych journals, and prepared to catch up on some reading. I'd just immersed myself in an article on the psychological development of premature infants when the service called.

"Good, you're home," said the operator. "I've got a Sergeant Michael Sturgis on the line. It's the third time he's called."

"Please put him through."

"Certainly, Doctor. Go ahead, sir. Doctor's on the line."

"Alex?" The connection was peppered with static, but the urgency in Milo's voice was clear.

"What's up?" I asked.

"Del said you wanted to talk about Radovic. Go ahead."

I told him about the bodyguard's following me and purchasing *The Wretched Act.*

"A sculpture?"

"More than just a sculpture, Milo. It combines elements of Jamey's father's death and Chancellor's murder. Radovic paid a lot of money for it. You might want to ask him about it once you locate him."

There was no reply, only crackles and pops.

"Milo?" I said, wondering if we'd been cut off.

"We've located him," he said softly. "He's lying a few feet from where I'm standing, gutted like a fish."

"Oh, shit."

"Wait, there's more. We've got an eyewitness to the knifing. There were two guys involved. Bikers. One skinny, the other a veritable tub of lard."

"Jesus. Where did it happen?"

"Near Bitter Canyon, off the Antelope Valley Highway. We need to talk, Alex. Soon."

"Name it."

"Whitehead and Cash are still here beating their meat, but they're splitting in a couple of minutes. I volunteered to handle the paper work, so I'll be here for a while. It's a forty-minute ride, give or take ten on either side. Leave in an hour, so you don't pass anyone on the freeway; it's an open road and every car's visible. Know how to get here?"

"Four-oh-five north?"

"Right. Stay with it past the merge with five, then hook east on fourteen, toward Lancaster and Mojave. You'll pass Soledad Canyon, Agua Dulce, and the L.A. Aqueduct. Bitter Canyon's a few miles before Palmdale. The highway cuts through high desert, and the exit road will drop you a thousand feet. It's damned deserted out here, so don't get spooked. Just keep going until you see an old Texaco station. The meat wagon will probably be there. You won't be able to miss it."

22

THE NORTHERN edge of the Valley began to bleed off into empty stretches just past San Fernando. As I turned onto the Antelope Valley Highway, the wayposts of prefab civilization—Colonial Kitchens, Carrows, Dennys, Pizza Huts—disappeared, and expanses of increasingly raw terrain slid into view: low sandstone hills parched white under a stubble of creosote and sagebrush, squat and pitiful against the distant black backdrop of the San Gabriel Mountains; long sashes of ravaged gravel pit; chaparral still scorched from last summer's brush fires; sudden flashes of brilliant canary yellow wildflowers.

As Milo had predicted, the highway was nearly empty, five barren lanes herringboned by exits leading to the canyons that ran the county line to its demise: Placerita, Soledad, Bouquet—whose rusty blue rock graced the patios and spas of many an L.A. dream house—Vasquez, Agua Dulce.

The Bitter Canyon turnoff was abrupt, a sharp downgrade that deposited the Seville on a narrow, squirming asphalt road, bordered by boulders and an occasional wind-savaged tree. Here, in the lowlands the hillsides were water-etched and craggy, a quilt of tans and reds washed with coy overtones of lavender and blue. The sky was overcast with heavy gray stratus clouds, and every so often a ray of sun escaped through a threadbare patch in the mist, casting a startling pinkish spotlight upon a favored section of rock. Incredible beauty, cruelly fleeting.

The Texaco station was fifteen miles down the road, rising from nothingness, straight out of a time warp. A pair of prewar pumps sat in the middle of a treacherously furrowed dirt and gravel yard, fronting a one-bay white frame garage of equivalent vintage. Occupying the bay was a green bubble-backed '39 Plymouth.

Attached to the garage was a shack that served as an office, its dirty windows obscured by piles of paper. A few yards down the road was a frame café sporting twin antique Coca-Cola disks on either end of a faded sign that said SAL's and a crowing-cock weather vane atop a tar paper roof. The cock postured arrogantly, unmoving in the still desert air.

The café looked as if it hadn't done business in a while, but a fleet of official vehicles had encamped around it. I pulled the Seville between a familiar bronze Matador and a mobile crime lab van and got out.

The northern corner of the yard was cordoned off by string attached to makeshift posts. Taped to the string were LAPD tags. Within the cordoned area technicians stooped and squatted, wielding scrapers, hypodermics, brushes, and plaster-casting material. Some worked on a pearl gray RX-7; others, on the area around the car. On the ground nearby was a sausage-shaped lump, encased in a body bag. A few feet from the bag a roan-colored stain spread its tentacles across the dirt. A Chinese man in a dark suit hovered over the body, talking into a hand-held cassette recorder.

A county ambulance was parked just outside the tape, its engine still running. A uniformed attendant stepped out of the ambulance's passenger door and looked around. His eyes finally settled on Milo, who was leaning against one of the gas pumps, writing in his notepad.

"Okay?"

My friend said something to the Chinese man, who looked up and nodded.

"Okay."

The attendant gave a hand signal, and a second attendant got out from the driver's side and flung the rear doors open. A stretcher materialized. Within seconds the body had been lifted nonchalantly and deposited with a dull thud in the rear of the vehicle. The ambulance departed, leaving behind a small dust storm.

Milo saw me and put the pad away. He flicked dust off his lapel and laid a heavy hand on my shoulder.

"What happened?" I asked.

"About eight this morning Radovic powwowed with two bikers right over there and got sliced up." He pointed to the bloodstain. "From what our witness saw, sounds like it was a prearranged meeting to pull off some kind of dirty deal. But the deal went bad."

I looked at the stain, then at the empty grizzled hills.

"Why all the way out here?"

"That's what we're trying to find out. Park ranger's due any minute. Maybe he can shed some light on it."

He pulled a package of mints out of his pocket and offered me one. I took it, and both of us sweetened our breaths.

"Way I figure it," he said, "one of the parties knew the area, the other didn't, and the station was used as a landmark. Which, under normal circumstances, would have been an excellent idea because the place is usually deserted. The station, the greasy spoon over there, and fifty acres on either side of the road are owned by an old man named Skaggs who lives in Lancaster and rarely opens up anymore. I just finished interviewing him, and he told me forty years ago there used to be an army base a few miles down the road and the café was a 'jumpin' joint'—outdoor bandstand, great steaks, illegal hooch. But today we're talking ghost town."

Shading his eyes with his hand, he looked into the sunlight and scanned the terrain, as if seeking confirmation of his assessment.

"From what I can gather, he considers the café a symbol of his wife; she was Sal. When they were in business, he pumped gas while she did the cooking. She died in 'sixty-seven, and he never got over it. So when he starts thinking about her and gets really low, he drives down, sits at the counter, and reminisces. Which is what happened last night. It was the twentieth anniversary of her death. He'd pulled out their wedding album and gotten all weepy. When he couldn't take it anymore, he threw on some clothes, grabbed the album and a quart of Jack Daniel's, drove over, locked himself in, and got shitfaced. He's a little hazy about time but figures he got here around eleven and dozed off around one. At eight he was awakened by shouts. At first he thought it was an evil booze dream, but then his head cleared, and he realized someone was out there. He peeked out through the window, saw what was happening, and crouched behind the counter. Poor old guy was so scared he stayed there for three hours before calling anyone."

He glanced at the old Plymouth.

"That's his car. No one saw it because he'd parked it in the garage and locked the door."

"Lucky for him."

He shook his head.

"It was no accident. We found a piece of rubber hose attached to the exhaust pipe. Needless to say, we're going to be looking after his health. He's far from the perfect eyewitness but good enough to renew my faith in God."

"What did he see?"

"By the time he woke up things had already gotten nasty. Radovic and the bikers were shouting at each other. Skaggs isn't sure, but he thinks the leather boys said something about Radovic's not keeping his end of a bargain, and Erno responded in his usual endearing manner: laughed, cussed them out and put up his fists. At that point things moved pretty fast. The fat biker must have blinked wrong because Radovic hit him, floored him with a fist in the gut and a fast chop under the bridge of the nose. Skaggs says he went down easy, like a 'soft sack of shit.' But the skinny one was another story. When he saw his buddy laid out like that, he pulled out a chain and a buck knife and went into a street fighter's crouch. Radovic reached into his pocket—we found another Beretta on the body—but Skinny was too fast. He got the chain around Radovic's neck, jerked him close, and stepped straight in with the knife. The ME looked at the wounds and said permanent damage was intended: There was a forward thrust that pierced the liver and several up-and-down saw cuts. Also a throat slash, which appears to have been done after he was dead—your basic street fighter's coup de grace. Afterward Skinny revived Fatso, and the two of them split. Skaggs heard an engine starting, but he was hiding so he didn't see the vehicle."

"One vehicle? You'd expect two bikes."

"The old man claims he heard only one, and the techs found only one set of unaccounted tire marks, so it looks like they doubled up on one chopper. Romantic, huh?"

He ran his hand over his face and stared at his shoes.

"I looked at the body myself, Alex. He was thoroughly eviscerated. You know how I felt about the guy, but that's still no way to go."

We began walking away from the crime scene, drifting toward the roadside and keeping parallel to it. There was a large bolt in the dirt, and Milo kicked it. A flock of crows rose, squawking over a distant hilltop.

"Tell me more about that sculpture he bought," he said.

"A heavy lump of clear Lucite, with all kinds of toys molded inside to create a tableau."

"A Ken doll hanging, you said?"

"From a noose, with a knife in his belly. What really grabbed my attention was the title. *The Wretched Act.* It's a phrase Jamey used to describe suicide."

"And the artist is another one of those geniuses from the university."

"Right. A kid named Gary Yamaguchi. According to the others, the closest thing Jamey had to a friend. He was seen going off with Jamey and Chancellor."

"Tell me more about the toys inside the plastic."

I realized that I hadn't looked at the sculpture that closely. Concentrating, I tried to recall the details of the scene.

"It was a takeoff on a teen-ager's bedroom. Football pennants, a diary, miniature pill vials—empty ones—a toy knife, fake blood."

He frowned.

"Doesn't sound like something worth bidding for. Anything else?"

"Let's see—some photos of Barbie, a Beatles poster, love letters."

"What kind of love letters?"

"Miniatures. One-inch scraps of paper with 'I Love You' all over them."

"All that to dress up Ken with a knife in his gut, huh?" He shook his head. "Art."

We walked a bit.

"The bikers," I said, "they keep cropping up."

"Uh-huh."

"Doesn't that put a new cast on the Slasher case?"

"It complicates matters, but if you mean, does it help Cadmus, the answer is no. All it might boil down to is that Chancellor and Cadmus's little cutting club had two more members than we thought. Which makes sense—we never found anyone who saw Chancellor cruising Boystown, and a guy like him would be damned conspicuous. He was an executive type, used to delegating odd jobs. So he could have sent the bikers to snare pretty boys and bring them to the mansion, then let them stay for the party."

"Which means the bikers may have killed him."

"We found the knife in Cadmus's hand. What does that make him, an innocent bystander?"

"A psychotic bystander."

"Then why wasn't he killed, too? You're reaching, Alex."

"Maybe," I said, "but what's Radovic's connection to all of it?"

"Could be he found out what was going on during his nights off, and when he tried to blackmail the bikers, things got out of hand."

"Then why was he following me? And why was he so intent on buying *The Wretched Act?*"

He sighed.

"Look, I'm not saying that's the way it actually went down. Just that it's goddamned complicated and far from a reprieve for Cadmus." He clenched his jaws and breathed in deeply. "Maybe Radovic really was trying to clear Chancellor's name—even assholes have bursts of altruism— and he thought you might know something useful because you were Cadmus's therapist. Or maybe his motives were impure, and he thought you might be able to give him some dirt for the same reason."

"I hadn't treated Jamey in five years."

"How was he supposed to know that? What if Cadmus rambled on about what a great doc you were and Radovic thought you were still in the picture?"

I remembered what Andrea Vann had told me that first night at Canyon Oaks: that Jamey had spoken of me fondly. When he was lucid.

"That still doesn't explain why the bikers ransacked Gary's place."

"You want me to play Answer Man? Okay. Yamaguchi was a member of the cutting club, too."

My mind rebelled at the thought of another Project 160 member indicted for murder.

"That's ridiculous."

"Why? You yourself said he was seen going off with Chancellor and Cadmus."

"If he were a murderer, he wouldn't advertise it in a sculpture."

"It's been known to happen. Few years back one of those British crime writers made a good case for a painter named Sickert being Jack the Ripper. The guy did paintings that were damned close to some of the murder scenes. And from what you told me about Yamaguchi, rationality isn't his strong suit. Shoot enough speed, and the old cerebral cortex starts to look like Swiss cheese."

"When I saw him, he was hostile, but he was rational—"

"Point is, Alex, I could stand here and theorize all day, which would be a great parlor game for the whodunit crowd. But without evidence the whole thing translates to *bullshit*. Bikers, Cadmus, back to bikers again. A goddamn roller coaster. And roller coasters always make me puke."

He lengthened his stride and jammed his hands in his pockets.

"What really gripes me," he said, "is that we've already done a damned good search for those assholes. Spent weeks running down dozens of leads and listening to Whitehead's pearls of wisdom. Visited every S and M bar in L.A. and saw enough leather to upholster the state. We even pulled a couple of guys out of undercover— guys Narco'd taken a lot of time to plant in the outlaw gangs. All for nothing."

"You've got a physical description to go on now."

"What? One fat, one skinny? For some reason—undoubtedly sociological—those assholes tend to fall into two categories: *gordos disgustos* or speed freak anorexics. *Fat and skinny* eliminates exactly zero percent of the population."

"The old man saw them. Couldn't he tell you more?"

"Sure. The fat one was bald—or maybe he had real short hair—with a big or maybe medium beard that was either black or brown. The skinny one had long hair that was straight or wavy or curly and a mustache—no, make that a mustache and a beard." He sighed disgustedly. "Eyewitnesses are notoriously inaccurate when it comes to physical description, and this one's an eighty-year-old depressive coming out of a heavy drunk. I'm not even totally convinced he heard any of the conversation he reported. I need something solid, Alex. I've put in an order to have Pacific Division go down to the Marina and toss Radovic's boat. Maybe we'll even find the sculpture and learn that it's crammed full of emeralds. Or coke."

"Just like in the movies."

"Hey"—he grinned—"this is L.A. Anything's possible, right?" The grin faded. "I want to talk to Yamaguchi. Where can I find him?"

"He drifts around downtown. I got to him through the gallery, but it sounded as if he were planning to leave L.A. He may be gone by now."

He took out his book and wrote down Gary's name and the address of Voids Will Be Voids. I thought of something.

"There was a little blond girl with him who looked as if someone might have cared for her once upon a time."

"Name?"

"He called her Slit."

"Sweet. I'll run a check with Juvie. Let's head back. I want to put a couple of calls through."

We turned around and walked back toward the café. When we reached the Matador, Milo got in and began talking into the radio. While I waited, I peered inside the café. A small, shriveled man in a plaid flannel shirt and overalls stood behind the counter, scouring the chrome-lipped top with a wet rag. The counter stools were chrome-legged mushrooms with red leather tops. An inert Black Forest cuckoo clock hung on the knotty pine wall, next to a third-rate oil painting of Lake Tahoe. Strains of country music—George Jones lamenting that his blood could start a still—floated forth from a cheap transistor radio.

The music was overtaken by engine sounds from the north. I turned and saw a jeep appear to float over the horizon. It sped on and slowed down at the cordon. The driver stared at the crime techs, then coasted to a halt in front of the café, turned off the motor, and got out. The jeep bore the emblem of the Parks Department, and the man wore a ranger uniform. He was in his forties, skinny, and sun-cured with generous features, round wire-rim eyeglasses, and an Abe Lincoln beard. Wisps of yellow hair sneaked out from under the brim of his Smokey the Bear hat. The back of his neck was the color of steak tartare.

"Sergeant Sturgis?" he asked.

"That's him over there."

"Bill Sarna." He extended a hand as hard and dry as rawhide.

"Alex Delaware."

"Sergeant?"

"Consultant."

That puzzled him, but he smiled through it. I looked over at Milo.

"He should be off in a moment."

He glanced at the café's open door.

"I'm going to go see how Asa's doing. Come on in when you're ready."

He removed his hat and entered Sal's.

Several minutes later we joined him at the counter. Inside were more third-rate landscapes, more time warp ambience: a shelfful of Depression glass; a tool and die company calendar dating from 1967, a wall menu listing steak and eggs for $1.95 and nickel coffee. Cobwebs tapestried every corner. The place smelled stale and musty, like the mausoleum it was.

"Hello, gents," croaked the old man. He was moving a lot without accomplishing much—darting, pacing, scrubbing nonexistent stains, patting, wiping. His face had a caved-in look, the legacy of several years of toothlessness; his hyperactivity seemed theatrical, a charade designed to coat the place with the veneer of vitality.

Sarna stood. He and Milo introduced themselves.

"Like to offer you fellows coffee or something," said the old man, "but I been a little lax about provisions."

"That's okay, Asa," said the ranger. "Next time."

"You betcha. Chicken-fried steak and buttermilk biscuits with snap beans and chicory coffee. Maybe next time?"

"Sure." Sarna smiled. "Looking forward to it." He put a hand on Skaggs's shoulder, told him to take care of himself, and led us out of the café.

"How's his mind?" asked Milo.

"Good enough for eighty-three."

"What about as a witness?"

The ranger put on his hat and adjusted it.

"Sometimes he gets a little lost in wishful thinking."

"Terrific. Has he been suicidal before?"

Sarna looked surprised.

"Before?"

As Milo told him about the hose around the exhaust pipe, his face grew grim. The mustacheless beard made him look like an Amish elder.

"That's news to me. I've always thought of him as a solid old guy with too many memories. As far as being a quality witness, I couldn't say."

"He have any family?"

"Not that I know of."

"Who can I talk to about looking in on him?"

"There's a senior citizens' group at the Baptist church, but as far as I know, Asa's a nonbeliever. If you want, I can ask around."

"I'd appreciate that, Bill."

Up the road the technicians had started to pack up.

"My captain said it was a nasty one," said Sarna, watching. "Biker cutting?"

Milo nodded.

"We get a few of those each year, mostly in Angeles Crest. Which club was involved?"

"We don't know. Skaggs couldn't identify any colors."

"What about the victim?"

"The victim wasn't a biker."

"Hmm. That's worrisome. Most of our calls are the result of those turkeys getting blasted on booze and crank and tearing away at each other. But for the most part, they've stayed away from the straights. Hope this isn't the start of something. Do you need help with your search?"

"No, thanks. The search is over. We sent guys out in all directions hours ago, but they didn't find a thing. Later the techs told us that the tire tracks pointed back to the highway."

"That means they could have headed into one of the northern canyons or back into the city. When did it happen?"

"About eignt this morning."

"Then it's too late to do anything about it. Asa give you any physical description?"

"One was fat; the other was skinny. Which clubs ride around here?"

"The major ones—Angels, Mongols, Satan's Disciples—as well as a bunch of smaller packs that come and go. They tend to headquarter in Foothill Division—Tujunga, Sunland—and use parkland for partying."

"Is this parkland?"

"No. Originally it was owned by the army. Then it was transferred to private ownership. But once in a while we patrol here anyway. The surrounding canyons have been earmarked for recreational development, and unless you've got a map, the boundaries are tricky. If you're asking whether this is a hub of biker activity, it isn't."

"What kind of criminal stuff goes on here?"

"In Bitter Canyon specifically? Not much. Once in a great while we come across a body that was killed elsewhere and dumped. Then there's the usual petty stuff—teen-agers drinking, poachers bagging tortoises. Nothing heavy."

"What I'm getting at is this," said Milo. "Our victim may have been engaged in a blackmail scheme. The homicide could have resulted from a payoff gone bad. Can you think of any reason someone would come all the way out here to transact business?"

Sarna removed his glasses and grew contemplative.

"Just that it'd be far from prying eyes. It's a darned quiet place, Milo. No tourism to speak of, because it's not as pretty as some of the other spots. The lake's impressive, but it's inaccessible for fishing or water sports. Lately there's been a little more traffic because of the power plant—surveyors, architects, construction people—but even they're few and far between."

"What kind of power plant?" I asked.

"Hydroelectric."

"From a lake?"

Milo looked at me curiously, but he didn't cut me off.

"It's more than the lake," said Sarna. "Bitter Canyon's not really a canyon at all. It's a water-filled volcanic crater surrounded by sloping mountain walls and fed by underground streams. It's the streams that make the difference, because you get constant replenishment. The estimates run into the billions of gallons. Untapped." He'd segued into a lecture and was enjoying it. "There's a ten-year plan with two long-range goals: to harness the water for enough energy to meet the needs of the north-

ern Valley and to establish an emergency drought control
reservoir that interfaces with the aqueduct."

"Sounds like the quiet days will be over."

"Once the construction gets going. It's a huge under-
taking—forty-five million dollars for the plant alone and
another twenty-five million for the town that's supposed
to grow around it. They've been talking about it for
years. It got a kick in the pants a few years back when we
had that drought and all the fancy restaurants stopped
serving water with dinner. Then the rains finally came,
and things quieted down. They revived it about two years
ago, but it took quite a bit of backroom politics to push
through a bond issue to finance it."

"Environmentalists?" I asked.

"No. Like I said, except for the lake itself, which few
people ever see, it's not particularly pretty around here,
and the locals are more interested in jobs than preserving
creosote. But there was a conflict-of-interest matter that
took a while to resolve; the company that owned the land
was the prime bidder to build the plant."

"Cadmus Construction?"

"That's right," he said, surprised. Then he looked at
us with sudden insight. "Homicide cops from West L.A.
That case, huh?"

"Bill," said Milo, leaning forward conspiratorially, "we
don't know yet. And we'd appreciate it if this conversation were kept under wraps."

The ranger drew a line across his lips.

"Sealed."

"Muchas gracias." My friend smiled. "These construction types who've been passing through, where do they
go?"

"To the northeast rim of the crater. It's the only place
you can get a look at the entire lake. They stand there
and draw plans."

"Do they ever get down to the lake itself?"

"Nope. It's a two-day descent for an experienced
climber. With pitons and rope."

"How about giving us directions so we can take a look
ourselves?"

"What are you driving?"

Milo pointed to the Matador.

The ranger shook his head.

"Forget it unless you feel like hiking. The road ends four miles before the viewpoint. It's four-wheeler terrain. I'll take you in the jeep."

We hurtled south over a progressively deteriorating road, the ride bone-jarring, the view through the window flaps of the jeep a horizontal slash of ghost-pale rock, infinite and inert. But Sarna made it come alive, giving names to the scrub—greasewood, honey mesquite, rabbit brush—directing our eyes toward rare oases of activity—a flock of birds feasting upon a bitter cherry bush, an alligator lizard scurrying across the spines of a fan palm—extolling the beauty of a single, time-ravaged digger pine, describing the savagery of a hard winter in the high desert and the resilience of those creatures that survive.

Throughout it all Milo slumped in his seat, nodding at the appropriate time, his mind fixed upon a different kind of savagery.

The transition from blacktop to dirt caused the jeep's chassis to vibrate like a bowstring. The dirt turned to sand, and our wheels kicked up a dust storm. Sarna seemed to view it as a challenge, maintaining his speed and playing with the gears in lieu of braking. Milo and I held on to our seats.

We climbed and dipped through the scrub, then climbed again. Remembering what Milo had said about roller coasters, I looked over and saw him: shut-eyed, tight-lipped, and honeydew green.

The jeep continued to rise. Sarna gave one final feed of gas, and we lurched to the top before reaching a shadowed plateau. He came to a halt, set the parking brake, and bounded out.

"We've got to take the last bit on foot."

We got out and stood facing a stand of pines. Most of the trees were dead—hollow gray hulls with jagged, dry spikes for branches, some felled, others tilting improbably out of the parched earth. The live ones didn't look significantly better. The space between their trunks was filled by eye-searing flashes of gray-white light, and we were forced to look down.

Sarna found a pathway through the trees. We followed him, ankle-deep in leaf dust, stepping gingerly over brittle spindles of dead branches. Once Milo snagged his trouser leg and had to stop to free himself. He still looked ill, but his color had returned to normal.

Beyond the trees was a clearing, and as we neared it, the gray-white light grew unbearably intense. We walked haltingly toward open ground, shading our eyes with our hands. Sarna stopped along a sloping, sandy rim blemished by random mounds of rock. And beyond the rim, the white-hot light.

"It's hard to see at this time of day," said the ranger. "But if we stand over there, we can probably get enough shade. Be careful, the ground tilts sharply."

He led us to the shelter of one of the rock formations, a pile of boulders topped by an overhanging sandstone shelf. We stood under the shelf and looked out.

The lake was an opal set into the sun-gilded earth. Its surface was as brilliant as a crystal mirror, so static that it seemed artificial. A single step out of the shade turned it into a blinding disk of luminescence, as Milo quickly learned.

"Jesus," he said, shielding his face and returning to shelter.

Sarna lowered the brim of his hat and nodded.

"The setting sun hits the rocks at an angle that sets off one heck of a refraction. It's another reason few people come up here."

"It's like a goddamn sheet of plate glass," said Milo, rubbing his eyes.

"That's what the Spanish thought, too. They named it El Cañón Vidrio, which later became vulgarized to Bitter Canyon. Which is a shame, don't you think? Because on top of being a heck of a lot prettier, the Spanish is accurate."

"*Vidrio,*" said Milo.

"Sure," said the ranger. "The glass canyon."

23

SARNA DROPPED us off back at the café, and Milo spent another half hour talking to Asa Skaggs, making small talk and trying to find out if he remembered seeing anyone matching Jamey's, Chancellor's, or Gary's description in the recent past. The old man stopped scouring a cold griddle and thought, scratching his head and sucking on his toothless gums.

"Yamagooch—that's a Jap name, ain't it?"

"That's right."

"We used to have Japs around, in the relocation camp up near Mojave."

"During World War Two?"

"You bet. Later they let 'em out and put 'em in the army, and I hear they done pretty well—tough little monkeys."

"I was thinking a bit more recently, Mr. Skaggs."

"Hmm. No, haven't seen any Japs since then. Plenty of 'em in the city, though. Near San Pedro Street. They call it Little Tokyo now. Got a lady in town, Alma Bachman, who likes to drive over there and eat raw fish. Says it makes her feel younger, which don't make much sense, does it?"

"Not much," said Milo.

"You remember those days pretty well, don't you, Mr. Skaggs?" I said. "During the war and right after?"

"You bet."

"Do you remember the man who bought the army base?"

"Mr. Black Jack Cadmus? Hard to forget him. Now, that was a gentleman, the kind you don't see no more. Carried himself like a king. Beautiful clothes, down to the spats. Sometimes he'd drive up to look at the lake and stop in for a fill-up and a window wash. I remember

293

the car. Twenty-seven Bugatti. Forty-one Royale, the one with the big monobloc straight eight and the twin-choke carburetor. Jet black and big as a bus. He'd had it restored in Italy and shipped over. The way the thing was put together you had to strip the whole engine down if you needed to work on the valves. Maintenance alone cost enough to support half a dozen families for a year, but that's what the man was like. High style, only the best for him. Once in a while, if I was changin' oil or checkin' the tires, he'd come in here, sit right where you're sittin'. Have a cup of coffee and a chocolate roll—the man loved chocolate. Sal used to say he coulda been a movie star with that black hair and them white teeth."

"Did he ever bring anyone with him?"

"Nope. All by his lonesome. Drove the Bugatti as far as it would go, and then he'd hike around for a couple of hours. I'm saying that 'cause sometimes he'd come back all dusty and I'd kid him. 'Been climbin and gettin' into mischief, Colonel Cadmus?' You could talk to him like that; he had a sense of humor. And he'd smile and answer back, 'Communin' with nature, Asa. Gettin' back to basics.' "

The old man winked and lowered his voice.

"I never asked him about it, but I think he was up there writin' poetry."

"Why's that?"

"He used to carry this little book with him and one a them fancy gold-tipped fountain pens. One time, when I was cleaning the windows, he left it open on the seat. I got a quick gander, and it was laid out in these little paragraphs, like poetry. When he saw me lookin', he closed it real quick. Probably didn't want to be thought of as no nancy boy."

Milo smiled.

"What did the book look like?" I asked.

"Smallish, leather."

"Black leather?"

"Darkish is all I recall. Coulda been black."

"Did you ever read what was inside?"

"Nope. Never got that close."

"But you're pretty sure it looked like poetry."

"You bet. What else would a real man been ashamed of?"

* * *

We exited the café. The crime techs had departed, and the road was as silent as a graveyard.

"What were you getting at?" asked Milo. "Poetry and all that."

"The book Skaggs described matches the one in *The Wretched Act*," I said, "which, now that I think about it, didn't fit with the rest of the sculpture. Everything else in the scene was miniaturized, but the book was full size. Way out of proportion. On top of that it looked more like an antique than a teen-ager's diary. Gary had scrawled 'Diary' on it in lavender, but it was a sloppy job—totally out of character with his style. He's compulsive, Milo. In all the other pieces he took pains to be precise."

A hawk rose over the darkening hills and began circling. Milo stared up at it.

"I know," I said, "there are thousands of black books in this world. But *glass canyon* was one of Jamey's pet phrases when he hallucinated. He used it the night he called me; it means this place was on his mind. Ordinarily you could brush that off, because he's psychotic and a lot of experts, including Mainwaring, don't put much stock in psychotic speech. But Radovic got killed out here. Is that coincidence?"

Milo ran his hands over his face, grimaced, and cleared his throat.

"Let's roll it back for a minute," he said. "Once upon a time Old Man Cadmus used to drive up here—to the glass canyon—hike around, and write poetry in a black book. Forty years later his grandson—who's a poetry freak and *hallucinates* about glass canyons—rips off his boyfriend and a tag-along chicken and busts a serial murder case wide open. Then the boyfriend's bodyguard buys a punk sculpture to get hold of the black book, uses it to blackmail two bikers, and gets butchered for his trouble."

He looked at me.

"Enough to make your head hurt, isn't it?"

He walked to the Matador, got in, and closed the door. I watched him pick up the radio speaker and talk into it for several minutes, nodding and brushing the hair out of his eyes. Then he hung up and climbed out of the car, looking preoccupied.

"Pacific Division just started the search of Radovic's boat. Someone had already been there and tossed it good. They left behind guns, knives, and a wad of cash he had hidden in the base of the steering wheel. Also a power drill, a pile of plastic chips and dust and the rest of the toys from the sculpture—the guy I spoke to got a big kick out of hari-kari Ken—but no black book. According to Skaggs, nothing changed hands between Radovic and the bikers, which by itself wouldn't be enough to convince me of anything. But the fact that people went to the trouble of burglarizing the boat means they were still looking. So either they found it or Radovic stashed it somewhere clever and it's still around."

A sudden rush of cold air blew in from the south. Milo tightened his tie, and both of us buttoned our jackets. The sky had darkened to charcoal splashed with indigo and coral. The hawk became a faint black crescent, then disappeared. And all around, a primeval silence.

"I can just see it," said Milo. "The golden arches'll be over there, right next to the Taco Bell, which'll be belly to belly with Ye Olde Bitter Canyon Souvenir Shoppe— wiseass postcards and plastic models of the power plant. Progress."

I got caught up in his imagery, visualizing high concrete towers jutting brazenly out of the low, silent hills, the modular claws of a prefab town strangling the solitude. Then I remembered something Heather Cadmus had told me.

"Milo, Jamey and Chancellor met at a party thrown by Dwight Cadmus for the money people behind a Cadmus construction project. It was a large-scale deal, and Chancellor was a major investor. Be interesting to find out what that project was, wouldn't it? And the exact nature of Chancellor's involvement."

His eyes widened with interest.

"Very." He laced his hands behind his neck and thought out loud. "Which means getting access to all of Chancellor's financial records. Which, on top of being a major procedural hassle because it would give chest pains to plenty of biggies, would have to go through Dickie Cash— Chancellor's bank's in Beverly Hills. Given Cash's level of industriousness, count on at least a month. And if he's in on it, Whitehead'll have to be, too. Along with all our so-called superiors, which in Trapp's case is a gross inaccuracy. You met those guys, Alex. Far as they're concerned, the Slasher case is solved. They're gonna be real enthusiastic about dealing with this."

"Radovic's murder doesn't bother them?"

"Radovic is a throwaway, a three F: Find it; file it; fuck it. Quoth Charming Cal to Dickie when I wasn't supposed to be listening: 'The faggot was lucky. This was faster than AIDS. Har-har.' "

He grimaced. "Must be nice to be that concrete, huh? Put everything in neat little cubbyholes."

"I think I can find out about the project," I said, "without going public."

When I told him how, he was pleased.

"Good. Do it. If you get something, we'll dig deeper." He looked at his watch.

"Better be getting back."

"One more thing," I said. "I know you're convinced of Jamey's guilt, but it wouldn't hurt to consider other alternatives."

"You got some, toss'em at me."

"For one, someone should be taking a closer look at Canyon Oaks Hospital. The night Jamey escaped no one was at the desk. Maybe that kind of incompetence is typical, but maybe it's not. The nurse in charge had piled up lots of debts. She quit soon after Jamey was arrested and left town with a brand-new car."

He smiled faintly.

"Been doing a bit of detecting?"

"A bit."

"What's her name?" he asked, pulling out his notepad.

"Andrea Vann. She's a divorcée traveling with a little boy." I gave him the Panorama City address.

"What kind of car'd she buy?"

"Mustang."

"I'll run a trace on the registration, see what comes up. Anything else?"

"Mainwaring. He has a reputation for being pliable when it comes to a buck. Not a bad choice if you wanted to stash someone away with no questions asked. He bent the rules by letting the Cadmuses bring in their own nurse. Could be he bent a few more."

"You talked to the guy. Did you pick up anything iffy?"

"No," I admitted. "His treatment wasn't particularly creative, but it was adequate."

"Anything you would have done that he didn't?"

"I would have talked more to Jamey, attempted to get a picture of what was going on inside his head—which isn't to say that I would have succeeded. But Mainwaring didn't even try. Jamey had consistent hallucinations. Months before he was committed he was saying the same things as he was the night he called me. Someone more openminded might have been curious about it." I paused. "Or maybe Mainwaring knew and chose to suppress it."

Milo raised his eyebrows.

"Now you're talking conspiracy, my friend."

"Just throwing stuff out."

"Let's get back to these consistent hallucinations. What did Cadmus talk about besides glass canyons?"

"He used the word *stink* a lot. The earth was stinking and bleeding. Rankstink. Bloody plumes. White zombies. Needle games."

He waited a few moments.

"Anything else?"

"Those are the most repetitive elements."

"Any of it meaningful to you?"

"Now that I know about the power plant, I suppose there could be an ecological flavor to it—bleeding the earth, stink as a symbol for pollution."

"How does 'needle games' fit in with that?"

"Needle games and miles of tubing," I recalled. "When I first heard it, I thought he was expressing his fear of treatment. Of course, back then I thought 'glass canyon' meant the hospital."

"What about 'plumes' and 'zombies'?"

"I don't know."

He waited awhile before asking:

"That it?"

When I nodded, he put the notepad away.

"I don't know," I said, "maybe Mainwaring's right and I'm overinterpreting. Maybe it's just crazy talk that doesn't mean a damn thing."

"Who knows?" said Milo. "Over the years I've learned to respect your intuition, pal. But I don't want to raise any unrealistic expectations. You're a long way from restoring Cadmus's virginity."

"Forget virginity. I'd settle for the truth."
"Sure of that?"
"Not really."

When I walked through the door, Robin gave me a mischievous smile.

"A sweet young thing named Jennifer has been calling every half hour."

I kissed her and took off my jacket.

"Thanks. I'll call her after dinner."

"Dinner is pizza and a salad from Angelino's. Is she as cute as she sounds?"

"Absolutely. She's also a former . . . student. And seventeen years old."

Pretending to count on her fingers, she said:

"Less than half your age."

"Now that's a grim thought."

She came over and nuzzled my ear.

"That's okay. I'll still love you when you're old and gray." She touched my hair. "Grayer."

"Gee, thanks."

"So tell me, do all your former students call you *Alex* in that breathlessly eager way?"

"Only the cute ones."

"Swine."

She bit down on the ear.

"Ouch."

She drew away, laughing.

"I'm putting the pizza in the oven and taking a bath while it warms. Here's Jenny-poo's number. Why don't you call her, *Alex,* and when you've worked yourself up sufficiently, come in and join me?"

Handing me the number, she sashayed away.

I dialed and got Mrs. Leavitt.

"Oh, you just missed her! But she should be back in a couple of hours."

"I'll try back later."

"Please do, Doctor. I know she wants to talk to you."

I heard the bath water running. There was another call I wanted to make, and I went into the library and leafed through the Rolodex.

Unsure whether Lou Cestare was still wooing fat cats on *The Incentive* or back at the Willamette Valley estate,

I dialed the yacht and got a taped message to call Oregon. The Willamette number was another tape, informing me that it was after hours but that in case of emergency Mr. Cestare could be reached through a beeper code. I punched the code and was connected to a preschool voice.

"Hello, this is Brandon Cestare. Who is this, please?"

"Hello, Brandon. My name is Alex. May I please talk to your dad?"

"Are you a client?"

"Yes. My name is Alex."

"Hi, Alex."

"Hi. Is your dad there?"

"He's in the bathroom."

"How about your mom?"

"She's breast-feeding Hillary."

"Oh. How old are you, Brandon?"

"Five and a half."

"Do you know how to write?"

"Just printing."

"If I spell my name, could you print it on a piece of paper and give it to your dad when he gets out of the bathroom?"

"Yes. Let me get a piece of—"

The end of his sentence was cut off by Lou's voice ("Who is it, Bran? . . . Thanks, tiger. . . . No, that's all right, I'll talk to him. . . . What? . . . No, you don't have—Brandon, it's not necessary. I've—okay, okay, don't get upset, sure, let me explain it to him.").

Cestare came to the line, chuckling.

"It's Lou, Alex. Brandon insists on writing your name down."

"Put him on." I laughed.

The boy returned and said, "What's the letters?"

I dictated my name, and he read it back to me.

"Perfect, Brandon. Now, could you please give it to your dad?"

"Yeah. He's right here."

"Thanks. Bye."

"Byc."

"Hi again," said Cestare.

"You've got a conscientious staff, Lou."

"Train 'em young. What's up?"

"I need some information on a recent bond issue. The Bitter Canyon Power Plant."

"Good bond, but you've got enough long term in your portfolio."

"I'm not interested in buying, just in finding out some of the details."

"What kinds of details?"

"Some background on the issue. Who bought into it in a big way."

Sudden wariness crept into his voice.

"Why do you want to know this?"

"It's related to a case I'm working on."

That silenced him for a moment.

"What does psych have to do with a power plant?"

"I'm not free to get into that, Lou."

"You know something about the issue that I should?"

"No. I—"

"Because I'm into it sufficiently heavy to get burned if something goes wrong. If there's even the slightest nuance of a problem, I want to know about it. Right now."

"Is it a shaky issue?"

"Hell, no. It's a triple A-rated, MBIC-insured." He paused. "But so were the Washington Power bonds. The whole damned investment business is based on faith. And considering the debacles of the last few years, it doesn't take much to shake the faith. If there's going to be a sudden sell on Bitter Canyon, I want to be at the head of the line. Now, what's your connection to it?"

"I can't tell you, Lou."

"I don't believe this! You call me at home in order to pump me and then refuse to tell me why. Alex, you and I—"

"Lou, this has nothing to do with finance. I haven't heard anything even hinting the bond's in trouble. Fact is, I don't know a damn thing about it. It's the people behind it that I'm interested in."

"Which people?"

"Ivar Digby Chancellor. Beverly Hills Trust. The Cadmus family. Any connections between them."

"Oh. That case."

"That case."

"What's your connection with it?"

"Defense consultant."

"Not guilty by reason of insanity?"

"Something like that."

"From what I hear you've got your work cut out for you. Kid's supposed to be really crazy."

"You get that from the *Wall Street Journal?*"

"The financial whiz grapevine. Anytime a major corporation's involved in something nasty, we money types make it our business to assess the impact."

"And?"

"And the general consensus is that the impact is zilch. If the kid had control of the corporation and planned to turn the lake into a giant Jacuzzi, there might be something to worry about. But in his condition that's hardly likely, is it?"

"Hardly."

"Something the matter, Alex?"

"No. About Chancellor—"

"Gay as a blade but a smart fellow and a hell of an arm twister—the right combination of creativity, caution, and *cojones*. Beverly Hills Trust is one of the strongest small banks on the West Coast. Chancellor took good care of his depositors. put through enough smart deals to beat the big boys on interest rates without overextending himself. Made money the old-fashioned way: by inheriting it and watering it until it grew nice and tall. If you're rich enough, you can get away with liking young boys and wearing eye shadow. What else do you want to know?"

"Was he involved in setting up the Bitter Canyon deal?"

"Most probably. As a skid greaser. He'd been dealing with the Cadmuses for years and had plenty of clout with the Water and Power boys, so his influence could only be salutary. But his *major* involvement was when it came to buying. BHT was a major purchaser of the initial short-term serials. I remember that because by the time the offering came out, all the serials had been snapped up. I was curious who got them and did a little research. He also bought into the long terms. Let me move to the phone by the computer, and I'll punch in the data."

He put me on hold and returned in a moment.

"Okay. I'm calling it up right now. Bitter Canyon Consolidated System Power Revenue Bonds, Series of 1987—here we are. It's a state bond, not a muni, because there's no municipality of Bitter Canyon yet. We're talking seventy-five million dollars in revenue—fifteen thousand lots of five-thousand-dollar bonds at par. Eighteen million were in serials maturing from 1988 through 2000, staggered toward the end; the rest, in long terms: one-third twenty-year maturities; one-third, twenty-fives; and one, thirtics. Nineteen million each."

"What was Chancellor's buy-in?"

"Wait a sec. I've got that on another file. Okay, here it is. Now, this isn't rock solid precise 'cause there may have been some under-the-table trading, but it's pretty damn close. According to my data, BHT snapped up ten million of the scrials— including the shortest terms, which were the most desirable—and another ten in long terms. That's through the bank. Chancellor may have bought more for himself personally, but it'd be difficult to trace that."

I calculated mentally.

"Over a quarter of the total. Isn't that a big purchase for a small bank?"

"Sure is. It's also atypical for any bank to get that heavily involved in long terms, especially considering the downward trend of the bond market over the last few decades. But Chancellor was known as someone who bought aggressively when he believed in something. No doubt he figured to sell at a premium in the secondary market."

"How'd he get such a large share?"

"The Cadmuses and the government gave him the inside track because a big buy by BHT was mutually beneficial. When a savvy investor demonstrates that kind of confidence in an issue, it raises the general level of enthusiasm."

"Where did the rest go?"

"The serials were evenly distributed among several major financial institutions: other banks; savings and loans; brokerage houses; insurance companies. As were a healthy chunk of the long terms, with a little left over for a few eagle-eyed independents such as yours truly."

"Sounds like a hot issue."

"Red-hot. By the end of order-taking period all of it was gone. What does that have to do with defending the Cadmus kid?"

"Probably nothing. Let me ask you one more thing: Could a prior agreement by Chancellor to buy large numbers of bonds influence approval of the issue itself?"

"As a guarantee? Sure. If there'd been initial feasibility issues regarding the project, it couldn't hurt to have a major supplier of project revenues lined up a priori. But that wasn't the case with Bitter Canyon, Alex. The reason it was a hot issue was that the setup was a sweet deal all around. The Cadmus family's owned the land since the war. They bought it dirt cheap from the army and could afford to sell it back at a very substantial discount and still make a whopping profit. That profit, in turn, enabled them to put in a highly competitive bid to build the plant. And I do mean *highly*. That allowed the bond's interest to come out at half a point to a point over market. These days that's a hell of a lot, and since everyone's projecting lower rates in the foreseeable future, the premium could be juicy."

"One hand washing the other."

"Exactly. It makes the world go 'round."

"I've heard there was some opposition. Conflict-of-interest questions."

"Nothing substantial. Some of the other construction companies tried to raise a fuss, but it died in the back rooms. Most of them weren't big enough to put together a project of that size. The two companies that were couldn't come close to competitive bids. Pushing the objection would have raised the risk of a public outcry over expense padding—which they're all guilty of—and major delays. The surrounding municipalities and DWP wanted the project to be approved quickly and were exerting pressure to speed things up. Being seen as obstructionist would have been a major liability, politically speaking."

"Make waves and forget future contracts."

"A little more subtle than that, but you've got the general idea. Politically speaking, this was easy street, Alex—no Sierra Club types screaming about sacred cactus, high rates of local unemployment. Going to be lots of smiling faces when they break ground."

"When's that supposed to happen?"

"Early next year. Right on schedule."

"And Chancellor's death has had no effect?"

"Why should it? Sure, people are going to be looking

at who takes over the bank. If it's a moron, you're going to see a slow, steady trickle of withdrawals—nothing sudden, because everyone gets hurt in a run. But that's an internal issue that has nothing to do with Bitter Canyon. Or the bonds."

"What *could* affect the project?"

"Nothing smaller than your basic act of God—always nice to blame Him when things go wrong, isn't it? The lake evaporates overnight; Cadmus Construction turns socialist and converts to a macramé factory—I don't like the tone of this conversation. What the hell are you getting at, Alex?"

"I don't know, Lou. I really don't."

"Listen, I don't want to come across hysterical, but let me explain my position. In general, I stay away from bonds. Both for myself and in managing portfolios. Historically they haven't performed well, and at best you're protecting your flanks. But I have some clients who insist on them: conservative types like you and fools who are so rich they've deluded themselves that they have enough money. So I keep my eye out for good issues and buy in quickly. It doesn't happen often, but Bitter Canyon was one of those times, and I got in heavily. So far I've made a lot of people happy with it. But if it slides, those same people are going to be very unhappy. Murderously so. No matter that last year I was Midas. One mistake and I'm as popular as Arafat at the B'nai B'rith. All those years of charisma building down the proverbial crapper."

"Like I said, Lou, I haven't heard anything. If I do, I'll call you."

"You do that," he said fiercely. "Collect. Twenty-four hours a day."

24

I GOT to campus at seven the next morning. Although the psych building was locked, a side door was open, as Jennifer had promised.

The lab was two floors below ground level, at the end of a murky hall, just past an animal dormitory that smelled of rat chow and dung. She was waiting in the windowless room when I got there, seated at a gray metal table, flanked by stacks of books, photocopied journal articles, and a pad of yellow legal paper. An Edward Gorey poster graced the rear wall. To the left was a black-topped lab table, its gloss dulled by years of scalpel nicks; to the right, a barracks of cages. Atop the table was an open dissection kit and a spool of electrode filament. The cages percussed with activity—dark, oblong blurs banded with white, scurrying from side to side: hooded rats. They seemed especially restless, interrupting their exercise only to scratch, chirp, suck the spouts of their water bottles, or gnaw the bars in protest of man's inhumanity to rat. Some of them had sacrificed for science, their heads topped by pink caps of paraffin. Underneath the wax, I knew, was exposed brain tissue, strategically lesioned. Extending from the center of each cap was an inch of filament—electrode lead wire—that quivered with each movement of the skull that housed it.

"Alex." She rose quickly, as if startled. A rat squeaked in response to the movement.

She'd dressed completely in black: bulky sweater; skin-tight denims; high-heeled knee boots. Her tawny hair was shower-damp; her face, freshly scrubbed. Black plastic triangles hung from her ears. Her fingers jitterbugged on the table top. A dramatic-looking and very attractive young lady. Less than half my age.

"Good morning, Jennifer."

"Thanks for coming down. I know I wasn't too forthcoming last night. I didn't want to get into it over the phone because it's so complex."

"If you know something that can help Jamey, I'm all ears."

She looked away nervously.

"I'm not—I may have overstated myself. It's all conceptual at this point."

I sat down, and she followed suit.

"What's on your mind?" I asked.

"You remember I said his mental deterioration had intrigued me for a while? Well, the points you raised crystallized that intrigue: the lack of psychopathy; the contradiction between his supposed mental state and a serial murder profile; the visual hallucinations; the questions about drug use. I thought about it for a long time and kept going in circles. It was maddening."

After picking up a pen from the table, she used it as a conductor's baton, punctuating the rhythm of her speech.

"Then I realized that I'd been proceeding bass-ackwards, trying to adapt the facts—*the givens*—to an unverified hypothesis: that he was both psychotic *and* a serial murderer. The key was to throw all that out and start from scratch. Conceptually. To establish alternative hypotheses and test them."

"What kinds of alternatives?"

"All the permutations. Let's start with *murderer but not psychotic*. Jamey's a sadistic, homicidal psychopath who's been faking schizophrenia in order to escape responsibility for his crimes. It's a tactic that's been used before by serial killers—the Hillside Strangler, Son of Sam—totally in character with a psychopath's manipulative nature. But from what I've read, it doesn't work very well, does it?"

"No, it doesn't," I said. "Juries are suspicious of psychiatric testimony. But a defendant facing overwhelming evidence might still chance it."

"But Jamey could have avoided capture in the first place, Alex. There's no reason someone that bright—given the assumption that he's not psychotic—would allow himself to be caught red-handed and then rely on a low-return strategy. Besides, the psychosis wasn't something he just tossed on like a sweater. He was deteriorating long before he was arrested. *You* don't think he was faking, do you?"

"No," I said. "He's been suffering too much for too long, and it's gotten worse. The day I talked to you guys he threw himself against the walls of his cell and ended up with a concussion. It was bloody. Even a prison guard who'd been sure he was malingering had second thoughts when he saw it."

She turned her head toward the cages, watched a rat wiggle its snout through the bars, and winced.

"That's horrible. I read about it in the paper, but there were no details. How is he?"

"I don't know. I've been removed from the case and haven't seen him since."

That surprised her. Before she put the surprise into words, I said:

"In any event, you don't have to convince me he's not a psychopath. What's your next hypothesis?"

"*Psychotic but not a murderer.* The problem of the visual hallucinations remains, as does the general drug abuse issue. But both could be explained by the possibility that he was schizophrenic *and* a drug user."

"Simultaneously?"

"Why not? I know drug abuse doesn't cause schizophrenia, but hasn't it been known to put some people—borderline types—over the edge? Jamey's never been well adjusted—at least since I've known him. So, couldn't he have dropped acid or PCP and had a bum trip that loosened his ego boundaries and caused a psychotic break, then continued to take dope afterward?"

"Jen, according to almost everyone, he was antidrug. Nobody's ever seen him take anything."

"What about Gary? Did you find him?"

"Yes, and he did say Jamey was a user. But he'd inferred it from Jamey's behavior and admitted he'd never actually seen him trip out."

"So at least it's still an open issue," she insisted.

"The big problem with hypothesis number two," I said, "has nothing to do with drug use or psychosis. If he's not a murderer, how did he end up with a knife in his hand?"

She hesitated.

"Here's where it gets a little theoretical."

"Okay."

"What if he was set up? It would handle several conceptual problems at once. The question was *how*. And once I got on that track, it led me to the third alternative, the one I think provides the best fit because it eliminates all the inconsistencies: He's neither a murderer *nor* truly schizophrenic. Both the crime scene and his mental deterioration are the products of a psychobiological manipulation."

"Meaning?"

"Chemical mind control, Alex. Psychological poisoning. Someone used hallucinogens to drive him crazy. And planted him at the murder while he was stoned."

"That's a quantum leap," I said.

She reached across the table and grabbed my hand.

"I know it sounds far-fetched, but just hear me out."

Before I could reply, she was off.

"The concept isn't really that weird after all. Didn't the field of psychedelic research develop precisely because psychiatrists were looking for drugs that could simulate schizophrenia? In fact, before the term *psychedelic* was coined, LSD, psilocybin, and mescaline were called psychotomimetics; they *mimic* psychosis. And until the hippies gave it a bad name, LSD was considered a research wonder drug because it had the power to create an externally induced *model* psychosis. Psychotherapists started taking it to find out what their patients were going through, and pharmacologists studied the molecular structure in order to discern the neurobiologic—" She stopped, looked at our hands, and pulled away, embarrassed, then tried to hide it by rearranging her books.

"What am I going on about?" she said. "You know all this."

"Jennifer, I don't think your theory's far-fetched at all—as a theory. In fact, drugs have been in the back of my mind since I first got involved in the case. Because I've been searching for a way to absolve Jamey. So nothing would make me happier than to find out he's a victim and not a victimizer.

"Unfortunately," I continued, "once you get past theory, there are some serious problems. The night he was committed to Canyon Oaks, he was tested for LSD, PCP, and other street drugs and found negative." If

Mainwaring could be trusted. "And even though there are similarities between drug intoxication and schizophrenia, you know as well as I that they're far from equivalent states. Drug trips are more stereotypic and visually disruptive. Schizophrenia's primarily auditory—"

"But Jamey had visual hallucinations."

"He *may* have—some schizophrenics do—but the majority of his disturbances have been auditory. He heard voices. That's much more consistent with psychosis. And his deterioration's been chronic. Drug trips are generally short-lived. Someone would have to be virtually force-feeding him LSD to keep him that crazy. You'd just about need an IV drip."

"Which you could do in a hospital."

"But not in a jail."

She was silent but undaunted. After tearing a sheet of paper off the legal pad, she began writing.

"I'm making a list of all your objections. What else?"

"Okay. Even if we could prove he was doped up the night of Chancellor's murder, there's physical evidence connecting him to six other slashings. Was he doped up and planted at all those murders? Then there's the matter of his escape. How did he get to Chancellor's house from Canyon Oaks? Even if he were stoned, you'd expect him to have some memory of that night."

She scanned her notes, then looked up.

"What do you mean by physical evidence?"

"I don't know the details," I said, omitting to mention Heather Cadmus's lavender dress.

"If it's fingerprints, they can be lifted and transferred. Anything else is even less reliable. I've been reading up on forensic biology, and it's not nearly as scientific as most people think. Two experts can examine the same physical evidence and come up with diametrically opposite findings. Just like psych."

I smiled.

"As far as the escape," she said, "what if it wasn't an escape at all? Suppose someone set it up as an escape and then snatched him out of the hospital and dumped him at Chancellor's?"

I thought of Andrea Vann's new Mustang and wondered about that. But if the escape had been a kidnapping, why had he been allowed to call me?

"Now," she said, returning to her notes, "the issue of nonequivalency between drug trips and psychosis. What you say is true as far as LSD and most of the common hallucinogens are concerned. But it doesn't exclude some other drug, one that causes long-term disturbance and distorts auditory perception."

"And is easy to administer covertly," I added. "Orally or by injection. And unlikely to be tested for routinely. You're talking about the ultimate psychotomimetic."

She bobbed her head enthusiastically.

"Exactly!"

"Any suggestions?"

"No. I thought you might know."

"Nothing comes to mind," I said. "But I'm no expert in psychopharmacology."

"It's a researchable issue," she said, staring into my eyes. "I've got time. How about you?"

I thought for a moment.

"Sure," I said.

"Great!"

We walked south across the science quad, toward the medical center. It was seven-thirty, and the campus was beginning to fill: huffing joggers; preoccupied grad students; premeds and predents, burdened by book bags and self-doubt. It was one of those mornings that draw people back to L.A. despite the craziness, the air ocean-washed and astringently cool under a deep blue sky. Jennifer drew her serape around her and talked animatedly.

"At first I approached the issue from a purely cognitive perspective. Could you scramble someone's mind using purely psychological techniques?"

"Brainwashing?"

"Yes, but *relentlessly*—to the point of severe psychosis. Like what Charles Boyer tried to do to Ingrid Bergman in *Gaslight*. But that's movie stuff. In real life it wouldn't work; stress by itself isn't enough. I mean, think about the greatest stress a person could go through—the Nazi concentration camps, right?" Her lids lowered and closed for a moment. "My dad spent his adolescence in Auschwitz, and lots of his friends are survivors. I've talked to them about it. The trauma affected them for life—anxieties, depression, physical problems—but none of them actually went *crazy*. Daddy verifies that. The only people he remembers exhibiting psychotic symptoms were those who were psychotic when they entered the camp. Does that square with the data?"

"Yes. And with clinical experience. Over the years I've seen thousands of children and families under incredible stress, and I can't recall a single instance of stress-induced psychosis. Human beings are remarkably resilient."

She considered that, then said:

"And yet it's pretty easy to elicit psychoticlike behavior in rats and monkeys with stress. Dr. Gaylord's shown that. Electrify the floors of their cages, prevent escape, shock them at random intervals, and they just curl up, defecate, and withdraw. Do it long enough, and they never recover." She stopped and thought for a moment. "Human beings are a lot more complex, aren't they? As organisms."

"Yes." I smiled. "As organisms."

We walked the rest of the way in silence, arrived at the Biomedical Library five minutes before opening and filled the time by drinking coffee from a vending machine in an open courtyard. The walk had heightened the color in Jennifer's face, bringing a dusty rose flush to the surface of her tanned skin. Young skin, free of the tributaries etched by experience. Her hair had dried, and it shimmered in the sun. Her eyes mimicked the sky.

She put her books down, held her cup with both hands, and chattered animatedly between swallows. With each exclamation she edged closer to me, grazing my arm with tentative, darting touches, as if testing the surface of a hot iron. Several male students noticed her, then the interaction between us. I thought I saw a couple of them smirk.

"Let's go," I said, looking at my watch and tossing my coffee cup into a trash bin.

We entered the library just behind two dental students carrying bone boxes and found an empty oak table near the periodicals rack.

"How do you want to go about this?" she asked.

"Let's sit down and make a list of relevant topics, divide them between us, run each one down in the card catalog, then go into the stacks and track down the most promising ones. We can do a general scan first and bring back anything definitive."

"Sounds good. How about using the computer for the more recent stuff?"

"Medline?"

"And *Psych Abstracts*. I think they've got *Chemical Abstracts* online as well."

"Sure. Take it wherever the references lead you."

"Great—uh, do you have a faculty account? They won't run searches without guarantee of payment."

"No, my faculty appointment's across town. But they've done courtesy billing before through the pediatrics department. Use my name, and if you have any problems, I'll talk to them."

We made the list, divided it, agreed to meet at eleven-thirty, then parted ways—age-congruently: She made a beeline for the computers, and I spent an hour thumbing through the card index and jotting down call numbers before entering the twelve-story data silo known as the BioMed Stacks.

My search began in the psychiatry section and progressed through neurology and psychobiology. As I zeroed in on topics, the references grew progressively esoteric and wide-ranging. At the end of two hours I'd sifted through scores of documents and learned little.

As Jennifer had noted, psychedelic research had begun as an attempt to replicate psychosis, and the articles from the thirties through the fifties were, for the most part, dry treatises, preoccupied with molecular structure and laced with cautious optimism about future benefits to schizophrenia research. I came across Hoffman's description of the synthesis of LSD and other landmark references, but none of them dealt with the issue of premeditated psychological poisoning.

In the sixties the scientific climate changed. I'd been a college student then, too intent on studying to get side-tracked to biochemical recreation. But I remembered how Leary, Alpert, and others had begun to imbue drugs with philosophic, religious, and political properties—and the flood of bandwagon-jumping drug abuse that had ensued when the wrong people listened.

The sixties articles brought back those memories—chronicles of tragedy delivered in the matter-of-fact prose of clinical case histories: bum trippers leaping out of ten-story windows in spread-eagled flights of Icarian omnipotence, running naked down the freeway, cooking their arms in vats of boiling water, an orgy of self-destruction.

As psychiatrists and psychologists busied themselves developing treatments for drug poisoning, notions of scientific value vanished. Although the specter of permanent psychosis in psychologically healthy users was raised, researched, and eventually discarded, hallucinogens were deemed especially dangerous for borderline personalities and others with "weak ego boundaries." LSD was the most frequently cited culprit, but there were others as well: amphetamines, barbiturates, and a psychedelic named DMT and labeled the businessman's lunchtime high because it provided a sudden, intense trip of forty-five minutes to two hours.

Two things about DMT caught my eye: Sometimes lunchtime lasted longer than expected—aberrant bad trips had been known to last four or five days—and unlike LSD, its effects were potentiated—*intensified*—by the administration of Thorazine and other phenothiazine tranquilizers. I remembered Jamey's uneven response to medication, the up-and-down pattern that had puzzled and frustrated Mainwaring, and wondered if potentiation could have caused it. If he'd been poisoned with something like DMT, Thorazine would have made him crazier instead of more lucid. But DMT was too unpredictable for the type of calculated mind control Jennifer had suggested.

I read on and found articles on hashish, psilocybin, mescaline, and a quaint concoction combining both of them with LSD and DMT, known as STP. One piece that intrigued me was a collection of case histories by a research group at the UC San Francisco Medical School, which described STP as "biochemical Russian roulette" and noted that it had been the party drug of choice for outlaw motorcycle gangs. But that infatuation had been brief, for the cocktail had proved too volatile even for the beasts in leather. Bikers again. I tossed that around for a while, came up with nothing.

A footnote in a 1968 review made note of a drug called Sernyl, a short-term anesthetic developed by Parke, Davis for field use by the military but abandoned because, when overadministered, it had produced psychiatric symptoms.

Sernyl intoxication could resemble acute schizophrenia, to the point of causing auditory hallucinations. But according to the author of the review, its effects were so frightening—often creating the illusion of death by drowning and other horrors—that he didn't believe it had much potential for abuse. Ten years later Sernyl would be known primarily by its street names—hog, crystal, DOA, angel dust, PCP—and emerge as the main recreational drug of the inner-city ghettos. So much for prophecy.

PCP had been one of the first things I'd thought of after hearing Jamey's garbled speech on the phone and learning about his symptoms, which included some classic PCP reactions: sudden agitation and confusion to the point of violence, paranoia, auditory hallucinations, and a wind-down period of deep depression. PCP could be administered orally, and its effects lasted from hours to weeks. But as with DMT, that range was unpredictable. On top of that, PCP reactions were heavily dose-dependent: Small amounts could cause numbness or euphoria; moderate amounts, analgesia. The psychosis elicited by overdose could progress quickly to coma and death, and the difference between toxic and lethal blood levels was infinitesimal. Which means that a constant diet of PCP could just as easily kill someone as make him crazy. Too volatile to count on in a program of calculated psychological poisoning.

And there was another problem with PCP, the one I'd raised with Jennifer: Mainwaring had found none of it in Jamey's blood.

If the psychiatrist could be believed.

If he couldn't, what was the alternative? An evil doctor scenario, the healer using his skills to fashion madness? It had surface attractiveness. Solving the problem of dosage calculation; a "biochemical engineer" could have known how to adjust drug levels with the precision required for mind control. But past that point it fell apart. For Mainwaring had entered the picture long after Jamey had begun deteriorating. And even if he'd been involved before then, what motive could he have to poison his patient?

A discordant collage ran through my mind: punk sculptures, black books, power plants, and bloody bolts of lavender silk. I heard Milo chiding, "Another conspiracy, pal?" and realized that I'd let the intellectual ruminations of a seventeen-year-old—albeit a brilliant one—rope me into a guessing game.

Intellectual exercises for the idle, I thought, looking at the pile of books before me. A waste of time.

But I continued reading anyway. And proved myself wrong.

I found two promising references. What had seemed at first a perfunctory allusion to psychological poisoning in a Swedish article on chemical warfare led me to the botanical section of the stacks, in search of a monograph by McAllister et al. of Stanford University. But the book was missing. I took the elevator to ground level and went to the front desk on the off chance that it had been checked out and returned but not yet reshelved. The librarian was a husky black quarterback type who spent five minutes computer punching and page flipping before returning, shaking his head.

"Sorry, sir. That hasn't been checked out. Which means it's probably circulating within the library. Sometimes people take books to the Xerox machines and leave them there."

I thanked him and searched the area around the machines but didn't find it. Trying to spot a single volume in a place as vast as BioMed made the old needle-in-the-haystack game look easy, so I went looking for my second reference, taking the stairs down to the lowest level of the stacks, four stories belowground.

I found myself in a musty corner of the basement, surrounded by floor-to-ceiling metal cases jammed with antique volumes—collections deemed marginally relevant to high-tech medicine and sequestered like senile oldsters.

It was a bibliomorgue, silent and dim, the ceiling a tangle of exposed pipes, the walls mildewed and rust-spotted. One of the pipes had sprung a slow drip, and a pool of water had collected at the base of one of the cases; some of the books were softened and curled by moisture.

Many of the volumes were foreign: Latin, German, or French. Most were dog-eared. I had to squint to make out faded titles on weathered spines. Finally I found what I was looking for and carried it to a reading cubby.

It was bound in stiff white canvas that time had darkened to café au lait, a seventy-year-old volume, the size of an art book, filled with thick pages of elegant type and vellum inserts festooned with handcolored engravings. *The Taxonomy and Botany of Phantastica and Euphorica: The Products of a Search Among the Primitives for Narcotic Alkaloids* by Osgood Shinners-Vree, MBE, A.B., A.M., Ph.D., D.Sc., Professor of Botany and Botanical Chemistry, Oxford University, Research Fellow, The British Museum.

I turned to the introduction. The writing was pompous and a tad defensive, as professor Shinners-Vree attempted to justify a decade of jungle-hopping in search of mind-altering herbs.

"The history of human experimentation with the vegetal environment in order to manipulate the sensoria is as old as Mankind," he wrote. "But only in this century has Science developed the techniques to elucidate the chemical properties of the species I have classified *phantastica*, for the *betterment* of Mankind. Such benefits lie primarily in the treatment of the dementias and other nervous and mental diseases, but doubtless others will accrue as well."

The first chapter was a history of witchcraft in medieval Europe. Shinners-Vree's thesis was that witches had been skilled apothecaries who had used their talents for "unwholesome commerce"—pharmacologic hit women selling their services to the "less moral members of the Upper Classes."

Hired by the nobility to poison political and personal enemies, witches concocted brews containing:

Phantasticants of an alkaloid nature including, but not limited to, Black Henbane *(Hyoscyamus niger)* and the various derivatives of Belladonna *(Atropa belladonna)*. These flora have the ability to simulate fits of confusion and madness that persist from days to weeks and are, in larger concentrations, lethal. The highly skilled crone could be depended upon to blend the alkaloids in her brew with such precision that the outcome of imbibing was highly predictable: transient confusion, prolonged dementia, or *mortis*— all were at her command.

Thus, the witch of the Middle Ages was no more than a clever chemist, though she encouraged false attributions of demonic power in order to create an aura of omnipotence. The same can be said of the shamans and voodoo priests of Haiti and other Caribbean islands. The mental and physical disturbances brought about by their so-called spells are nothing more than intoxication achieved through the cunning use of alkaloids.

In Chapter Two Shinners-Vree charted his travels to Latin America and noted that "an unusually high concentration of mind-altering plants are indigenous to the New World. The *gi-i-wa* puffball of the Mixtecs, the sacred mushroom known as *teonancatl* (divine flesh) by the Aztecs, the tree fungus of the Yurimagua of Peru, the hex potion *ayahuasca* distilled by the Zaparo from the *banisteriopsis* vine as described by Villavicencio (1858)—all can be said to produce alkaloid exudates similar, chemically, to that obtained from *Atropa belladonna*. All are Phantasticants, all worthy of further study.

"I, however, have chosen to concentrate my attentions upon a specific source of belladonna: the tree datura, specifically the subgenus *brugmansia,* because of its unique vegetative properties. The remainder of this volume will be dedicated to that end."

I flipped through the illustrations—vivid and detailed renderings of shrubs and small trees, all sporting broad leaves, drooping, trumpetlike white or yellow flowers, and large, smooth, podlike fruit—and jumped into Chapter Three.

As the intrepid Professor S-V told it, *"Brugmansia* is the archetypical Phantasticant, both because ingestion of its various parts produces behavioural states that mimic, uncannily, the symptoms of acute dementia and other mental diseases and because of the degree of human control that can be exercised over its effects."

Human control. I read on, heart pounding:

Such control is due to the fact that *brugmansia* shrubs tend to mutate spontaneously and rapidly and that these mutations can be easily propagated by sticking a piece of stem in moist earth. So simple is the process that, in principle, even a dull child could rise to the task.

I have discovered in the valleys below the High Andes, the prevalence of curiously malformed "races" of the species, some so misshapen that any resemblance to the parent plant has disappeared. Remarkably, each has unique and predictable Phantasticant properties, caused, no doubt, by minute chemical alterations. Use of these races is not peculiar to one tribe. The Chibchas, the Chocos, the Qechuas, and the Jívaros are only some of the primitives who have grown expert in its application. (Matters of personal safety prevented contact with several of the others.)

The Indians use these "races" quite specifically. One is earmarked for the disciplining of wayward children, who are forced to drink a potion of its seeds ground up in water. Auditory disturbances follow, during which long-dead ancestors appear and admonish the youngsters. Another is believed to reveal the existence of treasures buried in graves; still another, to prepare warriors for battle by presenting to them the macerated faces of those they must kill. Though I have not witnessed this firsthand, I have been told that one of the more savage tribes employs a "race" of *b. aurea* to intoxicate the wives and slaves of dead warriors so that they acquiesce without struggle to being buried alive with their masters.

The "races" vary in potency, with the shamans of each tribe quite knowledgeable as to which are weak and which are strong. What is most remarkable, in fact, is the degree of sophistication with which these so-called primitives are able to manipulate the human mind through the selective application of intoxicating alkaloids.

I put the book down, feeling chilled and queasy. A little more than a year before I'd stepped into a greenhouse of horrors—horrific clones, the product of one madman's revenge against the fates. Now here I was, once again, confronting Nature at her most perverse. My thoughts were interrupted by footsteps. I saw Jennifer, carrying an armful of books, descend the stairs and head toward the section where I'd found Shinners-Vree's book.

"Hi," I said, and she jumped, arms flying out reflexively, books tumbling to the floor. She put her hand over her heart and turned toward me, pale and wide-eyed.

"Oh." Deep breath. "Alex. You scared me."

"Sorry," I said, getting up and walking to her side. "Are you okay?"

"Fine," she said hastily.

I stooped and collected the books.

"Silly of me to be so jumpy," she said. "It's just that it's spooky down here." Nervous laughter. "As if we're the first people to come down here in ages."

"We probably are," I said. "What are you looking for?"

"An old botany book. I've found something, and it's the original source."

"Come with me," I said, and led her to the cubby. After laying the books down, I lifted the big canvas volume.

"This it?"

She took it and thumbed the heavy pages.

"Yes!"

"You wouldn't happen to have been drawn to it by a reference in an anthro monograph from Stanford? McAllister, et al., 1972?"

She looked at me, astonished, then pulled a thin volume out of the pile on the desk, opened it, and read:

" 'The Use of Herbaceous Anticholinergic Alkaloids in the Maintenance of Social Order: The Brugmansia Rituals of the Indians of the Valley of Sibundoy, Southern Colombia. McAllister, Levine, and Palmer. How did you know?"

"A footnote in a piece on chemical warfare. What about you?"

"A cross reference from an anthro journal on live-burial rites. Amazing."

"Great minds traveling in the same direction."

We moved from the cubby to a large table. She listened while I summed up the Shinners-Vree book, then lifted the McAllister monograph and said:

"The Stanford group retraced Shinners-Vree's steps, Alex. Used his book and went into the Sibundoy Valley, searching for hallucinogen cults. McAllister was the prof; the other two were grad students working under him. When they got there, they found things virtually unchanged from the way Shinners-Vree had described them: several small, obscure tribes living in the jungles at the base of the Andes, cloning *brugmansia* and using it for every aspect of their life—religion; medicine; puberty rites. The Colombian government was planning a highway that threatened to destroy the jungle and eradicate the tribes, so they hustled to collect their data.

"Levine was into the biochemical variations between the clones. He found that the psychotomimetic ingredient in all of them was some kind of anticholinergic alkaloid—very similar to atropine and scopolamine. But his analysis failed to pinpoint the minute differences between the clones, and I never found any further publications of his, so his research may have come to nothing.

"Palmer was more culturally oriented. And a lot more productive; the book's her master's thesis. Do you suppose they put her name last because she was a woman?"

"It wouldn't surprise me."

"Thank God for feminism. Anyway, her research was a detailed description of how anticholinergics were used for social control. Her main hypothesis is that for the Indians, drugs took the place of God. In the discussion section she speculates that all religions had their origins in psychedelic experiences. Pretty radical stuff. But the main thing, Alex, is that those Indians knew exactly which clone to use to elicit exactly the symptom they wanted. That's proof it can be done."

"Atropine poisoning," I said. "A modern-day witch's brew."

"Exactly!" she said excitedly. "Anticholinergics block the action of acetylcholine at the synapse and screw up nervous transmission. You could thoroughly mess someone up by using them. And a psychiatrist wouldn't think to screen for them routinely, would he?"

"Not unless they were abused on the street. Did you come across anything like that?"

"No, and I combed the psychopharm indices. In minute dosages, atropine and scopolamine are relaxants, and they're used in over-the-counter medicines—sleep remedies; allergy potions; those little patches you put behind your ear to combat seasickness. But years ago they were prescribed in higher concentrations, and there *were* major side effect problems. Scopolamine was given to women in labor in order to help them forget the pain.They mixed it with morphine and called it twilight sleep. But it damaged the fetus and caused psychotic attacks in some patients. Atropine was used for Parkinson's disease, as an antispasmodic. It reduced the tremors, but patients started to become pseudosenile—forgetful, confused, and paranoid—a real problem until they developed synthetic drugs with milder side effects."

Pseudosenility. That recalled something—the shadow of a memory—but it darted through my mind like a minnow and hid behind a rock.

"And at the turn of the century," she went on, "there used to be something called antiasthma cigarettes, belladonna blended with tobacco. Dilated the bronchioles, but too many puffs and it caused major freak-outs: delirium, hallucinations, and *profound memory loss.* Which is another important point: Anticholinergics destroy the memory. If Jamey were stoned on them, you could pick him up, set him down, manipulate him like a puppet. Ask him about it the next day, and he'd have forgotten all about it."

She stopped, caught her breath, and opened her notebook.

"Something else," she said, flipping pages rapidly. "I found this little ditty on the symptoms of belladonna poisoning and copied it down."

She handed me the book, and I read out loud:

" 'Mad as a hatter, dry as a bone, red as a beet, and blind as a stone.' "

"Dry mouth and flushing," I said. "Parasympathetic effects."

"Yes! And when I read it, I remembered the day Jamey got all agitated in group. And the other times I saw him freaking out. Alex, during each episode, he was *highly flushed!* Red as a beet! Breathing hard! I'm sure I mentioned it."

"You did." And so had Sarita Flowers. And Dwight Cadmus, describing the night Jamey had torn apart his library. I concentrated and reeled in the exact words: *red and puffy and breathing hard.*

Looking at the books she'd collected, I asked: "Anything there on drug interactions?"

She extracted a thick red volume and handed it to me.

I turned to the section on anti-Parkinsonian drugs and scanned it. The warning to physicians was midway through the paragraph on counterindications and had been placed in a black-bordered rectangle:

Anticholinergics were potentiated by Thorazine.

Administration of most of the standard antipsychotic tranquilizers could prove harmful, even fatal, to Parkinson's patients and others who'd been given atropine or one of its derivatives, scrambling the nervous system and creating intense deleria and pseudomadness. *Pseudosenility.*

That set the minnow free and allowed me to net it: The throwaway I'd picked up that first night in the lobby of the hospital—*The Canyon Oaks Quarterly*—had featured an article on anticholinergic syndrome in the elderly, the misdiagnosis of senility caused by drug-induced psychosis.

If Jamey had indeed been poisoned with belladonna derivatives, the drug Mainwaring had pumped into him in the name of treatment had plunged him into a man-made hell. The evil doctor scenario was looking better and better.

I put the book down and tried to look calm.

"This is it, isn't it?" said Jennifer.

"It fits," I said, "but you'd need *brugmansia* clones to pull it off. Where would you get hold of something like that?"

"From someone who'd been to the jungle," she said, "before they bulldozed through it. A botanist or explorer."

I picked up the Stanford monograph and scanned it. At the end of the text were several pages of photographs. One of them caught my eye.

It was a stone carving, an idol used in a hallucinogenic burial rite. I looked at it more closely: a squatting toad with the face of a slit-eyed human, a plumed helmet atop the rough-hewn head. Crude yet strangely powerful.

I'd seen one just like it not too long ago.

Turning quickly to the front of the monograph, I read the names of the authors: Andrew J. McAllister, Ronald D. Levine, Heather J. Palmer.

Heather J. Palmer. A name out of a newspaper clipping. A June wedding in Palo Alto. The bride's mother

was a stalwart of the DAR. Her late father, the diplomat, had served in Colombia, Brazil, and Panama, where
the bride had been born.

The future Mrs. Dwight Cadmus had done field work
after all.

25

"THE AUNT," said Milo. "Jesus. This case is a goddamn cancer. Every time you turn around, it's spread somewhere else."

He warmed his hands on the coffee mug, took a bite of bagel, and went back to reading the McAllister monograph.

The rains had started late in the afternoon, gathering strength with ferocious haste, courtesy of a tropical storm blown inland. The last time it had come down this hard, the canyons had turned to fudge sauce and a healthy chunk of Malibu had been washed into the ocean. Despite its outward frailty—perched flamingolike on stilts and cantilevering improbably over the hillside—my house had withstood all previous onslaughts. But that didn't stop me from stockpiling sandbags and fantasizing about arks as each new sheet of water slapped against the redwood siding. Outside, the glen seemed to be melting, and I was shot through with melancholy and that special California sense of transience.

Lightning splintered the sky, and thunder applauded. Milo read while I fidgeted.

"This *brugmansia* is nasty shit," he said, peering at the pages. "Any number of ways to hit someone with it—tea, soup, food, cigarettes."

"Some preparations can be absorbed through the skin," I said. "There's a section later on about poultices."

"Wonderful. And Auntie's an expert on it." He frowned and slapped his hand on the table hard enough for the mug to dance. "Paying a quack to blitz a kid's mind. Very cold. Do you think at some level he understood what was going on? All that talk about zombies?"

"God only knows."

"Jesus, Alex. I hate family stuff. Pure shit, and the richer the family, the worse it smells. At least the poor

folk do it honestly—get pissed at each other, grab the
Remington off the rack, and blast away. These upper-
crust assholes don't even have the guts to act out their
own passions. Probably delegate their bowel movements.
'Grimes, take a shit, please.' 'Yes, madam.' " He shook
his head and took a long swallow of coffee.

"Besides lacking subtlety," I said, "blasting away with
the Remington gets you caught."

He looked up.

"Yeah, I know. There's still no solid evidence. Rub it
in."

"They looked everywhere for the book?"

"No," he growled. "We used volunteers from the Braille
Institute, let them tap around the deck for a coupla
minutes with their little white canes, and called it a day.
What do you think?"

"Excuse *me*, Sergeant."

"Hmmph," he mumbled, and returned to the book,
humming off key: "Rainy days and Mondays always bring
me down."

"It's Thursday."

"Whatever."

I went into the kitchen to get another cup of coffee.
Sitting on the window ledge and drinking, I waited for a
lull in the downpour. When none came, I put on my
raincoat anyway, stuck an old cowboy hat on my head,
and went down to the garden to check the koi.

The gravel around the pond had loosened, and the azaleas drooped defeatedly. But the water level was a good
six inches from overflowing, and the fish seemed to be
enjoying themselves, careening playfully in the turbu-
lence, pecking at the rain-packed surface of the water,
creating kinetic rainbows that sparkled through the gloom.
When they saw me, they raced forward and slurped at
the moss rock, bumping and grinding in a frenzy of fat,
wet polychrome bodies. I took some pellets out of the
feed canister and tossed them in.

"*Bon appétit*, fellows." I crossed the garden to take
a look under the house: muddy but intact, just a bit
of erosion. Some of the sandbags had gotten wet.

I dragged them out of the rain and had started to stack
them when I heard Milo call:

"Phone, Alex."

After scraping my shoes off, I climbed back up to the
terrace. He was holding the receiver with one hand, the
monograph with the other.

"Some guy who claims he's your broker. Very fast
talker."

I took the phone.

"Hello, Alex? Lou. Anything you want to tell me
about the Bitter Canyon bonds, yet?"

I glanced over at Milo. He sat hunched, chin in hand,
immersed in a chapter on rites and spells.

"Not yet. Give me a couple—"

"No sweat, Alex. I already unloaded it. After we spoke,
I went digging and found a slight trickle oozing out of
Beverly Hills. No big block sales, just a few odd lots here
and there, but there's definitely been some quiet selling.
Might mean nothing, but then again, it might. In any
event, I'm out."

"Lou, I—"

"Don't worry, Alex. I sold at a good premium and
made a tasty short-term capital gain. My clients are pleased,
and my charisma remains unscathed. If it crashes, I'll
look like Nicodemus; if not, we still did okay. So thank
you, Doctor."

"For what?'

"Information. I know you couldn't say anything, but
nuance was enough. The market runs on it."

"If you say so. Glad to help."

"Listen, I'm fueling up *The Incentive* and heading down
your way en route to Cabo San Lucas. Going to be
looking for white sea bass and the late albacore run, plus
there's a rumor the tutuava have returned. I'll be docked
at Marina Del Rey for a couple of days, tying up some
loose ends with a client. How about I call you and we
take lunch?"

"Sure, Lou," I said absently. "That would be great.
Listen, can I ask you a technical question—"

"That's what I'm here for."

"Not about finance. About boats."

Milo stopped reading.

"If you're looking to buy, I know someone who's got a
very clean thirty-foot Boston whaler. Probate situation—"

"Not in the market," I said, then looked out at the
downpour. "Yet."

"What then?"

"Lou, if you wanted to hide something on a boat, where would you put it?"

"Depends on the boat. *The Incentive*'s got all sorts of nooks and crannies, all that teak. If there's enough wood-work, you could hollow out a compartment virtually anywhere."

"No, I mean so even the pros couldn't find it."

"The pros?"

"The police."

Milo looked up and stared at me.

"Alex," said Cestare, "what the devil are you up to?"

"I'm not up to anything. Consider it a theoretical question."

He gave a low whistle.

"In some circuitous way this is related to Bitter Can-yon, isn't it?"

"It could be."

Silence.

"How big a thing are you trying to hide?"

"Say, five inches by eight."

"How thick?"

"An inch."

"That small, huh? For a minute you had me worried you were getting into something felonious. Cocaine trans-port, et cetera. But even coke wouldn't be worth smug-gling in such a small quantity . . . unless, of course, it were a private stash and you—"

"Lou," I said patiently, "I'm not a dope smuggler. Now where would you hide—"

"A five-by-eight-by-one *thing?* Let's see, have you tried the sea strainer?"

"What's that?"

"In a motorized boat—we are talking about a stinkpot, aren't we?"

I held my hand over the speaker and asked Milo:

"Radovic's boat motorized?"

He nodded.

"Yes."

"In a motorized boat, seawater is used to keep the engine cool. The sea strainer is basically a duct that runs through the boat, carrying the water to the engine and keeping it free of debris. You've got hatches on both ends. If I really didn't want something to be found, I'd use the one in the hull. You'd have to swim underwater to stash it. Is this *thing* perishable?"

"Yes."

"Can you use it in the kitchen? Animal, vegetable, mineral?"

I laughed.

"Anyway," he said, "I'd wrap it in something to protect it, unscrew the strainer hatch, stick the *thing* in, close it up, and forget about it. Sound like what you're after?"

"Could be. Thanks, Lou."

"Think nothing of it. We're a full-service brokerage house. Oh, one more thing, Alex."

"What's that?"

"Brandon says hello. You've convinced him he's an executive."

"Hello back to Brandon."

I hung up. Milo stood over me.

"So?" he said.

"Do you know a good frogman?"

The wind came in hard, cold gusts separated by ominous moments of frigid silence. The strongest blasts bent the masts of the smaller sailboats, causing them to whipsaw and dance. The air was a gumbo of bilge, gasoline, and sweet coastal air, lightly salted.

"This is supposed to blow over by evening," said Milo, drawing his yellow slicker tight and hugging himself. His pale face had pinkened in the chill, and his eyes were red and watery. The slicker made him look like a big school kid. "We can wait. You don't have to do it now."

The man in the wet suit looked out at the marina. Cinder skies had turned the water a deep, angry gray. Gray flecked with frothy white. Shark-fin waves threw off mottled highlights of pea green as they climbed, peaked, and rolled to sudden collapse. The man watched it for a while, white-lashed eyes compressed to a squint, young, freckled face stolid and still.

"S'okay, Sarge," he said. "I've seen worse."

He rubbed his hands together, checked his tanks, inspected the tool bag hanging from his weight bag, and stepped to the flimsy aluminum rail. Another diver climbed out of the cabin and flippered over. His face was equally young: shelf-chin, gray eyes, pug of a nose.

"Ready, Steve?" he asked.

The first man grinned and said, "Let's do it."

They pushed their masks down, climbed over the rail, held on, and curled their bodies, as sleek and black as bull seals. Without a word they went over, piercing the skin of the water and disappearing.

"Pacific Division rookies," said Milo. "Macho surfers."

We were standing on the bow of Radovic's boat, a fifteen-year-old Chris Craft labeled *Sweet Vengeance* in chipped gilt script, its fiberglass dull and scarred, its sloping deck caked with fish scales, grime, and black algae and badly in need of repair. The deck fixtures had been dismantled. Some hadn't been replaced. A fisherman's chair lay on its side. Several bolts had rolled into a corner. A rotting ribbon of kelp floated in a deepening pool of muddy water.

The door to the cabin had been left open, revealing a cramped interior made claustrophobic by jumbled clots of clothing and stacks of cartons. The boat had been taken apart.

"Looks as if the Braille people were thorough," I said.

"Oh, yeah," said Milo. "Dogs and all." He pulled out a handkerchief, blew his nose, and looked down at the water. Suddenly a face slap of wind whipped up the waves, and the boat lurched. Both of us grabbed the rail for support. The deck was slimy-slick, and I had to struggle to keep standing. Milo's feet slid out from under him, and his knees gave way. A fall looked inevitable, but he stiffened, put his weight on his heels, and fought to remain upright. When the wind died down, he was swearing and his face had started to turn green.

"Terra firma," he said weakly. "Before I heave my chowder."

We walked off the boat gingerly and waited on the dock, wet but stable. Milo breathed deeply and stared out at the angry harbor. Forty-foot craft bobbled like bathtub toys. His complexion remained pallid, tinted with olive.

"You okay?"

He puffed out his cheeks, exhaled, and shook his head. "Motion sickness. Had it since I was a kid. Lost my sea

legs the moment we climbed aboard. That last roll was
the final straw."

"What about Dramamine?"

"Dramamine makes it worse."

"There are patches you can stick behind your ear.
Laced with scopolamine."

"Very funny."

"No, I'm serious. Anticholinergics are great gastric
relaxants. It's one of their legitimate uses."

"I'll pass."

A moment later:

"Are those patches prescription or over-the-counter?"

"Prescription. But you can get anticholinergics over
the counter, if that's what you're asking—sleep remedies
and decongestants."

"Could you hoard enough over-the-counter stuff to
poison someone?"

"I doubt it. There are other ingredients in the pills,
many of them in much higher concentrations. Like adrenaline in decongestants. Too much of it, and the heart
gives out. A hoard with enough anticholinergic to cause
psychosis would be so loaded with adrenaline it would
kill the victim first. And even if you knew enough chemistry to extract what you wanted, it wouldn't give you the
desired effect. Jamey showed a progression of symptoms
that varied over time: He was drowsy when that was
called for, agitated on cue. We're talking about a manu-
factured psychosis, Milo. *Custom-tailored* to fit the needs
of the poisoner. Unadulterated atropine or scopolamine
couldn't be counted on to give you that much control. If
he was poisoned, it was with weird stuff. In combinations."

"Designer drugs."

"Exactly."

He turned up his collar and began rocking on his heels.
I noticed that his color had returned: the power of intellectual distraction. After several silent minutes he said:

"I'm going back to the car, try County again. The
resident I spoke to sounded sharp, but I want to connect
with the head guy."

He walked away with long, purposeful strides, leaving
me alone on the wharf. A hundred feet away was a
marine filling station with a minimarket just beyond the
pumps. I bought bad coffee and a glazed doughnut, stepped

under an awning, and sipped and ate as I watched a big sparkling yacht fill its tanks. Twenty minutes later Milo returned, notepad in hand. He looked at *Sweet Vengeance*.

"Nothing?"

"Not yet. How's Jamey doing?"

"Still stuporous. It was a serious concussion. There doesn't seem to be any major brain damage, but it's too early to tell. Vis-à-vis poisoning, the bloodwork's still at the lab, should be back in a couple of hours. I asked them to rush it, but apparently it takes time for technical reasons. The guy in charge—neurologist named Platt, sounds very on top of things—was pretty skeptical about the whole idea of atropine psychosis. Said the few cases he'd seen were Parkinson's patients, and even those were rare because they use different drugs now. He'd never heard of its being done deliberately. But he also said that if the tests do come out positive, they've got something that can pull him out of it relatively quickly."

He raised the notepad, shielded it from the rain, and read:

"Antilirium. It unblocks the damage done by atropine and cleans up the nerve endings. But it's strong stuff in its own right, and the kid's pretty beat-up to risk it without chemical confirmation. For now, they're putting him on unofficial detox. The only visitors have been Souza and the aunt and uncle; Mainwaring hasn't been there for four or five days. They're trying to keep an eye out without letting on and haven't seen anything fishy, but if the stuff's that absorbable, Platt admitted it could be slipping in anyway. He said the best they can do in the meantime is log meticulously and keep taking blood. He's handling all the kid's medication personally."

He looked at his watch. "What's it been, forty minutes?"

"Closer to half an hour."

"Ugly out there. They say sharks like this kind of weather. Gets the predatory juices flowing."

"They had enough air for at least an hour. More, if they're as experienced as they seemed."

"Oh, they're experienced all right. Hansen—the one with the big chin—moonlights as a scuba instructor. Steve Pepper was an all-Hawaii surfing champion. I'm glad they did it, but they're still nuts to go out there." He pushed a shock of hair out of his face. "The impetuousness of

youth, huh? I think I had it once but can't remember that
far back. Speaking of which, can your little friend Jennifer be counted on to keep quiet about all this?"

"Absolutely. It started out for her as an intellectual
lark combined with real compassion for Jamey, but when
reality sank in, she was pretty scared."

"Hope she stays that way. Because if it turns out to be
poisoning, we are dealing with heavy-duty evil."

"I impressed that on her."

The surface of the water broke with a splash. One
head, then another, appeared. Masks were pushed back;
mouths, thrown open.

"Yo! Sarge!

"We got it, sir!"

The divers hoisted themselves on deck, pulled off their
flippers, and leaped nimbly off the boat. Hansen handed
something to Milo.

"The hull hatch was soldered shut," he said, "so we
had to pry it off, which took awhile 'cause one of the
screwdrivers snapped. But once we did, it was a piece of
cake. Steve stuck his hand in, and bingo. It was wedged
about six inches up, positioned so the strainer was still
open. Looks like the plastic kept it dry."

Milo inspected the package in his hands. The book
appeared intact, swaddled in layers of clear Teflon bags
that had been heatsealed. The word *Diary*, scrawled in
lavender, was visible through the plastic.

"Excellent work, gentlemen. I'm going to notify your
watch commander. In writing."

Both men grinned.

"Anytime, Sarge," said Pepper, teeth chattering. Hansen slapped him on the back.

"Now go get warmed up."

"Yes, sir."

They jogged off.

"Come on," said Milo. "I want the lab to look at this.
Then we'll find a quiet place to read."

26

A BORED-LOOKING desk sergeant opened the door of the interrogation room and told Milo he had a call. He left to take it, and I picked up the black book and started to read.

What Old Man Skaggs had believed to be poetry was, in fact, a collection of impressionistic jottings, Black Jack Cadmus's version of a journal. The entries varied from incomplete sentences to several pages of inspired prose; on some days he'd written nothing. The handwriting was expansive and backslanted, so ornate as to verge on the calligraphic.

He was most expressive when writing about land purchase and management: how he'd cadged three hundred acres of orchard out of a San Fernando farmer at a bargain price by charming the man's wife "told her the pie was the best I'd ever eaten and complimented the baby. She leaned on the rube and we cut the deal that afternoon"; the maximum number of bungalows that could be constructed on a desert plot in the east end of the Valley; the most economical way to supply water to his projects; a Mexican crew boss who knew where to get cheap labor.

By comparison, his personal life had received short shrift in the sections that I read; his marriage, the births of his sons, even the beginnings of his wife's mental deterioration were most often relegated to single-sentence status.

One exception was a rambling August 1949 analysis of his relationship with Souza:

> Like myself, Horace has pulled himself up out of the gutter. We self-made men have plenty of be proud of. Give me one bootstrap yanker for a hundred

of those California Club pansies sucking their allowances straight from Mama's teat; Toinette's old man was one of those, and look how fast he slid down once he was forced to deal with the real world! But I think the experience of climbing to the top also leaves us with some scars, and I'm not sure old Horace has learned to live with his.

His problem is that he's too damned hungry—too damned intense! Took the thing with Toinette way too seriously. She told me he misunderstood; she never thought of him as anything more than a chum. Then to run like a mutt to fish-faced Lucy, only to have her throw him over for the medico! He smiles through it all, like a good little gentleman, but it worries me. I know he's always thought I should have cut him in as a full partner. But lawyering—even good lawyering—just doesn't put you on a par with the man who does all the thinking and the risk taking! Even after the war I continue to outrank him.

So I figure down deep he's got to hate my guts, and I'm wondering how to diffuse it. I don't want to cut the ties; he's a first-class maneuverer and a good friend to boot. Asking him to be Peter's godfather was what the hoity-toities would call a gracious gesture on yours truly's part, but the bottom line is bucks. So maybe I'll add on to his Wilshire parcel as a bonus, it's prime, but I'll have a lot more soon when the Spring St. deal goes down. A little charity camouflaged as gratitude could go a long way. Got to keep H. in his place but also make him feel important. Now if only he'd hitch himself up with a nice girl—preferably one that has nothing to do with me!

Milo returned, green eyes suffused with excitement.

"That was Platt. The blood tests are positive for anticholinergics. Lots of it. He was blown away, wanted to know when it would be okay to write it up for a medical journal."

He sat down.

"So now"—he smiled—"we've got more than theory."

"When will they be giving Jamey the Antilirium?"

"Definitely not today, probably not tomorrow. The head injury complicates things; it's hard to know how much of the stupor comes from the concussion and how much from the dope. They want him to be stronger before they give his nervous system another jolt."

He eyed the book in my hands.

"Learn anything?"

"So far only that Jack Cadmus's and Souza's views of their relationship don't jibe."

"Yeah, well that sometimes happens, doesn't it?"

He held out his hand, and I gave him the diary.

"Now that we've got method, it would be nice to firm up some motive before I call in Whitehead and the gang. How far'd you get?"

"August ninth 'forty-nine."

He found the place, backtracked a few pages, read for a while, and looked up.

"Arrogant son of a bitch, wasn't he?"

"The scars of a self-made man."

Twenty minutes later he found the first entry on Bitter Canyon.

"All right, here we go—October twelfth 1950: 'I'm in a good positon on the Bitter Canyon base because Hornburgh came to me rather than vice versa. That means the army wants to get rid of it quickly and they know I can come up with quick cash. But why? From the way Hornburgh threw around the Hail, Comrades bunkum, he'll be trying to jew me down by playing on my sense of patriotism. When he does, I'll turn it back on him. Ask him if a decorated hero isn't entitled to a fair deal from his Uncle Sam. If he keeps on buddying up, I'll ask him what he did in the war; Horace has checked around and says he was a West Point pansy who spent his entire tour pushing paper in Biloxi, Miss.' "

Milo turned a page.

"Let's see, now he's off on something else—a downtown office building . . . he's going to have to bribe someone to get a zoning variance . . . okay, here it is again. 'Hornburgh took me for a tour of the base. When we got close to the lake, it seemed to me that he looked a little antsy, though it may have been the heat and the light. The water's like a giant lens; when the sun hits it a

certain way, it's blinding—damn near unbearable—and a
milquetoast like Hornburgh is used to being pampered.
As we drove, his jaw kept flapping; the man may be a
colonel, but he blabs like a woman. Gave me the whole
song and dance about the potential for development:
houses; hotels, maybe even a golf course and country
club. I let him go on then said, "Sounds like the Garden
of Eden, Stanton." He nodded like a dummy. "Then
how come"—I smiled—"the army is so damned eager to
dump it?" He stayed smooth as cream, yammered about
needing to let go of the land due to congressional restric-
tions and peacetime budget concerns. Which is a lot of
gobbledygook, because the army does as the army damn
well pleases—hell, they say Ike will be the next pres, so it
can only get better. So the whole situation bears watching."

Milo hunched forward and peered at the diary.

"Back to the office building again." He frowned, running his index finger over the yellowed pages. "The bribe
worked. . . . Here's something on the wife. They were
invited to a party at the Huntington Sheraton, and she
stood in a corner and wouldn't talk to anyone. It pissed
him off. . . . C'mon, Bitter Canyon, where are you. . . .
Wouldn't it just be my luck for that to be all of it?"

He perused silently through September and October,
pausing from time to time to quote a passage out loud.
The quotes painted Jack Cadmus as the quintessential
robber baron—ruthless, single-minded, and self-obsessed—
with occasional lapses into sentimentality. The man's feelings toward his wife had been a combination of rage,
bafflement, and compassion. He professed his love for
her but viewed her weaknesses with contempt. Terming
his marriage "deader than Hitler," he described the mansion on Muirfield as "a damned crypt" and berated Antoinette's doctors as "Harvard-educated quacks who pat
my back with one hand while dipping into my pocket
with the other. All they have to offer are idiot grins and
jargon." He'd escaped the emotional void by embracing
work, power brokering and putting together one deal
after another, playing the high-stakes poker game known
as big business with an almost erotic zeal.

"Aha, here we go again," said Milo. "Wednesday,
November fifteenth: 'I've got Hornburgh and the damned
U.S. Army by the short hairs! After plenty of phone

bluffs I agreed to come down for another tour of the base. Once I arrived, Hornburgh made a pathetic attempt at flexing his own muscles—sent word that he'd be tied up in ordinance inventory for a while and had his driver zip me around in a jeep. Far as I could tell, nothing much was going on; the place looked empty. Then we passed a group of wooden bungalows on the east end and a passel of MPs marched out from between the buildings, all stiff and deadly serious. Looked like an escort, so I took a gander, and when I saw who they were guarding, I nearly jumped out of the jeep and went for his throat.

" 'That evil little weasel Kaltenblud! We zipped by fast, so I only saw him for a second, but I'd know that face anywhere—Lord knows I looked at it enough times! He was on our roundup list for Nuremberg, but we never got him—always seemed to be one step ahead. It made me suspect the damned CIA pansies had spirited him away in order to use him for dirty work, but questions to that effect got the usual hush-hush gobbledygook. Now, the proof!

" 'Damned unjust to let the weasel go after all the misery he caused, but no use making a stink, the war's over. On the other hand, no harm in using it to squeeze Hornburgh's nuts, is there? Because if what I'm thinking is true, the nervousness and all that eagerness to sell the base makes a lot of sense. However, I didn't choose to spring it on him today. Just filed it away for use.' "

"Ever hear of this Kaltenblud?" asked Milo.

I shook my head.

He thought for a moment.

"The Simon Wiesenthal Center keeps tabs on those assholes. I'll give them a call soon as I finish this." He returned to the diary. "Oh, shit, another digression. Now he's into a land swap with a bunch of Indians from Palm Springs. Old Black Jack was everywhere." He flipped pages impatiently.

"Okay," he said several minutes later, "this sounds like the showdown. November twenty-ninth: 'Over lunch at my office, I sprang Kaltenblud on Hornburgh. Told him if the weasel was at the base, I knew what kind of dirty work had been going on and understood damn well why they wanted to dump the place. At first he hemmed and hawed, but when I told him we could either cut a fair deal or let the newspapers dig around, he fessed up. Just as I thought, they'd saved the bastard's neck, brought him over on a private military transport, and set him up with a lab at the base. Little weasel didn't care who he did his dirty deeds for—U. Sam or Schicklgruber. Just went on his merry way and left behind tons of poisonous garbage—which, after I leaned on him for a while, Hornburgh admitted they buried underground. He insisted it was done safely, in metal canisters, supervised by the Corps of Engineers, but I've got no confidence in those yahoos, having seen plenty of messes they've created. So, as far as I'm concerned, the place is sitting on a land mine. One earthquake or Lord knows what else, and the poison could leak out into the lake or plume underground. A sucker deal if I ever heard of one! I figure they picked me for the sucker because I was buying more and faster than anyone and they thought I'd snap it up, no questions asked. Ha! By the time I left that office, it was they who were the suckers and I got everything I asked for:

" 'A. The land, at a price so cheap it borders on free. Every damned square foot except I set aside a little for Skaggs, because his wife's a damned good cook and he does a fine job on the Bugatti. B. They furnish me with signed and certified geological reports stating the place is virgin-clean. C. All documentation of Kaltenblud's dirty work destroyed clear to Washington. D. The weasel himself must be eliminated in some sanitary fashion just in case he gets big ideas and starts yapping. Hornburgh claimed that had been their idea all along, he'd outlived his usefulness, but I won't be satisfied until I see a photo of him with pennies on his eyelids.

" 'So as soon as all that goes through, I'll own Bitter Canyon free and clear. Doesn't look like there's much I can do with it for the time being, but it was a gift, so I can afford to wait. Maybe someday I'll find a way to clean it up, or maybe it can be exploited in some other way, like for storage or dumping. If not, I can just hold on to it, use it as a private getaway. Toinette's behavior is forcing me out more and more, and despite all the rottenness underneath, there's a kind of bleak beauty to the place—kind of like Toinette herself! Anyway, for what I paid, I can afford to let it go fallow, and after all, isn't being wasteful a sure sign a man's really made it?'"

"Poisoned earth," I said. "Plumes. Jamey was making sense all along."

"Too much sense for his own good," said Milo, standing. "I'm gonna make that call."

He left and returned a quarter of an hour later, holding a scrap of paper between thumb and forefinger.

"The folks at Wiesenthal knew him right away. Herr Doktor Professor Werner Kaltenblud. Head of the Nazis' chemical warfare section, poison gas expert. He was supposed to be indicted at Nuremberg but disappeared and was never heard from again. Which could make sense if the army kept its bargain with Black Jack."

"Black Jack would have demanded it."

"True. So the prick's definitely dead. The researcher I spoke to said he's still on the active file, considered one of the big ones who got away. He pressed me for what I knew but I stonewalled him with vague promises. If this thing ever resolves, maybe I can keep them."

He began to circle the room.

"A power plant built on tons of poison gas," I said. "Now you've got your motive."

"Oh, yeah. Seventy-five million dollars' worth. Wonder how the kid got hold of the diary."

"It could easily have been by accident. He was a voracious reader, liked to go rummaging around old books. The night he was committed to Canyon Oaks he tore apart his uncle's library, which could indicate he'd found something there before and was looking again."

"Buried for forty years among the limited editions?"

"Why not? After Peter died, Dwight was Black Jack's primary heir. Suppose he inherited the old man's books but never bothered to look at them? He didn't impress me as a bibliophile type. If he and Heather had come across the diary, they would have destroyed it. It was undisturbed because no one knew it existed. Until Jamey found it and realized how explosive it was. Chancellor had gotten him interested in business and finance, put him to work doing securities research. He had to know how heavily Beverly Hills Trust had invested in the Bitter Canyon issue, and he went straight to Chancellor and told him he'd bought a lot of potentially useless paper—

OVER THE EDGE

twenty million dollars' worth that couldn't be unloaded without attracting unwanted attention."

Milo had stopped pacing to listen. Now he stood with one palm pressed against the tabletop, the other rubbing his eyes, digesting.

"Your basic extortion/elimination scenario," he said softly. "With a bunch of extra zeroes tacked on. Chancellor confronts Uncle Dwight with what he's learned from the diary. Maybe Uncle knew about the gas, maybe not. In either case, Chancellor's chafing to get rid of those bonds and demands that Uncle buy them back. Uncle balks; Chancellor threatens to go public. So they arrange a buyout. It would have to be gradual, under the table, to avoid scrutiny. Maybe Chancellor even tacks on interest to compensate for pain and suffering."

"Or demands a premium price."

"Right." He thought for a while, then said:

"Fast Talker told you there's been some slow selling of the bond, which could mean Uncle's letting a little trickle back onto the market, but just like Chancellor, a little's all he can afford to let go of. That leaves him doubly at risk—building a plant on all that gas and paying for it himself."

"Tight squeeze," I said.

Milo nodded. "Time pressure, too. Uncle can't keep buying those bonds back without the corporate ledgers' eventually starting to smell bad. He searches for a way out, finds himself thinking how nice life would be if Chancellor—and the kid—were out of the picture. Tells his troubles to wifey-poo, who's an expert on blitzing people out with herbs, and they cook up a plan that will eliminate all their problems: Cut up Chancellor and set the kid up for the murder."

He stopped, thought, continued:

"You realize, that this doesn't mean the kid didn't kill anyone. Only that he might have been under the influence when he did it."

"True. But it does say something about culpability. He was set up, Milo. A disturbed kid pushed over the edge slowly, with exquisite care, until he was ready for a locked ward. After hospitalization the poisoning continued; the Cadmuses found themselves a doctor who'd do anything for a buck, including breaking his own rules to allow a private nurse to work there. Ten to one, Surtees's real job was administering the daily dose. Under Mainwaring's supervision."

"Surtees," he muttered, writing in his notepad. "What was her first name?"

"Marthe with an *e*. If that's her name at all. None of the nursing registries have ever heard of her. She vanished the day after he broke out. Just like Vann, who just *happened* to have stepped away from her desk. The whole thing stinks, Milo. He was allowed to break out, then taken to Chancellor's house and . . ."

"And?"

"I don't know." Translation: I don't want to think about it.

He put the notepad down and said he'd put a trace on both the nurses. "Maybe we'll even get lucky."

"Maybe," I said gloomily.

"Hey, don't overwork your empathy glands." Gently: "What's the problem, still thinking about guilt and innocence?"

"Don't you?"

"Not when I can avoid it. Gets in the way of doing the job." He smiled. "Course, that doesn't mean you civilized types shouldn't."

I stood up, pressed my palms against the green walls of the interrogation room. The plaster felt soft, as if weakened by the absorption of too many lies.

"I was hoping there'd be a way to find him truly innocent," I said. "To show that he hadn't killed anyone."

"Alex, if it turns out he was under the involuntary influence of drugs, he'll never see a day in jail."

"That's not innocence."

"But it is, kind of. There's something called the unconsciousness defense—applies to perps who commit crimes while unaware of what they're doing: sleepwalkers; epileptics in seizures; head injury victims; the chemically brainwashed. It's almost never used because it's even harder to prove than dim cap; real unconscious felonies are pretty damned rare. Only reason I know about it is an old guy I busted several years ago. Strangled his wife in his sleep after his doctors had fucked up his medicines and derailed his circuits. It was bona fide, backed up by real medical data, not just psych stuff—no offense. Even the DA bought it. They let him off at the prelim. Free and sane. Innocent. Souza'll be sure to jump on it."

"Speaking of Souza," I said, "there's something else to consider. He was the one who found Mainwaring. And Surtees. What if he's in on it and the whole defense is a sham?"

"Then why would he call you in and subject it to scrutiny?"

I had no answer for that.

"Listen, Alex, I like the general flavor of what we've come up with. But that doesn't mean we're even close to knowing what actually happened. There are lots of question marks. How did the diary get from Chancellor to Yamaguchi? How did Radovic know to look for it? Why was he following you around? And where do Fat and Skinny figure in? And what about all those other Slasher victims? I'm sure I could come up with a few more if you gave me some time. Point is, I can't afford to sit around and speculate, can't keep cowboying this thing much longer without clueing in Whitehead and the others. And before I do that, I'd prefer something more solid than old books to back me up."

"Such as?"

"A confession."

"How do you plan on getting that?"

"The honorable way. By intimidation."

27

THE STORM continued to rage, battering the coastline and dressing it in graveclothes of fog. Pacific Coast Highway was closed to nonresidents past Topanga, because of mud slides and poor visibility. The highway patrol was out in force, setting up roadblocks and checking IDs. Milo grabbed the magnetic flasher from the dash, opened the window, and slammed it onto the roof of the Matador. Having returned a drenched arm to the wheel, he steered onto the shoulder and sailed past the jam of high-priced buggies.

He braked at the command of a CHP captain, engaged in the ritual exchange of police banter, and drove on. As we hit the highway, the Matador's tires spun and skidded before attaining traction. He slowed down, squinted, and followed the taillights of a BMW with vanity plates proclaiming it HALS TOY. The police radio belched out a litany of disaster: fatal crackups on the Hollywood and San Bernardino freeways; a disabled truck obstructing the Cahuenga Pass; killer surf jeopardizing what remained of the Santa Monica Pier.

"Goddamn city's like a spoiled brat," he growled. "Minute things aren't gorgeous it falls apart."

To the left was the ocean, roiling and black: to the right, the southern edge of the Santa Monica Mountains. We passed through a section of highway that had been decimated by slides two years ago, the hillsides skinned like a slaughterhouse steer. Art and chemistry had come to the rescue: The denuded earth had been preserved under an immense sheath of pinkish brown fiberglass— the kind of trompe l'oeil topography used on movie sets, complete with molded furrows and simulated scrub. A Disneyland solution, synthetically perfect.

The house was two miles into Malibu, on the wrong

side of the Pacific Coast Highway, segregated from sand and sea by four lanes of blacktop. It was a small fifties ranch structure, a single story of white texture-coated stucco under a low, flat composition roof, the entry side coated with used brick, the sole landscaping beds of ice plant that hugged a rising asphalt driveway. Attached to the house was a double garage. Where the front lawn should have been was all oil-stained concrete.

Parked in front was a pea green Mercedes sedan. Through its rainclouded windows came a flash of white—a doctor's coat, draped over the passenger seat.

"I think I've got it down pretty good," said Milo, parking close to the house and turning off the engine, "but do me a favor and keep your ears open. In case he tries to snow me with technical stuff."

We got out and made a dash for the front door. The bell was out of order, but Milo's knock evoked a quick response—a slice of thin face through a door barely edged open.

"Yes?"

"Police, Dr. Mainwaring. Sergeant Sturgis, West L.A. Division. I believe you know Dr. Delaware. May we please come in?"

Mainwaring's eyes caromed from Milo to me and back to Milo, settling, finally, on a spot somewhere in the middle of my friend's thick torso.

"I don't understand—"

"Be happy to explain it, sir"—Milo smiled—"if we could just step out of this monsoon."

"Yes. Of course."

The door swung open. We walked through, and he backed away, staring at us, smiling nervously. Stripped of his white coat and status, he was far from impressive: a stoop-shouldered middle-aged man, undernourished and overworked, wolf face dotted with a day's growth of white stubble, hands clenching and unclenching at his sides. He wore a bulky gray fisherman's sweater over rumpled olive twill trousers and scuffed bedroom slippers. The slippers were cut low and revealed marble-white flesh veined with blue.

The interior of the house was musty and so devoid of style it had been rendered psychologically invisible: a boxy white living room filled with bland furniture that appeared to have been lifted intact from a department store display; walls hung with the type of seascape and landscape that can be purchased by the pound. Beyond the half-open door at the rear of the room was a long dark hallway.

The adjacent dining area had been converted to an office, its table piled high with the same kind of clutter I remembered from Mainwaring's sanctum at Canyon Oaks. A framed snapshot of two sad-looking children—the boy seven or eight, the girl two years older—was propped against a pile of medical journals. There was food on the table: a wax carton of orange juice, a plate of cookies, and a half-gnawed apple, browned by oxidation. On the floor was one of those robot toys—a jet plane—that transform into three other objects when manipulated by small, nimble fingers. Beyond the dining area was a pistachio green kitchen, still resonating with last night's cabbage and boiled meat. A Bach organ fugue streamed out of a Montgomery Ward stereo.

"Make yourselves comfortable, gentlemen," said Mainwaring, gesturing toward a cotton couch the color and texture of congealed oatmeal.

"Thanks," said Milo, removing his slicker.

The psychiatrist took it and my London Fog, regarded them as if they were diseased.

"Let me hang these up."

He carried the garments through the half-open door into the hall and disappeared in the darkness long enough for Milo to grow antsy. But a moment later he returned, closing the door.

"Can I get you anything? Some coffee or biscuits?"

"No, thanks, Doc."

The psychiatrist looked at the cookies on the table, thought for a moment, then sat down, folding his spare frame into a brown velveteen armchair. After selecting a briar out of a rack on the coffee table, he packed it, lit, sucked, and settled back, exhaling bitter blue smoke.

"Now then, what can I do for you, Sergeant?"

Out came the notepad. Milo flashed a stupid grin.

"Guess it's a switch for someone like you, huh? Me taking notes while you talk."

Mainwaring smiled with just a trace of impatience.

"Let me just get a few details out of the way, Doctor. First name."

"Guy."

"As in Fawkes, huh?"

The smile widened condescendingly.

"Yes, Sergeant."

"Middle name."

"Martin." He looked at me quizzically, as if expecting a secret eye signal or other evidence of a camaraderie. I turned away.

Milo put the pad on his knee and scrawled.

"Guy Martin Mainwaring . . . okay . . . and you're a psychiatrist, right?"

"That's correct."

"Which means you charge ten bucks an hour more than Dr. Delaware here, right?"

Mainwaring's eyes narrowed with hostility as he looked at me again, unsure what game was being played but aware, suddenly, that I was on the other team. He kept silent.

"The accent's British, right?"

"English."

"Where'd you go to school? In Britain?"

"I attended the University of Sussex," the psychiatrist recited crisply. "Upon earning my M.B.—"

"M.B.?"

"It's the English equivalent of the M.D.—"

"What does the *B* stand for?"

"Bachelor."

"So you're a Bachelor of Medicine, not a doctor?"

The psychiatrist sighed.

"It's called that, Sergeant, but it's equivalent to an American medical doctorate."

"Oh. I thought they called doctors Mister in Britain."

"Nonsurgical physicians are addressed as Doctor, surgeons as Mister. One of our funny little traditions."

"What do you use here in America?"

"M.D. To avoid the type of confusion you just experienced." When Milo didn't say anything, he added: "It's all quite legal, Sergeant."

"Confusion is right. Probably be more simple if I just called you Guy, huh?"

Mainwaring bit down on the pipe and puffed furiously.

"You were telling me about what you did after you got your . . . M.B., Doctor."

"I was awarded a residency at the Maudsley Hospital in London and was subsequently appointed to a lectureship there in the department of psychiatry."

"What'd you teach?"

Mainwaring looked at the detective as if he were a dull child.

"Clinical psychiatry, Sergeant."

"Anything in particular?"

"I instructed the house staff in comprehensive patient management. My specialty was the treatment of the major psychoses. The biochemical aspects of human behavior."

"Do any research?"

"Some. Sergeant, I really must ask—"

"I'm asking 'cause Dr. Delaware has done a lot of research, and when he talks about it, I always find it interesting."

"I'm sure you do."

"So what was your research about?"

"The limbic system. It's a part of the lower brain that's related to emotional—"

"How'd you study it—examine people's brains?"

"On occasion."

"Live brains?"

"Cadavers."

"That reminds me of something," said Milo. "There was this guy Cole; they executed him last year in Nevada; he used to go into sudden rages and strangle women. Killed anywhere from thirteen to thirty-five. After he was dead, some doctor lifted his brain in order to study it, see if he could find something to explain the guy's behavior. That was awhile back, and I haven't heard if he found anything. Has it been written up in some medical journal?"

"I really wouldn't know."

"What do you think? Could you look at a brain and say anything about criminal tendencies?"

"The origins of all behavior are in the brain, Sergeant, but it's not quite as simple as merely looking—"

"So what did you do with those cadaver brains?"

"Do?"

"How'd you study them?"

"I conducted biochemical analyses on homogenized—"

"Under a microscope?"

"Yes. Actually my use of human brains was infrequent. My usual subjects were higher-level mammals—primates."

"Monkeys?"

"Chimpanzees."

"You figure there's a lot to learn about human brains from looking at monkey brains?"

"Within limits. In terms of cognitive function—thinking and reasoning—the chimpanzee brain is significantly more limited than its human counterpart. However—"

"But so are some people's brains, right? Limited."

"Unfortunately that's true, Sergeant."

Milo inspected his notes and closed the pad.

"So," he said, "you're quite an expert."

Mainwaring looked down with forced modesty and polished his pipe with the edge of his sweater.

"One tries one's best."

My friend swiveled toward me.

"You were right, Dr. D. He is the right person to talk to." Back to Mainwaring:

"I'm here for a little medical education, Doctor. An expert consultation."

"Regarding what?"

"Drugs. How they affect behavior."

Mainwaring tensed and glanced at me sharply.

"In relationship to the Cadmus case?" he asked.

"Possibly."

"Then I'm afraid I can't be of much help, Sergeant. James Cadmus is my patient, and any information I have is privileged."

Milo got up and walked over to the dining room table. He picked up the photo of the two children and examined it.

"Nice-looking kids."

"Thank you."

"The girl kind of looks like you."

"Actually both of them resemble their mother. Sergeant, ordinarily I'd be pleased to help, but I have a staggering amount of work to do, so if—"

"Homework, huh?"

"Pardon me?"

"You took the day off to work at home."

Mainwaring shrugged and smiled.

"Sometimes it's the only way to get through the paper work."

"Who takes care of the patients when you're gone?"

"I have three excellent psychiatrists on my staff."

Milo returned to the living room and sat down.

"Like Dr. Djibouti?" he asked.

Mainwaring tried to hide his surprise behind a veil of smoke.

"Yes," he said, exhaling. "Dr. Djibouti. And Drs. Kline and Bieber."

"Reason I know his name is when I called the hospital to talk to you, they hooked me up with the psychiatrist on call, who was Dr. Djibouti. Very nice guy. What is he, Iranian?"

"Indian."

"He said you'd been out for four days."

"I've had a nasty cold." As if illustrating, he sniffled.

"What do you do for it?"

"Aspirin, fluids, rest."

Milo snapped his fingers and gave an aw-shucks grin.

"That's it, huh? For a minute I thought I might pick up a medical secret."

"I wish I had one to offer you, Sergeant."

"What about chicken soup?"

"As a matter of fact, I cooked a pot last night. A noble palliative."

"Let's talk about drugs," said Milo. "On a theoretical level."

"Really, Sergeant, I'm sure you're aware that my position as a defense witness for Mr. Cadmus precludes any discussion of his case with the police."

"That's not exactly true, Doctor. It's only your conversations with Cadmus, your notes, and your final report that are off-limits. And once you testify in court, even those will be fair game."

Mainwaring shook his head.

"Not being an attorney, I can't evaluate the validity of that assertion, Sergeant. In any event, I have nothing to offer by way of theoretical speculation. Every case must be judged on its own merits."

Milo leaned forward suddenly and cracked his knuckles. The sound made Mainwaring flinch.

"You could call Souza," said the detective. "If he decides to be straight, he'll admit I'm right and tell you to cooperate. Or he might advise you to stonewall while he pushes enough paper to stall me—to avoid looking like a patsy; lawyers like to play power games. In the meantime, you'd be wasting time: taken out of this nice warm house; forced to take a long ride in this kind of weather; sitting in an ugly room down at the West L.A. station; cooling your heels while Souza and the DA sling fifty-dollar words at each other. All at the expense of your paperwork. And after it's over, chances are you'll still be required to talk to me."

"To what end, Sergeant? What's the purpose of this?"

"Police business," said Milo, opening the pad again and writing in it.

Mainwaring bit down hard on the pipe.

"Sergeant," he said between clenched jaws, "I do believe you're trying to bully me."

"Far from it, Doc. Just trying to show you your options."

The psychiatrist glared at me.

"How can your ethics allow you to participate in this type of outrageousness?"

When I didn't answer, he stood and walked to a phone resting on an end table. He lifted the receiver and punched three digits before putting it down.

"Just what is it you want to know?"

"How different drugs affect behavior."

"On a theoretical level?"

"Right."

He sat down again.

"What kind of behavior, Sergeant?"

"Psychosis."

"Dr. Delaware and I have already discussed that, as I'm sure he's told you." Wheeling on me: "Why in blazes are you pursuing a dead issue?"

"This has nothing to do with Dr. Delaware," said Milo. "Like I said, it's police business."

"Then why is he here?"

"As a technical adviser. Would you rather he wait in another room?"

That suggestion seemed to alarm the psychiatrist.

"No." He shrank back defeatedly. "What's the difference at this point? Just get on with it."

"Great. Let's talk a little about LSD, Doc. It simulates schizophrenia, doesn't it?"

"Not very effectively."

"No? I thought it was a pretty good psychotomimetic."

The use of the esoteric term raised Mainwaring's eyebrows.

"For research purposes only," he said.

Milo stared at him expectantly, and he threw up his hands.

"It's difficult to explain in a brief discussion," he said. "Suffice it to say that an educated party would never confuse LSD toxicity with chronic psychosis."

"I'm willing to be educated," said Milo.

Mainwaring started to protest, then straightened his shoulders, cleared his throat and assumed a pedantic tone.

"Lysergic acid diethylamide," he intoned, "evokes an acute, rather stereotypic psychoticlike reaction that once caused some researchers to view it as an attractive tool for study. Clinically, however, its effects differ significantly from the symptoms of the chronic schizophrenias."

"What do you mean by *significantly?*"

"LSD intoxication is characterized by florid visual distortions—arrays of colors, often dark green or brown; dramatic changes in the shapes or sizes of familiar objects—and overwhelming delusions of omnipotence. LSD users may feel huge, godlike, capable of anything. Which is why some of them jump out of windows, convinced they can fly. When hallucinations occur in schizophrenia, they are typically auditory. Schizophrenics hear voices, are tormented by them. The voices may be muddled and indistinct or quite clear. They may admonish the patient, insult him, tell him he is worthless or evil, instruct him to carry out bizarre behaviors. While omnipotent feelings can exist in schizophrenia, they usually ebb and flow in relation to a complex paranoiac system. Most schizophrenics feel worthless, entrapped, insignificant. Threatened." He sat back and smoked, trying to look professional but not succeeding. "Anything else, Sergeant?"

"I've seen LSD trippers who were hearing things," said Milo. "And plenty who were pretty paranoid."

"That's true," said Mainwaring. "But in LSD abuse the auditory disturbance is generally secondary to the visual. And quite often subjectively positive. The patient reports sensory enhancement: Music sounds fuller, sweeter. Humdrum sounds acquire richer timbres. The paranoia you cite is typical of the *unpleasant* LSD experience—the so-called bum trip. The majority of LSD reactions, however, are experienced as positive. Mind-expanding. Which is in stark contrast with schizophrenia, Sergeant."

"No happy madmen?"

"Unfortunately not. Schizophrenia is a disease, not a recreational state. The schizophrenic rarely experiences pleasure. On the contrary, his world is bleak and terrifying; his suffering, intense—a private hell, Sergeant. And prior to the development of biological psychiatry, that hell was often permanent."

"What about PCP?"

"Cadmus was tested for it. As he was for LSD."

"We're not talking about Cadmus, remember?"

Mainwaring blanched, blinked, and struggled to regain pedagogic aloofness. His lips tightened, and a white ring formed around them.

"Yes, of course. That's exactly why I didn't want to have this discussion—"

"How's that cold?"

The white ring expanded, then disappeared as the psychiatrist forced his face to relax.

"Much better, thank you."

"Figured it had to be 'cause I haven't heard you sniff since that first time. Four days, you say?"

"Three and a half. The symptoms have just about disappeared."

"That's good. Weather like this, you have to be careful. Stay away from stress."

"Absolutely," said Mainwaring, searching the detective's face for hidden meaning. Milo responded with a blank stare.

"Is there anything else I can help you with, Sergeant?"

"We were talking about PCP," said Milo.

"What would you like to know about it?"

"For starters, how well it mimics schizophrenia."

"That's an extremely complex question. Phencyclidine is a fascinating agent, very poorly understood. No doubt the primary site of activity is the autonomic nervous system. However—"

"It drives people crazy, doesn't it?"

"Sometimes."

"Sometimes?"

"That's correct. Individuals vary greatly in their sensitivity. Some habitual PCP abusers experience euphoria; others become acutely psychotic after a single dose."

"Pychotic as in schizophrenic?"

"It's not that simple, Sergeant."

"I can deal with complexity."

"Very well." Mainwaring frowned. "To discuss schizophrenia intelligently, one must bear in mind that it isn't a single disease entity. It's a collection of disorders, with varying symptom constellations. Moderate-dose PCP reactions conform most closely to the type we call catatonia—disturbances of body posture and speech. But even catatonia is divided into subtypes."

He stopped, as if waiting for his words to crystallize. Hoping he'd said enough.

"Go on," said Milo.

"What I'm trying to emphasize is that phencyclidine is a complex drug with complex, unpredictable reactions. I've observed patients who manifest the mutism and grimacing of *stuporous* catatonia, others who display the waxy catalepsy of *classical* catatonia—they become human manikins. The ones *you'd* be most likely to come into contact with display symptoms that uncannily resemble an *agitated* catatonia: psychomotor agitation; profuse but incoherent speech; destructive violence directed against the self and others."

"What about paranoid schizophrenia?"

"In some patients large doses of phencyclidine can cause auditory hallucinations of a paranoid nature. Others respond to high-dose abuse with the kind of grandiosity and hyperactivity that leads to a false diagnosis of unipolar affective psychosis—*mania,* in lay terms."

"Sounds like a hell of a psychotomimetic to me, Doc."

"In the abstract. But by itself that's meaningless. All the commonly abused drugs are potentially psychotomimetic, Sergeant. Amphetamines, cocaine, barbituates, hashish. Even marijuana can cause psychotic symptoms when ingested in sufficient dosage. That's precisely why any psychiarist worth his salt will observe his patient carefully and test for drug history and the presence of narcotics in the system as a differential prior to establishing the diagnosis of schizophrenia."

"That kind of screening is routine?"

Mainwaring nodded.

"So what you're saying is that although drug reactions can mimic schizophrenia, it would be hard to fool a doctor."

"I wouldn't go quite that far. Not all doctors are sophisticated about psychoactive agents. An inexperienced observer—a surgeon, a general practitioner, even a psychiatric resident who lacked familiarity with drugs—might conceivably mistake drug intoxication for psychosis. But not a board-certified psychiatrist."

"Which is what you are."

"Correct."

Milo got up from the couch, smiling sheepishly. "So I guess I've been barking up the wrong tree, huh?"

"I'm afraid so, Sergeant."

He walked over and looked down at Mainwaring, put away his pad, and began extending his hand. But just as the psychiatrist started to reciprocate, he pulled it back and scratched his head.

"One more thing," he said. "This routine screening, does it include anticholinergics?"

The pipe in Mainwaring's mouth trembled. He used one hand to hold it still, then removed it and made a show of examining the tobacco within.

"No," he said. "Why would it?"

"I've done a little research of my own," said Milo. "Found that atropine and scopolamine derivatives have been used to drive people crazy. By South American Indians, medieval witches."

"The classic belladonna potion?" said Mainwaring off-handedly. Both hands were shaking now.

"You got it."

"Interesting concept." The pipe had gone out, and it took three matches to relight it.

"Isn't it?" Milo smiled. "Ever seen it?"

"Forced atropine intoxication? No."

"Who said anything about forced?"

"I—we were talking about witches. I assumed you—"

"I meant any type of atropine intoxication. Ever seen it?"

"Not for years. It's extremely rare."

"You never did any research or writing about it?"

The psychiatrist grew reflective.

"Not to my recollection."

Milo cued me with a look.

"There was an article in *The Canyon Oaks Quarterly*," I said, "about the importance of screening elderly patients for anticholinergics so as not to misdiagnose senile psychosis."

Mainwaring bit his lip and looked pained. He stroked the stem of his pipe and answered in a low, shaky voice.

"Ah, yes. That's true. Many of the organic anti-Parkinsonian agents contain anticholinergics. The newer drugs are cleaner in that regard, but some patients don't respond to them. When the organics are used, medical management can get tricky. The article was intended as a bit of continuing education for our referral sources. We try to do that kind of—"

"Who wrote it?" asked Milo, staring down at the psychiatrist.

"Dr. Djibouti did."

"All by himself?"

"Basically."

"Basically?"

"I read an early draft. He was the primary author."

"Interesting," said Milo. "Seems we have a little discrepancy. He says you collaborated. That the original idea was yours, even though he did most of the writing."

"He's being gracious." Mainwaring smiled edgily. "The loyalty of an associate. In any event, why the fuss over a little—"

Milo took a step closer, so that the psychiatrist had to crane his neck to look up at him, put his hands on his hips, and shook his head.

"Doc," he said softly, "how about we cut the crap?"

Mainwaring fumbled with the pipe and dropped it. Ashes and embers scattered on the carpet. He watched them glow, then die, looked up with the guilty terror of a child caught masturbating.

"I have absolutely no idea—"

"Then let me explain it to you. Just a couple of hours

ago I had a meeting with a whole bunch of specialists at County Hospital. Professors of medicine. Neurologists, toxicologists, bunch of other ologists. Experts, just like you. They showed me lab reports. Drug screenings. Explained everything in terms a cop could understand. Seems James Cadmus has been systematically poisoned with anticholinergics. For a long time. During the period he was under your care. The professors were pretty damned horrified about a doctor's doing that to a patient. More than willing to testify. They even wanted to file a complaint with the medical examiner's. I held them off."

Mainwaring moved his lips soundlessly. He retrieved the pipe and pointed it like a pistol.

"This is all rubbish. I haven't poisoned anyone."

"The professors thought otherwise, Guy."

"Then they're bloody wrong!"

Milo let him stew for a while before speaking again.

"Talk about your Hippocratic oath," he said.

"I tell you I haven't poisoned anyone!"

"Way the professors figured it, you slipped it to him every time you medicated him. Not only was it subtle, but there was an added benefit: seems Thorazine and the other medicines you gave him supercharged the anticholinergics. *Potentiation* they called it. The equivalent of a massive OD."

"You put him on a pharmacologic roller coaster," I said. "The electrochemical properties of his nerve endings were being constantly altered. Which is why he showed such a strange reaction to the medication: settling down one day; going out of control the next. When his body was free of anticholinergics, the antipsychotics did their job properly. But in the presence of atropine they were turned into poisons, which could also explain the premature tardive dyskinesia. Isn't one of the main theories about TD that it's caused by cholinergic blockage?"

Mainwaring dropped the pipe again, this time willfully. He put both hands in his hair and tried to melt into the chair. His face was as white and moist as boiled haddock; his eyes were feverish with fear. Beneath the bulk of the sweater his chest moved shallowly.

"It's not true," he muttered. "I never poisoned him."

"Okay, so some stooge did the actual dosing," said Milo. "But you're the expert. You ran the show."

"No! I swear it! I never even suspected until—"

He stopped, groaned, and looked away.

"Until when?"

"Recently."

"How recently?"

Mainwaring didn't answer.

Milo repeated the question, more sharply. Mainwaring sat frozen.

"Have we reached an impasse, Doc?" thundered the detective.

No response.

"Well, Guy," said Milo, opening his jacket to reveal his shoulder holster and fingering the handcuffs that dangled from his belt, "looks like it's you-have-the-right-to-remain-silent time. No doubt you want to dummy up until you talk to a lawyer. Do yourself a favor and get one with heavy-duty criminal experience."

Mainwaring put his face in his hands and hunched over.

"I've done nothing criminal," he muttered.

"Then answer my goddamn question! How long have you known about the poisoning?"

The psychiatrist sat up, ashen.

"I swear, I had nothing to do with it! It was only after the—after he'd already escaped that I grew suspicious. Following my meeting with Delaware. He kept pressing me about drug abuse, badgering me about hallucinatory content, the idiosyncratic response to phenothiazines. At the time I dismissed all of it, but it had been such a puzzling case that I started thinking—about the drug abuse issue in particular, wondering if there could be some merit to it—"

"Where did your thinking lead you?" demanded Milo.

"Back to Cadmus's medical chart. When I reread it, I began noticing things I should have noticed before—"

"Hold it!" I said angrily. "I read that chart. Three times. There was nothing in it to indicate atropine poisoning."

Mainwaring shivered and laced his fingers together, as if in supplication.

"All right, you're right. It's not—wasn't the chart. It was . . . hindsight. *Recollections.* Things I hadn't recorded —things I *should* have recorded. Discrepancies. Discrepant symptoms. Deviations from the norm. Flushing, disorientation, confusion. The precocious tardive syndrome. I'd just written the article on anticholinergic syndrome, and it had passed right under my nose. I felt like a bloody idiot. An EEG at the outset might have put me right on it. Atropine causes mixed rapid and slow brain wave activity, reduced alphas, increased deltas and betas. Had I seen that kind of pattern, I would have caught it, known what it meant from the outset. But the EEG never got done; the bloody radiologist balked. You read the chart, Delaware; that's in there. Tell him about the radiologist's balking, go on."

I looked away from him, attempting to suppress my disgust, fixing my eyes on a seascape so muddily rendered it had managed to make Carmel look ugly.

"Guy," said Milo scornfully, "am I hearing right? Are you trying to tell me that you—an expert, a *board-certified imperial poobah*—were fooled?"

"Yes," whispered Mainwaring.

"That's a crock," I said.

With a glance Milo told me to back off. He bent over so that his nose was an inch from Mainwaring's. The psychiatrist tried to pull away but was stopped by the back of the armchair.

"Okay," said the detective, "let's go with that for a minute. Let's say you were fooled."

"It's humiliating, but it's tr—"

"You think that kind of ignorance is gonna buy you bliss?" snarled Milo. "You just admitted you figured it out after you spoke to Delaware. You've known about it for over a week! Why the hell didn't you say anything? How could you let that kid continue to go through that kind of suffering?" He waved his notepad in Mainwaring's face. "*Intense suffering, bleak and terrifying,* a goddamn *private hell?* Why didn't you stop it!"

"I—I was going to. Took the time off to formulate—to plan how to go about it."

"Oh, Jesus, more bullshit," said Milo disgustedly. "How much did they pay you, Guy?"

"Nothing!"

"Bullshit."

The door to the hallway opened, and a woman stepped into the room. Young, dark, conspicuously voluptuous in a flame red turtleneck and tight jeans. Brassy brown eyes shielded by long black lashes. The sculpted cheekbones and full dark lips of a young Sophia Loren.

"It's not bullshit," she said.

"Andrea!" said Mainwaring, with suddenly renewed vigor. "Stay out of it. I insist!"

"I can't, darling. Not anymore."

She walked over to the armchair, stood next to the psychiatrist, and placed a hand on his shoulder. Her fingers uncurled, and Mainwaring shuddered.

"He's not a coward," she said. "Far from it. He's trying to protect me. I'm Andrea Vann, Sergeant. I'm the one they paid off."

Milo's interrogation of her was as rough as any I've ever seen him do. She took it unflinchingly, sitting on the edge of the sofa, straightbacked and stoic, hands folded motionless in her lap. Every time Mainwaring tried to intervene on her behalf, she silenced him with a steely smile. Eventually he gave up and withdrew to brooding silence.

"Run that by me again," demanded the detective. "Someone leaves five thousand dollars in cash in your apartment along with a note telling you there'll be another five if you leave your post on a certain night, and you don't ask questions."

"That's right."

"That kind of thing's an everyday occurrence for you."

"Far from it. It was unreal, like winning the lottery. The first good luck I've had in years. It bothered me that someone had broken into my place, and I knew the money was dirty; but I was dirt poor and tired of it. So I took it, changed my lock, and didn't raise a peep."

"And tore up the note."

"Tore it up and flushed it down the toilet."

"Very convenient."

She said nothing.

"Remember anything about the handwriting?" asked Milo.

"It was typed."

"What about the paper?"

She shook her head.

"The only paper I was looking at was green. Fifty-dollar bills. Two packages of fifty each. I counted it twice."

"I bet you did. Did you ever stop counting long enough to wonder why someone wanted you off the ward that night?"

"Of course I did. But I forced myself to stop wondering." Milo turned to Mainwaring.

"What would you call that, Guy? Repression? Denial?"

"I was greedy," said Vann. "Okay? I saw dollar signs and blocked everything else out. Turned my brain off. Is that what you want to hear?"

"What I want to hear is the truth."

"Which is exactly what I've been giving you."

"Right," said Milo, and busied himself with note taking. She shrugged and asked if she could smoke.

"No. When did you decide to switch your brain back to on?"

"After Jamey was arrested for murder. I realized then that I'd gotten myself into something big. I got scared— really scared. I handled it by insulting myself calm."

"What?"

"I kept telling myself I was an idiot to let anxiety get in the way of good fortune. Over and over, like hypnosis, until I calmed down. I wanted the second five thousand, felt I deserved it."

"Sure, why not? Honest wages for an honest night's work."

"Now look here," said Mainwaring. "You—"

"It's all right, Guy," said Vann. "He can't make it any worse than it is."

Milo crooked a thumb at Mainwaring.

"How long have you and he had a thing going?"

"Almost a year. Next Tuesday's our anniversary."

"Happy anniversary. Marriage plans?"

She and the psychiatrist exchanged meaningful looks. His eyes were wet.

"There were."

"Then why all the pissing and moaning about poverty? Soon you would have been a doctor's wife. Until then he could have loaned you money."

"Guy's as broke as I am." She scanned the shabby room. "Do you think he'd be living like this if he weren't?"

Milo turned to Mainwaring.

"That true? And don't bullshit me, I can check out your finances in an afternoon."

"Go ahead. There's nothing to check. I'm bloody busted."

"Bad investments?"

The psychiatrist smiled bitterly.

"The worst. A rotten marriage."

"His wife's an evil bitch," spit Andrea Vann. "Cleaned out their joint accounts, attached his earnings, took the children and every stick of furniture, and rented a twelve-room mansion in Redondo Beach—five thousand dollars a month plus utilities. Then she filed a deposition full of vicious lies, claimed he was an unfit father, and had his visitation cut off. He has to undergo a full psychiatric evaluation in order to see his children!"

"Had," corrected Mainwaring. "The matter's moot now, Andy."

She turned on him.

"Don't be so goddamned defeatist, Guy! We've messed things up, but we haven't killed anyone!"

He withered under the heat of her words, gnawed at a knuckle, and stared at the carpet.

"Let's get back on track," said Milo. "You say the second five thousand came a week later."

"Five days," she said. "Same as the other two times you asked. The story won't change in the retelling because it's true."

"And Guy, here, knew nothing about it."

"Absolutely nothing. I didn't want to get him involved, didn't want to jeopardize his custody fight. My plan was to put away the money for a nest egg, so that we could start fresh. I was going to surprise him with it after we were married."

"The Mustang part of that nest egg?"

She hung her head.

"How much did it cost?"

"Two thousand down, the rest on payments."

Milo pulled out a piece of paper and handed it to her.

"This your loan contract?"

"Yes. How did—"

"You registered it in your own name but told the dealer you were Pat Demeter. Gave a Barstow address. How many of those payments did you plan on making?"

She looked up defiantly, eyes the color and heat of mulled cider.

"All right, Sergeant, you've made your point. I'm a lying bimbo with the ethics of a—"

"Who's Pat Demeter?"

"My ex-husband! A snake. Beat me and stole every penny I owned and shoveled it up his nose. Tried to turn me into a coke whore and threatened to maim Sean when I refused. I'm not telling you this to get your sympathy, Sergeant. But don't waste any on him either. When they come to him to collect for that car, it won't even start to make up for what he did to me!"

"Demeter's your married name?" asked Milo dispassionately.

"Yes. The first thing I did after the divorce was change my name back. Didn't want anything to remind me of that scum."

"Where's your son?"

She stared at him hatefully.

"You're a sweet soul, aren't you, Sergeant Sturgis?"

"Where is he?"

"With my parents."

"Where with your parents?"

"In Visalia—yes, I know you can get the address. They're good people. Don't drag them into this."

"Why'd you send him away?"

"I was scared."

"Because Cadmus had been arrested."

"No. There's more if you'd just let me get it out!"

"Go on."

She caught her breath.

"It was after the second payoff arrived. Whoever brought it got into the apartment again. Through the new lock—a dead bolt, supposed to be burglarproof. They put the money on the lid of the toilet bowl, left the door wide open. It felt . . . contemptuous. As if someone wanted to let me know how expendable I was. I drove straight to Sean's school, picked him up and took him to a friend's, went back to the apartment, and packed—"

"By yourself?"

"Yes. There wasn't much." She waited for another question.

"Keep going," said Milo.

"I waited until after dark to put the stuff in the car. Just as I was about to drive away, these two guys appeared out of nowhere, on both sides of the car, yanking on the door handles, saying they wanted to talk to me, trying to force their way in. I barely got it locked in time."

"What did they look like?"

"Scuzzy. Outlaw bikers. I know the type because there are lots of them around Barstow, and during the few times in his life that Pat worked, he pumped gas at a station where they used to hang out."

"Recognize these two?"

"No."

"What did they look like?"

"The one on the passenger side was fat and bearded. The one close to me was a hairy animal. Unshaven, big mustache. Big hands—at least they looked big pressed against the glass. Weird, dead eyes."

"Eye color? Tattoos? Distinguishing marks?"

"No idea. It was dark, and all I could think about was getting out of there. They were pounding the glass, rocking the car, snarling. I tried to back out, but they'd parked their chopper up against my rear bumper. It was a big bike and I was afraid I'd get jammed up and be trapped. So I screamed and leaned on the horn, and Mrs. Cromarty—the landlady—came out. The hairy one had a hammer; he was about to smash the window. But Mrs. Cromarty kept shouting, 'What's going on?' and coming closer. That scared them off. The minute they were gone I got out of there. Drove around for hours before I was sure I hadn't been followed, finally picked up Sean, and came here to Guy's."

"Who was absolutely shocked by the whole thing."

"As a matter of fact, yes. When he told you he'd been fooled, he was being truthful. It was only after I told him about the money that he started to suspect something. We're not saints, Sergeant, but we're not the people you're after."

"And who might those be?"

"The family, of course. They're the ones who hired that Surtees cow to give him the poison."

"How do you know she did it?"

"She had daily access to him."

"So did others. Including you and Guy."

"We didn't do it. We had no reason to."

"Poverty's a hell of a motivator."

"If we'd been paid off, why would we stick around?"

Milo didn't answer.

"Sergeant," said Andrea Vann, "there was no logical reason for Marthe Surtees to be there. She was weird, poorly trained. Guy accepted the family's story about wanting one-on-one care, because people in that situation are highly stressed and he was being compassionate, but—"

The detective wheeled on Mainwaring:

"How much did they pay you to let her in?"

"Two thousand."

"Cash?"

"Yes."

"The uncle give it to you directly?"

"Through the lawyer. Souza."

"These people are filthy rich," said Vann. "Their type runs the world by manipulating people. Can't you see that they manipulated us?"

Milo scowled.

"So now you're victims, right?"

She tried to lock eyes with him but gave up and pulled out a pack of cigarettes. Milo let her light up and began pacing the room. From outside came the sweet, liquid tones of a steel-drum symphony—raindrops dancing coyly on hollow stucco walls. When he talked again, it was to Mainwaring.

"Way I see it, Guy, you're in the crapper, ready to be flushed. If you've lied about not participating, I guarantee I'll find out and bust you for attempted murder and accessory to murder. But even if you're telling me the truth, you're up to your neck in malpractice and whatever else they charge doctors with who allow their patients to be poisoned. Hope you know how to whittle or work a cash register or something, 'cause practicing medicine sure as hell isn't in your future. Not to mention fatherhood."

"Bastard!" hissed Vann.

"Same goes for you," said Milo. "No more RN; byebye, Mustang. And if old Pat ever had designs on getting custody of little Sean, he'll have his chance real soon."

She choked back a cry of rage.

"Damn you, keep her out of this!" shouted Mainwaring.

Milo smiled.

"Now how the hell can I do that, Guy, when she put herself right in it?"

Mainwaring looked at Vann, and what little composure he had gave way. His mouth began to tremble, and the tears that had pooled in his eyes overflowed and trickled down his unshaved cheeks. She ran to him and held him, and he began to sob. It was a pathetic scene that made me want to disappear. I looked at my friend to see if it had affected him and thought I noticed something—a flicker of empathy arcing across the ravaged terrain of his face. But it didn't last—if it had ever existed.

He observed them with clinical detachment, sternly watched them share their misery, before saying:

"On the other hand, maybe there is something I can do."

They broke apart and gazed at him in supplication.

"I'm not talking salvation, you understand. Just a little damage control. Cooperation traded for sealed records. And I'm not guaranteeing I can pull it off, gotta clear it with the brass. Plus, even if we do strike a deal, I doubt you could stay in California. Understand?"

Dumb nods.

"But if you help me get what I want, I'll do my damnedest to keep things quiet enough for you to start up somewhere else. You want to talk it over, that's okay."

"We don't," said Andrea Vann. "Just tell us what you want."

Milo smiled paternally.

"Now that," he said, "is what I call a positive attitude."

28

IT WAS a small, sad room filled with bored, sweating men, and by nightfall the air had soured.

Whitehead dozed in a grubby blue armchair, shoeless, mouth agape, a disk of chewed gum wadded on the wall behind his head. Cash sat on a plastic-topped end table, next to a lamp, its shade half shredded, its base a headless golden female torso, extravagantly bosomed and freckled with white where the paint had chipped off the plaster. He smoked a cigarette down to the butt and added it to the pile in the gold scallop ashtray.

Milo hunched on the edge of the bed, at the foot end, drinking a Diet Coke and reading his notes. I sat cross-legged at the head, my back to the gold-flocked wall, trying, without much success, to get into the latest issue of *Consulting and Clinical Psych*.

At first glance the bed seemed the natural place to settle: a California king-sized water mattress covered with a luridly turquoise velveteen spread, so expansive that it virtually filled the room. But the other detectives had taken care to keep their distance throughout the hours of waiting.

The video equipment was set up on a sticky woodgrain vanity table. Before it sat a technical sergeant named Ginzburg, bald, mustachioed, with a bull neck and shoulders to match. Having checked and double-checked every switch and knob, he contented himself with cold coffee and a book of mathematical puzzles. The trash can overflowed with empty styrofoam cups, taco sauce containers, crumpled napkins, and wax paper greased to translucence. A half-eaten burrito stiffened next to the video monitor.

Displayed on the screen was the room next door: the Scheherezade Suite of the Studio Love Palace. The suite

was no more than a room, set up identically to the one
we were in, with the exception that the bed was covered
in scarlet satin—upon which lay a gray man. But that
kind of hyperbole seemed appropriate in a palace that
was no more than a peeling motor court, a sordid little
retreat just off Ventura, in the east end of Studio City, a
forgotten finger of the Valley that reaches into the cookie
jar called Hollywood. The sign on the roof advertised
ADULT MOVIES and EROTIC MASSAGE, the former exempli-
fied by a peep-show channel on the TV, the latter by a
vibrator gizmo attached to the bed. Both were coin-
operated; both had been tried by Cash and found lacking
("Call this a massage? 'Bout as energetic as a hand job
from a corpse" and; "Look at that, Cal. The guy's a
stone junkie, and she's got scars and a twat you could
drive a truck through. Couldn't pay me to fuck her by
proxy").

There was sudden movement on the monitor: Mainwaring getting up from the bed, walking back and forth,
and approaching the wall that separated the rooms. He
licked his lips and stared up at the hanging plant that
housed the hidden lens.

"Goddammit," said Ginzburg. "There he goes again. I
told him not to do that."

Cash stretched and yawned.

"Maybe I should go in there and remind him."

Milo looked at his watch. "No," he said. "Too close
for comfort."

Cash consulted a wafer-thin gold watch.

"What, eight-thirty? Thing's supposed to go down at
nine-four-five."

"Let's play it safe. Just in case."

Cash looked at Ginzburg, who'd returned to his puzzles, then back at Milo.

"Whatever. But if he keeps doing it, I'm gonna go in
there and kick his ass." As if on cue, Mainwaring went
back to the bed and lay down with one arm over his eyes.
One of his feet wagged like a puppy's tail. Cash watched
him for a while, then said: "How long have we been
here, five hours?"

"And eighteen minutes," said Ginzburg.

Cash looked at Mainwaring again, then asked Milo:
"What do you figure the chances are of this panning out?"

"Who the hell knows?"

"Got to learn to live with ambiguity," said Ginzburg.

"Yeah, right." The Beverly Hills detective lit another cigarette.

"Could you cool it with the smoke?" said Ginzburg. "Place smells like cancer."

"Fuck," said Cash, going into the bathroom and closing the door.

Milo chuckled.

"Nothing like forced intimacy, huh, Lenny?"

Ginzburg nodded, picked up the burrito, looked at it, and threw it into the trash. It landed with a thud that opened Whitehead's eyes.

"Where's Dick?" he asked drowsily.

"In the john," said Ginzburg. "Beating off."

Whitehead's forehead creased. He got up, put two sticks of gum in his mouth, began chewing, and walked to the TV. Fumbling in his pockets, he came up with a palmful of change.

"Shit, all nickels. Anybody got quarters?"

Ginzburg ignored him. Milo produced three coins.

"Keep the volume down," he said, handing them over.

" 'S it time?" asked Whitehead.

"Not yet. But let's play it safe."

Whitehead looked at his watch, mumbled, "Eight thirty-four," and dropped the quarters into the slot atop the TV. Seconds later a loop called *Jungle Love* came on: a jerky, hand-held pan of a plywood-paneled room, followed by a long shot of a naked black couple squirming on a daybed in time to a rhythm-and-funk beat. The camera zoomed in drunkenly on contorted faces, fingers kneading nipples, then a series of gynecologic close-ups that revealed the man to be exceptionally well endowed.

"Figures," said Whitehead disgustedly, but he kept his eyes glued to the screen.

The door to the bathroom opened, and Cash came out, zipping up his fly.

"Good morning," he said to Whitehead, who nodded absently. Then Cash saw the movie and settled back down on the end table to watch.

At nine-ten the phone rang. Ginzburg picked it up, said "Yeah," several times, and hung up.

"That was Owens in front of the 7-Eleven on Lankershim. Might not mean anything, but two sleazes on a Harley Hog just turned east on Ventura. One was a porker."

"All *right*," said Milo. He checked the blackout drapes to make sure no light was escaping. Cash went over to the TV and turned off the sound, extinguishing, midnote, the sounds of heavy breathing and the sympathetic rasp of an asthmatic saxophone. He watched for a few seconds, proclaimed the woman on screen a pig, and drew away. Whitehead continued to stare at the silent images, jaws working, then realized he was the sole voyeur and reluctantly switched off the set. He pulled out his .38 and inspected the barrel.

Ginzburg sat up straight and fiddled with his machines. Cash walked over and eyed Mainwaring.

"Cool fucker," he said, "lying there like that."

"Don't bet on it," said Ginzburg. "Look at that foot."

Twenty-five minutes passed uneventfully. The momentum that had begun with the phone call from Owens began to dissipate. After three-quarters of an hour it was gone, and a numbing cloud of torpor descended on the room. I found the shifting levels of arousal draining, but Milo had warned me about that. ("Trapp's impressed with your good citizenship—quote: 'First shrink I ever heard of who wasn't a crybaby pinko' unquote—so I can probably arrange it. But it's boring, Alex. We're talking brain death.")

Nine forty-five came and went noiselessly.

"Think they'll show?" asked Cash. "Think it's them?"

"What's the matter," said Ginzburg, "you got something to do?"

The Beverly Hills detective thumbed his chest and answered in a jive whine.

"I *always* got me something going down, my man. Something *sweet* and *fuzzy*, you dig?"

"Yeah, right," said Ginzburg sullenly.

"Hey! What's eating *you?*"

Ginzburg shook his head and picked up his puzzle book. He tapped the point of his pencil against his teeth and started scribbling.

Cash muttered something unintelligible and returned to his perch on the end table. After pulling out a cigarette, he lit up and blew the smoke toward the monitor. If Ginzburg noticed, he didn't let on.

"Hey, Dick," said Whitehead, between chews, "how's it going with the screenplay?"

"Real good. They're looking at it over at MGM. Seriously."

"Oh, yeah? Anybody in mind to play you?"

"Maybe Pacino, maybe De Niro."

"Right," muttered Ginzburg, suppressing a snicker.

Cash flicked an ash toward the monitor. "Whatsamatter, Lenny, baby, you jealous—"

"Shut up!" whispered Milo, pointing toward the door. From the other side came noises: the trace of a shuffle; the hint of a scrape; the mouse squeak of a heel lowering softly. As brief as a heartbeat, but for vigilance, inaudible.

All eyes fixed on the monitor.

A knock sounded on the door of the Scheherezade Suite. The speaker on the vanity table transformed it to a hollow bark, Mainwaring sat up, eyes nightmare-wide.

Another knock.

"C'mon, answer it, asshole," whispered Cash.

The psychiatrist pulled himself to his feet and stared at the camera, as if awaiting rescue.

"Oh, no," murmured Ginzburg. "Wet pants time."

"If he doesn't answer it," whispered Milo, "let's go out there and bust them."

"For what?" asked Whitehead. "Loitering? We need conversation."

"Anything's better than letting them go."

The sheriff's investigator grimaced and chewed faster.

"Snap out of it, goddammit," urged Ginzburg. "Do you believe this? The chickenshit's going into lens hypnosis."

Mainwaring kept staring. A third knock got him moving. He went to the door, opened it, and was pushed backward, as if by a storm gust. Stumbling and tripping, he landed on the bed, winded and terrified.

The door closed. Two dark figures entered the room. Split-second blurs of hirsute face flashed across the screen then faded to black before they could be processed mentally; the bikers had turned their backs to the camera.

Ginzburg tinkered, distancing the lens and endowing the blackness with texture and contour: greasy leather, filthy denims. To the left, a bald head atop a bottom-heavy mound larded with excess flesh, the neck supporting it segmented like a rolled roast. Inches to the right, a rangy, lean physique topped by stringy dark hair under a Marlon Brando cap. Both bikers had their hands on their hips. Mainwaring's face was a pale wisp floating in the space between their elbows.

The camera picked up glints of metal: The skinny one held a buck knife parallel to his leg; the fat one made tiny circles with a chain.

"Uh-oh," said Milo. "Rough stuff right away. Let's position." He bounded up, sprinted to the door, and pulled out his .38. Easing the door open, he stuck his head out, looked both ways, and closed it softly. "Clear. The bike's at the back of the court, near the alley. I'm gonna let the air out, then come back and stay outside their door."

Cash went and stood next to Milo. Whitehead padded over to the connecting door and gave each leg a limbering shake. Both men drew their weapons.

"All right, fuckbrain," Skinny was saying, inching forward menacingly. "What's all this about having something to sell?"

"I've already discussed that with Heather Cadmus," said Mainwaring.

Both the bikers laughed. The movement caused the fat one to shimmy gelatinously. *Soft,* Old Man Skaggs had said. *Like a soft sack of shit.*

"Same cue?" asked Cash.

Milo nodded.

"Let's still try for incriminating conversation followed by safe body language. We want their weapons down to avoid a hostage grab or a reflex slash. But if they even get close to cutting him, go for the diversion: Pound the walls and run out screaming. Cal and I will break down both doors simultaneously." He craned to get a look at the screen. "Where's the blade, Lenny?"

"Still down at his side," said Ginzburg. "I wish they'd turn so I could get a snap of their faces."

"I'm gone," said Milo, opening the door and slipping out silently. Cash shut it after him and took his place.

Mainwaring propped himself on his elbows. The fat biker took a waddling step and shoved him down.

"They just pushed him," said Ginzburg evenly. Cash and Whitehead tensed. "He looks all right. The one with the knife is running his fingernail over the edge of the blade, could be a precursor—no, he's keeping it down, looks like he's just playing with it. Fatso's still swinging the chain."

"I asked you a question, fuckbrain," said Skinny. The speaker on the video recorder had distorted his voice, but it sounded vaguely familiar. I longed for a look at his face. As he talked, his head bobbed, revealing an earlobe and the ends of a mustache behind the mop of hair. But that was all.

"C'mon, putz, turn around and say cheese," urged Ginzburg, one index finger resting upon a circular red button.

"It will do you no good to harm me," said Mainwaring with sudden forcefulness. "My information is locked safely away and accompanied by instructions to deliver it to the police if I don't return home by a designated hour. Mrs. Cadmus knows that."

"Har," said Skinny. He looked at Fat, who giggled appreciatively. "Mrs. Cadmus knows a lot of stuff."

"Bingo," said Cash. "Keep talking, fucker."

"Then I assume we can proceed with business," said Mainwaring calmly, and he sat up.

"I take back everything," whispered Ginzburg. "Guy's got balls."

"Then I assume we can proceed with business," exclaimed Fat, mimicking Mainwaring's English accent in a high, shrill voice. He feinted toward the psychiatrist, as if to shove him down again, then retreated and giggled, turning in the process and revealing his face. Ginzburg began pushing the red button rapidly, snapping still photos off the videotape and displaying them on a split screen. He depressed a lever and Fat's face loomed large: bullet head shaved naked; bushy black eyebrows; lumpy, swinish features under a massive black beard.

"I'm glad we have an understanding," said Mainwaring. Fat passed his chain from hand to pudgy hand and laughed again.

"D'you believe this shit?" he asked his partner. His voice was still high—incongruously so coming from that massive body—and I began to wonder if it was his natural way of talking.

Skinny bent his right arm.

"Whoa," said Ginzburg, "he's got the blade in his palm. Holding it out."

"Palm is bullshit," said Cash. "Movie stuff. You want to cut someone you grab the hilt and chop down. I just got through telling them that at MGM."

Whitehead looked at the connecting door, then at his right foot.

"Now what?" he asked.

"No change."

"See this?" said Skinny. "Its name is Pigsticker. Don't fuck with us. We'll turn you into fucking summer sausage."

"It's wintertime." Fat laughed. "How about hot pastrami?"

"Nah," said his partner, "fuckhead doesn't have enough fat on him. Cut him up find and nothin' but dry bones and shit."

"Closer to the bone, sweeter the meat," said Fat. "Yum."

"You got a point there."

"Wonder how his toes slice. Like butter, you think?"

"Nah. Too scrawny. Maybe with wire cutters, though."

"D'ja bring the cutters?" asked Fat excitedly.

"Nah. Just Ol' Pigsticker."

Mainwaring sucked in his breath.

"Got something to say, fuckhead?" asked Skinny.

"Mrs. Cadmus—"

"Far as Mrs. Cadmus is concerned, you're dead meat. She gave us carto blanco to do with you whatever the fuck we feel like."

"Yeah." Fat smiled, stroking his beard. "We could dice you, slice you, or cut you into julienne strips. Just like a Veg-o-matic."

"And forfeit my information?" asked Mainwaring, voice beginning to quaver.

Skinny moved around to the right side of the bed, inches from the psychiatrist, the knife still resting in his hand. It was then that I got a good look at him.

"That's Antrim," I said. "Souza's chauffeur."

"You sure?" asked Cash.

"A hundred percent."

"Quiet," said Ginzburg. "This may be it."

Antrim had lowered the knife so that it was leveled at Mainwaring's groin.

"Get ready," said Ginzburg.

"How 'bout," said Antrim, "you forfeit your nuts?"

Mainwaring looked at him blankly, then lashed out violently with a rabbit punch, connecting with Antrim's wrist. The knife went flying. Antrim howled with pain and threw himself on the psychiatrist. Fat let out a high-pitched scream and dived into the melee.

What followed next was a cop show scripted by a speed freak.

"Now!" shouted Ginzburg, rising to his feet. With one hand he manipulated the camera controls; with the other he pounded the wall. His mouth was wide-open, and he was howling, "Freeze! Police!" like a banshee.

Simultaneously Cash flung the door open, two-handed his revolver, and bolted through, while Whitehead splintered the connecting door with a single kick and charged into the Scheherezade Suite.

I sat there, immobile, watching it all on the monitor:

Fat and Antrim pummeling the unseen Mainwaring; faces raised suddenly in panic; a dive for the knife. Doors breaking; Milo lumbering into the room, gun drawn, stomping a groping hand, yelling, "Freeze, fuckers! Drop the knife! Drop it! Drop the knife! Drop the knife! Drop it! On the ground! On the ground!"

Antrim backed off. Cash retrieved the buck knife, wrapped it in a handkerchief, then dropped it in his pocket. Whitehead made a flying tackle at Fat. Milo yanked Antrim to his feet, cuffed him to the bedpost, and used plastic ties to bind his feet.

Whitehead was still trying to roll Fat off Mainwaring, groaning at the effort. Cash joined him. The two of them pulled hard on Fat's arms, fought to hoist him upright. Unable to cuff him because the arms couldn't reach around the obese body, they called for more plastic ties.

Mainwaring sat up, bloody and bruised. Smiling with satisfaction.

"Stand the fuck up," gasped Cash, still struggling with Fat. "Fucking . . . rodeo . . . event."

Fat squirmed in their grasp, jiggling, squealing, gnashing his teeth, spitting in Whitehead's face. The sheriff's investigator struck out impulsively, slapping the fat face hard. Knocking the beard askew. A high-pitched wail.

"Huh?" said Whitehead as he ripped away the false hair. "What the—"

"Get the eyelashes, too," said Cash.

Off came the thick black fringes.

"Aahh!" cried the naked face, doughy and porcine and androgynous. A booted foot stamped the carpet, and tears coursed down the blubbery cheeks.

"Who—*what* the fuck are you?" asked Cash.

"Aahh!" Fat snuffled and snapped like a wild boar in a trap, bared its teeth, and tried to bite off one of Whitehead's jug ears. He recoiled and slapped it again.

"Hurt her again, and I'll kill you," howled Antrim, thrashing in confinement. "Hurt her again, and I'll—"

"Shut the fuck up!" screamed Whitehead. "What the fuck is going on here?"

"Aahh!" cried the hairless face.

"Hurt her agai—" Milo jammed a handkerchief in Antrim's mouth.

"Aahh!"

"This is weird," said Ginzburg, mopping his forehead.

I got up and made my way through the splintered doorway.

Mainwaring was in the bathroom, dabbing at his wounds with a damp washcloth. Whitehead stood guard over Antrim. Milo was on the phone, and Cash was still staring at the hairless woman, looking nauseated as he half demanded, half pleaded, "What are you? What the fuck are you?"

"Her name is Marthe Surtees," I said. "She was Jamey's nurse."

The room grew silent.

Marthe Surtees managed somehow to curtsy.

"Hello, Dr. Delaware," she said sweetly. Batting her lashes, the suety face blotched with patches of adhesive and strands of false hair. "How nice to see you again."

29

MILO SPEARED a new potato, rolled it in butter, and ate it. He'd finished one loin lamb chop, and three others crowded his plate. I swallowed a cube of filet mignon and washed it down with a swallow of Grolsch.

It was 10:30 P.M., and we were the chophouse's last customers. But the bar at the front was packed three deep and resonant with mating sounds.

"William Tull Bonney," he said, wiping his face. "As in Billy the Kid. Claims he's a lineal descendant. Used Antrim as an alias, 'cause that was the name of Billy's stepfather."

He looked at the remains of his gin and tonic, considered a reorder and turned, instead, to his water glass, which he drained. Pulling a piece of paper from his breast pocket he unfolded it. He leaned forward, squinting, and read in the dim light of the glassed candle.

"Once we ID'd him and fed him into the computer, it just kept printing and printing. This is just an abstract, your basic American success story. Born in Mesilla, New Mexico, mom a boozehound, dad unknown. Truant from day one. Drunk and disorderly at the age of eleven—how's that for precocious? Vandalism, fire setting, string of juvenile assaults and robberies. Bunch of suspected rapes and at least one murder—mutilation cutting of an Indian girl—that no one could prove but everyone knew he did. This was at sixteen. County-raised till he was eighteen. Out for a year, came to California, busted within a month for attempted murder—bar knifing up in Kern County—took a year in the county jail, got extra time for attacking a guard and sundry other bad behaviors, placed in some rehab program, where he learned auto mechanics, got a job as a grease monkey when he got out, lost it for beating up the boss. Busted for a string

of armed robberies and assaults. Graduate school at
Soledad, where he hooked up with the Aryan Brother-
hood, absorbed a bit of two-wheeler philosophy. Upon
release, rode with an outlaw gang called the Ghouls, up
near Fresno, busted for second-degree murder—gang war
cutting—case dismissed on a technicality raised by his
attorney, Horace Souza, Esquire."

He turned the paper over.

"Now for the illustrious Marthe Surtees aka Wilhel-
mina Surtees aka Billy Mae Sorrell aka Martha Sorrel
aka Sabrina Skull."

"Sabrina Skull?"

"As in cranium. Gang name—she was a Ghoul mama.
Social history similar to Antrim's—drugs, booze, and
pulling the legs off tiny animals—except that she got a
shitload of psychiatric treatment and avoided imprison-
ment as an adult. One disorderly conduct bust, case
dismissed. Only reason I could get anything on her was
that the Fresno DA has a file on the Ghouls in which she
figured prominently: she liked to hurt people."

"Is she a real nurse?"

"Oh, yeah. When she got out of youth camp, some
federal grant paid her tuition at a fly-by-night operation,
and she got an LVN. When the Ghouls weren't partying,
she free-lanced at old-age homes. Left the last one under
suspicion of stealing drugs, but no charges were filed.
Then she disappeared. Turns out she and Antrim were
living in a cabin out in Tujunga. Stuck in the middle of a
hundred acres of forest owned by Souza. Birds, bees,
outdoor plumbing, a portable TV, and plenty of crack.
Place was a sty. I saw it this morning. In one corner was
a fiberboard closet—starched white dresses on one side,
smelly black leather on the other. Two drawers at the
bottom, crammed with theatrical make-up, beards, mus-
taches, hairpieces, some very smarmy S and M mags."

"Charming," I said.

"Yeah. And romantic, too." He gave a cold laugh,
reached for the mint jelly, and prepared another lamb
chop for surgery. "Antrim caved in the moment we got
him alone. Said he'd cooperate if we went easy on her;
he'd done all the knife work anyway. We told him there
were limits to the kind of flexibility you could muster in
this kind of case, and besides, she'd been the one to

poison the kid. Asshole started crying—do you believe that?"

He shook his head and chewed a piece of meat into oblivion.

"Anyway, inside of an hour we had the whole story, pictures included. He'd buried them under the floorboards of the cabin along with his notes. All part of his insurance policy."

He'd shown me the snapshots before dinner. The story they told was a familiar one. But the players had been surprising.

"Planning on using them?" I asked.

"Can't see why we'd need to at this point. But they do help clarify matters, don't they? Give the case a little context. Now all we need are some numbers. Which our guest should be able to provide." He shot his Timex out from under his cuffs. "Twenty more minutes if he's punctual. Let's finish up."

Eighteen minutes later the door to the bar opened, and clamorous waves of conversation spilled through. When it closed, a narrow young man stood in the doorway, suspended in the silence, eyes blinking furiously behind gold-rimmed glasses as they adjusted to the dimness of the dining room. He wore a dark suit and tie that blended with the somber paneling and carried a large attaché case that seemed a prosthetic extension of his right arm.

"Looks like our boy," said Milo, and he got up and escorted the newcomer to our table. As he walked, the man placed both hands on the case and carried it gingerly, as if it housed something alive and excitable.

"Mr. Balch, this is Dr. Alex Delaware. Alex, Mr. Bradford Balch. Esquire."

Balch's hand was fine-boned and cold. I let go of it and said:

"We've spoken on the phone."

The attorney looked blank.

"You called me to arrange a visit to the Chancellor estate."

"Oh, that," he said, and pursed his lips. The memory of being used as an errand boy tasted bad. "Why's he here?" he asked Milo.

"Consultant."

Balch regarded me with distrust.

"I thought you were working for Mr. Souza," he said.

"I was. Not any longer."

"What are you here for? To check me out psychologically?"

"We've done all the checking out we need to," said Milo. "Have a seat and let's get down to business."

"Sergeant," said Balch, "I insist that we talk alone."

"Your insistence has been duly noted," responded Milo, holding out a chair. "Have a seat."

"I'm serious, Sergeant—"

"Balch"—Milo sighed—"you're in big trouble, and I'm letting you take a lot more than you're giving. So don't waste my time with power plays, okay?"

Balch blushed, and his eyes dropped to the floor. He sank down abruptly in the chair, swinging the case onto his lap, embracing it. Up close he looked very young— apple-cheeked and sandy-haired, the hair short and neatly parted, with a sprig of cowlick at the tag end of the part. His clothes were expensive and traditional but a trace ill-fitting—button-down collar a half size too large, silk rep tie just a smidgeon off plumb. He seemed imprisoned in them, like a boy forced to be a man.

"Drink?" asked Milo.

The attorney frowned prudishly.

"I just want to get this over with and get out of here."

"Sure," said Milo. "This has to be ticklish for you."

"Ticklish? It's a breach of ethics. Violation of confidentiality. If it ever gets out, I'm finished. Be lucky to get work as a paralegal."

"No reason for it to get out."

"So you say." Thin, manicured fingers played with the clasps of the attaché.

"It's tough," agreed Milo. "Damned if you do, damned if you don't."

"Look," said Balch, "how was I to know the signature was forged? Mr. Souza vouched for it. Mrs. Cadmus was right there."

Milo's eyes hardened.

"No one expected you to be a mind reader," he said. "Just to follow the goddamn notary rules: No stamp unless you personally witness the signature."

"But there was absolutely no reason to suspect forgery," insisted Balch without passion. "The trust had a routine provision for mental incompetence: transfer of funds back to the guardian upon written request. In view of the beneficiary's mental status, it wasn't illogical for Mr. Cadmus to activate it."

"For the kid's own good, right?" asked Milo.

"There were documents attached certifying incompetence," said Balch. "It wasn't illogical," he repeated.

"Not illogical," agreed Milo. "Just fraudulent."

"I had no knowledge of that."

"I believe that," said Milo. "You were slipshod, not crooked. That's why I'm giving you an opportunity to do penance."

Balch looked ill.

"The whole notary thing was a pain in the ass," he said. "Souza's idea. He said a trust and estates man should be a notary, in order to streamline things. I thought it more appropriate for a secretary. I should have insisted."

"Gotta listen to the boss, right?"

"Shit," muttered the attorney, and looked at Milo's drained gin and tonic.

"Sure you won't have that drink?" asked the detective.

"No—oh, why the hell not? Tanqueray on the rocks with a twist."

Milo disappeared into the bar and came back with the drink. After loosening his tie, Balch tossed it back quickly.

"It was Nixon who ruined things for notaries, wasn't it?" said Milo. "Donating all that stuff for tax write-offs, inflating the values—how was the notary supposed to know he'd be liable. I mean, this was the president, the big boss." He smiled. "Seems bosses have a way of screwing the little guy over, huh?"

Balch bristled, clearly miffed at being characterized as a little guy. He stirred the ice in his glass and asked:

"What I want to know is how you found out about it."

"Little birdie with big ears."

The attorney thought for a while, then groaned.

"Oh, shit. The chauffeur. He was there the whole time, waiting to take Mrs. Cadmus home. I never assumed he was paying attention to what was going on. Should have, the guy always impressed me as a sleaze— how much did you pay him, Sergeant?"

Milo ignored the question.

"Shit," said Balch, looking ready to cry.

"Think of it this way," said Milo consolingly. "There's a positive side. You're the first one in the firm to find out about the boss's imminent decline. Gives you a head start on the job market. Where'd you go to school?"

"Penn."

"Ivy League. You shouldn't have any problem."

Balch drew himself up and tried to look dignified.

"I'll be fine, Sergeant. Can we get down to business?"

"Sure. Hand over the stuff; once I'm satisfied everything's there, we'll shake hands like gentlemen."

"Before I hand over anything, I want your assurance that my name will never come up in any part of your investigation. And that no one will ever know where you got the documents."

"The case is too hairy for me to promise you anything more than I'll try my best."

"Not good enough," snapped Balch.

Milo picked up a lamb bone and gnawed at it.

"How about Cub Scout's honor?" he said, crossing his heart.

"Dammit, I'm serious, Sergeant!"

Milo put one palm on the table and leaned in close, waving the bone like a scimitar. His brows knitted, and the candle highlighted the grease on his lips, creating an altogether menacing visage, a pirate sniffing plunder.

"So am I, Counselor," he said. "Dead serious. Now open that goddamn case."

30

WALKING NEXT to Antrim was like wearing a cobra for a necktie. The fact that he was cooperating was singularly unreassuring; I knew what he was capable of in an instant of rage. But his presence was an important part of the setup, and I'd gone too far to turn back.

The decision to use him—and me—had been made after three hours of meetings behind closed doors. Milo had come to my house and told me about it.

"We had him call and say everything was taken care of, but it's only a matter of time before they realize he's been busted. Their kind of money means mobility: Learjets; Swiss accounts; villas on islands that don't extradite—look at Vesco, still out there, flipping off the government. Which means if we don't move fast, we're at risk for losing the big fish."

"What do you want from me?"

He told me and followed it by assurances not to feel pressured. I considered the alternatives, measured the risks, thought of a 3:00 A.M. crisis call and all that had happened since, and asked:

"When do you want to do it?"

"Tonight."

They removed Antrim from his cell that evening. Bathed him, fed him, and fetched him coffee. Exchanged his prison jump suit for a full set of livery. Drove him to the cabin in the woods. And when the call had come, he'd handled it with surprising aplomb considering the ring of big, angry men surrounding him. Surprising until you realized that he was a killing machine whose twisted circuitry lacked a conduit for worry or self-doubt. With one exception: an unfathomable vulnerability when it came to a fat, hairless woman.

A police officer had actually driven the Rolls. A tall,

thin, mustachioed man who, in the dark, looked enough
like Antrim to be his twin. But two blocks from our
destination, he'd turned into a Hancock Park cul-de-sac,
parked, and stepped out. Within seconds the chauffeur
had materialized from behind the trunk of a big maple, in
the grip of two plainclothesmen. Uncuffed and unbound.
They walked him right up to the open car door, blocking
any escape. Let go of him and watched as he slid behind
the wheel.

"Drive carefully," said Milo, lying on the floor of the
passenger compartment, the nose of his .38 pressed against
the back of the driver's seat. "One fuck-up, and Ms.
Skull does very hard time."

"Yo," said the chauffeur casually. He wheeled the big
car toward Wilshire, made a quick left turn, cruised for a
hundred feet, and turned again, floating smoothly into
the circular driveway. A silver Mercedes 380 was already
there.

"Okay?" he asked. "Should I get out?"

"Yeah," said Milo. "Remember, all eyes are on you."

Antrim turned off the engine, got out, and held the
door open for me, ever the faithful retainer. I exited, and
we walked together toward the building. He seemed relaxed. I watched his hands, his feet, the dark eyes that
moved like dung beetles scurrying across sandstone.

We approached the front steps. The door opened, and
Antrim's mustache curved upward in a smile. My throat
tightened: Was the cobra coiling?

A man stepped out and stood on the top step, with one
hand wedged in the door to keep it open.

Until then, despite Milo's rationale, the whole thing
had seemed an unnecessary bit of production for a walk-on
scene. But when I saw Souza, I knew there could have
been no other way.

"Good evening, Doctor," he said testily. He wore
evening clothes that made him look like a well-fed penguin: black silk tuxedo; starched white evening shirt perforated with tiny gold studs; plum-colored bow tie and
cummerbund; patent leather pumps as shiny as molten
tar.

"Good evening." I smiled.

"I hope this is as urgent as you made it sound. The

Cadmuses and I have an important social function this evening."

"It is," I said, with one eye still on Antrim, wondering if he'd recite his lines or try a last-minute improvisation.

The silence couldn't have lasted longer than a second, but it seemed eternal. Antrim had stepped back. Behind me. I wanted to turn, to see his face, gauge his intentions. But I couldn't risk cuing Souza to anything out of the ordinary. So, instead, I looked at the attorney, searched his eyes for absorption of a silent message. Saw only flat brown. But where was the cobra—

"Uh, Mr. Souza."

My body tightened.

"What is it, Tully?"

"The car's low on gas. Want me to fill it?"

Bravo.

"Go ahead," said Souza. "Be back in half an hour to take us to the Biltmore."

Antrim touched the visor of his cap, pivoted, and walked toward the Rolls. Souza used his fingers to push the door open.

"Come," he said impatiently.

Inside, the law building was shadowy and cold, the marble floor amplifying every clack of Souza's glossy shoes. He walked under the winding staircase, toward the back of the mansion, moving briskly for someone of his age and build. I followed him past the law library and the photocopy room and waited as he swung open carved double doors.

The paneled walls of the dining room seemed fleshlike in the soft light, each knot a spiraling black eye. The stone mantel housed a spitting tangerine fire that, from the look of the logs, had been burning for a while. A portable Chinese rosewood bar had been wheeled next to the oval Victorian table, which had been set with cut-crystal decanters and silver-jacketed tumblers. Icy facets picked up the firelight and winked it back prismatically. The tabletop gave off a burnished glow, like a lagoon at sunset. The silk rug glimmered like iridescent moss. Very elegant. Deathly quiet.

The Cadmuses were seated next to each other, on one side of the table. Souza took his place at the head and motioned me across from them.

"Good evening," I said.

They looked up long enough to utter frozen greetings, then pretended to be fascinated by their drinks. The room was sweet with burning cedar, heavy with the echoes of attenuated conversation. Souza offered me a drink that I declined. While he poured himself a bourbon, I gazed across the table.

Dwight looked bad, diminished by stress. In the two weeks since I'd seen him, he'd lost weight. His tuxedo bloused, and his shoulders rounded under some invisible burden. He'd removed his glasses and placed them on the table; the skin under his eyes was loose, dull, smudged with fatigue. Next to the spectacles was an empty tumbler. The film coating its sides said it hadn't been empty for long. One of the decanters was within reach. Between it and the tumbler was a hyphen of wet blisters: droplets of spilled booze.

Heather still looked girlish. Her hair had been piled high, revealing a long, porcelain neck circled by a diamond choker. Her ears were small, thin, elfin. A carat of blue-white diamond graced each lobe. She wore a gown of midnight blue chiffon. Her arms were white tendrils filmed by see-through sleeves. Between choker and décolletage was a milky triangle of chest, faintly freckled and furrowed by the merest hint of cleavage. Wind streaks of rouge above her cheekbones gave her lady-in-waiting features a vaguely feverish cast. Above her wedding band was a ring set with a pear-shaped sapphire the color of a newborn baby's eyes. Her tumbler looked untouched, filled with something rosy and sparkling.

"This had better be important," said Dwight, words thickened by alcohol.

"Darling," said Heather, in her little-girl voice, touching his arm gently.

"No," he said angrily. "Haven't we been through enough?"

She smiled at me, apologetically, and removed her fingers from his sleeve. He reached for the decanter and poured himself a double. She turned away, embarrassed, as he drained his glass.

Souza had seemed to ignore the exchange. Now he drew closer, cleared his throat, and said:

"Doctor, just what are these medical developments you were so insistent upon discussing?"

"They're more than developments," I said enthusiastically. "I think I've solved all your problems for you. Proved that Jamey was innocent—at least in a legal sense."

"Really?" A millimeter of smile, a mile of scorn.

"Yes. I've asked the doctors at County General to run some lab tests to verify this, but I believe he was poisoned with a class of drugs called anticholinergics. They disrupt nervous transmission and cause exactly the type of psychotic symptoms he displayed. If I'm correct, he'd be no more responsible for his actions than a somnambulist. Certainly you could use that to get him off."

"Poisoned?" said Dwight. He stared at me with sick fascination, the kind of pained look the respectable reserve for carny freaks and comics dying onstage. Then he raised his drink to his lips and snorted disgustedly.

His wife shushed him with a finger to her lips.

"Go on please, Doctor," said Souza. "How did you arrive at this intriguing hypothesis?"

"Too many things didn't fit. The slashings weren't the work of a psychotic. And Jamey's psychiatric history was puzzling, even for a schizophrenic. He'd present symptoms that were typical for chronic psychosis one day, atypical the next, shift abruptly between lucidity and delirium. The night he called me he was able to converse, when I saw him shortly after, he was unreachable— stuporous. His response to Thorazine was strange, too: up and down, like a roller coaster. And he developed premature neurological reactions to his medications, the kind of thing you usually see in patients who've been treated for years. The more I thought about it, the more toxic it sounded; something, some foreign substance, was making his nervous system go haywire. I raised the point with Dr. Mainwaring but abandoned it because he assured me he'd tested Jamey for all the common narcotics. But afterward—after I left your team, Mr. Souza—I couldn't stop thinking about how wrong everything seemed. Off kilter. I started wondering if there was some other class of drugs that Mainwaring hadn't tested for—something a doctor wouldn't normally think of because it was rarely abused. I tried to call Mainwaring to talk to him about it but wasn't able to reach him. In fact, I'd started to think he might be avoiding me—perhaps at your request, Mr. Souza. But today I called Canyon Oaks, and his secretary said she hadn't heard from him in days and was starting to get worried. Has he been in touch with you?"

"No," said Souza. "Perhaps he took a couple of days off. Impulsively."

"He didn't strike me as an impulsive person, but perhaps he did. Anyway, I did some research on my own. No need to go into the technical aspects right now, but suffice it to say that I've come up with a group of chemicals that fit perfectly—anticholinergic alkaloids. Atropine, scopolamine, belladonna extracts. You may have heard of them."

Heather looked at me raptly, like a coed with a crush on her professor, and shook her head.

"Vaguely," said Souza.

"They were used extensively in the Middle Ages to—"

"Middle Ages," said Dwight. "This is pure crap. Psychological bullshit. Who the hell would poison him?"

"Please excuse my husband's tone," said Heather, "but his point is well taken. How in the world—and why—would anyone want to poison Jamey with these . . . anticole . . ."

"Cholinergics." I smiled. "That I don't know. I suppose it'll be up to the police to look into it. But in the meantime, if the lab tests pan out, we've got a way to get Jamey off the hook. And to help restore him to normality! Because if he has been given belladonna, there's an antidote, a drug called Antilirium that can reverse its effects!"

"That *would* be something," said Souza. "These tests. Who's running them?"

"The neurologist who's caring for Jamey. Simon Platt."

"And you simply called him and requested that he run them?"

I smiled, shrugged, produced my best boyish grin.

"I told him I had your permission. I know it's a little irregular, but given the seriousness of the issue—the threat to Jamey's sanity and his life—I didn't think you'd mind. And please don't come down on Platt for not verifying it with you. He and I know each other; we're both med school faculty members. So he took me at my word."

Souza folded his arms across his barrel chest, looked at me sternly, permitted himself an avuncular smile.

"I admire your resourcefulness and your dedication," he said, "if not your disregard for the rules."

"Sometimes"—I smiled—"the rules have to be bent a little to get at the truth." Looking at my watch: "The results should be in by now. I have Platt's beeper number if you want to call him."

"Yes," said the attorney, rising. "I believe I do."

"Oh, come on, Horace," said Cadmus. "You're not taking this seriously."

"Dwight," said Souza sternly, "Dr. Delaware may or may not be correct. And though he's overstepped his professional bounds, it's clear that he's done so because he cares about Jamey. The least we can do is investigate his theory. For the boy's sake." He smiled down at me. "The number, please."

I pulled out a scrap of paper and handed it to him. He snatched it up and walked to the doors. Swung them open and came face-to-face with Milo and Richard Cash. And behind them, a sea of blue uniforms.

31

Arrogance can be comforting, the belief that one is a blossom of cleverness springing from a dung heap of stupidity a snug bit of emotional insulation. But it's a risky delusion, leading to ill-preparedness, a sudden lack of balance, when reality comes crashing down and clever is no longer good enough.

It was that kind of vertigo that caused Souza to sway at the sight of the police, his lawyerly self-assurance crumbling like old cheese. But his recovery was quick, and within moments his features had reconstituted themselves into a dignified mask, as cold and immobile as one of the marble busts that dominated the corners of the room.

"What's this about, Sergeant?" he asked Milo.

"Loose ends," said the detective. He was carrying a large briefcase, and he stepped in, reached for the rheostat inside the doorway, and spun it. As the wattage climbed, the room was stripped naked, transformed from a hushed, private world into four walls filled with expensive clichés, every nick, glitch, and faded spot confessing its existence under the heartless flood of incandescence.

Cash entered and closed the door, leaving the uniformed men outside. He took off his shades, folded them away, straightened his tie, and looked around the room appreciatively, settling his gaze on a print above the mantel.

"Currier and Ives," he said. "Nice." Milo had positioned himself behind Souza, and the Beverly Hills detective walked over and stood behind the Cadmuses, taking a tactile tour along the way, inquisitive fingers caressing the polished contours of marble, porcelain, hardwood, and gilt before coming to rest at the lower hem of his suit jacket.

The Cadmuses had reacted characteristically to the intrusion, Dwight darkening with bewilderment and annoyance, Heather straight-backed and still, as outwardly self-possessed as a prom queen. I saw her hazard a quick look at Souza, then return her attention immediately to her husband's quivering profile. As she watched his jaws work, one delicate hand took flight and rested on his sleeve. He didn't seem to notice.

"Horace," he said. "What is this?"

Souza quieted him with the lift of an eyebrow, looked back at Milo, and indicated the decanters.

"I'd offer you gentlemen drinks, but I know it's against regulations."

"If you have plain soda water, I'll take some," said Milo. "How about you, Dick?"

"Soda's fine," said Cash. "On the rocks, with a twist."

"Yes, of course," said Souza, smiling to conceal his pique and pouring the drinks.

The detectives took them and found seats. Milo slumped down between Souza and me, putting his briefcase on the floor next to my legs. Cash sidled next to Heather. He took in her jewelry with hungry eyes, shifted his scrutiny to the swell of her breasts. She pretended not to notice but, as he kept staring, fell captive to a tiny, reflexive squirm. Dwight noticed the movement and swung his head around. Cash met his eyes defiantly, then buried his smirk in bubbles. Dwight looked away furious, checked his watch, and glared at me.

"*You* called them in, didn't you, Delaware? Played hero without letting us know because of some half-assed theory." He put his glasses on and barked at Souza: "Horace, first thing tomorrow I want you to file a malpractice suit against this—"

"Dwight," said Souza quietly, "one thing at a time."

"Fine. Just as long as you know where I stand." He looked down his nose at Milo. "We need to be out of here soon, Officer. There's a major fund-raiser at the Biltmore, and I'm on the dais."

"Kiss off tonight," said Milo.

Dwight stared at him, incredulous.

"Now wait one sec—"

"In fact," added Cash, "kiss off a whole bunch of tonights."

Dwight's nails dug into his placemat. He started to rise.

"Sit, sir," said Cash.

"Darling," said Heather, exerting subtle pressure on her husband's sleeve. "Please."

Dwight sank down. The icy contours that anger had etched upon his face began to melt around the edges, softened to slush by a cloudburst of fear.

"Horace," he said, "what the hell are they talking about?"

Souza tried to placate him with an avuncular smile.

"Sergeant," he said to Milo, "I represent Mr. and Mrs. Cadmus's legal interests. Surely, if there's some issue that needs to be discussed, you can take it up with me and allow them to fulfill their social obligations."

Milo hadn't touched his soda. He held it up, squinted as if inspecting for taint, and put it down.

"Sorry," he said. *"That* would be against regulations."

"I'm afraid I don't understand," said the attorney coldly.

In lieu of a reply, Milo got up, opened the doors, and stood aside as a young uniformed officer wheeled in a video monitor on a stand. Atop the monitor was a Betamax recorder. Both monitor and recorder fed into a battery pack.

"Set it up there," said Milo, pointing to the far end of the table. The officer complied, working quickly and competently. When he was through, he gave Milo a hand-held remote control unit and asked if there was anything else.

"Nothing for now, Frank. Stay close."

"Yes, sir."

Dwight had followed the installation with a baffled look on his face. Now he filled his tumbler with scotch and emptied it. His wife watched him drink, allowing herself a momentary look of loathing. Erasing it quickly, she pulled a white silk handkerchief out of her evening purse, dabbed at her lips, and held on to it, veiling the lower part of her face. The gray eyes visible above the silk were still, yet dilated with interest. But not in her husband, for when he spoke again, they failed to follow him.

"This is damned outrageous," he said, trying to sound authoritative. But his voice had risen in pitch, leavened by anxiety.

Milo pushed a button and the monitor lit up, pushed again and the tape began to roll. The screen filled with a series of numbers—LAPD file codes—which gave way to a medium shot of a small yellow room, unfurnished except for a metal table and chair.

On the table were an ashtray and a pile of Polaroid pictures. On the chair sat Tully Antrim, dressed in a blue jump suit, eyes furtive, a cigarette smoldering between the fingers of one hand. The other lay flat on the table, big-boned, scarred, terminating in blunt fingertips capped by dirty nails. At the upper right edge of the picture was a dark fuzzy shadow of vaguely human proportions: the back of someone's head.

Antrim picked up the cigarette and inhaled. Blew smoke through his nostrils, looked up at the ceiling. Picked something out of the corner of his eye. Coughed and stretched.

"Okay, Tully," said the shadow, speaking in Milo's voice. "Let's go through that again. Who was the first?"

Antrim picked up a photograph and flexed it.

"This one."

"You've just identified Darrel Gonzales."

"Whatever."

"You never knew his name?"

"Nope."

"Did you know him by any other name?"

"Nope."

"Little D? Tinkerbell?"

Antrim dragged on his smoke and shook his head. "Never heard any of that."

"Where did you meet him?"

"Boystown."

"Where in Boystown?"

Antrim bared his teeth, amused.

"I think it was near Larabee. Just off Santa Monica. That what I said the first time?"

"Tell me about the pickup," said Milo.

Antrim yawned.

"Again?"

"Again."

"Yo. We cruised Boystown looking for someone to off. A scuzzy one, zoned-out, so there wouldn't be any problem getting him in the van, you know? Found this one, agreed on a price, and he climbed on in."

"Then what?"

"Then we drove around, got him blasted on downers, played with him, and offed him in the van."

"You and Skull?"

Something savage came into Antrim's eyes. He pulled the cigarette from his mouth, ground it out on the table-top, and leaned forward, hands warped into claws, lower jaw extended prognathically.

"I told you before," he said between clenched teeth, "I did it all, man. All she did was drive. Got it?"

Milo said, "Uh-huh," and looked at his fingernails. He waited until Antrim had relaxed before asking his next question.

"How'd you kill him?"

Antrim nodded his approval of the question.

"First I cut him a little," he said blithely. "Then I used the silk to choke him out; then I cut him up some more—that was my orders, to make it look like a psycho. Afterward I dumped him."

"Where?"

"Some alley off Santa Monica. Near Citrus, I think."

"Why there?"

"That was the orders—between this street and this street."

"Which streets?"

"La Brea and Highland."

"That was your dumping zone?"

"Yup."

"Was it the same way for each of the killings?"

"Yup. Except the streets changed for each one."

Milo pulled out a map, unfolded it in front of Antrim, and pointed.

"These dots are where we found the bodies, Tully. The numbers refer to the sequence of the murders, one for the first, two for the second, et cetera. You dumped them from east to west."

Antrim nodded.

"How come?"

"That was the orders."

"Any idea why?"

A shake of the head.

"Never asked," he said, lighting up another cigarette.

"Ever wonder why?"

"Nope."

Milo put the map away and said:

"What about the blood?"

"What about it?"

"The blood in the van. How'd you handle that?"

"We had tarps. What wouldn't wash out we burned later. The metal we hosed down. It wasn't no big deal."

"Who was the second one?"

Antrim examined the photos, picked up a pair.

"One of these, they look kind of the same."

"Keep looking. See if you can remember."

Antrim lowered his face, chewed his mustache, and stuck out his tongue concentrating. A mop of hair fell across his forehead.

"Yo," he said, letting one photo fall to the table and waving the other. "This one. The bigger one."

Milo examined the snapshot.

"You've just identified Andrew Terrence Boyle."

"If you say so, chief."

"You didn't know his name either?"

"Nope. Didn't know any of their names, except the nigger."

"Rayford Bunker."

"Not that name. Quarterflash."

"How come you know that?"

Antrim smiled.

"He was an uppity type, you know? Kept bragging, batting his lashes and singing, 'I'm Quarterflash, I'm a hot flash. I'll suck your trash for cash.' Some shit like that." Antrim gave a disapproving look, took a drag on his cigarette. "Pushy little nigger faggot. I cut him more than the others before I choked him out. To teach him a lesson, know what I mean?"

There was the sound of scratching, an arm moving. Milo finished writing and asked:

"Who was number three?"

Antrim sifted through the pile of photos.

"This one. I remember the freckles. He looked like a kid."

"Rolf Piper," said Milo. "He was sixteen."

Antrim shrugged. "Whatever."

It went on that way for a while, Milo questioning, Antrim expounding casually on the mechanics of murder. Then the interrogation began delving into greater detail: dates; times; weapons; the victims' clothing.

"Did any of them struggle, Tully?"

"Nope."

"None of them resisted at all?"

"Too zoned."

"Zoned on what?"

"Downers, hash, wine. Whatever."

"Which of them drank wine?"

"Don't remember."

"Think for a while."

A minute passed. Antrim wiped his nose with his sleeve.

"Come up with anything?"

"Nope."

"What did you do afterwards, Tully?"

"Afterwards?"

"After you dumped them."

"Cleaned up. Like I said."

"Where?"

"At the cabin."

"Which one?"

"You been there."

"Tell me anyway."

"In Tujunga. Up past La Tuna."

"Who owns the cabin?"

"Souza."

The attorney stirred at the mention of his name but remained detached, knitting his hands in front of him. Dwight turned and stared at him wildly, but Souza ignored him.

"Horace Souza?" asked Milo. "The attorney?"

"That's right."

"Did Horace Souza rent it to you?"

"No. We lived there free."

"Why is that?"

"It was part of the deal. Remember?" Antrim licked his lips and looked around the room. Bored.

"Thirsty, Tully?"

"Dry mouth. All this talking."

"How about a cup of coffee?"

"You got soup?"

"I think there's soup in one of the vending machines."
"What kind?"
"I think it's chicken soup. Want some?"
Antrim thought about it.
"No vegetable?" he asked.
"I can check. What if there's only chicken?"
Antrim contemplated his choices.
"Then I'll take a regular glass of water."
Milo moved off camera. Antrim dealt with the solitude by closing his eyes and dozing in his chair. Several minutes later Milo came back and handed him a paper cup.
"No soup, Tully. Here's the water."
"That's cool," said Antrim, gulping noisily. He put the empty cup down with a satisfied exhalation.
"Want more?" asked Milo.
"Nope."
"Okay, let's get back on track. You said after you dumped the bodies, you and Skull cleaned up. How?"
"Hosed the van, burned whatever needed burning."
"Where'd you do the burning?"
"That old barbecue pit near the cabin. The one I showed you."
"What about after cleanup? What'd you do then?"
Antrim looked perplexed.
"Something confusing you, Tully?"
"Nope. Hard to remember."
"Why's that?"
"We didn't do any one thing afterward. Sometimes we ate; sometimes we partied. Depending, you know?"
"You ate and partied after you dumped them."
"Yup. One time—after the nigger—we drove downtown and saw a movie."
"Where was the theater?"
"Off Spring. Near Fifth, I think."
"Did you take the van?"
"Nope. The Hog."
"Your Harley?"
"Right."
"What movie did you see?"
"Some fuck flick—*The Dirty Talkers, Dirty Talk*. Something like that."
"Okay," said Milo. "Anything else you want to tell me about the killings?"

Antrim grew thoughtful.

"Just that it wasn't personal," he said.

"What do you mean?"

"We didn't know those faggots. We were doing a job, that's all."

"Following orders?"

"Yeah."

The screen turned dark, and another set of numbers came on. When the room came into view, Cash and Whitehead were in it, standing to the side, taking notes.

"The date is Thursday, December tenth, 1987. This is the fourth in a series of interviews with suspect William Tull Bonney, also known as William Antrim, concerning his participation in a series of homicides, details of which have been enumerated in a previous tape. The present interview is being conducted at Parker Center. Mr. Bonney has been informed of his rights and has acknowledged his comprehension of such. He has repeatedly been offered the right to consult an attorney and has refused each time. He has been examined psychiatrically and found mentally competent to participate in decisions concerning his defense. He has consented, in writing, to these interviews and to their video and audiotaping. Any comments, Mr. Bonney?"

"You said it all, chief."

"And you still don't want a lawyer?"

"No way. A lawyer got me into this, right?"

"Mr. Antrim, if you change your mind, inform us immediately, and an attorney will be supplied."

"I won't. Let's get it over with."

Milo continued reciting:

"Present at the interview are Los Angeles County Sheriff's Deputy Calvin W. Whitehead and Detective Sergeant Richard A. Cash of the Beverly Hills Police Department." At the mention of his name Cash touched his forehead with his index finger and gave a small salute. "I'm Detective Sergeant Milo B. Sturgis of the Los Angeles Police Department, West Los Angeles Division."

Antrim seemed more animated than in the previous tape, shifting his position. Posing. He lit a cigarette, ran his fingers through his hair, and smiled. Mugging for the camera.

"Okay, Tully," said Milo, "in previous interviews you

told us how and when you killed Darrel Gonzales, Matthew Alan Higbie, Rolf Piper, John Henry Spinola, Andrew Terrence Boyle, and Rayford Antoine Bunker."

"Those are them."

"Now let's talk about two other murders. Richard Emmet Ford and Ivar Digby Chancellor."

"Sure," said Antrim. "What do you want to know?"

"Everything," growled Whitehead.

Antrim looked at him, then back at Milo, as if to say, "What's his problem?" He pulled out a cigarette and put it in his mouth.

Milo lit it for him and said:

"Why don't you start from the beginning."

"There was a bunch of beginings."

"Such as?"

"The beginning of the job was when we took the kid out of the hospital, the beginning of the cuttings—"

"Which kid are you referring to?"

"The Cadmus kid. The one who was locked up."

"James Cadmus."

"Right."

"Let's start with him," said Milo.

"Yo. I drove out to the hospital—"

"When?" asked Whitehead.

"I don't know, when was it about four, five weeks ago?"

"What day of the week was it?" asked Cash.

"Thursday."

"How do you know that?" demanded Whitehead.

"All of them happened on Thursdays."

"Why's that?"

"That was the orders. Go out on a Thursday and off a faggot."

"You didn't ask why?" asked Whitehead skeptically.

Antrim shook his head.

"Why not?" pressed the sheriff's investigator.

Antrim narrowed his eyes and grinned.

"Just doing my job, chief."

Whitehead looked as if he'd just swallowed sour milk. Folding his arms across his chest, he stared down at Antrim and snorted derisively.

"What's the matter?" said Antrim, looking injured. "I

been giving you what you want, and you still keep getting on my case."

Whitehead leaned over him.

"You're shit, Tully. I may have to hang around you, but I don't have to like the smell."

Antrim's lower jaw shot out. One hand balled into a fist. He clamped the other over it, as if subduing a rabid animal. His face went rigid, eyes flashing poisonously.

"C'mon," urged Whitehead, bobbing his head. "Make my day."

Cash and Milo stared at him.

"Scum," said Whitehead.

Antrim spit on the ground and turned his back on all three detectives.

"Take me back," he said.

No one answered.

"Come on, Tully," said Milo after a while.

"Take me the fuck back, man. I don't wanna talk no more."

"Was it something I said?" mocked Whitehead.

The screen went black for a second. When it came back on again, Milo was alone with Antrim, who sat hunched over the table, spooning something out of a bowl. He slurped, wiped his mouth, and put the spoon down. The ashtray overflowed with butts. Next to it stood a can of Pepsi.

Milo reiterated his speech, had Antrim repeat his refusal to consult an attorney, then asked:

"Ready, Tully?"

"Yo. Just keep that stupid fuck out of here, man. He comes in, I dummy up."

"Okay, Tully. It'll just be you and me, okay?"

"Stupid fuck's got an *attitude*. Someone's gonna clean his fucking clock one day."

"More soup?" asked Milo.

"No, thanks. Go ahead."

"We were talking about the murders of Richard Emmet Ford and Ivar Digby Chancellor. You were telling me how you drove to the hospital to get James Cadmus out of the hospital. Which hospital was that?"

"The nut farm where he was. Out in Agoura."

"Remember the name?"

"Canyon Oaks."

"Go on."

"I drove out there around two."

"A.M. OR P.M.?"

"A.M. I got there late. The freeway was jammed up, some kind of crash. I got a scanner in the van, so I heard about it, got off in Canoga Park, and took surface streets. Took a while to find a safe place to park, but I found one. Then I waited. The plan was for Skull to dose the kid up with something that would zone out his head but still let him walk. That way she could lead him out and bring him straight to the van. When she went in the room, he looked like he was sleeping, so she took the straps off before giving him the needle. But as soon as she stuck him, he freaked out and yanked it out. Hit her upside the head and knocked her cold. Just for a minute, but by the time she woke up he was gone. She went looking for him and found him, in one of the conference rooms, talking on the phone to the shrink."

"Which shrink?"

"Delaware."

"How do you know it was Dr. Delaware?"

"She heard him call him by name. Sounded like he was trying to get help. So she got up behind him, got an arm around his neck, and gave him the needle again. Hard. But there must have been too much stuff in it or something 'cause he went out completely and she had to drag him out of there. I seen her coming, jumped out, and threw him over my back. He was dead weight—skinny but heavy, know what I mean? Took a while to get him in the van and all gagged and tied, but I finally did it. Got the hell out of there."

"You and Skull?"

"No. Just me. She met me later. Near Chancellor's house."

"When was this?"

"When she met me?"

"When you left Canyon Oaks."

"Maybe around three-thirty."

"And when did she meet you?"

"Maybe around four-thirty."

"How did Skull manage to drag him out without someone noticing?"

"No one was around. The bitch in charge had been

paid off to make that happen. Ten grand—five and five. I know, 'cause I brought the bread to her place.''

"Which bitch is that?"

"Vann. A real cunt. She treated Skull like shit." He closed his eyes for a second, smiled dreamily. "We had plans for her."

"Where'd you go after you left the hospital grounds?"

"Back toward L.A."

"Anywhere in particular?"

"Boystown."

"Do you remember your route?"

"Yeah. The freeway was still jammed up, so I took side streets to Reseda, got back on and got off at Laurel. Drove to Santa Monica and turned left."

"East."

"Yeah."

"Go on."

"I trawled Santa Monica and picked up the whore— Ford."

"Where'd you find him?"

"Street corner near Western."

"What'd you do with him?"

"Same as the others: talked cash, got him in, dosed him up, and choked him."

"To death?"

"Nope. Just unconscious. Then I gagged him and tied him and stashed him next to Cadmus." Antrim laughed.

"What's funny?" asked Milo.

"I used to drive this meat truck, for this sausage company over in Vernon. Hauled pig carcasses. This was kind of the same thing."

"Where'd you go after you'd tied up Ford?"

"Up to Chancellor's place."

"Remember that route?"

"Santa Monica to Sunset, west into Beverly Hills to the hotel, then north and up a ways. Big white place behind walls."

"Where was Skull?"

"Side street off Doheny. I picked her up."

"What'd you do when you got there?"

"Place was locked, electric gate. We had a plan to get in—part of the orders. There was a squawk box. Had to push the button a bunch of times before Chancellor answered. He sounded out of it, like he'd just woke up. Said, 'Who is it?' and Skull answered in a kid's voice—"

"A kid's voice?"

"Yeah. Like a sixteen-year-old. An impression, you know? She's got a talent for that kind of thing," he added, proudly, "does Bugs Bunny, Minnie Pearl, Elvis. You should hear her."

"I'll be sure to," said Milo. "What did she say to Chancellor?"

"She told him she was a friend of Jamey's, that they'd had an accident and he was there with her, hurt bad. You could hear Chancellor get all uptight, breathing hard over the squawk box. He said he'd be right down. I pulled Cadmus's body out of the van and laid it in front of the gate. Skull backed down the block, cruised slowly; you can't park overnight in Beverly Hills, and we didn't want to attract no attention. I waited off to the side of the gate. After a few minutes I could hear Chancellor coming. The gates opened, and he came out in this faggy dressing gown. When he saw Cadmus, he gave a yell. I jumped him, hit him hard, and put a choke on him—to put him out, just like Ford. Then Skull cruised by with the van, and I loaded Chancellor and Cadmus in it. Tied up Chancellor and drove through the gate. Closed it and hauled all of them up to the house. He was heavy."

Antrim stretched, pulled out a cigarette, and lit up, contentedly, as if rewarding himself for a job well done. When he showed no intention of saying anything further, Milo said: "What'd you do once you got up there?"

"Dragged them all into the house."

Antrim blew smoke rings at the ceiling.

"Then what?"

"Dosed up Cadmus, choked Ford and Chancellor with the silk, cut them up, and hung Chancellor from the ceiling."

"Why'd you hang him?"

"That was the orders. Truss him up with the pool rope and hoist him up. Ball-busting job, man. He was big."

"What about the position of his hands?"

"The what?"

"The way you positioned his hands after you hung him. Was that part of the orders, too?"

"Oh, that. Yeah, it was. Tie him up and wrap his hands around what was left of his cock."

"Any idea why?"

"Nope," said Antrim. "Maybe it was his idea of a joke."

"Whose idea?"

"Souza's. Though I never did see him joke much."

Milo shut the monitor off and looked around the table. Dwight had gone bed sheet white. Heather continued to use the handkerchief as a veil. Souza sat as impassively as a cigar store Indian.

"Any comments?" Milo asked him.

"None whatsoever."

"Horace," said Dwight in a shaky voice. "What he said—"

"Is utter nonsense," spit Souza. "Tully's always been unstable, prone to wild fantasies. I knew that when I hired him, but I felt sorry for him and I was able to keep him in line. Until now."

Dwight looked at Milo.

"He's highly credible," said the detective calmly. "He knows details that only a perpetrator or an observer could have known. The physical evidence backs him up one hundred percent. Marthe Surtees verifies it all independently."

"Dwight," said Souza reassuringly, "this is absurd. A travesty that will be set right. In the meantime, I strongly advise you, as your attorney—and friend—not to say another word."

"He can't function as an attorney in this case," said Milo. "He's a suspect."

"He ain't much of a friend either," drawled Cash.

Heather dropped her veil and touched her husband's cheek with her fingertips.

"Darling," she said, "listen to Horace."

"*Darling*," mimicked Cash. "That's a good one."

"Don't talk to my wife that way," said Dwight.

Cash looked at him scornfully, turned to Milo, and smiled. "Rich folk," he said. "Put 'em in shit up to their chins, and they think it's a beauty bath."

"Horace," said Dwight, "what the hell is going on?"

"*I'm* going to tell you what's going on," said Milo.

And he got up, picked up his briefcase, and walked with it to the far end of the table.

"On the surface it's complicated," he said, "but when you get down to it, what we have here is just another dirty little family squabble. Soap opera stuff. Dr. Delaware could probably give you the psychological reasons for it, but I'm going to stick to the facts."

He opened the briefcase, drew out some papers, and spread them on the table.

"I never knew your dad," he said to Dwight, "but from what I've learned, he sounds like a guy who liked things simple." He lifted a sheaf of papers. "Take this will, for example. Estate of this size and you'd figure it might get all complicated. But no, he had two sons; he divided everything right down the middle—almost. Fifty-one percent to your brother, forty-nine to you." He paused. "Must have seemed unfair, huh? Especially when you were such an obedient kid and Peter was such a flake."

"Father would have changed the will eventually," said Dwight reflexively. As if it were a well-rehearsed line. "If he'd lived long enough."

"Hush," said Souza.

Milo smiled. "I guess you can keep telling yourself that if it makes you feel better."

Heather let her veil drop. The face behind the silk was tight with anger. Gripping her husband's sleeve, she said:

"Don't respond to him, darling. Don't let yourself be demeaned."

"He's already been demeaned plenty," said Milo. "And not by me."

She let go of the sleeve and didn't answer. Her silence made Dwight dip his head and look at her.

"I need to know what's going on," he said weakly.

She avoided his stare and turned away. The evening purse was in front of her, and she plunged her fingers into its sequined folds and began kneading, furiously.

"Anyway," said Milo to Dwight, "no use speculating what might have happened. Point is, your dad didn't live long enough to change anything, and Peter ended up with the lion's share. Which could have been a real disaster, even with all your hard work and the help of Faithful Friend Horace, here. Because at some point, if he wanted to, Peter could have taken over the company, sold it to an outsider, run it into the ground, whatever. Lucky for you, he had the courtesy to die prematurely."

Dwight lifted a finger and pointed it at Milo. "If you're suggesting that I viewed my brother's death as good luck, you're damned—"

"Take it easy," said the detective. "I'm not suggesting anything—only you know how you felt about it. Let's stick with the evidence." He put down the papers he was holding and retrieved some others. "Like Peter's will. As straightforward as Daddy's—everything passes on to Peter's sole heir, James. One funny thing about it, though. Every other Cadmus family document I could find was drawn up by Souza and Associates. But this was handled by a San Francisco lawyer named Seymour Chereskin."

"One of Peter's hippie pals," said Dwight. "Long hair and beard, dressed in buckskins and beads."

"He's a professor of law now," said Milo. "At UC Berkeley. And he has clear memories of drawing up the will. Especially all the pressure he got from Souza not to do it. Even to the point of being offered five thousand dollars as an incentive."

Dwight looked at Souza.

"It made sense for our firm to handle it," said the attorney. "Peter's holdings were enmeshed with those of the corporation and yours, Dwight. I wanted to keep things consistent. To avoid a disaster. Chereskin looked like Charles Manson. Who knew what he'd do?"

"He's a Harvard grad," said Milo.

"That didn't mean much in those days, Sergeant. I was concerned he'd pull some hippie stunt."

"He tells it differently. That he was clear about what he was going to do and laid it out for you. Even sent you a copy. But you kept the pressure up. Flew up in person to lean on him. He got the distinct feeling you were heavily into control."

"That's ridiculous. Peter had a history of being duped by unsavory types, and I was simply attempting to protect him from himself."

"Noble of you," said Milo, examining the document again. "My legal adviser tells me Chereskin did a bang-up job, very straightforward and sensible."

"It was a competent effort," said Souza.

"Straightforward," repeated Milo. "The inheritance was set up as an irrevocable trust fund for Jamey, with his uncle as the guardian. Payouts were to start at the age of eighteen and continue through thirty-five. At thirty-five, full transfer of ownership. Standard spend-thrift and ill health clauses. Chereskin even recommended that you be the trustee because of the linkage with corporate affairs. So I guess your fears were unfounded, huh? Unless, of course, you had something else in mind."

"Such as?"

"You tell me."

"Sergeant," said Souza, "you burst in here and ruined our evening under the guise of revealing hard facts. But all we've heard so far are tedious rehashes and rude implications."

"Gee," said Milo. "Sorry about that."

"We're both sorry," said Cash.

Souza sat back, fought to appear casual, and succeeded. He reclined further, and the light cast shiny white tiger stripes across the pink surface of his head.

"Onward," said Milo. "After Peter died, his will was probated, making a small child the majority owner of Cadmus Construction. How'd you feel about that, Mr. Cadmus?"

"Damned fine!" said Dwight stuffily. "It's a family business. It should support the family."

"I understand that," said Milo. "But didn't it bother you that after all your work, here you were again in the number two position? That one day Jamey would be able to waltz in and take it over from you?"

Dwight shrugged.

"I thought about it when he was young, figured we'd cross that bridge when we came to it."

"Nice of him to go crazy and cross it for you."

"What are you saying?"

"The ill health clause," said Milo. "In the event of mental incompetence, control reverts back to the guardian—you. A month ago you had Souza put it into effect. Gave yourself one hundred percent control over the family fortune."

"I did nothing of the damned sort!"

"Sure about that?"

"Of course, I'm sure."

Milo went back to the briefcase and took out another piece of paper.

"Here. Take a look at this."

He passed it to Dwight, who read it, mouth agape.

"I've never seen this before," he said.

"It's got your signature on it. Notarization and all."

"I tell you I never signed this."

Now it was Milo's turn to sit back.

Dwight kept staring at the document, as if hoping it would explain itself. Finally he put it down, shaking his head, looking around the room.

"I signed your name," said Heather softly.

"What!"

"To save you the trouble, darling. It was just a matter of time before it had to be done."

"You did it without *asking* me?"

"I knew it would be hard for you. I was trying to spare you the pain."

Dwight shook his head in disbelief.

"How'd you get it notarized?"

She bit her lip.

"Faithful Friend Horace leaned on one of his associates to do it," said Milo. "For your own good, of course."

Dwight glared at Souza, then looked at his wife as if seeing her for the first time.

"What's going on, Heather?"

"Nothing, darling," she replied tensely. "Please stop responding to him. Can't you see what he's trying to do?"

"Nothing like a surprise, huh?" said Milo. "Don't go away. I've got more."

"Then spit it the hell out," said Dwight.

"Hey," said Milo, "I don't blame you for being angry. If I were in your situation, I'd be angry, too. You bust your butt to keep the company going and fifty-one percent of the profits go to a playboy brother who never lifted a finger to earn his keep. Then he dies, and all of that money passes to his kid—who *you* get stuck raising."

"I wasn't stuck with anything," said Dwight. "He was family."

"Sounds good," said Milo. "How did your wife feel about it?"

Heather glared hatefully at Milo.

"After all," continued the detective, "raising *this* kid couldn't have been a picnic—too smart for his own good, a nasty mouth, antisocial. And to top it all, gay. When he started hanging around with Chancellor, it must have been where-did-I-go-wrong time, huh?"

"You'd know about that kind of thing, Sergeant," said Souza dryly.

"Still," continued Milo, "all that could have been tolerated. But not his threatening to blow you out of the water financially."

Comprehension spread across Dwight's face like a malignant rash.

"I don't know what you're talking about," he said shakily.

"Sure you do. The same old story—playing it straight and getting tripped up by bad luck. You went into the Bitter Canyon project thinking it was the deal of a lifetime. Daddy'd left a giant parcel of land ripe for development. A sweetheart situation if there ever was one. You could sell the land to the state cheaply enough to put in a winning bid on the construction and still make a massive profit. Like playing blackjack with yourself—you couldn't lose. Digby Chancellor thought it was sweet, too. Bought a major chunk of the bonds at par and got ready to rake in the profits. Imagine how he felt when he found out he'd invested in poison gas."

"According to the reports I had, that land was clean," said Dwight. "There was no way to know."

"Stop chattering," said Souza furiously. "There's no need to defend yourself."

"No, there wasn't any way to know," commiserated Milo. "Like I said, bad luck. And if Jamey hadn't found an old diary of your dad's, no one would have known. But he did, and he told Chancellor. Who put the squeeze on."

Dwight gave an embittered laugh.

"So that's what it was," he said. "A diary. I never knew Father kept one."

"Where did Chancellor say he got the information?"

"He—"

"Oh, for God's sake," said Souza disgustedly.

Dwight regarded the attorney with a jaundiced eye. Played with his glasses and said:

"He said he'd gotten hold of some old business records. Wouldn't say how, but I suspected Jamey, because
he was a rag picker—always poking around where he
shouldn't have. When I asked Dig for proof, he handed
me a Xerox of Father's description of the gas storage.
Then he demanded I buy back his bonds at a premium. I
told him he was crazy. He threatened to go public if I
refused, promised me he'd bring down the company. I
tried to bluff him, said he'd never do that because it
would break him, too, but he said he'd sue for fraud and
win. That he'd enlist Jamey as a co-complainant and the
court would dissolve the corporation and award them the
assets. *Them,* as if they were married. He was a ruthless,
perverted bastard."

"Who else knew about the squeeze?" asked Milo.

Dwight looked sharply at Souza.

"Horace did. I went to him for advice on how to
handle it. Told him we hadn't started digging yet and
there was time to pull out."

"What did he advise you?"

"That pulling out would damage the company perma-
nently. He said to go ahead as if nothing had happened.
That he'd find a way out, but I should start paying in the
meantime."

"Did you?"

"Yes."

"For how long?"

"About a year."

"How frequent were the payoffs?"

"Nothing regular. Dig called and we traded."

"Cash for bonds?"

"That's right."

"How'd the transactions take place?"

"I kept several accounts at his bank. We met in his
office, I signed a withdrawal slip, and he took it from
there."

"What about the bonds?"

"They found their way into my safe-deposit box."

"Must have hurt," said Milo.

Dwight winced.

"Toward the end it got worse," he said. "He kept
demanding I buy more and more."

"Who knew about it besides Souza?"

"No one."

"Nobody in the corporation?"

"No. It was a personal account."

"How about your wife?"

"No."

"Big thing like that and you didn't discuss it with her?"

"I handle the finances in the family. We never talk about business."

"When did you decide to get rid of Chancellor?"

Dwight shot out of his chair. "I don't know a damned thing about that!"

He backed away from the table, knocking his tumbler over in the process. Standing pressed against the paneled wall, he turned his head from side to side, as if searching for an escape route. Cash looked meaningfully at Milo, who gave his head a brief shake. The Beverly Hills detective stayed in his place, but his eyes were vigilant.

"Why don't you sit down?" suggested Milo.

"All I did was give in to blackmail," said Dwight. "I was exploited. I had nothing to do with anything else."

"Two people threaten to ruin your life. All of a sudden one's dead and the other's locked away in the booby hatch. Pretty convenient."

Dwight was silent for a moment. Then he gave an odd smile and said:

"I figured I was entitled to a stroke of good luck."

Milo looked at him, then shrugged.

"Hell," he said, "if you can live with it, I can." Pulling a tape recorder out of the briefcase, he set it on the table. The flick of a switch evoked a hiss of white noise and over it the sound of a phone ringing. On the third ring the phone was answered.

"Hello," said a familiar voice.

"It's Tully, Mr. Souza."

"Hello, Tully."

"Just called to tell you everything went perfect."

"I'm glad to hear that."

"Yeah, two birds with one stone. The broad—Vann—was shacking up with Mainwaring. We took care of both of them—"

"No need to go into detail, Tully."

"Okay, Mr. Souza. Just wanted you to know it was clean—bare hands, no weapo—"

"That's enough," snapped Souza.

Silence.

"Thank you for calling, Tully. You did well."

"Anything else you want me to do, Mr. Souza?"

"Not at the moment. Why don't you take a couple of days off? Relax, rest up."

"I could use some rest, Mr. Souza. My knuckles are real sore." Phlegmy laughter.

"I'm sure they are, my boy. I'm sure they are."

"Bye, Mr. Souza."

"Good-bye."

Milo turned off the recorder.

"You goddamned bastard," said Dwight, and he began moving toward Souza. Cash sprang up, took him by the arms, and held him back.

"Settle down," he said, and steered Dwight to the far side of the table, near the video screen. With a firm hand on a heaving shoulder, he pressed him into a chair. Staying on his feet, he took a watchful position behind the enraged man.

Dwight brandished a fist at Souza and said, "Bastard."

Souza gazed at him, bemused.

"Any comments now?" Milo asked the attorney.

Souza shook his head.

"Would you like a lawyer before we go any further?"

"Not at all. However, I could use a martini. May I fix one?"

"Suit yourself," said Milo.

"Would anyone else care for a drink?" asked Souza.

No one answered, so he smiled and leaned toward the portable bar, mixing gin and vermouth, slowly. Picking an olive out of a silver dish, he dropped it into the drink, watched it bobble, and sat back down. Taking a small sip, he ran his tongue over his lips, the picture of contentment.

"Damn you, Horace," croaked Dwight. "Why the hell—"

"Oh, shut up," said Souza. "You're being tiresome."

"The *why* is fairly mundane," said Milo. "Money, power, the usual stuff. It's the *how* that tripped us up. Until we found out about Mrs. Cadmus's special talents with drugs."

A fresh wave of horror swept over Dwight's face. He

stared across the table at his wife, begging for denial. Instead, she lowered the veil and shot him a defiant look of cold disdain.

"When did you first get the idea?" Milo asked her. She ignored him, and he continued:

"The way I see it is you've hated Jamey for a long time. Been fantasizing about getting rid of him. When Souza told you about Chancellor's little squeeze, the two of you decided the time had come to go ahead with it."

Heather's mouth began to tremble, and she seemed about to say something. Then Souza cleared his throat, and she turned toward him. The look that passed between them renewed her resistance, and her eyes narrowed and hardened, darkening to the color of storm clouds. Sitting taller, she met Milo's gaze unflinchingly, looking through him as if he didn't exist. The entire exchange had taken a second, but Dwight hadn't missed it. He made a low, choking sound and sagged in his chair.

"Talk about your two birds," said Milo. "You probably considered killing both of them outright but decided it might look too cute, maybe cause us to snoop around the family fortune. Not to mention probate court and inheritance tax. But murdering Chancellor and setting up Jamey as a psycho killer would have given Hubby access to the money without any of those hassles. A year later Jamey could die in jail or on the back ward of some hospital; at that point it wouldn't really make a difference. Couple of years later Hubby could meet with an unfortunate accident—maybe even go crazy and kill himself, 'cause that kind of thing runs in the family, doesn't it? Leaving you with all of it."

Heather laughed scornfully. Souza said, "Ridiculous." Milo nodded at me.

"If anyone knew how to drive someone crazy, you did," I told her, and gave a summary of her thesis research. She seemed unaffected by the recitation. But from the numb, sick look on Dwight's face, it was clear that he'd never taken the time to learn about his wife's scholarly efforts, had never seen her as other than the dutiful helpmate.

"You did it subtly," I said. "Poisoned him slowly over a one-year period with belladonna clones, slipping the drugs into his food, his milk, his mouthwash, his tooth-paste. Gradually elevating the dosages. Your knowledge of organic anticholinergics enabled you to pick drugs and mix them to evoke exactly the type of symptom you wanted—agitation one day, depression the next. Para-noia, auditory hallucinations, visual scrambling, stupor—you'd learned how to create all of them from the Indians in the jungle. And if you wanted something different, there was always the occasional chaser of a synthetic agent—LSD, PCP, amphetamine. Volunteering at the drug rehab center gave you access to street drugs. The police have found two kids—so far—who've admitted selling to you.''

She blinked rapidly. Said nothing.

"Oh, God," said Dwight. Cash watched him carefully.

"Jamey's psychological history made things easy for you," I continued. "He'd never been well adjusted, so no one would be surprised when he went off the deep end. You took him to the point of severe psychosis and had him committed. Canyon Oaks was chosen because Souza knew Mainwaring could be manipulated with money. And you lost no time taking advantage of that. Marthe Surtees was brought in as a private-duty nurse, and she took over the poisoning—at your direction. Meanwhile, Mainwaring was treating what he thought was schizo-phrenia with phenothiazines, which, when combined with the anticholinergics, toxified Jamey's nervous system fur-ther. Surtees says she gave you a daily report on his status. When things got too severe, you had her back off. When he started looking better, he got another jolt. Even his arrest and incarceration in the High Power block didn't put an end to it. Surtees had to bow out, but someone else took over. Someone who had a valid rea-son to visit him frequently. Someone who could sit with him for extended periods of time without attracting un-due attention. Put a fatherly arm around his shoulder, give him sips of juice. Someone who was supposed to be his advocate.''

I glared at Souza.

"Absurd," he said. "Wild speculation.''

Heather nodded in agreement but distractedly, as if performing by rote.

"The two of you are quite a pair," I said, focusing on

Souza. "While she worked on Jamey, you had Antrim
commit the Lavender Slashings. Those seven boys were
human sacrifices, picked at random, dumped like garbage. They died so that you could set up Chancellor and
Jamey as sex killers, make Chancellor's death look like a
party gone bad. Every detail was planned and premeditated. The bodies were dumped in a westerly pattern that
reversed itself when Chancellor was killed—to make it
appear as if the chain had been broken. The slashings
took place on Thursday because Chancellor had to be
murdered on Thursday—the night his bodyguard was off.
You even provided a garrote which would incriminate
Jamey: strips cut from Heather's lavender gown, which
she took pains to tell me he'd stolen. Everything was
going as planned until Jamey managed to knock out
Surtees and call me."

"Dr. Delaware"—Souza sneered—"you flatter yourself with too much self-importance."

"Not really," I said. "I know I was nothing but another pawn. You knew I'd been Jamey's therapist, had
been told he spoke highly of me, and you weren't sure if
he'd blurted out anything important that night. So you
decided to *co-opt* me. You even used those very words—'I
want to co-opt you, Doctor'—playing with me. Because
that's your view of life, a game. One big tournament with
expendable players. Once I'd agreed to join your team,
you made a point of emphasizing that anything I learned
would be confidential, ostensibly to protect Jamey but
really to protect yourself."

"I simply reminded you of well-established ethical principles," said Souza. "Principles that you've violated
egregiously."

"You strung me along," I continued, "until you were
sure I knew nothing incriminating. Then you fired me.
Funny thing is, by hiring me, you bought yourself some
new trouble—Erno Radovic."

Mention of the bodyguard's name caused Dwight's eyes
to widen. Cash peered down at him watchfully.

"We'll never know why Radovic decided to poke
around," I said. "Maybe it was loyalty to his boss. More
likely he'd overheard Jamey and Chancellor talking about
Bitter Canyon, suspected it might have something to do
with Chancellor's murder, and decided to learn enough

to put on a squeeze of his own. He might even have known about the diary, looked for it, but couldn't find it. When you hired me, he did a background check, found out I'd been Jamey's psychotherapist, and suspected the same thing you had: that I'd been privy to secret information. So he started following me, and I led him—unwittingly—to the diary. When he read it, he realized he was on to something big and called Dwight, demanding cash and letting him know he meant business by having the payoff take place on the road to Bitter Canyon. Dwight called you, and you dispatched Antrim and Surtees to take care of business."

"That's conspiracy to commit murder," Milo told Dwight, who avoided scrutiny by covering his face with his hands. "What'd you think when you found out Radovic had been gutted, Dwight? Another bit of good luck?"

No answer.

The silence stretched like taffy. Souza snapped it.

"Sergeant," he said, putting down his martini, "it's been intriguing. Are we free to go now?"

"Go?"

"Exit. Leave. Fulfill our social obligations."

Milo concealed his incredulity behind an angry laugh.

"That's all you have to say?"

"Surely," said the attorney, "you don't expect me to take any of this seriously?"

"Not impressed, huh?"

"Hardly. You march in here with your paraphernalia and your battalion and present a loosely connected pastiche of ramblings, hypotheses, and wild speculation, the kind of case for which I could obtain a dismissal during prelims."

"I see," said Milo, and he read him his rights.

Souza listened, nodding approvingly, like a schoolmaster conducting an oral exam, remaining unruffled even after Milo had drawn his arms behind him and cuffed him. It was then that the full extent of his disturbance hit me.

I shouldn't have been surprised, because it had been simmering inside him for forty years: the pain and humiliation of living under the shadow of another man. Of losing a woman to him only to see her atrophy and die, of *running like a mutt* to her sister, only to be rejected again. Of yearning for full partnership and having to settle for token rewards. The constant relegation to second fiddle.

Black Jack Cadmus had understood what that kind of thing could do, and it had worried him.

"So I figure down deep he's got to hate my guts," he'd written, *"and I'm wondering how to diffuse it."* His solution had been cynical and self-serving: *"A little charity camouflaged as gratitude could go a long way. Got to keep H. in his place but also make him feel important."*

But in the end it had been Souza who'd diffused it himself, defending against his feelings by prostituting himself emotionally, deifying the man he unconsciously despised and worshiping him dutifully, maintaining the adoration even after death: Faithful Retainer Horace, with no family of his own, always available for the crises that seemed to afflict the Cadmuses like some morbid allergy to life. On twenty-four-hour call, ever ready to serve.

Reaction formation Freud had termed it: the embrace of noble deeds in order to mask festering impulses. It was a tough defense to maintain, like walking a tightrope backward. And it had become the modus operandi of Souza's adult life.

But his anger when I'd asked him about his involvement with the Cadmus family was evidence that the grout around the edges of his defenses had begun to come loose. Softened by the heat of pent-up rage. Eroded by time, opportunity, and the availability of another Cadmus woman. The release of his passions had turned him into a murderer, a life taker of monstrous proportions, but like all grotesques, he'd shunned his reflection.

Now the mirror was being held before his eyes, and he'd withdrawn behind a wall of denial. A *belle indifférence* that Marie Antoinette would have been proud of.

Milo finished reading and looked from Heather to Dwight.

"Eeny meeny miny," said Cash, reading his mind.

Before he made his choice, the door opened, and Cal Whitehead walked in, dressed in a bottle green suit with white-piped lapels and carrying a gleaming lizardskin case, its handle wrapped in clear plastic and tagged. Managing to chew gum and grin at the same time. Swinging the case onto the table, he said: "How come all the long faces?"

"Just wrapping up," said Milo. "Mr. Souza's not impressed with our case."

"Tsk-tsk," said Whitehead. "Maybe this'll help."

He donned plastic surgical gloves, pulled a tagged key out of his pocket, and inserted it into the lock of the case. "You're a very confident lady," he said to Heather, "leaving this right in your bureau drawer, tucked underneath all those nice silk undies. Right next to your diaphragm."

A turn of his wrist opened the case. The interior was thick lavender velvet. Twenty hexagonal depressions had been formed in the velvet. Occupying each one was a small crystal jar held in place by a velvet strap, containing grayish and brownish powders and coarser substances that appeared to be dried leaves and twigs. Strapped to the lid of the case were a small porcelain mortar and pestle, a porcelain dish, three metal hypodermic syringes, and a platinum cigarette lighter.

"Best-looking works I've ever seen," said Whitehead. "Very ladylike."

Heather pulled up her veil again. Stared at the evening purse. Souza looked up at the ceiling, seemingly oblivious. A log crackled in the fireplace.

"Still not impressed?" asked Whitehead with feigned hurt that turned suddenly to genuine annoyance. He reached inside his jacket and pulled out a stack of photographs.

"Detective Whitehead," said Milo, but before he could complete his sentence, the sheriff's investigator had fanned the photos like a deck of cards and begun dealing. First to Souza, who ignored them, then to Heather, who took one look and let out an agonized moan, a gargling, raw noise from deep in her belly, so primal and painracked it verged on the unbearable.

Tearing at the pictures with palsied hands, she succeeded only in bending them. Moaning again, she lowered her head so that her brow was level with the table edge and began to dry-retch.

"What are those?" said Dwight sharply.

"You wanna see them, too?" said Whitehead.

"Cal," said Milo meaningfully.

Whitehead dismissed him with the wave of a hand. "Sure, why not?" And he tossed a handful in front of Dwight, who scooped them up, inspected them, and began to tremble violently.

I understood the reactions because I'd seen the pictures: grainy black-and-white snapshots, taken surreptitiously through door cracks and behind lace-curtained windows but clear enough to do damage—Heather and Souza making love. In his office, she lying belly down on his carved desk, skirt hiked over her narrow hips, placid and bored, as he pumped, squinting, grinning, from behind. In his bedroom, on a four-poster bed, she taking him in her mouth, wide-eyed, one spidery hand compressing a meaty buttock. In the back seat of the Rolls, a two-backed beast contorting amid a disarray of hastily unfastened clothing. And so on. A graphic chronical of adultery, repugnant yet possessing the smarmy allure of crude pornography.

His insurance policy Antrim had called the photos. A nasty collection assembled over a two-year period. Rendered feasible because he was a servant and servants were psychologically invisible. Just as his presence had been overlooked during the false notarization of the trust fund, so had his hungry, jailyard eyes been disregarded in the heat of the rut.

Heather dry-heaved again.

Dwight stood and shook a finger at her.

"You goddamn slut!" he shouted across the table. "Goddamn lying whore!"

The epithets jerked her upright. She pulled herself shakily to her feet. Eyes wild, cheeks spotted with color, hair coming loose on one side, fingers groping at the clutch purse. Sobbing. Breathing hard, on the verge of hyperventilation.

"Two-faced bitch," spit Dwight, shaking his fist at her.

"Easy," said Cash, with one hand on his shoulder.

"You," said Heather, sobbing, gulping air. "You . . . have the . . . nerve . . . to preach . . . to me. . . ."

"Two-faced whore!" he roared. "This is the thanks I get. Fucking bitch."

"Who are . . . you to . . . judge?" she screamed, raising her hands, the fingers curling into talons.

He held up a snapshot. "I kill myself for you, and this is my thanks!"

"I don't . . . owe you . . . anything."

He reached across the table, picked up the decanter, and threw whiskey in her face.

She stood there drenched, shuddering, mouth working soundlessly.

"Enough," said Milo.

"Come on," said Cash, holding Dwight back. "Settle down."

"Fucking frigid whore!" screamed Dwight, flailing at her.

She wailed and pulled something out of the purse. A shiny little revolver, not much bigger than a derringer. Silver-plated, engraved. Almost toylike. Two-handing it, she aimed it at her husband.

Three .38 police specials were out in a flash, trained on her.

"Put the gun down," said Milo. "Put it down."

"You worm," she said to Dwight, still fighting for control.

"Wait a second," he said feebly, and retreated a step.

"The nerve of you . . . to preach to me. You worm." To no one in particular: "He's a worm. A sick worm."

The gun wavered.

"Put it down. Now," said Milo.

"Come on, Heather," said Dwight, sweating, holding one hand against his chest in a futile effort at self-protection. "Stop it. There's no need to—"

"Oh." She laughed. *"Now* he's scared. *Now* he wants to stop it. Gutless, castrated *worm.*" To no one in particular: "He's a eunuch. And a murderer, too."

"Please," said Dwight.

"What else would you call someone who found his brother . . . his own brother . . . strangling to death . . . playing a hanging game and strangling to death . . . strangling? Who saw that and didn't cut his own brother down? Who let him die like that? Strangling . . . what would you call that?"

"I'd call that pretty low," said Whitehead, and he put his .38 down on the table and sauntered nonchalantly between her and Dwight. Smiling, chewing.

Milo cursed under his breath. Cash kept his gun arm

rigid, put his other on top of Dwight's head, and prepared to push him to the ground.

"Don't try to save him," said Heather. "I'll kill you,
too."

Cash froze.

"Put down your gun," she said.

Cash shook his head. "Can't do that."

The refusal didn't seem to bother her.

"Worm," she snarled. "Gets drunk and *confesses* to
me. 'I killed my brother, I killed my brother.' Blubbering
like a baby. 'Have to make it right by taking in his son.
Have to do right by Jamey.' " She raised her voice to a
high-pitched scream. "Who raised the little bastard, *you?*
Who put up with his abuse, his evil mouth? He was *your*
penance, but *I* got crucified."

She steadied the gun.

"Come on, little lady." Whitehead smiled. "Guns aren't
for pretty little ladies—"

"Shut up," she said, trying to peer around his bulky
body. "I want the worm."

Whitehead laughed heartily.

"Now, now," he said.

"Shut up," she said, louder. Whitehead creased his
forehead irritably. Forced a smile.

"Now come on, honey. All that tough talk's fine for
TV, but we don't want any trouble now, do we?"

"Shut up, you idiot!"

Whitehead's face puckered with anger. He stepped
forward.

"Now cut the crap, lady—"

She looked at him quizzically and shot him in the
mouth. Aimed the gun at Dwight but was cut down by
thunder. Bullet after bullet hit her slender body, tearing
it, buffeting it. Smoky holes perforated her gown, the
blue chiffon reddening wetly, then blackening as she
sank.

The doors to the dining room burst open. A surge of
blue. Uniforms, armed with shotguns. Horrified looks,
falling faces. Milo explaining to them as he rushed over
to examine Whitehead's prone form. Calling for an ambulance. The bark of static. The hum of procedure. Cash,
silent, ashen, relinquishing Dwight to a pair of officers.
Holstering his gun. Loosening his tie. Dwight, staring at

his wife's corpse. At scarlet spatters on waxed pine paneling. A pool of blood gleaming obscenely on the table. Collapsing in a dead faint. Dragged away.

Souza had sat through it all, silent, removed. Two pairs of hands took him by the armpits and hoisted him up. He surveyed the carnage, clucked his tongue.

"Come on," said one of the cops.

"One second, young man." The imperiousness in his voice made the policeman stop.

"What?"

"Where are you taking me?"

"To jail."

"I know that." Irritably. "*Which* jail?"

"County."

"Excellent. Before we leave, I want you to make a phone call for me. To Mr. Christopher Hauser. Of Hauser, Simpson, and Bain. The number is on a card in my wallet. Inform him that the location of our breakfast has been changed. From the California Club to the County Jail. And tell him to bring a pad and paper. It will be a working meeting. Have you got all that?"

"Oh sure," said the cop, rolling his eyes.

"Then repeat it back to me. Just to be sure."

32

THREE WEEKS after Souza's arrest, Gary Yamaguchi and Slit (née Amber Lynn Danziger) were found in Reno by a private detective agency hired by the girl's parents. They'd been living in an abandoned trailer on the outskirts of town, subsisting on handouts and her earnings as a part-time counter girl at Burger King. Upon return to L.A. she was released to her parents and Gary was taken into custody as a material witness. When Milo questioned him about the diary, he adopted the same kind of robotic indifference he'd shown me in the alley behind Voids. But a stay in the County Jail and a slide show of the Slasher victims' bodies, donated by the coroner, made him somewhat more cooperative.

"The way he tells it," said Milo over the phone, "Jamey called him and asked to get together about a month or so before he was committed. They met at Sunset Park, across from the Beverly Hills Hotel. It was a hot day, but Jamey was wearing a raincoat. Yamaguchi said he looked like a street nut—dirty, staggering, talking to himself. They sat down on a bench, and he started rambling about this book he had that was so important he could be killed for it. Then he pulled it out of his coat, shoved it in Yamaguchi's hands, and told him he was the only friend he had, that his mission was to keep the book safe. Before Yamaguchi could say anything, he ran off.

"Yamaguchi figured the whole thing was a paranoid delusion, said he considered tossing the book in the nearest trash can. Instead—he can't say why—he took it with him, stuck it in a drawer, and forgot about it. After Jamey was committed, he wondered if there had been something to the story, but not enough to examine it. After Chancellor was murdered, he pulled it out and started reading. But he claims he found it boring and gave up after the first few pages. It was then, he says,

423

that he decided to use it. For art. Jamey had told him about his father's suicide, and he combined it with the murder scene and stuck it in a sculpture. He seemed to think it was funny, something about death being the source of all true art."

"He never read the book through?"

"If he did, he didn't catch on to the Bitter Canyon bit because he never tried to exploit it."

"He wouldn't," I said. "He fancies himself a nihilist. Takes pride in being apathetic."

Milo thought for a moment.

"Yeah, you could be right. When I asked him if he thought the book might be important when he encased it in plastic, he gave this snotty smile and said it was an irrelevant question. When I pressed him, he said he hoped it was because the idea of someone's hanging it on his wall without knowing what he had was hilarious. Then he laid on a bunch of crap about art and bad jokes being the same thing. I asked him if that's why the Mona Lisa was smiling, but he shined me on. Weird kid, but as far as I can tell, he has no connection to any of it, so I turned him loose."

"Any indication of why Jamey hid the book from Chancellor?" I asked.

"Nope."

"I was thinking," I said, "that they could have had a falling-out. Jamey wanted to use the diary to stop the construction, and when he saw that all Chancellor cared about was saving his own skin, he took it and left it for safekeeping with Gary. Because Gary was a nihilist and would never use it."

There was a long silence.

"Could be," said Milo. "If Jamey was rational enough to put that all together."

"You're probably right. It was wishful thinking. He was pretty muddled by then."

"Not so muddled he couldn't reach out for help."

I said nothing.

"Hey," said Milo, "that was your cue to recite something about the indomitability of the human spirit."

"Consider it recited."

"Consider it heard."

After he hung up, I finished my breakfast, called the

service, and told them where I'd be. There were three messages, two from people wanting to sell me something and a request to phone a Superior Court judge, a man I respected. I called his chambers, and he asked me to consult on the impending divorce case of a famous film director and a famous actress. According to the director, the actress was a cocaine freak on the verge of psychosis. According to the actress, the director was venal, cruel, and a rabid pedophile. Neither really wanted their five-year-old daughter; both were determined the other wouldn't get custody. The actress had spirited the child to Zurich, and it was possible I'd be able to fly there at her expense to conduct my interviews.

I told him it sounded like a mess of the worst kind: flaming narcissism combined with enough money to pay lawyers to keep it messy for a long time. He laughed sadly and agreed but added that he thought I'd be interested because I liked excitement. I thanked him for thinking of me and politely declined.

At nine o'clock I went down to the garden to feed the koi. The largest of the carp, a stout gold and black *kin-ki-utsuri*, which Robin had named Sumo, sucked on my fingers, and I patted his glossy head before climbing back up to the house. Once inside, I straightened up, switched a few lights on, and packed a carry-on. Then I called Robin at her studio and told her I was leaving.

"Have a good flight, sweetie. When can I expect you back?"

"Late tonight or tomorrow morning depending on how things go."

"Call me and let me know. If it's tonight, I'll wait up. If not, I'll stay here late and finish the mandolin."

"Sure. I'll phone by six."

"Take care, Alex. I love you."

"Love you, too."

Throwing on a corduroy sportcoat, I picked up the carry-on, walked out to the terrace, and locked the door behind me. By ten-thirty I was pulling into Burbank Airport.

33

THE HOSPITAL sat on a promontory overlooking the ocean, swaddled in acres of jade green clover that rolled and tumbled into the Monterey mist. It was a paragon of low-profile architecture, caramel-colored bungalows cast haphazardly around a two-story administration building, the complex veined with stone pathways and flower beds, half shaded by the spreading branches of coast live oak. Dagger points of red tile roof intruded upon a cobalt sky so pure it bordered on the unreal. At the junction of land and sky a single twisted Monterey pine clawed at the heavens. Below its careening trunk, patches of yellow and blue lupine flowed like paint spills down a sloping green canvas.

The drive down from Carmel had been a quiet one, broken only by the hiss of the ocean, the chug of the rented Mazda, and the rare, startling bellow of a lust-filled sea lion bull. I thought of the last time I'd been there, with Robin. We'd come as tourists, for a week in spring, doing the things that tourists do on the Monterey Peninsula: a visit to the aquarium, seafood dinners under the stars; windowshopping the antique stores; lazy love-making on a crisp, foreign bed. But now, sitting on a redwood bench near the edge of the cliff, peering through salt-eaten diamonds of chain link as the Pacific foamed like warm ale, those seven days seemed like ancient history.

I turned, looked back toward the bungalows, and saw only strangers in the distance, sheeplike Grandma Moses people, sitting, strolling, reclining on elbows that disappeared in the clover. Talking, responding, rejecting, ignoring. Playing board games and tossing Frisbees. Staring blankly into space.

The beach below was glossy and white, striped by the

receding tide, dotted with a tortoise brigade of moundlike rocks. Between the rocks were mirrored tide pools, bubbling with the respiration of trapped creatures, mustached by dendrites of eelgrass. A pelican's horizontal reconnaissance broke the stillness. Diving suddenly, big wings rasping, the bird aimed for a mirror, shattered it, and rose triumphantly with a beakful of squirm before sailing off toward Japan.

Fifteen minutes later a young woman in jeans and red smock brought Jamey to me. She was blond and braided, with a round, pensive, farm girl face, and had drawn red daisies on her nurse's badge with a felt-tipped pen. She held his arm as if he were her steady boyfriend, let go reluctantly, sat him down next to me, and told me she'd be back in half an hour.

"Bye, James. Be good."

"Bye, Susan." His voice was hoarse.

When she was gone, I said hello.

He turned to me and nodded. Squinted up at the sun.

He smelled of shampoo. His hair had been cut short, and the beginnings of a mustache sprouted on his upper lip. He wore a maroon Izod shirt so new it sported box creases, gray sweat pants, and running shoes without socks. The clothes bagged on him. His ankles were thin and white.

"Beautiful out here," I said.

He smiled. Touched his finger to his nose. Slowly, as if performing a test of coordination.

Several minutes passed.

"I like to sit right here," he said. "Get lost in the quiet."

"I can see why."

We watched a flock of sea gulls peck at the rocks. Breathed in nosefuls of brine. He crossed and uncrossed his legs. Put his hands in his lap and gazed out at the ocean. Two gulls got into a fight over something edible. They kicked and squawked until the weaker one backed off. The victor bounced several yards away and feasted.

"You look good," I said.

"Thank you."

"Dr. Levi told me you're doing amazingly well."

He got up and gripped the chain-link fence. Said something that was drowned out by the waves. I got up and stood next to him.

"I didn't hear you," I said.

He didn't respond. Just held on to the fence and swayed unsteadily.

"I feel prety good," he said after a while. "Achey."

"Are you in pain?"

"A good pain. Like a . . . good night's sleep after a strenuous day."

Moments later:

"Yesterday I took a walk."

I waited for more.

"With Susan. Once . . . maybe twice . . . she had to hold me up. Generally, my legs were okay."

"That's great." At first the neurologists hadn't been certain if the damage done to his nervous system would be permanent. But he'd regained function rapidly, and I'd been told this morning that optimism was called for.

A minute of silence.

"Susan helps me a lot. She's a . . . strong person."

"She seems very fond of you."

He looked out at the water and began to cry.

"What is it?"

He continued to weep, let go of the fence, stumbled, and sat back down on the bench. Wiping his face with his hands, he closed his eyes. Tears seeped out.

I put a hand on his shoulder. Touched jutting bone covered by the merest sheath of skin.

"What's the matter, Jamey?"

He cried some more, composed himself, and said:

"People are being nice to me."

"You deserve to be treated nicely."

He hung his head, raised it, and began moving slowly along the rim of the cliff, taking small, tentative steps, holding on to the fence for support. I stayed by his side.

"It's . . . confusing," he said.

"What is?"

"Dr. Levi told me I called you. For help. I don't remember it," he added apologetically "Now you're here. It's as if . . . nothing happened in between."

He backed away from the edge, turned around, and walked in the direction of the bungalows, holding out his arms for balance, moving slowly, carefully, like someone getting used to a false limb. I walked with him, forcing myself to slow down, sinking ankle-deep in clover.

"No," he said. "That's not true. A lot's happened, hasn't it?"

"Yes, it has."

"Terrible things. People are gone. Disappeared."

He bit back more tears, stared straight ahead, and kept walking.

Fronting the bungalows, two hundred yards in the distance, was a picnic area, redwood tables and benches, the tables shaded by candy-striped umbrellas. A red figure rose from one of the benches and waved. Jamey waved back.

"Hello, Susan," he said, although she couldn't hear him.

"It's normal," I said, "for someone who's gone through what you have to be confused. Give yourself time to get reoriented."

He smiled faintly.

"Sounds like you've been talking to Dr. Levi."

"Dr. Levi's a very smart woman."

"Yes." Pause. "She told me you were friends."

"She was a psychiatric resident when I was a graduate student. We were on a crisis team together. You're in good hands."

He nodded.

"She's putting me back together again," he said softly, then veered toward a stand of cypress.

We passed a middle-aged couple sitting on a blanket with a girl of around eighteen. The girl was chubby and wore a shapeless, colorless smock. She had a painfully beautiful face dominated by vacant eyes and long dark hair that she knitted, using her fingers as needles—wrapping, twisting, letting go, starting all over again. Her father wore a dark suit and tie and sat with his back to her, reading Michener behind dark glasses. Her mother looked up sheepishly as we walked by.

We passed through a clearing in the trees, into a cool shady bowl, cathedraled by branches, padded with dry leaves. Jamey found a stump and sat on it. I leaned against a trunk.

"Your finding Dr. Levi for me," he said. "It's strange."

"How so?"

He cleared his throat, turned away, embarrassed.

"You're safe now," I said. "It's okay to talk. Or not to."

He pondered that. Wet his lips with his tongue.

"I called you and you responded. You helped."

His incredulity was sad. I said nothing.

"Before, if I needed a doctor, Uncle Dwight generally—" he stopped himself. "No, that wouldn't make sense, would it?"

"No."

He looked around at the columns of tree trunks and said:

"Too cold in here. Can we walk some more?"

"Sure."

We climbed the lawn toward the hospital in silence. He tried putting his hands in his pockets, but his legs buckled, and he started to fall. I took him by the arm and held him upright.

"Let's rest," I said.

"Okay."

He folded like a deck chair, allowed himself to be lowered to the lawn. Touched his nose again and said:

"I'm getting better at it."

"You're healing."

Several minutes later:

"They all hated me," he said. Matter-of-factly, without self-pity. But his eyes were tortured, and I knew what they were asking: What did I do to make them feel that way?

"It had nothing to do with you," I said. "They dehumanized you in order to justify what they did to you."

"Disappeared," he said unbelievingly. "Right off the screen. So hard to believe." Picking a dandelion husk out of the clover, he brushed it against his lips, rubbed it awkwardly between his fingertips, and watched the silky threads float skyward.

"That's me. Sailing through space with no . . . moorings."

"Do you like that?"

"It's freedom. Sometimes."

"And the other times?"

"It's terrifying," he said with sudden passion. "Makes

me want to be . . . subterranean. Packed tightly. Do you know what I mean?"

"I know exactly what you mean."

He exhaled audibly, closed his eyes, leaned back, and warmed his face in the sun. His forehead grew wet with perspiration, though the bluff was cooled by an ocean breeze. Opening his mouth wide, he yawned.

"Tired?"

"They stuff me with food. Red meat for breakfast. It makes me . . . logey."

Several moments later:

"They're very nice to me."

"I'm glad. Dr. Levi tells me you're sleeping better."

"Somewhat. When the pains don't come."

"The memory pains?"

"Yes."

"They sound rough. Like bad dreams."

"Maybe they are. I don't know."

"They must be pretty frightening."

He looked down, and his pupils dilated, black intruding on blue.

"I can just be lying there. Not doing anything. And something—something dark . . . and ugly floats up in the front of my brain . . . forces itself into consciousness."

"What kind of dark thing?"

"That's just it, I don't know. Sometimes it seems like . . . trash. Something rotten. Fetid. A clot of garbage. I can swear I smell something, but when I try to focus on it, there's no odor at all. Does that make sense?"

When I nodded, he continued.

"A few nights ago it seemed like the shadow of a monster—a friend . . . Jack the Ripper hiding behind a grimy stone wall. That sounds . . . deranged, doesn't it?"

"No," I assured him. "It doesn't. Any other images?"

"I don't know . . . maybe. It's definitely ugly. Insistent . . . scratching against the inner surface of my forehead but . . . hiding. Lurking. Maybe it's insectile, I don't know. I can't get hold of it. So frustrating."

"Like a word on the tip of your tongue?"

He nodded.

"It's maddening. Makes my head throb."

"Brain strain" Deborah Levi had called it. *"There's a ton of repressed material fighting to push through prema-*

turely. When he tries to force it, he gets severe headaches that keep him awake at night. He calls them memory pains. I've told him they're his body's way of saying slow down, that he needs to pace himself, not to push it. He's still highly compromised, Alex. His bloodwork's clear, but for all we know, he may still be toxic at some subclinical level. Not to mention all the shit he's been through."

"What do you think?" he asked.

"It's normal for your situation," I said. "It will pass."

"Good," he said, visibly relieved. "I value your opinion."

A red blur moved peripherally: Susan rising from her bench again. Standing, in anticipation.

"Dr. D.," he said, "what's going to become of me? Afterward. After I'm all patched up?"

I thought awhile before replying—long enough to choose my words but not so long as to make him anxious.

"I know that question seems overwhelming now, but when the time comes for you to leave, it will be manageable. Maybe even answer itself."

He looked at me doubtfully.

"Think of a calculus text," I said. "Open it in the middle, and it's incomprehensible. Start at the beginning and progress steadily, and when you reach that same spot in the middle, it just glides by."

"Are you saying it will be . . . a simple . . . stepwise progression?"

I shook my head.

"Far from it. There'll be constant challenges. Times when you seem stuck and aren't moving at all. But if you take it at a reasonable pace—value yourself, care for yourself, allow yourself to be helped—you'll handle the challenges. You'll surprise yourself at how well you cope."

He listened, but edgily. Like someone who'd craved ice cream and had been offered celery.

"Do you still remember my number?" I asked.

He recited the seven digits automatically, then looked amazed, as if he'd spoken in tongues.

"Call me if you want to talk," I said. "Dr. Levi says it's okay. When you're through up here, we'll get together, do some planning. Okay?"

"That would be—I'd like that—I'll look forward to that."

Susan had started walking toward us. He saw her and stood. Extended his hand.

"It was good to see you," he said.

I shook the hand, released it, and put my arms around him. Heard a sharp intake of breath, a suppressed sob, the sound of a lost child finding a familiar signpost. Then two whispered words:

"Thank you."

About the Author

With over two million copies of his best-selling novels in print, translations into numerous foreign languages, and receipt of both the Edgar and the Anthony awards, Jonathan Kellerman has received wide acclaim as a contemporary master of the psychological thriller.

Born in New York City in 1949, he grew up in Los Angeles, graduated from UCLA, and received a Ph.D. in clinical psychology from the University of Southern California, where he is currently clinical associate professor of pediatrics in the School of Medicine. Prior to earning his doctorate Kellerman worked as a cartoonist, illustrator, editor, teacher, and musician. During the course of his career as a psychologist, he cofounded and directed the Psychosocial Program at Children's Hospital of Los Angeles, headed a psychological consulting firm, conducted research in behavioral medicine, and acquired a national reputation as an authority on childhood stress.

In addition to *When the Bough Breaks, Blood Test* (both available in Signet editions), and *Over the Edge,* Dr. Kellerman has written two nonfiction books and well over one hundred scholarly articles, chapters, reviews, and abstracts in the field of psychology. His short fiction and essays have appeared in *Alfred Hitchcock's Mystery Magazine, Los Angeles Magazine,* the *Los Angeles Times,* and *Newsweek.*

He lives in Southern California with his wife, novelist Faye Kellerman, and their three children, and is currently at work on a major crime novel.

AFTERWORD

WHILE PRACTICING clinical child psychology full-time, I wrote three novels, hunched in my unfinished garage, hammering away at a quirky, bruised IBM Selectric, breathing in Liquid Paper fumes, keeping company with spiders and other creepy-crawlies. Because I was faced with a full patient roster and the joys of marriage and family, my writing time was apportioned to the quiet period between eleven p.m. and two a.m. I think of those three books as my Nocturnal Triangle.

The first novel so composed was *When the Bough Breaks*. Derived in part from my experiences treating children traumatized by abuse, it proved to be a hard sell. Written in 1981, finally sold in 1983, *Bough* was held for publication until 1985 because the publisher was queasy about the subject matter. My advance payment came out to three bucks an hour. To everyone's surprise—most of all the publisher's—the book became a word-of-mouth bestseller. (Thank you, dear readers.)

Despite the apparent lack of financial reward from writing fiction, I was so jazzed at finally "becoming" a novelist that I created my second novel, *Blood Test*, over a frenzied, three-month period, well before *When the Bough Breaks* was published. Novel Number Two, a testament to my obvious feel for the slick and the nakedly commercial, arose, in part, from my many years dealing with the psychosocial needs of children with cancer and their families. Darker than *Bough*, *Blood Test* scared the publisher even more, but like *Bough*, it garnered rave reviews. The book was lost in a warehouse in Nebraska but it, too, became a word-of-mouth bestseller in softcover. You, dear reader, weren't deterred by publishing snafus.

Over the Edge is the third garage novel and it materialized after I sat back and focused on what I was really writing about—what really *mattered* to me. Though high-profile horrors such as abuse and cancer had formed the apparent foci of my first two novels, I realized that what unified *Bough* and *Blood Test* was a theme that had emerged from my work—from my *identity*—as a psychologist: *Failure to deal with the past—with the emotional past—often dooms families to confronting their worst nightmares.*

Over the Edge represented a new level of maturity for me as a novelist. Without sacrificing the passion for writing that had fueled the manic production of *When the Bough Breaks* and *Blood Test*, this book forced me to look deep into my own soul and to think long and hard about whether I had anything valuable to say.

Edge was a true labor of love, created with greater care and pacing and craftsmanship than I had ever exercised. I sweated to create a labyrinthine plot that would be complex without being complicated, strove to build a novel word by word, saying more with less, and fought to up the personal ante posed by two surprise bestsellers. Knowing that, if this book worked, I might indeed be able to embark on a career as a novelist.

Edge was embraced lovingly by the reading public, remained on the *New York Times* bestseller list for thirteen weeks, and went into multiple printings. Thank you again, dear reader. Thank you so very much.

Since then, I've written fourteen other novels in as many years, all of them warmly accepted. Each book is harder to write than its predecessor, as I continue to raise the bar in order to create believable and engrossing stories with endings that offer satisfaction without being facile, stretch to keep characters fresh, and play with the language in an inventive manner. I'm not complaining. I hate being bored and love the challenge of my job. And though I continue never to take commercial factors into consideration, I never take my readers for granted.

After the success of *Over the Edge*, I spruced up the garage and bought myself a word processor.

This book occupies a special place in my heart. I hope you enjoy it.

Jonathan Kellerman